EXILE ON BRIDGE STREET

EXILE ON BRIDGE STREET

A NOVEL BY
EAMON LOINGSIGH

VOLUME TWO OF THE
AULD IRISHTOWN TRILOGY

THREE ROOMS PRESS
NEW YORK

*Best when read with J. S. Bach's *Suite for Solo Cello no. 2 in D Minor, BMV 1008 Sarabande*

Lyrics from song "Haul Away Joe" (traditional) used in this book.
Lyrics from song "Old Fenian Gun" by P. O'Neill used in this book.
Lyrics from song "Dear Old Skibbereen" by Patrick Carpenter used in this book.
Words from medieval Requiem Mass hymn "Dies Irae" used in this book.

This book is fiction. Although many characters retain their original names and many events are historically accurate, the story as a whole is fiction.

Exile on Bridge Street
A NOVEL BY
Eamon Loingsigh

"Volume two of the Auld Irishtown Trilogy"

ISBN 978-1-941110-42-3 (print)
ISBN 978-1-941110-43-0 (ebook)
Library of Congress Control Number: 2016936894

COVER AND INTERIOR DESIGN:
KG Design International
www.katgeorges.com

DISTRIBUTED BY:
PGW/Ingram
www.pgw.com

Three Rooms Press
New York, NY
www.threeroomspress.com
info@threeroomspress.com

FOR UNCLE JIMMY "MAC"

A kind soul, unfairly treated

Auld Irishtown Characters:

Narrator
William Garrity—*Teenage Irish immigrant*

The White Hand:
Dinny Meehan—*Gang leader*
The Swede—*Enforcer*
Vincent Maher—*Enforcer*
Tommy Tuohey—*Irish traveler, enforcer*
Lumpy Gilchrist—*Accountant*
Mickey Kane—*Dinny's cousin*

Dockbosses:
Wild Bill Lovett—*Red Hook, old Jay Street Gang leader*
Cinders Connolly—*Jay & Fulton street terminals*
Harry "The Shiv" Reynolds—*Atlantic Avenue Terminal*
Cute Charlie Red Donnolly—*Navy Yard*
John Gibney "The Lark"—*Baltic Street Terminal*

Lonergan Crew:
Richie Lonergan—*Leader*
Abe Harms—*German Jew, Richie's right-hand*
Petey Behan—*Feuds with Liam Garrity*
Matty Martin—*Follower*
Timothy Quilty—*Follower*

The Black Hand:
Frankie Yale—*Leader in Brooklyn*
Jack & Sixto Stabile—*Father & son owners of Adonis Social Club*
Paul Vaccarelli—*Old Five Points leader, ILA VP*

International Longshoreman's Association:
Thos Carmody—*Recruiter*
King Joe—*VP, New York City*
T. V. O'Connor—*President*
Henry Browne—*ILA leader in the Navy Yard*

Police:
William Brosnan—*Detective*
Daniel Culkin—*Patrolman, son-in-law of Brosnan*
Ferris—*Patrolman*

OTHER GANG MEMBERS:

Mick Gilligan—*Low-end White Hand follower*

Eddie Hughes—*White Hand Gang member*

Freddie Cuneen—*White Hand Gang member*

The Simpson brothers, Whitey & Baron—*White Hand Gang members,*
WWI soldiers

Joseph Flynn—*Drunkard, childhood friend of Lovett's, WWI soldier*

Johnny Mullen—*White Hand Gang member, WWI soldier*

Happy Maloney—*White Hand Gang member, WWI soldier*

Quiet Higgins—*White Hand Gang member, WWI soldier*

Gimpy Kafferty—*White Hand Gang member, WWI soldier*

Fred Honeybeck—*White Hand Gang member, WWI soldier*

OBSCURES AND EXTRAS:

Mr. Lynch—*Greenwich Village saloon owner, Hibernian societies*

Mrs. McGowan—*Mother of McGowan*

Emma McGowan—*Sister of McGowan*

Rose Leighton—*Sadie's mother*

Frank Leighton—*Oldest Leighton brother, manager at Kirkman Soap Factory*

Tiny Thomas Lonergan—*Lonergan child*

Ms. Gilligan—*Wife of Mick Gilligan*

Sammy de Angelo—*Italian hit man*

Seamus "Red Shay" Meehan—*Dinny's uncle*

Lefty & Costello—*Two followers of Tanner Smith*

James Cleary—*Garry Barry follower*

EXILE ON BRIDGE STREET

T'was a Day for Legends

"HER EXILED CHILDREN IN AMERICA ARE not hatched of the city's womb," Paddy Keenan once said, his back to me as he tapped a barrel of ale in the daybreak darkness, only amber beginnings of light under the bridges rising and reaching up toward the coal-soot windows outside the Dock Loaders' Club. Always there at first of light. Fixed on that constant position of change, the passing through of poles and the inequitable polemic between the remembrance of night and the unknown day, we lived. Do we always live hovering, be sure.

I was but a stripling back then. A slight teenage soldier of the dawn in Brooklyn's Irishtown, up and ready for the day's labor with the many of us. Wool caps donned, and ties and coats and boots and tools aplenty in the saloon corner.

I think back now on what Paddy'd meant, the inner eye of an old man having the gift of vision, and seeing now as I can that he was alluding to our people's age-old struggle to survive in this ever-changing darkness to day. To be free to live as we, ourselves. An exiled and migrated people under demand again of assimilation.

Many Irish were berthed by ship here in Brooklyn two and three generations before I arrived in 1915. They'd been sent 'way by starvation and by British law, yet still retained the ways of their forebears by insulating themselves against the waterfront in their neighborhoods where, just like home, the oceanic winds and the brine in the unsettled sea air create a sense of timelessness again. The aura of the past felt to be within our grasp and endlessly repeating itself in the now.

Back when, our mother's land and her milk was still fresh on our lips here in America, and the egg of our discontent a great hunger thriving. In his off-handed way, Paddy was right, this timeless and unsettled air and the sorrowful poetry of our past gave us to thinking that we were not of New York City's womb at all. We were still but children having crossed the Atlantic, exiled from the mother. Long without her, but never forgetting. Never forgiving.

Oh, the police and the papers called us many things in our day during the Great War. Always had, of course. But it was as a gang we became known. The term originally came about because as longshore laborers of the busiest port in the world, we had pier gangs, deck gangs, hull gangs, hatch gangs, and many others. They all served a purpose in the loading and unloading of ships. But collectively we were known as "The White Hand," in opposition to the Italian longshoremen of South Brooklyn and their leaders, "The Black Hand," that sought to take over the tribute money we'd always imposed in the north on waterfront businesses and immigrant laborers. But it was ours from the start, and although the Italians played hard, in those days we played harder still.

They called us these things to degrade and disparage us. To change us. But our deeply held ideas, the ways of our people remembered, were inherited over many, many generations. The unified disbelief in foreign law and the rejection of the overarching establishment of organized logic that'd been bequeathed us were universally present in each individual in Irishtown and along the waterfront. And it's that cynicism that kept us alive too, for we could not trust in their ways. Ask any Irish woman or man why we bear such great distrust in law and they'll tell you, that the foreigners' ways had never benefitted our like and repeatedly proved itself our greatest enemy, endlessly throughout our history. The culmination coming in the 1840s that sent us to roadside graves, coffin ships, and if we were lucky, to the shores of Brooklyn and elsewhere. No no, we could only believe in the ways of our own. The endless past endlessly being relived and seen in everything, everywhere.

And only from the womb of this collective psyche is our type of hero born. The martyr! Sweet and fatal. The martyr forever relegated to breaking his body against a greater power. In America or Ireland, the weight of organized logic pressing down on us, an Irish chieftain bulbs out of the crush. Made a leader for his flouting their power with a reckless courage. Creates and enforces our own law by the old codes. And finally, after having his people divided by the greater power, is murdered by one of his own. Another Irish leader martyred for the bogland of our history.

I am William Garrity and it's me who tells this story you now, many years on. Although I come from a long line of oral storytellers, I became known in Brooklyn as a thief of pencils. An old man now I am, and I slowly stand from my writings and hobble to the kitchen with an empty teacup. It shakes in my straining. I have the mind of an able youngster, I'll have you know, but it's true my body is that of a tin-can old man. Bockety and stiff. In the kitchen I steep the next cup and lean on the blackthorn. The same kind of cane my father took out of the chimney the day I left with him for the country train and the Atlantic steamer that took me across, steerage class. The same weapon used in the faction fights of lore, I lean on now.

Shuffling with it, I wobble back to my typewriter, pencil and papers and look out the window over the harbor where I spent the breadth of my life. And I think of the man who taught me about that great harbor. And taught me to be a man too. His name was Dinny Meehan. The leader and the spirit of all us who ran with him back in our day. A great ghost of our past, was he, there always to remind us that to create is to truly rule. In him, there was always that sense of timelessness that stood erect in the unsettled air and, as if by some imagining, the streets of Brooklyn were paths in open fields, the buildings ancient Irish mountain shields.

By the time Dinny was eleven years old, two older brothers, two younger sisters, his mother, and his uncle "Red Shay" had all died or been killed. Two other girls married off to Albany to a Phelan family. The last son of the once great Meehan clan of Hudson Street in Manhattan, he was forced to cross the East River to Brooklyn at the turning of the century with his Irish-born, sick father. On a windy day he landed on Bridge Street in old Irishtown, and started as a no one. His father soon dead, he an orphan. A gypsy boy. The son of an exiled child and a hallowed apparition of our past rising up. Taking power by force and violence. Killing Christie Maroney, a gang leader who sought to sell Irishtown to outsiders. Dinny Meehan, he who spited law by being found innocent of murder charges and brought together an army of early rising soldiers with whom I fell in with, joined. It is for Dinny Meehan this story is told by myself, a thief of pencils in a place where the written word was seen as dangerous, and evidence.

Back in our day, the territories were held down by dockbosses and went from the Navy Yard down to Red Hook where our people had controlled labor for many years. All of the dockbosses had followers, but each and every one reported to Dinny Meehan at 25 Bridge Street, a saloon underneath the Manhattan Bridge that we called the Dock Loaders' Club, though there was no sign outside stating such a thing. All orders emanated from it where Dinny Meehan held power, and down through the terminals where the dockbosses held sway in his name. It was a system that had worked for many years before

my arrival when my father sent me, the youngest son to
New York just months ahead of the Easter Rising in Ireland
to secure passage for my mother and sisters. I'd been
sent to work with my uncle, who was well established himself in Brooklyn with the International Longshoremen's
Association—another of the gang's enemies. Soon enough
though, my uncle and I had a falling-out that left me homeless in an Irishtown winter. It was then I was picked up off
the street and taken to Dinny, surrounded by his bodyguards and rowdies. He put me to work on the docks and
running messages from one terminal to the next. And
with the work I saved every dime earned to get my mother
and sisters out of the Great War's way, and out of the way of
the Brits too, our ancient enemy who would come to clean
the Easter Rising up as they'd done throughout history,
with our own blood.

My mother and sisters facing the hoary tradition of
British reprisals, Dinny vowed to help me get them out.
The price was high though. He wanted my uncle, for uncle
Joseph was a union recruiter in Brooklyn. I paid that price
in full too. A heavy one. It's too hard for me to openly say
what I had done to him. But done, it was.

"Do you know what done means?" Dinny had asked me,
his wide, muscular jaw flexing as he stared at me with
stone-green eyes. "Done means done."

My own uncle, stabbed and left to the flames we'd relit
in Brooklyn. The Irish once again taking hold of power
and claiming the inherited land where the waterfront
zephyrs timelessly blew in our ears and in the poetry of our
pained remembrances. All this happening at the same
time bold Irish rebels stormed Dublin on Easter Monday
in 1916 to declare their independence from the British
Empire. And I took my uncle's life to begin my own journey
into manhood. Rising up and out from the child in me.

Just like the rebelpoets of Dublin, we in Brooklyn had so
much against us. So many elements; dock and shipping

companies wanting to control their profits, unions vying for power over labor, Italians groping to the northern piers, American law demanding our subservience and the threat of revolt within our own gang. Alone, Dinny Meehan put an ingenious plan in place and our gang made a violent declaration on the waterfront. The White Hand took power back on the lucrative Brooklyn docks when three hundred and fifty angry Irish went from pier to pier and beat any man refusing to pay us tribute. Burned down their strongholds too. I was there. And although we had many battles in those times, t'was a day for legends, that one.

In Ireland, the Easter rebels were executed right off. In Brooklyn we were jailed. We ruled the marine terminals here, where the riches of hard labor fed the tenements that lined the waterfront among the factories and storing houses. Young men on the streets and docks of Brooklyn bound together by old codes and who were not hatched of the city's womb at all, but by the mother of our discontent.

Come then, to hear a shanachie in his dying days, where within the story alive and well is the struggle for America in its fertile bights between the tenebrous morn and the wet of breaking day round New York Harbor.

CHAPTER I

The Butcher's Apron

April, 1916

"Liam," a voice says to me, and I feel a poking in my back. I sit up and open my eyes and see the bars, zoo bars they seem, and on the other side of them is Head Patrolman William Brosnan in dark police blue, his face covered by an open newspaper, legs crossed on the angled desk. The thudding pain through my head begins to beat. I want only to sleep away from things. To let myself off from this. Sleep being my only escape. I lie back again.

I am among three other teenagers sleeping off a drunk, curled up and rag-haired and open-mouthed on the cement floor. Inside the cell and awake next to me is the bony face of Richie Lonergan staring forward on a bench and stern and untroubled by guilt. Next to him is the long Cinders Connolly, dockboss of the Fulton and Jay Street Terminals with his toothy smile and hair falling in thick shards over the shorn sides above his ears.

"They let us starve," I mumble, falling asleep on the cold pavement floor behind bars. I can't really say why that sentence comes to my lips. But it does. It comes as if it had been whispered in my ear while I slept. Or told me so many times as a baby that it has become so ingrained that there is no stopping it from bubbling, circling through the many thoughts that cross my dreaming mind confusedly. A back-drop. In the distance but always there. April of 1916 being a month and year never to be forgotten, true, but the long history behind it. Deep in our minds. There for us. Always. "They let us starve."

I dream off. Into the black I go; the bright of day is painful to my eyes; I am then enclosed in a constant rain. A crack in the cement floor where I lie, and in my dreaming becomes a great fissure where we are all separated by a flood that opens into an ocean until I flinch and wake. Open my eyes again. Feel the great pain in my temple and the back of my head. I try to remember why I am in a cell, but my head cannot configure and organize my thoughts. Still dazed. The guiltless childhood gone from me now. Behind me. Brooklyn has its way and takes my purity. The tender boy wrenched open by crime and orphaned by a watery divide. I roll over to my back and lay a hand across my forehead, putting things together best I can.

After beating every man not associated with us, then burning Red Hook, hilarity and drinks ensued the previous night. Our songs bouncing off tenement walls as we strode through them with starry-eyed children in windows watching the midnight celebrants. Watching their heroes in their bands and bunches gloating and crowing at the night, and for taking back power on the waterfront from all those that had challenged us. The rarest of all things Irish being victory, Dinny Meehan's name once again rings out in triumph. His name repeated over and over throughout the night, even though no one ever admits to knowing him.

Then we were arrested. A customary thing for the gang, but the first for myself.

"Ya ain't learned to hold the drink yet," Cinders says, leaning toward me with a smile, elbows on knees, the gang's youngsters Petey Behan, Timothy Quilty, Matty Martin, and I in various states of awakening on the cell's floor. Abe

Harms, Richie's best friend is sitting next to him on the bench whispering whispers to him, as he's known to.

I look back again toward Richie, who has only one leg. Richie Lonergan is the leader of us teenagers not only because his mother and father were in gangs, which makes him royalty, but because he is the fiercest fighter among us and has the coldest of looks in his gray-eyed stare. He even put one of Dinny's dockbosses, Red Donnelly, to sleep in a fistfight that I saw with my own eyes. But Abe Harms gives Richie his ideas through whispers and is always at his ear. In the cell among us there are some eight other men of differing ages and languages. Three of color and plaintive and soliciting barefaced pity from Brosnan and Brosnan's son-in-law, young patrolman Daniel Culkin.

Stretching along the floor and holding my head in pain, I look up to the bars holding us in, and up again I look to the cutting shine and buzz of electricity exposing me to its unnatural light, a knife through my throbbing head. Lying there, I can't remember all that happened over the previous days, only flickering memories that dance remorsefully in my mind. Death and violence still so new to me. And under the cover of the silence that binds all of us in the gang, protects us even, the idea of death churns and circulates in me with the alcohol strewn and diffusing in my blood. Shame colors me, and my thoughts are blackened with the guilt of killing. Killing. Shame cataracts over me. Crushes me. My shy and youthful West Ireland nature bared out. Here now caged by law. My head aching and flat on the hard floor, I cover my eyes from the drone and hum of the straining light above that exposes me. Buzzes in its false burnished shine and bares me to its bright brandishing. Electricity still so rare in the waterfront neighborhoods I'd lived in since emigrating and which did not exist on the farm where I was raised in County Clare, Ireland. I want nothing more than for it all to go away so I can wake again far from here. Far from the terrible things I've done. Far from the thoughts too of my dead uncle, of whom I simply cannot allow myself to think.

The bars that hold me are a sign, I know. A notice of my fault and sinful acts. I am a criminal among criminals. An animal of men, even as I am not yet a man. Still, the world finds me and places me here. Somehow knows that my thoughts flash with the culling of blood and acts of fire and violation. Seeing it in my eyes. Finding me, as law is known to do, locking up offenders.

Of a sudden there are slurs between Richie Lonergan and two other men within the narrows of our cell and quickly we all rise from the cement floor, fists at the ready. I am dizzy and tingling and almost lose my breath, but hold my hands clenched, black spots appearing in my speckled vision.

Cinders is between Richie and the others with his wide hand spread open across the teen's chest as he warns off the two men. Patrolman Culkin is clanking on the bars with a blackjack and a melee between prisoners is somehow avoided. Richie then sits down among the cover of our numbers unaffected by the excitement. Unaffected by anything, ever, it seems. By the look in Richie's gray, high-cheeked eyes, he'd have as much issue in killing a man with his fists as hammering a hot rivet into a steel plate.

A few moments later I watch as Richie unplugs the strut of wood at the end of his leg, unravels the adjoining straps underneath his trousers but does not complain of pain nor discomfort. Just lets the leg breathe and sit there, laying across the bench dumb and limp, scarred where it was hastily sewn shut above the knee when he was eight years old, iron trolley wheels severing it downright. The flat look in his bone-drilled eye sockets revealing a great shortage of the humility and diffidence in which I was raised and know. He and many others reared by families starved out of Ireland during the Great Hunger causes me to think that it wasn't only food they were shorted, but coming across left them barren of the great modesty we are known to possess. Lost to distrust forever and carried down to his generation.

"Are we getting out of here?" I ask, crouching against a wall and pushing hair out of my face.

"We'll be out soon," Cinders assures with his toothy grin, long broad shoulders leaning forward, coat a size too tight, which reveals his bony wrists and knuckly, muscular hands. A gentler soul, Cinders always has kindness for the people he feels a kinship toward, but to him outsiders can never be trusted and beating them into their place with fists or a cudgel is part of being the dockboss of the Jay Street Terminal and the Fulton Ferry Landing.

"Will we?" I ask.

Cinders nods. Seeing that I am anxious and burdened with fear, he leans close to my ear, "Just don' say nothin'. Ya don' say a thing to these tunics. Don' answer the questions, just say ya don' know. Nothin' else. Ya never heard o' nobody named Joe Garrity. Ya don' even know anyone named Liam Garrity, right? Ya don' know no one named Dinny Meehan and ya don' even know me either. . . . I don' know you. What's ya name?"

"Patrick Kelly," I say, having been trained to know the answer to that question.

"Petey? What's ya name?" he whispers.

"Patrick Kelly," Petey Behan says, yet leers in my direction.

"Who's Dinny Meehan?"

"Don' know," we all whisper back like good students.

Cinders smiles again, nods and looks out the bars toward Brosnan and Culkin, "Everyone's Patrick Kelly."

Through the bars I look toward Brosnan myself, the Head Patrolman at the Poplar Street Station. He looks back toward us with a look of concern over his newspaper. He is a man on the take, Brosnan is. But no one talks about it. When we burned Red Hook and took back the docks on that day for legends, he was paid to look the other way until after we'd finished. Then he came with the cuffs and a big black Irish cigar hanging out the side of his head. We called his like "tunics," because that's what they wore, big blue tunic coats like the bobbies in London. An Irishman from Dublin, he spends his take on his pregnant daughter—Patrolman Culkin's wife. His relationship to Dinny is complicated though, but officially they are enemies, Brosnan seeing Dinny as a low-classed Famine-Irish descendent, Dinny seeing Brosnan as a "souper," which in the old country referred to those who were bribed out of their Catholic religion, toward English Protestantism for a bowl of soup to quell the rattles of hunger. Giving away our sacred ways to the enemy of us. The enemy who let us starve if we didn't turn. That's how we all felt about an Irishman who wore the tunic of Anglo-Saxon law. British or American, didn't matter.

But the concern in Brosnan's wrinkles is valid. A patrolman's salary is barely enough to pay for a working class tenement, the cheapest rooms in the same neighborhood that is run by Dinny Meehan's men. Not only is he reliant on Dinny's money so he can one day retire, but he also has no choice but to accept Dinny's handouts. If refused, his safety walking around the streets of Brooklyn after dark could not be guaranteed, as Dinny Meehan controls everything there. Everyone pays Dinny Meehan tribute. For most people, paying tribute to Dinny means giving part of their earnings. For patrolmen, it means accepting money.

When, one day, great change comes to New York as it has all along, and the rising current against gangs in Brooklyn sweeps William Brosnan in, his loyalty to the vows he has given to the letter of the law will be questioned. When this happens, he will be made to choose between the law that employs him, or to Dinny Meehan. Brosnan knows that if and when change finally comes to Brooklyn and the gangs are outlawed—as they already have been in

Manhattan—a terrible and bloody surge will separate us all. A surge that could easily take his life, or that of his son-in-law Culkin. Or any of us.

From my cell I watch Brosnan look away from the newspaper for a moment, worried. The black cigar wriggling from the side of his mouth and the forehead of him made long by the comb-back, wet-black hair. He knows what Patrick Kelly means. He knows because he's Patrick Kelly too. Right along with us, even though he is not as vigorous and dependent to loyalty as we are. He knows the consequence of spiting that code, too. Our code put forth by Dinny Meehan and the violent and looming men around him that enforce it, such as The Swede, Vincent Maher, and Tommy Tuohey and many others who will never bow to Anglo-American law. Never, for it's bred in them.

Yes, the worried wrinkles on Brosnan's face as he looks upon us are valid, surely. Because when the time comes that he must choose, both himself and his son-in-law will be caught in the rising flood and the ripping currents of clashing wills. The tumult of change is forever hardest come in the old insulated neighborhoods of New York City. "Here t'is," Brosnan's voice booms out, pulling the newspaper back up to his face. "Listen to this headline: 'Riots on the Brooklyn Waterfront Claim Six Lives: Seventy-Nine Reported Injuries: Two Missin'."

Brosnan reads on of "the staggerin' evidence of this borough's gang infestation" and how two men were murdered on Tuesday in a Red Hook saloon that was torched afterward, four more in front of the New York Dock Company and then yesterday "a band o' men moved from pier to pier and laid down their own brand of law, culminatin' in the fire-bombin' o' the New York Dock Company's land holdin's and the International Longshoremen's Association stronghold at the Red Hook docks" and the next part he reads makes Cinders chuckle, "We believe we have the leader in custody; his name is John 'Non' Connors."

"Why do they think Non's the leader?" Tim Quilty asks next to me, rubbing sleep from his eyes. "He's one o' us, he ain't no leader." Cinders shooshes him.

"'Cause that's what they was told, right, Cinders?" Petey says from the floor, not so much a question as an indictment. "Right, Brosnan?"

"Shut ya head." Patrolman Culkin stares at Petey through the bars and out of the side of his head, the police cap tilted over an eye. Crossing in front of Brosnan on the other side of the bars as us, Culkin wields his blackjack and points it at Petey and threatens to take him out of the cell for a ripe beating. But Petey Behan never stops talking. He is the blathering type, to be sure. I look at him with his wide shoulders and short build standing next to Richie and Abe now and threatening Patrolman Culkin in kind. Being short always seems to make Petey more aware of other people's weaknesses. Mine being fear, he pounces on me for it. But we are on opposite sides for many reasons, Petey Behan and myself. He, along with all of Richie Lonergan's teenage followers were always closer to Bill Lovett's side, while it is to Dinny Meehan I pay respects, along with most others. Years earlier Lovett was the leader of the Jay Street Gang, Jay Street running parallel to Bridge Street, where Dinny's White Hand Gang was headquartered. In a deal making Lovett the dockboss of Red Hook, Dinny enveloped the members of the Jay Street Gang into The White Hand before I ever arrived in Brooklyn. But Bill Lovett would never be as loyal to Dinny as his other dockbosses. And neither would Bill's followers, like Petey Behan and the other boys.

As for Non Connors, he was Lovett's right-hand man in the Jay Street Gang, and later down in Red Hook too. It was news to all of us that Connors was being called the leader of The White Hand by the newspapers, but it wasn't news to Brosnan and Culkin.

Brosnan continues reading, "Why his devotees call 'em 'Non' is a mystery, but the deeply ingrained sense of contrarianism in his demeanor may help our readers see into the dark soul of the gang's chief," Brosnan laughs aloud at the journalist's waxing on the fraudulent leader. "As it's these young men, teenagers even, that have it in them to disagree fer the simple sake o' disagreein'."

"The simple sake o' disagreein'," Cinders repeats in a mocking whisper, looking at us boys. "That's why we fight, eh?"

"Shaddup," Culkin says to Cinders daringly.

Brosnan pulls from the Irish-brand Na-Bocklish cigar in his mouth as I look up at his pensive face. The lines around his eyes pinching, jaw adjusts in worry as he looks at his son-in-law, the husband of his pregnant daughter and father of his only grandchild who is not wise enough to avoid challenging prisoners that own the streets he patrols. Not wise enough to know that Dinny Meehan and the long line of young men that follow him make enough booty off these fertile docks to feed every open Irish mouth in the breezy neighborhoods from the Navy Yard on down to Red Hook with enough left over to hire the best lawyer in Brooklyn: Michael "Dead" Reilly.

"What's the news in Ireland?" Cinders changes the topic while looking at me.

"Well the law's closin' in on them rebel bhoys in the GPO," Brosnan says.

He goes on to describe the men of the Easter Rising as "damn fool Fenians" and that the people of Dublin are throwing the contents of their chamber pots on them as they are being marched through the streets as prisoners.

"Imagine the wreckage they've made o' the city, if ye can," Brosnan says to Cinders through the bars. "It's burnin' as we speak. And fer what? The idiots've been offered Home Rule for Ireland the day the Great War ends and they go'n undermine it. Even the Irish papers're against 'em."

I hold my tongue as I'm told. Even when a shoneen and a souper like Brosnan is at his boasting. Every Irish man and woman knows the British Empire's promises mean nothing. Home Rule for Ireland had been debated for many years to no avail and no one believed England would suddenly, willingly give up one of its colonies. Only a fool and a souper like Brosnan would say such things. Knowing my thoughts on the topic, Cinders watches me, though I make sure there's nothing to see on my face, even as it's about my own family Brosnan speaks, since my father and older brother are most assuredly involved in the rising, seeing as though they are proud Volunteers for the East Clare Brigade.

"What about out west?" I whisper.

"Out in the Irish countryside?" Cinders asks Brosnan.

"Few skirmishes," Brosnan says passingly. "Mostly quiet."

I take a deep breath and close my eyes.

"Don' worry, your Ma and sisters're fine," Cinders says to me.

"You don't know that," I say to him quietly and not as respectful as I should. "The British will come. And out there, there's no law holding them back from raping the countryside."

Cinders watches me closely again, knowingly, then nods when I look back at him.

* * *

TWO DAYS LATER WE ARE TRANSPORTED, then arraigned in front of Judge Denzinger and with our lawyer Dead Reilly talking for us and no witnesses, we are sent out of the courtroom with a callous brushing of the back of the judge's hand from above, perched upon his high bench. On the way out, a fat man with a long bushy mustache and a police tunic plops a fat finger on a piece of paper. "Patrick Kelly," I sign, and we are released from the Adams Street Courthouse.

As we come out from its arches, a gang of workers are clearing debris without noticing us and just as Reilly is to direct us on our next move, a wobbly, rusty train takes over our ears as it passes by above the street. Reilly waits with an air of importance and competence, one arm on Cinders's shoulder, the other on an elevated's girder like a man whose time is in great demand. As the chain of overhead cars slowly ambles north toward the Brooklyn Bridge and the Sands Street Train Terminal on the Myrtle Avenue El, Reilly explains, "Dinny wants the boys to go to the Lonergan bicycle shop and wait."

"That means stay there," Cinders says to us, wiping back the hair off his forehead as men drop broken bricks and worn timber joists from a scaffold on the third floor of the courthouse onto the bare pavement. "Stay there until notice. I'll get wit' Dinny and The Swede and send word for ya."

Reilly shakes hands with Cinders and heads back into the courthouse where all the other sleekly dressed men are heading, leaving us out for the wind. Leaving Cinders Connolly to the street too, and although he is about the same age as Reilly, the two men couldn't look more differently, as Cinders is dressed as a laborman like myself and the other boys with hard, scarred hands and a face that the weather makes its own.

"Richie?" Reilly calls back.

Richie limps up the cement stairs and in some strange sacerdotal edict, Reilly puts his hand on Richie's shoulder, the ordained standing a step lower and looking up to the bishop of the Adams Street Courthouse. After a moment of whispering Reilly shakes Richie's hand and nods at him with a resolute but fabricated dignity, then sends the boy back to us. With private messages for Cinders and Richie, I await my turn, but Reilly simply turns round and disappears within the archway. No messages for me from Dinny.

After some goodbyes, I watch Cinders run up the stairwell to the Adams Street Train Station above as the rest of us walk toward Bridge Street and the bicycle shop. I look up at Cinders as he disappears in the crowd along the raised train platform, his long strides and dark gray suit with workers' boots and big smile leaving me to the other teens.

"Lovett's still in," I hear Richie tell Harms up ahead of us, who whispers something back that I can't hear.

To my side, Petey Behan is talking with Timmy and Matty. "You think Bill Lovett's gonna be all right wit' every-thing? No, he ain't. Non Connors, his righthand man, takin' it as the lamb? Just like Pickles Leighton took the fall for Dinny back in 1913? Nah, that shit ain' gonna fly. Bill an' Non Connors go way back and so do we. Back before Bill started payin' tribute to Dinny. I know Dinny set up Non. And I'll bet Brosnan's in on it too. We all know it. Dinny don' want Bill gettin' too strong as the dockboss down in Red Hook, so he removes pieces. That's what all this is about. Ain't it?"

I look over to them and see Petey looking at me as he speaks. It's not long ago that him and I were at odds, fighting over a stolen coat that brought us to blows the same night my uncle was killed.

"Just wait," Petey says to the other boys, though staring toward me as we walk across York under the Manhattan Bridge abutment. "It'll all come around too, won' it, Liam?"

"What?"

"Yeah, ya think it'll all be all right now, don't ya? Like nothin' happened," he says walking next to me and looking up into my face. "Like ya jus' gonna take away one o' our best guys an' we won't do nothin' about it, right?"

"I didn't do anything," I say. "Dinny and Bill Lovett put aside their differences, Petey. For the good of all of us, we gotta stick together, just like Dinny says. I don't know what's going on with Non Connors, but they'll let him go."

"No, they won't," Petey says. "It was planned well ahead of our takin' back the docks. Planned with Brosnan and the tunics too. Dinny wants Lovett weak. You know that, I know that."

Up ahead of us, Richie and Harms slow down and watch. I look at Richie in hopes he'll put a stop to Petey's ballyragging me, but he just watches with his dead eyes on the corner of Adams and York.

"Ya think Lovett don' know what you do?" Petey says to me. "Ya walk around like ya some kinda royalty'r somethin'. Tellin' everybody what we do. Ya're a fookin' tout, ya know that?" Then turns round. "He's a fookin' tout, Richie."

"Do we have secrets here?" I shout back awkwardly, looking at Richie too. "No, we don't then. So what's a tout without a secret? I don't know what's going on with Non Connors, but why not let it all shake out first? That's your problem, Petey—you talk too much. Your mouth is going to get you hurt one day."

Petey looks up at me from his wide neck and shoulders. He shakes in anger and I can see his fists clenching.

"Go on, boys," a grocer woman says with a broom in her hand.

I back away from Petey and try going round him, but he won't let me, keeping me at bay with his left hand on my chest, his right fist held down behind him. I swipe at his left hand in anger and we stand chest to chest in front of the grocer woman, who calls back to her sons inside. Petey pushes up to his toes to get his face closer to mine while I lean into him. Bitterness fires inside me with my pumping heart and I imagine grabbing his throat and kicking him wildly. We then push each other away, but somehow I am punched in the mouth with a swiping swing that doesn't have much power behind it. The grocer woman yelps for her boys to hurry and when they come out of the store they stop to find Richie Lonergan's face, who they know very well and are in no hurry in confronting.

I feel at my mouth and there is a bit of blood on my fingers from it. And I feel the eyes staring at me too. All of them. Petey is at the ready with his fists and teeth clamped closed while the others turn toward me too, Timmy, Matty, and Abe Harms. Richie stares down the brothers from the grocers and I know quickly that I am in a bad place. Outnumbered and with no help at all, my loyalty tied closely to Dinny Meehan, theirs to Bill Lovett. The divide among us now feeling greater than it ever has been.

Feeling alienated by the Lonergan crew, I look away angrily. It's all too much for me, and if I'm to think clearly, I don't long to choose Dinny's side at all, even though he's vowed to help me get my mother and sisters to New York. Greater on my mind than any of it is what is happening in Ireland, my true home. The great country I was born to defend. My mind turns away from all of these demanded loyalties in Brooklyn to defending the motherland, particularly when she calls for me at her greatest time of need in this springtime of her awakening, 1916.

And with Petey ready to fistfight me and everyone staring, I decide right here and now that I am not for Brooklyn in the first place. Any of it. And that I am to be back home, to my birth land where the earth is always under my feet instead of cement and brick.

"Fuck off," I yell to Petey, point at him and Timmy and Matty and Abe and Richie. "The whole lot of you. I don't need any of this."

I turn and sprint. Back across York Street and jump ahead of a slow-moving trolley. I refuse looking back. Just run with tears of fury coming off my eyes. The shame of my uncle's death and of being jailed and alienated by everything else. The only things that slow me are McGowan's old boots that Dinny gave me, and the heavy thoughts weighing me down. The thoughts somehow pushing up from a dream I'd had of the small crack I saw on the cement floor of the jail cell. That the crack opened into a great fissure that separated us by a flood, which opened into an ocean. Sent us to different sides, forcing us all to choose. I keep running, though, as fast as I can. All the way to Sands Street do I run, thinking in my head that

I need nothing of the gang, having chosen my side. They don't care about what is top on my mind. Don't give a single care about my family caught in the coming troubles of war back home. My mother, who looked at me with the hopes of the Savior Himself when I left, is now the only person on my mind.

I couldn't have known it at the time, but I know now that she hoped for me to save her from the coming storm. She knew it was coming. Somehow she knew. She always knew things. She felt it coming last October, 1915, when I left Ireland. I'm sure of it. I can see it on her face now, in my memory. As I sprint along the sidewalks and storefronts, running and running, I think of her. Harder and harder I run to drive out my fury. And I think of her. My own mother. Caught in a rebellion among a war and no one seems to have the worry or the care of it. As I run up to the third level I think of her more. She looking up to me in a hope and I not doing a thing about it. And being sent into a jail for some reason that has nothing to do with the urgency of needing to get my mother and sisters out from the bloodshed they'll be faced with. To do the job my father sent me to do.

When the news broke a few days earlier of the Easter rebellion in Ireland, Dinny and I were with Tanner Smith in Greenwich Village. We'd passed a place called the County Claremen's protective, an Irish organization helping new immigrants from County Clare. So it's there I'll go for help. Among the gray clouds and the charcoal-blue sky, I look down from the Brooklyn Bridge trolley out into the big East River below. I think of my family and I think of fate. I think of my connection to my country and I think of who I am. And who I am going to be one day. That I wasn't born to be a foreigner to my own land like the rest. And especially not when it is my mother that calls for me. A deep and unnerving pain, her calling. I know too much of my land to forget her. To leave her forever.

I know now what I was born for. The same reason she bore
all her sons. To defend her; not for exile. To lend my body
to her struggle. Our struggle; not New York's. To join the
East Brigade of County Clare, Fifth Battalion with my
brother and father and be a man now. A man of fate. To
answer the calling of my flag, the Tricolour, that was made
with glory and humility by French seamstresses after their
own revolution. Made for the men that planned a rebellion in Ireland during the Great Hunger when the soul of
her had hit the lowest bottom. A bottom that lives in all of
us for all time because of the horror of eviction and
shallow graves and emigration and the witnessing of our
own Mother Ireland being brought to an undignified
bowing. To her knees begging for her children. Praying
for a mercy that was held against her by the theater of
words and promises, the cruelty of slight and neglect. The
silence that revealed their disdain. My own mother bent
and humiliated.

Again my eyes are filled with the tears of rage. Here she
is. She who has given so much of her to her sons as she sits
by the hearth pondering them. The mother in need now.
And during the blossoming of my fighting years. I am fifteen and ready. My brother Timothy a year older than I.
The two of us strong for her, for I know that she would not
grudge us for going out and breaking our strength and
dying for her. That she would know us faithful. That we
fight for her. And if I am to give my own life for her, would
I not be spoken of among my people for generations? That
I'll be remembered forever. Alive forever. Speaking forever, I'll be heard. Forever.

And won't it be said I am blessed for having the chance
to give my blood in a protest against her mistreatment?
And what of my father, who has longed to die for Ireland
and is now given his chance? What of him, I'm not sure.
And that of my sisters either. Clare is a long way from
Dublin where the rebellion is taking place, but my worry is

the whole of the land will be brought to its knees again by the flying of the butcher's apron above Ireland.

I am done then. I am leaving Brooklyn behind me forever. Forget Brooklyn as no more than a mistake in my life. It's not for me. To start anew now and to realize my missteps, is the best thing for me. I go now to see the Claremen's protective in Greenwich Village for my passage back home. Leave Brooklyn behind me.

CHAPTER 2

Pulcinella

May, 1916

THE MAN KNOWN ROUND AS "WILD BILL" Lovett, pale and thin and hard with the street-rearing of old New York City behind him already, steps out from the Doric columns and the long shadow of the Fifth Avenue Court inland of the Red Hook docks. With a hand of knuckles now scabbed over, he drops to his head a wool cap where hidden within the inner lining is a razor ring. He looks down from the top of the steps onto the street moving in front of his eyes. Carts and drays and sidewalks traversed by groups of whisking dresses grubby and browned along the hems. Men clopping along in work boots and leaning forward toward their destinations with old-country hats of various styles and the worn wool suits that hug the lifting of hard labor day in, day out. A filled-to-capacity, four-car trolley clanks through the middle of the cobblestones between the street that is walled in by masonry and brick buildings on the one side, the other is the sullied and grimy façade of the Fifth Avenue Court—this neighborhood's Parthenon satellite of Anglo-American law shadowing Lovett here.

Released, today it is his twenty-second birthday, though there will be no celebrations. Looking out over the South

Brooklyn streets, the cruelty in his eyes hidden within a gentle face and protruding ears. His body is slight and not tall; he gives everything he has to prove to men larger than him what great things loom inside, as Bill Lovett does not have it in him to follow others. And so, there is that great cruelty in his eyes betraying the innocent features. The lips red as if painted. The cheeks blushed by the cool air and the wing-like fawn ears all giving him the appearance of a young angel. The Italian laborers of Red Hook who fear not only his temper, but the violent men loyal to him, call Lovett "Pulcinella," a clown-like figure of their own lore. Standing among the courthouse pillars, it's only been a few days since he and Non Connors and others shot and killed three Italians and a pier house manager on Imlay Street at the foot of the New York Dock Company's head-quarters. The news quickly traveling through the Italian Red Hook and Gowanus neighborhoods that Il Maschio—Frankie Yale's Black Hand connection on the docks—was gunned down by Lovett and The White Hand. The Irish clown of the Red Hook docks, Pulcinella, whose cherubic appearance betrays the depraved man inside, had laid down his law in the neighborhoods in which the Italian lives in great numbers.

But to see his eyes is to know him. And to know him is to know it better to be away from him. He is a grandson of the exiled. His family's past smothered in the shame of a horrendous starvation and a grueling journey never recounted. Left only to the imagination of storytellers like those that told me, who tells you now.

Shoeless and emaciated, his grandparents landed in Brooklyn in 1848 from their native County Kerry and took to begging for scraps. His grandmother six months with child, face gaunt and pale. Weakened and choleric, her motions were slow and mouth stuck in an open position, eyes staring forward and unresponsive, stomach bulbous and half-covered by a fraying sack dress. Catholic, they could not find steady work in New York. One week after arriving, the police pushed them off the vacant lot where they slept without roof or cover. The local newspapers wrote that, "An extensive colony of Irish people who had settled on the vacant lots . . . which . . . from the number of pigs and dogs there, is known as 'Young Dublin.'" The same article described the area as a "pigdem" and wrote that the police had "rooted" them out.

Along with thousands of other newly landed Irish, Lovett's grandparents dug a hole in a foothill on a piece of land called Jackson Hollow just south of the Navy Yard. The police left them there since ownership of the property was in litigative dispute between the heirs of Samuel Jackson. Soon there was a baby, the eldest sister of Bill Lovett's unborn father. The baby breaking in a shallow, rain-puddled cranny on a night untamed dogs roamed Jackson Hollow, sniffing new mother's blood in the air. And so, they blocked off the entrance of their scalpeen home with long sticks and branches taken from trees that once grew all over Brooklyn. They stole a chicken from a child by beating him with their fists and running away with it. Then stole a pig too from another family. And a goat and slaughtered them all with sharpened rocks. When challenged by another starved Irishman for thieving, Bill Lovett's grandfather rose from their dirt hole with one fist clenched, hair falling out from malnutrition and only rags covering his groin and chest. The two men challenged each other in Gaelic, holding their sticks. One died.

In their generation, no Irish spoke about such things as the shame of destitution on their name. The embarrassment of want being the bane of pride. But Bill Lovett knew nothing of his family's struggle in Brooklyn and the Lower East Side of Manhattan when they arrived, for it had never been told him, yet the story thrives in him as it thrives in all the men I knew in Brooklyn. Told by the storytellers come out of Irishtown like The Gas Drip Bard, who gave way to Beat McGarry and finally down to myself, here. Giving allegories about innocence and cruelty. The backdrop of our story can be seen on each and every face that washes up. The innocence of appearance and in the cruel and inhuman eyes of Bill Lovett now as he steps quickly at a swift angle down the wide stoops of the Fifth Avenue Courthouse toward yelping children holding newspapers above their heads.

"Irish rebels to be executed, read it here!"

"Local gang men released after recent rampage, only one charged!"

"No mercy for those of the Easter rebellion, get it now!"

He drops a coin on one of the boys and flips through the April 29, 1916 morning edition, leaning on one leg propped on the bottom step of the courthouse. On page three he sees a small headline, "Brosnan made a detective for work breaking up gangs, jailing its leader John 'Non' Connors," and below reads the reporter's summary, "Brosnan vows to keep light of law along dark waterfront goings-on."

"Meehan and Brosnan," Lovett mouths and crumples the paper, dropping it on the ground by the feet of the newsies.

Adjusting his cap and immediately turning west toward the water, he crosses the street with purpose as the windswept faces of Frankie Byrne and two others, who had been awaiting Lovett's release on the corner of Union and Fifth Avenue, look toward him and wait for his order.

"Connors got the brunt," Byrne says. "Meehan's work, along wit' the tunics."

"I'm goin' to get Lonergan an' his boys," Lovett says. "Them yokes played right into it."

"Ya want ya piece?" Byrne asks.

They come in close to each other and exchange it. Bill places the .45 in his coat pocket while looking over shoulders; Jidge Seaman and Sean Healy watch too. With the wind forcing his eyes low he tells Byrne, "You're my right hand now. The time comes, we cut ties wit' Meehan an' them, I'll need ya right next to me. All o' yaz. You know like I do Meehan'll come for us. We gotta be ready, but we'll never survive under him. He kills us or we kill him. He'll keep us around long as he needs us. When he don' need us, he'll set us up like he did Pickles back in 1913, and like Non. Time comes, we'll keep Red Hook for our own in the south and never pay tribute to that fuck again. But we're gonna need Lonergan and the kids and we're gonna have to be quiet about it, right?"

Byrne and the others nod in agreement.

"I-talians in the ILA are weak right now, but that feller— what's his name? Used to run the Five Points Gang?"

"Vaccarelli, Paul Vaccarelli," Byrne says.

"Yeah, he's way up the ladder in the ILA now and all the I-talians follow him in Manhatt'n and New Jersey, but we can never let 'em cross the Gowanus Canal here in Brooklyn. We gotta keep 'em back—they can stay south down at the Bush Terminal. No I-talian labor allowed on the Red Hook docks, ever. Dig?"

"Yeah."

"Let one in, and they'll overrun us," Lovett says. "Meehan said anythin' to you guys about Connors? Deny settin' 'em up, what?"

"Nothin' to us," Byrne said.

"Won't even deny it," Lovett says, looking up Fifth Avenue, and as he walks away, yells back to them. "Go down to the docks 'til I come back. No I-talians!"

Byrne turns, walks toward the water at Red Hook, Seaman and Healy follow south on Fifth Avenue.

With a single-mindedness that he has come to be known for, Bill Lovett walks angrily in his workman's suit and beat boots. His quick steps move him ahead of a lazy horse clop-ping along in an aloof stride, the dray plopping at each step from a bockety wheel. Cheeks reddened in rage, teeth and fists clenched he stomps out into the street again, adjusting the cap over his eyes. Jogging across the way with a thin tie flying over his shoulder in the wind, he heads west on Union Street where an Italian woman sways slowly along the sidewalk with her children. Happening to look up, she sees the white man strutting toward her with a cold tilt to his head, fists at the ready. Grabbing desperately for her six-year-old and her toddler while dropping a sack, she yanks the children out from the man's way with herself leaning against a lamppost in safety. She notices her husband walking backward toward her. He is speaking the Italian language in a jovial tone to one of the neighborhood men up in a window.

"Giancarlo!" she screeches toward him.

The husband instinctively knows his wife's shrieking tone and wheels round just in time to notice the elfin man stamping toward him. Slyly, he spins out from the way and unplugs his derby respectfully, for the white man who chugs by has many stories that follow him.

"Pulcinella," he says the man's name under his breath, then motions vulgarly toward Lovett's back. *"Va fan culo, uh? Va a cagare."*

A half-block from the trolley stop, Lovett ducks into an unnamed saloon on Union and Hicks well before any expressways are built through the area. It is dark inside and he sits at the mahogany bar closest to the door. Those inside know his strange face. His bow-shaped ears, red lips, and the small frame that comes with great repute, ill or otherwise.

"Two beers, no foam," Lovett demands.

In the obscured light and the musky stink of old beer sunk deep in the walls he sits in anticipation, elbows to the bar showing his scarred hands. Five men enter behind him. A group of what some call "shenangoes," or floating migrant laborers that come for a single day's work unloading lighters and barges on the water, then evaporate into the city and the port saloons. Lovett downs one beer whole and looks up to the tender, twirls his finger for another round. Sets at the second and it is gone too. Soon three more men wander in—Scandinavians, though Lovett mumbles, "Austrians."

"Can I buy you a beer, sir?" one man offers.

"Nah."

The tender drops two beers in front of him and he pays, then takes one of them and drinks it down too. Sips on the fourth, burps silently through gritting teeth.

"Sammich? Soup?"

"Nah."

The tender looks away shyly, then back to Lovett, "Just get out? Glad to see someone's puttin' these fookin' dagos round here in their place. Ya know, if it were . . ."

"I don' know you," Lovett says.

The tender stops, walks down slowly to the other end of the bar.

Lovett hears behind him the mumblings of words, "Old Jay Street Gang" then, "Leader, Lovett" then, "White Hand in Red Hook."

He looks behind at the men that speak of him and one ducks out, bringing in a shock of spring light. Five minutes later that man arrives back again with two others.

Lovett finishes his beer and steps off the stool through the crowd, but is blocked to the door by a large man.

"Talk, Bill?"

"Who you?" he says, and slyly takes from the lining of his cap the razor ring and slides it on behind his back.

"One on one, I'll take ya," the man says simply.

The crowd of men listening opens outward, surrounding the two in the doorway. The large man has puffy fists and a thick build beneath the coat and although he is quite young, his hair is thinning. Lovett sees the man is nervous and as his opponent peels back his coat, Lovett slowly rolls his left shoulder to the man and drives the ring with a quick right swing that bounces off the man's orbital bone with a blatting sound.

The man begins to smile unfazed, but soon realizes he cannot now see from the eye. Touches it with his hand. Blood streaming down the sleeve of his white shirt. Moving to the left, Lovett swings again into other eye. The man begins losing his balance at the second landing and is now completely blinded, both eyeballs punctured by the razor ring. Lovett then swings three, four more times opening up the man's face with fleshy wounds and continues puncturing the top of the man's head when he goes to his knees, then resolves to kicking the man's head until he is no longer awake and sprawled dumbly among wooden chairs.

"Afoul it is," yells a squirrelly man with a northern European accent.

Lovett turns round at the circle, gnashes at them. Eyes alight. Legs bent, left fist clenched and right fist of a sudden holding a .45 with fresh wounds glistening at the knuckles again. He moves toward the door and two men jump from his way.

"Bill Lovett," he yells his own name at all inside, daring any one of them speak of this to the police. "Red Hook!"

He opens the door and walks out onto the bright sidewalk tucking the piece into his coat with his blood-ringed hand. From behind, he jumps a trolley bound for the Bridge District and although the standing driver sees him in the rearview, does not demand fare from the man sitting at the edge of his own seat and staring into his red fist pensively.

Jumping off at Bridge Street just a few blocks south of The White Hand headquarters, he walks himself into the Lonergan bicycle shop and finds Richie's teenage buddies loafing around the counter, Petey Behan, Matty Martin, and Tim Quilty.

"Lonergan," Lovett yells out. "Richie Lonergan."

"He's in za back, Bill," Abe Harms says with the accent of the Hun.

Walking past the boys, Lovett storms around the counter and as Lonergan appears from the back room with his fingers black from the grease of sprockets, Lovett grabs him by the collar, picks him up over his head, and slams the youngster to the ground with his might.

"The fuck's wrong wit' ya?" Lovett's face red and shaking, spittle dropping into Richie's face from gritting teeth. "Ya fookin' monkey. Ya're a fookin' monkey doin' tricks."

Yelling over Richie, legs spread around his body and holding him down by the neck and face, "I known ya since I'm six years old, Richie, and you was only what? A babe, that's all. And never had ya backstabbed me like ya have now."

"Why?" Lonergan says, looking up coolly without fighting back.

"Why?" Lovett yells looking back at the stunned Abe Harms and the rest of the Lonergan crew. "Why. Why. Why. Look what he done, Richie. Not only what he done, but he got you doin' it to me. Manipulated ya. Got ya doin' his tricks. Look at ya. Ya still don' even know what I'm talkin' about."

Lovett stands up, paces over Richie who comes to his elbows on the floor. Lovett jumps and pushes him back and puts one boot on the kid's neck, reaches down to Richie's leg and rips off the straps of his peg and yanks three, four times until it is finally free.

"Stay there," Lovett points to Richie's face, and holding the leg in one hand like a weapon walks across the faces of the other boys, Petey first, punching him across the ear until he holds his hands over his face. "Ya got somethin'?" Then to Harms, who looks away and toward the floor. He comes closer to him, the German Jew boy. Closer again, Lovett's chest against Harms's thin shoulder, slowly pushing him back. Forcing him back. Back more, slowly, coercing him into acting weak for him. Breathing deep and angrily into his ear and face, Harms just stares in the distance toward the ground without words. Avoiding the man's eyes until Lovett brings the wood leg up, smacking Harms in the lip with it, "I know ya think ya smart, you. How smart can ya be though, followin' Richie? Ya like a fookin' girl prancin' around waitin' for a man to tell ya what's right'n wrong. Waitin' for 'em to fuck ya head on straight. Ain' that right, Harms?"

"Yeah," he says, looking down and away.

"Richie?"

"Huh," Richie answers from the floor.

"Stay on ya back. . . . Ya listen to this heeb before me?"

"Nah."

"Seems like it. . . . I want ya to stop makin' it seem that way."

"A'right."

"Get against the wall," Lovett says to the four followers of Lonergan and pulls the .45 from his belt, kicks Tim Quilty in the pants. "Against the wall."

With heads pointed to the floor, eyes scared and stuck on Lovett, they walk ashamedly toward an empty wall in the bicycle shop.

"Stay there on ya back, Richie," he repeats, pointing with the gun, the wood leg in his left hand. "Faces against the wall. Faces, chest, peckers'n toes against the wall. Hands locked behind ya back."

Looking up from the floor, Richie watches emotionlessly.

"Which one first, Richie?"

Matty Martin winces and begins to cry.

"Martin," Richie says.

"On ya knees, Matty," Lovett yells. "Face on the wall, pecker'n chest too. Hands behind ya back. Lock ya fingers up."

The other boys look down at Matty, cheeks pressed to the wall. Lovett looks at them and pulls back the hammer and presses it against the back of Matty's hair.

"No, no, no, no . . ." Matty mumbles.

"Don' ya fookin' move from that wall, boy," Lovett says, points the gun toward the ceiling and fires and hits Martin in the head with the wooden leg at the same time.

Matty screams, falling to the floor. Feeling desperately at the back of his head for blood. Looking at his palms, white and dry. Feeling again, then rolling on the ground crying and holding his head.

"Get back against the wall, Matty," Lovett says. "Stand up. Up against the wall wit' the rest of 'em there. Matty."

"Okay."

"Get up there."

"Okay, a'right."

Pacing behind the backs of Harms, Behan, Quilty, and Martin, Lovett calls out, "Richie?"

"Yeah."

"Why do ya fookin' pieces of shit love when I'm weak? Why?"

"Don't."

"No?"

"No."

"This shop here, what is it?"

"Bike shop."

"No, it's boodle," Lovett says, dropping the leg. "A bribe to make ya Ma happy. And to keep you boys away from me. And who paid for it?"

"Dinny Meehan."

"Richie?"

"Yeah."

"Why'd Connors get set up? Why him?"

"He was yours."

"Richie?"

"Yeah."

"What'd Mick Gilligan ever do wrong? What? What'd he do that was so bad that you executed him at Meehan's order?"

"Gilligan went to you for a favor instead o' to him."

"Outta anybody to kill 'em, why'd Meehan choose you?"

"Show loyalty."

"Why's Darby Leighton eighty-sixt from workin' the docks?"

"He's Sadie's cousin, Pickles's brother."

"And what about Pickles?"

"Sadie's cousin too, set up back in '13."

"Harms?"

"Yez."

"Ya so smart, what happened to the money Wolcott'n the New York Dock Company commissioned Dinny Meehan for the Thos Carmody kill?"

"I uh . . . I'm not zo sure . . ."

"Ya don' know," Lovett says. "Ya got no idear, but ya the smart one. I'll tell ya what happened wit' it, it was used to pay off Brosnan'n the tunics to set up Non Connors. Make sense?"

"Well . . ." Harms says. "That's a theory."

"Yeah, a theory. Until I see Carmody's body somewhere, we're gonna assume it's the truth. But I gotta feelin' Dinny'll never take an order from some fat Puritan fookin' Anglo from Massachusetts who's in charge o' wage'n labor at the dock company. He don' take orders from nobody, ya know that. All o' ya know that. So, what's that mean if Carmody ain' dead?"

Harms begins to answer, but mumbles.

"Speak up."

"Maybe Volcott vill vant to know zat information."

"Yeah, Maybe Wolcott and his lackeys Silverman an' Wisniewski over at the New York Dock Company might wanna know that the man they paid Meehan to kill ain't dead. And since we're there talkin' wit' 'em, maybe he'd like to work somethin' out, him'n us. I mean, hey, we're the bosses of the Red Hook Terminals, right? The New York Dock Company's headquarters is in Red Hook, right? The White Hand Gang just firebombed the damn place and didn't even kill Carmody, the Brooklyn recruiter for the ILA, and he's supposed to be happy about it? Harms?"

"Yez?"

"Silverman's a heeb like you, you're gonna go'n find 'em, talk to 'em."

"I don't know zis man."

"Well," Lovett says coming up close to him again, his chest and breath against Harms's face. "Ya gonna talk to 'em. Find 'em. And we're gonna be quiet about it all. There's only the six o' us in here, so Meehan finds out anythin' about this conversation, I know who to look for. I'll hunt ya down, all o' ya. Yaz already got chumped by Meehan 'cause ya a bunch o' fookin' babies, all o' ya. But I hear anythin' back from Meehan about this conversation and I swear on my mother an' anythin' else, I'll open up ya heads like tomata soup, the fookin' whole lot o' ya."

Matty's legs begin shaking, tears streaming down his face.

"Matty?" Lovett says as Richie looks up from the floor. "Turn around, Matty. Turn around."

The boy turns around, his shoulders slumped and hair in his face.

"Shoulders against the wall," Lovett screams.

Matty trembles, pushes his shoulders back.

"What'll happen if ya talk to Meehan about any o' this?"

"I won't," he says, blubbering.

"Won't what?"

"I won't talk to no one, ever."

Lovett grabs him by the neck and throat and runs him up the wall with one hand, gritting and with eyes bulged and shaking in disgust, then points the gun up under Martin's chin toward the brain. "I'll take ya life. It'll be mine, forever. I'll hold it. And I'll walk wit' it and everyone'll know I have it."

At that moment mother Mary and daughter Anna Lonergan walk in, children among them with their wee hands held high to their mother and big sister and Willie Lonergan one year younger than Anna. Mary steps forward, her face maimed and discolored on one side where the man of the family had drunkenly thrown hot grease across her years earlier, disfiguring her and scalding the hair away forever just over the left ear.

"What happened, Richie?" Mary yelps in a panic as Martin is dropped to the ground. "What goes on in here?"

"Nothin', Ma," Richie says from the ground. "All's fine."

"What is yer notion comin' in here with all o' yer wild ginaker and yer ballyraggin', Bill?"

And young Anna, the lackeen, sees for the first time the ferocious look on Bill Lovett's face. An elf with his funny ears, red cheeks, and mean look on the mouth. And as she looks away from him, she looks to another face, Matty Martin's.

"Are ya okay, Matty?" she says, kneeling.

"I'm fine, stay away," he says, jumping to his feet.

Anna looks up as Matty struggles to hold back his tears, catching his breath. She looks up at the angry, wild face of Bill Lovett but does not seem outraged.

"He's just fine, girl," Lovett says as his tie again is stuck over his shoulder, then turns to Mary. "Get this, woman. You let Dinny g'ahead an' keep payin' the rent here."

"I do," Mrs. Lonergan says.

"But from today you'll pay a due every week to the Lovett Gang and ya won't say a damn thing to nobody about it either."

Lovett and Mrs. Lonergan hold eyes. And Anna stares at the man threatening her mother and holds close onto her arm as the man speaks in a terrifying tone. The children hiding behind skirts, tears on their cheeks and lips curled in cry. Tiny Thomas Lonergan too, all five years of him, scared by the threat in a man's voice again, like his father's, and is tearing up himself, hushed and pushed by the head behind the dresses of mother and older sister.

"My husband will have something to say about it," Mrs. Lonergan says softly, then looks away.

"Ya husband needs to be workin', Mary. We all know that. Send 'em every mornin' to Red Hook and I'll keep 'em busy. You're gonna run this bike shop from this point forward. You an' Anna and we'll keep supplyin' new bikes. Here's how it's gonna go. We're gonna stay quiet, all o' us. Right now, we ain' ready. I owe Meehan tribute every week from Red Hook. I'll give 'em back his own money from this shop here and it'll be even. But nobody says nothin' to 'em. Anybody talks," Lovett points toward the Lonergan children. "I'll take every last one o' these fookin' snotty fookin' mucks o' yours . . ."

"You're drunk," Mrs. Lonergan screams.

Gritting, Lovett grabs her by an arm and holds it over her head with a hard grip, pushing her backwards as Anna holds her from falling.

"Let 'er go," Anna screeches.

Harms looks from the wall toward Richie, who goes up on his elbows to watch.

"Ya fookin' ugly slattern whore," Lovett says, pushing her and Anna backwards over two bicycles and then wheeling around toward the boys with his .45.

Children are hugging each other, shrieking, convulsing, and unsure what to do with the fear that runs up in them. The littlest ones go to their mother and big sister who've fallen across a row of bicycles. Willie waits for his older brother Richie to move before going after Bill. Scared himself, Lovett pushes the stripling teen to the ground and points the gun at him, then kicks him in the kidneys.

"Six mont's," Lovett says, roaring toward Willie, then looks against the wall where four teenagers are smashed against it, over to Anna and Mary Lonergan standing and checking their wounds, then stares down to Richie on his back. "Six mont's and we'll make our move. . . . Petey an' Timmy?"

The two teens look back to him from against the wall.

"Ya tell ya older brothers they're wit' us. That they're in now, forever. Mary, ya tell ya husband he's wit' us too. Darby Leighton, Byrne, Seaman, Healy, and others. Six mont's and we'll make our move."

Squatting by her mother who is bleeding from an elbow and her back, Anna looks up to Bill Lovett. Sees that no one in the room challenges his command as he struts from one side to the other, bellowing and casting rules and orders. She watches Bill as he throws her brother's wooden leg toward him and tells him to get up. She is not outraged at his actions. Sees in him the violence that she knows from her father's actions, but does not feel the same disgust. Instead she sees in Bill Lovett all of the qualities of control and power that her father lacks. The dominance over others. The leadership. A violent demand for success unlike her father's violent demand for respect. Aroused by this man's will, she looks up from helping her mother and sees not hatred for the man that has wounded her here, not resentment as she has so often felt toward her father, but stimulated by the brutality she's come to know so well.

"All five o' ya, out the door. Go bring back five bikes so these women can get to work sellin' 'em. Ya got rent to pay, no more freeloadin' off Meehan. When the time comes I'll be in charge and the whole lot o' ya will be ruling ya own territories like Dinny's dockbosses. We're gonna get there, but we need six mont's o' quiet to build up. Richie?"

"Yeah."

"That day comes, you'll be my right hand. But get it, we need quiet. Silence. G'ahead an' do what Dinny an' his boys command for now. He'll be keepin' all o' ya away from me, so you'll be sent up north in the Navy Yard'n the other terminals. Do what they say. Wit'out question, but tell me about it right off. I wanna know everythin'. Understand?"

Everyone in the room looks at him, from the wall and from the ground.

"Understand?"

They all mumble in agreement, making sure not to attract too much attention on themselves as the five teens walk past the children and out the door to Bridge Street.

"Eh, Mr. Lovett?" Mrs. Lonergan says.

"Don' call me that."

"Well I just don' want to . . ."

"Whadda ya want? Say it."

"If yer to be the king round here someday soon, takin' me childers away from me . . . and me husband . . . won't ye need a wife fer to be known as . . ."

"Ma," Anna pulls on her mother's arm, yet looks toward the man for his reaction with a soft glance.

Bill looks at Anna with hard eyes, his cherub ears red and flayed out from the side of his head, bright lips and blushed cheeks. He looks at her body, gun in his hand, black tie still over his shoulder. He walks toward them as the children gasp again.

"This bike shop's yours now, Mary," Lovett says, staring into Mrs. Lonergan's eyes. "Ya husband an' the boys, they need to be workin'. You know that like I do. You're a businesswoman now. You're in charge here. When Dinny's men come to pay ya rent, just thank 'em. Don' talk. We're gonna move up, you'n me. All o' us. But there's only one way to move up, and that's to move someone else out. The world demands it. The strongest run it and I'll be the youngest ever to take over the docks."

Looking away from Mrs. Lonergan toward Anna, "Fourteen's too young yet. The day comes when I clap open Meehan's brain with this gun is the day I'll earn ya. 'Til then, I ain' nothin'r nobody but another laborer on the docks. The gang'll be ours, though, and your family will be on top. Mary an' Anna Lonergan, treated like queens ya will be, and wit' kids fat'n happy. I promise ya that. As a man, I promise it."

CHAPTER 3

The Old Protective

I LOOK IN WINDOWS. ALONE, IT takes me three long hours to find Greenwich Village from Park Row where City Hall watches the trolleys climb down from the Brooklyn Bridge. Now here on Hudson Street, I see scores of children I mistake for an entire class but are really only three mothers and some twenty-five kids with nosefuls of dirty fingers and a wave of high-pitched voices.

I ask an old man, "Do you know where I can find the County Claremen's old protective, uh, association?"

"Evicted Tenants Protective and Industrial Association?" he says with a toothless mouth and a melodious lilt.

"Yes."

"Go see Lynch in his tavern at 463." He points and shuffles off.

I come to a brick building on the corner and inside are the whites of eyeballs staring from the sides of sulky heads among the obscured light from the front windows. They look the same as the longshoremen of Brooklyn who wait for the flag, the whistle, and the shapeup in local saloons.

A very tall, sturdy man with a vest and full head of hair opens the growler hole behind the bar and takes some cash from a faceless hand outside, sends a filled cup through, then calls for me, "Help ye, bhoy?"

"Is there a Mr. Lynch here?"

He is looking in my eyes with a coldness about him that I can see he means to run this tavern as a real and respected business, "What's yer need?"

"I want to go back to Ireland and help set her free."

The men at the bar bob in a muffled, cynical laugh, holding their glasses of liquor in front of them.

"Is that all?" Mr. Lynch says, bringing more chortles.

I stare at him from the doorway.

"Don't stand there, bhoy, are ye in or are ye out? Make up yer mind."

I walk in.

"So," Mr. Lynch booms after dropping a beer for the man next to me. "It's a soldier ye wish on bein', like the ol' songs," he says, a dull light on one side of his face.

"Uh . . . I want to go and fight, yes."

"Ye know they've surrendered? The men in the GPO and the others," the tall man, Mr. Lynch, explains. "They'll be executed. And the locals, the Dubliners, even the Catholics there . . . spat on them bhoys as they was frogmarched t'rough the streets. Dumped chamber pots on 'em, they did."

"Why?"

"Lackeys, jackeens," Mr. Lynch says standing well above the other men hunched along his bar. "They see Home Rule as bein' put in place after the war, I s'pose. So why start an armed rebellion and ruin their city? That's what they say at least."

"But England will never follow through with Home Rule, not if the Ulstermen have something to do with it and there's no history that shows we should trust England."

"True t'ings, all that ye say there, but it's complicated. Here in the States, more and more we're seen as German sympathizers and with Roger Casement and the arms he tried to bring to Ireland t'rough the German cargo vessel, they've got their connection. . . . Think about it, bhoy, one-hundred t'ousand or more Irishmen have volunteered to fight with Britain against Germany. And this Easter

Rebellion is what, a t'ousand men or more? I support their efforts, don't hear me wrong, I want a free Ireland like the next fella, but those men're martyrs."

"What's wrong with martyrs?"

"Nothin', ye want to be one yerself?"

"Maybe I do."

"Then stow on a transport ship 'cause England's blockade won't allow ye go back Ireland way, but ye'll get caught 'cause every ship's searched in Dover'n Dunkirk."

I look down to the wooden floor, deflated.

"Where ye from, bhoy?"

"Tulla."

"Ah, father in the East Clare Brigade, is he?"

"He is, an' my brother too. Do you know what may've happened to them this week?"

"They was called off durin' the Risin' we heared, countermanded out in the country," Mr. Lynch said as the others mumble in confidence. "What's yer name?"

"Garrihy."

"Garrihy, eh? Tulla? Come on here, bhoy," Lynch says, touching his chin, then directing me to the end of the bar.

I sit up at the end with my elbows as we meet at opposite sides.

"Where've ye been stayin' here New Yark, Manhatt'n?"

"No."

"Brooklyn?"

". . . No."

"Well where then?" he says, standing tall. "Oh . . . ye don't talk, is that it. Yer as mysterious as the mist, aren't ye? Ye gotta be in Brooklyn then because they love bein' quiet. Irishtown is it?"

I am still quiet.

As he walks away, I call to his back, "How can I send a letter to my mother? I was sending her letters, but the return address was my uncle's place, but he . . . moved. And anyway, he won't give them to me."

He comes back and pushes his face close to mine, "Yer uncle's Joe Garrity, ain' it?"

I look at him and because of the shock, I'm not able to deny it right off.

"You an ILA bhoy down there? Brooklyn? The name Thos Carmody familiar? He's missin', ye know. Thos Carmody is. Know anythin' 'bout it, do ye?"

Again I'm taken aback.

"No, yer not ILA are ye? Yer Dinny's," he nods his head and grits his teeth in thought. "Bet ol' Dinny don't know ye're here neither."

A man sits at the bar and Mr. Lynch excuses himself. After serving a drink, he speaks with another man for a moment, who leaves out the front door. I have the look of torture in the face, unsure what to do with myself now with the idea of my returning home being shot to shit as it is.

"So," Mr. Lynch says returning. "Ye can't go home and join the Volunteers. Yer uncle's dead. Ye don't know what's been done with yer da or brother and yer mother's all alone in Tulla. Well, I'd be scared o' that too, for the Brits'll come and arrest all the suspected IRB and Volunteer men. Break up the brigades. Out in the country where there's no aut'ority is the most dangerous place fer a lone mother to be. Ye got sisters?"

"Two."

"Could get ugly for them, ye've a fair assessment on it. We've all got family back there, though, but we here can help in other ways. Our County Claremen's Evicted Tenants Protective and Industrial Association along with the Owen Roe and John Mitchel clubs and others here in the city have functions, and we send funds back to the place for various t'ings, freedom included. But now's a bad time fer goin' back or comin' here. Why not bring yer mother here after the war? And the sisters as well?"

I shrug my shoulders.

"I know ye want to fight and kill Brits, we all do, but the smart man . . . the t'inkin' man sees that it's a better life in America fer yerself and yer family, is it not?"

"My uncle thought so."

"Well," Mr. Lynch says, leaning on the bar closer to my face. "Maybe he chose the wrong side at the wrong time? Word was he had a mouth on 'em, but not the meat to back it, so someone cut 'em, burned down McAlpine's Saloon with himself in it. Is that what you heared?"

I don't answer.

"Some say t'was Dinny Meehan's men did it. The law locked up a good few of 'em too, but let 'em go all except one—Connors I t'ink's the name. The leader they're callin' him, Connors, but I know as well as the rest of us that whatever the gang tells the police in their blue tunics are no more than lies." Laughing, the tall man continues, "I heard a hundred dock men were arrested, all named Patrick Kelly, the entirety of 'em. Oh yeah, the Brooklyn bhoys have always lived under the cover of lies and silence, just like the White Boys of West Ireland back in the great day of Wolfe Tone and the Fenians. Some say that's where they got the gang's name from, and their code of silence too. And wouldn't that make sense, eh? White Boys and White Hand? Rebels the both, are they not?"

I'm watching and listening to Mr. Lynch behind his bar, fascinated by the stories and histories.

"There are ghosts of our past, ye know. They live among us too. Ye t'ink they don't? Even if they are mostly just remembrances. They live on. Within us all. In our stories too do they rise up like rebels against our oppressors. Martyrs who wish to die so that the children of the next generation have the stories of their blood-sacrifice held in the tears of those youths. That the demand for freedom to be ourselves, alone is worth their lives. To fight against the notion of becoming their enemy—does that make sense to ye? That there are a great many of us who don't wish on bein' Anglo-American here? Just as they didn't want to be Anglo-British over there?"

"It does."

"Oh, there's many-a story o' Dinny Meehan too, surely. Ye know he was born just a bit down the street here? Did ye know it? A lot's been said of the man. Did ye know too that almost everyone had died in his family within a matter of a year's time, they did. Even his uncle, the great Red Shay Meehan who was shot up by a bunch of Strong Arm Squad men dressed as laborers. A lot's been said of Dinny since he took his dyin' father 'cross the East River where on a stormy day the currents sent 'em to Bridge Street. And there was young Dinny Meehan, all eleven years of him holding up his father against the icy rain and the gales of a death blow bearing down on the ferry. But it was Brooklyn where he was reared by the streets and the docks. The last son of the once powerful Meehan clan. There are some who love to tell stories of him. It's true, too! Down in the auld Irishtown section, man named The Gas Drip Bard still tells those stories to this very day. And he tells 'em well too. Says, and I quote, 'Dinny's the last son who inherited a silent past. Whose history was obscured in lies by victors. In the shame of victims.' That's what the Bard says of him, ye know. Around 1912 auld Irishtown was bein' sold out by its own son, Christie Maroney. . . . Ah well," he says shrugging his shoulders. "No time for stories now but when ye've a moment, look up The Gas Drip Bard in Irishtown. An old man, a shanachie is he, whose words are like birds in their flight from Irish to English," he smiles. "Look 'em up and ask 'em about the rise o' Dinny Meehan and the gang known as The White Hand."

"I will."

Mr. Lynch smiles at me, "I s'pose ye just got outta the bullpen yerself. First time was it?"

I still don't answer.

"Yeah well, better not to commit, as they say. Listen, bhoy, I'll help ye. Do ye want to know why? I'll tell ye. For Dinny

Meehan's sake, I'll help ye. Only for his sake will I do it. So then, why not do this: write a letther. There's t'ree ports we can send it t'rough, so ye'll need to make two copies o' the letther. Most mail and packages from the United States'll be opened by British aut'orities to stop the money and weapons from flowin' in, so t'ree letters at t'ree ports are yer best bet," he counts them on fingers. "Foynes Harbor in Limerick, Galway Bay, and Kilronan on the Aran Islands which'll be ferried to Doolin and out to Tulla. When ye get word back from 'em, then ye can decide. It's not a smart man decides his life on a dime, bhoy. And I'll bet yer da didn't send ye here so ye'd come right back when the trouble started, am I right?"

"When my da came back from O'Donovan Rossa's funeral last year in Dublin, it was then he bought my passage and here I am."

"Yer a good lad. I can see it. Voice barely cracked but a big weight on ye, there. But if yer da was a Volunteer all along, sure he had a feelin' somethin' was on the rise. Now write yerself a letther right over there," he points to the wall opposite the bar, then turns to the rear room and yells. "Honora!"

From a back room adjoining the bar comes a woman with a large bun of hair on the top of her head, an apron in one hand and an open-mouthed one-year-old in another.

"This young man needs a sammich to write his poor ma a letther," Mr. Lynch says. "He misses her and wants to know if she's all right and he's hungry too. Can we make him one?"

"Sure we can," she says, then speaks to the baby. "Let's make the child a sammich, James, can we?"

I write my mother a letter, then copy it twice at a candlelit table where a long low bench is connected to the wall opposite the bar. When finished, I walk up to the bar with all three letters in my hand.

"Fine, fine," Mr. Lynch says smiling. "Do ye have money at least to pay fer postage?"

"Uh, well I have this," I reveal some change from my pocket.

"That won't even get ye home, bhoy."

"Consider it paid," a voice calls from among those at the bar.

When I look to the man with the offer, I recognize his face from the side as he drops some coins on the wet mahogany. Mr. Lynch thanks him and he stands from the bar, "C'mon, we're goin' back to Brooklyn, you'n me."

It is Tanner Smith.

"Bhoy," says Mr. Lynch. "Ye come here with an open hand and the old County Claremen's Association gives when ye need it most. The people o' Ireland are in need too, as ye know. Why not ask Meehan to pass the hat round the Dock Loaders' Club and we'll make sure it gets in the right hands? A few bits for the mothers and fathers back home fightin' an' sacrificin' fer the freedom?"

"I will, sir."

"Good lad."

Tanner takes me by the coat outside where we shield our eyes from the shining of the sun.

"Ya're a fool kid," Tanner says.

"What do you think Dinny will do to me?" I ask.

"I dunno. Ya was given a direct order and ya broke it. Stay at the bike shop and ya couldn't even do it. Listen, ya heard anythin' about Thos Carmody?"

"I haven't, but . . ."

"What?"

"Just that Mr. Lynch asked if I worked with him."

Nothin' lately 'bout 'em though? Thos Carmody? Like anyone seen 'em?"

"Nothing."

"Good."

"What do you think Dinny'll do to me?" I ask again.

"Let's go."

CHAPTER 4

Faction Fight

Under the echoes of the Manhattan Bridge sits the Dock Loaders' Club at 25 Bridge Street. It is there among the factories on the water where tug-pulled freight-lighters with many train cars on floating docks connect to the freight rails dug into the Plymouth and Jay Street cobblestoned streets, the tracks curving through sidewalks and entering buildings through red-bricked archways. Below the reverberations of great bridges and among factories and smokestacks and industrial rail tracks along the waterfront is where we call home, the east-end of Irishtown in the exact same windswept neighborhood our ancestors landed a generation or two earlier.

The events of April 1916 both in Brooklyn and back home in Ireland give me to thinking the world a violent place where the poor are ignored, put to use in labor, or reviled for their plaints. Made to fight amongst themselves for the right to charge tribute like some underground, unknown struggle. As a great writer once said, in the enormous posterior of the cities of my day there were garbage piles where its hated poor brawl each other for a place in life in the lowest of hierarchies, like underneath the bridges in Brooklyn.

Upstairs at the Dock Loaders' Club, the young men of The White Hand are divvying up the day's tribute given them by laborers and ship captains and warehouse and pier house supers. Dividing the spoils for owning sway in the ignored and lawless waterfront.

Downstairs through the front entrance I am forced in by Tanner Smith and see sitting at the end of the bar closest to the door is Bill Lovett of Red Hook, who turns round with a mug in his hand and looks straight into my eyes with Frankie Byrne at his side. Gibney The Lark and Big Dick Morissey, both of the Baltic Terminal, are there, as well as "Cute" Charlie "Red" Donnelly of the Navy Yard, their backs and necks wide over the mahogany trough like beasts of burden watering themselves up.

There among the gruff men is the beautiful, golden-haired Mickey Kane. Leaning against the bar with a charismatic smile and perfect skin along with Lovett and Byrne, Mickey has the look of a chosen one. Tall and broad-shouldered with thick hands and powerful thighs, his being Dinny Meehan's cousin got him elevated in status quicker than the rest of us. Although he had always been known as "the fair scrapper," Dinny made Lovett take him in as a regular down in Red Hook and, without anyone questioning it, Mickey provides Dinny with updates on Bill's comings and goings down at the furthest point from 25 Bridge Street and the southern-most territory of The White Hand.

In the bar where faces are only lit by the slow wick-flame in paraffin wax, there is a wash of names that come flooding through me as I see them. Picture them in my mind as I look back and search through the old memories in me. This story is about people. So many of them. So many stories I can't bear to exclude any. But looked at from afar it's easier to see them all. As a whole. Our struggle has always been ours to own. Ours to hide, even. They are a wash of names and faces that bubble up here and there, out of the foamy ocean chop of memory and story. Unrecognizable but for the desperate gasping for air before again the waves wash over them, awash in time. The Atlantic suck between

Ireland and New York enveloping the remembrances of them to tragedy's isolation. The tragedy of shame proscribing these names and faces by their deaths at sea and the class from which a death at sea or a tenement childhood in Brooklyn castes them. But to look at them from afar, as I wish you to do now, they're easier to see. And even though they come from modest stock and of the lowliest peoples, from "the blood of serfs," as it's been described, these men that raised me called themselves kings. The kings of Kings County. And so it is as kings their monikers describe them, such as "The King of the Pan Dance," Dan "Dance" Gillen, whose blood was mixed together, African and Irish, and "The Craps King of Ballyhoo," Chisel MaGuire in his old dusty top hat and coattails like some mid-nineteenth century immigrant. Even Dinny Meehan himself was called "king of a bunch o' low-breedin' diddicoys," by old William Brosnan. So many of them ran with us though, like Frankie Byrne and his followers. And the old storyteller Beat McGarry who talks too much and sits next to the silent drunkard Ragtime Howard. Not to be forgetting the Minister of Education himself, who doubles as the Dock Loaders' Club bartender, Paddy Keenan. Then there's the hangers-on like the bony Needles Ferry, mumbling Johnny Mullen, the half-Italian "Dago Tom" Montague, best friends Eddie Hughes and Freddie Cuneen, the Simpson brothers, the mental case Garry Barry and his lone crony James Cleary, Happy Maloney, the limping Gimpy Kafferty, and Fred Honeybeck. Most are there, but Mick Gilligan is not, since he's dead by now, shot in the back of the head by young Richie Lonergan. Nor is the secretive dockboss of the Atlantic Terminal, Harry Reynolds, present, as he'd already beat the place upon receiving his take from the divvy, as usual.

Tanner pushes the back of my shoulder while the men look upon me gravely. As we pass I see Petey Behan and the other Lonergan boys sitting around a small table with

half-drunk beers on it, eyeballs at the corners of heads
staring daggers at me.

"How go it, Tanner?" the pavee fighter Tommy Tuohey
says quickly while manning his post guarding the stairwell.

Tanner nods, then whispers to Tuohey, who runs
upstairs, knocks, grunts something when the door opens,
comes back downstairs, and throws a thumb over his
shoulder to us. "G'on up."

Vincent Maher opens the door, the grip of a .38 protruding from his belt, tight trousers clearly displaying his
phallus lying to a side. A gallous dresser, Vincent is. Vest
unbuttoned, belt unbuckled. Skinny and handsome and
full-haired and ready, he comes out to the hallway with
Tanner and myself and closes the door behind him.

"Listen, kid," Vincent says. "I'm gonna give ya the terms.
Listen. Shit's serious, a'right?"

"All right."

"It's four months t'day McGowan is killed up in Sing Sing.
We all know Lovett ordered it and Pickles Leighton got the
screws to do it from the inside. We all know Lovett was
behind it. Ain' no secret there. We might've won t'ings down
here in Brooklyn, but on the inside we lost. Pickles is still up
there now recruitin' guys in Sing Sing and when they get
out, we don' even know who they are, got it?" Vincent says to
me, wiping his nose with a knuckle in the dark stairwell, a
lone small window running light over his shoulder as he
speaks. "A man close to Dinny's heart, was McGowan, ya
know? Damn close. It was a hard war we won before you
even landed here. I don't blame it if ya don't appreciate it all
the way, but I'm here to tell ya it was a struggle to get where
we are now. I myself went to war right alongside McGowan
when I was your age . . . your age! And the man was a fookin'
soldier through to the heart of 'em. But lemme tell ya somethin', Dinny an' McGowan went way back. On the streets
together, no help from nobody. So Dinny . . . he's been
thinkin' a lot about McGowan t'day. About how close they

was, them two. And you. You too. Dinny started gettin' close wit' ya, so when he heard ya lam'd it to Manhatt'n on ya own? On this day o' days? Naturally, he's got a bit o' the mopes. Lookin' back on his ol' friend. Who he went to battle wit'? McGowan? Then this? Understand?"

"I do."

"Good, here's what I want ya to do. I want ya to shut ya hole when ya walk in there an' listen. Just listen's all. Can ya do that?"

"I can."

"Thanks again, Tanner," Vincent says, quickly moving the conversation toward him. "Ya hangin' out a bit?"

"For a while, yeah."

"Right, ya heard anythin' about Thos Carmody, the ILA feller?" Vincent winks.

"Heard he's missin'," Tanner says. "Real shame."

"Let's go," Vincent says, pointing in my face. "An' you. Just keep it shut, you."

As I pass through the door Vincent tightens his belt. But even back then I knew the face he had when violence was on the wing, and true enough, it was not there. I was safe.

In the office, the gang's chubby, idiot savant accountant Lumpy Gilchrist is slumping over his little desk in the corner, a cast of envelopes scattered about him and a broken pencil in his hand, unaware of my entrance entirely. The Fulton Ferry Landing and Jay Street Terminal dock-boss Cinders Connolly, who I shared a cell with, has turned round from his chair across Dinny's desk and looks at me lamentably. Dinny Meehan too is looking at me, a parting in his mane just left of the center separates two broad clumps of dark brown hair, shorn over the ears tight. Not surprised somehow, his face is almost smiling with agility and reserve like a lion panting or a king of some sunken, nameless and ageless practice that has for so long been ignored that it almost never existed, if not for his sitting atop its throne right here in front of me, the crowned head of lowly laborers in King's County itself. Eyes alert more than anyone I've met, then or now, bright and guarded and knowing and being of a culture older than ours. Older than my own father's, or his father even. Stones for eyes, a green and pale fuchsite shine, translucent as if they aren't there at all. But staring at me. Noticing everything. Seeing all. Over his thick shoulders are the industrial, open-shuttered windows and the New York skyline with the two bridges crossing over the East River. He is staring at me from his desk and with the expanse of the city behind him too. I look away. Unable to hold his stare, I look over his shoulder again where he is perched to overlook the docks and bridges. Then look back at him again with his thick jaw revealing within its hard curve over the neck and his piercing stare a purity of law, for which he violently oversees, violently defends. A law that is as rare today as it is ancient and logical and respectful of free men. I know his ways because he had already explained them to me, yet I ignored them. Took them for granted.

I look away again, then look back up and nod to the tall, tow-haired man on his right, The Swede, whose arms are folded angrily. The Swede he is called, but is not Swedish at all but looks the part of one. He refuses to acknowledge my nodding toward him and instead cynically looks down to me.

Staring at me as well, Cinders Connolly stands away from the chair he was occupying. Walking from it without being asked and looking at me too, grimly.

"Don' go," Dinny directs him while looking at myself, then nods for me to sit.

I do, gently.

Dinny tightens his tie although it is already flush on the collar, his hands large and muscular over the tiny knot and thin tie. He looks at me in a slightly pained squint. But just as he is about to speak, he stops. Stares. Watching me. Looking into me.

He is in the center of the room, Dinny Meehan. The center of all our lives. Surrounded like a mystical deity by men with the ability to do terrible things to others who threaten their leader. Lying about his very existence to outsiders in order to conceal him within the code. Inside our silence. Protecting our secrets from those who want us downed.

"Who's Dinny Meehan?" is the answer when someone asks about him. "Never heard o' the man. He live around here?"

Surrounding him, they do. Bad men, such as Tommy Tuohey guarding the stairwell downstairs, a man with a large build but handy with his fists due to his being bred from day one for gypsy boxing along the country boreens of Ireland. And Vincent Maher who guards the door to the second floor and who has no moral issue in both separating the virginity from a young female with his blood-filled cock as he does removing the life from a male with his snub-nosed, single-action revolver. And The Swede too, always at Dinny's right side by the window, a man freakishly tall and ugly and horse-faced, furiously paranoid and whose fist is as large as most men's faces and who has been known to punch the life out of people with a single looping and crushing swing, such as a Calabrian that stood up to him named Giovanni Buttacavoli, chronicled by the newspapers and word of mouth.

The three bodyguards stand watch around him while his dockbosses enforce his tribute along the waterfront docks, as has been done since their fathers and grandfathers arrived seventy years earlier. Dinny Meehan at the center. Nameless and faceless, if you ask about him. Yet seemingly always there at the center of our arrival and rule over Brooklyn longshore labor. He being our nous, embodying our intellect and knowledge, both a guide and creator even. A man whose reputation stands so far above the rest of us that some argue, such as Beat McGarry, that he is more than just a leader of labormen, but a man who saved

Irishtown and the old ways from the waves of time and
change that crashed across New York at the same moment
he surged to power like sparse light from darkness, a
countercurrent.

Staring at me, Dinny Meehan does. And even though he
is protected by many, he is not fragile by any means. Looking
at him is to feel it, and I can see that he is by far the fiercest
fighter of them all. Wide-set eyes, muscular brows, broad
jawline and shoulders with small ears and a tree-trunk
neck—that of a mauling dog. Ever since he'd taken power
on the docks in 1913, he has been challenged one on one to
some fifty or sixty fights and still now, undefeated. Perfect.
All knockouts, and with only cement or cobblestones or pier
planks to catch his flaccid victims. Russian, Italian, Polish,
Black, or Jew. Irish even. The biggest, rowdiest fighters
Brooklyn could muster from any reach. Not one even lasting
a full minute before Dinny comes to the inside of them,
blasting through their bodies and eventually up through
the face and jaw, the odds so much in his favor that no bets
are even taken any longer. Staring at me. Through me, with
his green-stoned eyes from his desk and me there, long and
skinny and young and unknowing, I open my mouth.

"I just want to know about my family."

"Little fuck," Vincent mumbles. "I told ya to shut it."

I look back at the man, Dinny Meehan at his desk, where
all attention is directed. He has only twenty-seven years, yet
somehow his patience comes to the fore. It was he that
brought us all together out of nothing, so I've been told.
He who now feeds the poor where this country chooses to
ignore them. Just like the British had when we died of the
starvation. Here, he finds them jobs, rooms, brings them
as one in a second-floor saloon by the docks amidst the
filth of factories, the fires of foundries and the enormous
transience of the elevated trains and bridges reaching
deep into the leaning tenements of the bulging under-
classes. All of this on him, and still he looks to me with a

great tolerance, patience.

"Connolly," he says after a good long silence.

"Yeah?"

"What was it ya said to all the new boys just the other day when . . . when all o' ya was outside just before we took back Red Hook?"

"I told 'em to listen to Richie. That any order Richie gives, treat it like it comes from Dinny."

Dinny nods.

"And what was it ya said to all the new boys just this mornin'?"

"Go to the Lonergan bike shop 'til ya hear word from us."

Nods again. Adjusts his shoulders inside the coat and swivels his neck. I look away from him for a moment. The top of his desk empty of all papers. All evidence. Dust accumulating on the most of it.

Dinny clears his throat and eventually speaks in a low tone, "I made a commitment to you."

I listen.

"That," he looks away, then looks back at me. "That I take seriously. If I were a man who said things he didn't mean, no one would care a shit for me. I take the things I say, the commitments I make, as somethin' carved into me, ya know? As somethin' all men around here can trust'll be done."

I agree with a nod.

"Do you know that the man you went to speak wit' today was a very close friend of my fam'ly? When I still had a fam'ly. Mr. Lynch and my father came from the same village, Coolmeen in Clare. His wife Honora met him at a County Clare ball that my father'd organized. She was an orphan girl sent to Ennis from a little place called Kildysart. Her fam'ly was a friend of my father's family, and we got her here, New York. My father . . ." Dinny looks up, but does not cross himself. "My father was buried in Calvary Cemetery in a respectable grave when I was eleven years old. I was the only one left wit' him. My mother and

brothers and sisters'd all died. But because of a man
Tanner Smith connected me wit'. . ." Dinny looks over to
Tanner, who calmly acknowledges. "The money he loaned
me . . . my father didn' have to be left in some pauper's
groundsweat. Now I have new fam'ly. There are many men
and women and children that we care for. In these neighborhoods. Because if we don't, no one will. So, people trust
us. Is that a fair statement?"

"Yeah," Maher says.

"True," Connolly agrees.

And everyone else in the room is with him. And I see that
they are raising me. That my childishness is small potatoes
compared with the vast operation that Dinny oversees. That it
takes a genius to keep together what we have here, with all the
elements that want us taken down. Our ways and our ancient
laws that inform us here in the new world is what makes us so
reviled by the many. Wolcott of the New York Dock Company
and his followers Silverman and Wisniewski who attempted to
control us. King Joe of the International Longshoremen's
Association along with the missing Thos Carmody and my
dead uncle Joseph who longed to enfold us in their syndicate.
Frankie Yale's man Il Maschio who was gunned down on
Imlay Street after threatening our sovereignty by crossing the
Gowanus Canal into the Irish north. Brosnan and Culkin of
the Anglo-American law whose job it is to bite at the wrists the
criminal activity we so blatantly flaunt. And even Lovett within
our midst, who'd love nothing more than to take the gang in
his own name by ripping the life out of Dinny himself. All of
them against our way. All of them using time against us while
we protest it. Dinny seeing them only as invading gangs or
opposing clans. Outsiders. Foreigners. Strangers. Intruders.
Infiltrators. Touts. Others. . . . Change. Only a man of great
ingenuity could succeed in stopping time and change. Halting
progress by summoning the ancient glories of our people.

He uses silence to sway me too, his hands folded and
head slightly atilt. To make me see it all, he sits quiet and

allows me to imagine on my own. To see him as who he is and what he has done. What he is still doing, for not only did he organize a great blow to take back the docks from the "others," a day for legends as we termed it, to not only win against the most absurd odds, but to know exactly where he'd land afterward. Where these enemies would be funneled and collect to again attack: Lovett. Lovett being the recipient of offers from our enemies through Red Hook in the south of our territories, Dinny will know from where these enemies will attack.

Everyone in the gang questioned why Non Connors, Lovett's right-hand man, was set up as the lamb. It's too obvious, some said. It gives Lovett momentum, others complained. But I see it now so clearly. By setting up Non Connors, Wolcott and the New York Dock Company, Frankie Yale and the Italians, King Joe and the ILA, Brosnan and the law would all go to Lovett to make a deal against Dinny and the power structure set up in old Irishtown. To divide and conquer us, as the Anglo-Saxon has always done. That the only way to take Dinny down, would be through Lovett. I look up to Dinny and see his brilliance for the first time, the bridges and skyscrapers over his shoulders and the breeze of the waterfront brine in our noses through the open iron shutters. He did it on purpose, setting up Connors so that he would know exactly where they'd strike next. Creating! Creating what would be seen as a weakness by outsiders, while making Lovett an enemy too for making deals with those outsiders. And I see too, looking at him at his desk now, that Dinny Meehan does everything with purpose.

"Why don' ya trust me?" Dinny asks, his thick, dark brown hair falling over his shorn ears in jagged shards. "Now I hear Petey Behan punched ya and ya ran away. Do ya remember what I said in the taxi we took together t'rough Manhattan earlier this year? Do ya remember?"

"I do."

"What?"

"You said draw a line and don't ever let anybody cross it again without a fight."

"We're a family here," Dinny says, spreading his hands across the room. "Some o' us don' act right and need to be handled. We don' go to Brosnan and the tunics for justice, though. The law ain' for us, it's for the ownin' class who can slip a piece o' change to the judge to get saved, make the laws themselves for their benefit—and for the rest? Who got nothin' but hope? It's to hell they're sent. We don' go to the papers to right a wrong either. Or the boss on-site for a slave's justice. We don' go to I-talians for nothin' and the ILA don' tell us what to do. Nah. . . . We take care o' our own problems. You, Liam. . . . Ya got a problem."

The other men in the room mumble in agreement.

"You know like I know," Dinny continues. "T'roughout time our people been crushed by others. They keep us poor and weak so that they can have touts among us who need handouts. To keep us small and controlled. If it weren't for touts among us, we'd have our own country where you'n I would still live, wouldn't we, Liam?"

"That's true. A big part of the problem, at least."

"Ya father told ya about 'em. They're always there among us. Always will be. That's why we take care o' things on our own. You . . . you got things ya gotta take care o' wit' Petey Behan, 'cause the rest o' us'll suffer if ya don't. Ya know why? Because if ya don' do somethin' about 'em, they'll see weakness in us. Weakness is opportunity, dig? Lovett an' Lonergan and every man down there are always, and always will be, waitin' for us to show weakness," Dinny opens his left palm out in front of him, open to the ceiling and says, "weakness," then does the same with his other palm, "opportunity."

I think about what he means.

"Now," he continues, The Swede staring down at me. "Can I have ya trust?"

"You can."

"Can I help bring ya mother an' sisters, Abby an' Brigid, to New York?"

"You can," I say.

"Can I help get ya own place where they can stay in a peaceful neighborhood? Like down by Prospect Park'r somethin'?"

"That sounds like a good plan."

"First though," Dinny raises a finger. "Ya gotta earn the trust o' these men. Earn ya name back. Show that you'll stand up for ya'self and for us and what we have together here."

I am following him.

"Do you knowhow you can do that? How you can earn their trust and earn ya name back?"

I think around in my head for the answer.

"He still don' get it," The Swede says, unfurling his long arms from their crossing and dangling them at his side in frustration.

"How can I do it?"

Dinny looks at me seriously, then speaks softly, "Ya gotta challenge Petey Behan."

"To a fight?"

Dinny nods, "Now."

"Right now?"

"Now," Dinny says, then turns to Vincent Maher. "Tell Tommy Tuohey to come up here."

Vincent immediately unlocks the door, "Tuohey? Come up."

"You have a short time now," Dinny says to me. "Ya boy is downstairs."

As Tommy Tuohey and Vincent Maher enter, Tuohey is blurting, "What's it I'm gonna learn the bhoy when it's Dinny beat me twice?" Tuohey then looks up to Dinny, "How's it? Why not yerself teach 'em?"

"I've already gave 'em advice and I don' think he's listenin'. What'd I teach ya about fightin', Liam? What? Were ya listenin' to me?"

Before I can feel scared about fighting, I am having to answer questions, "Keep my fists over my face and, uh, spread the legs for balance, I think you said."

"Dat's right giverteek, moraless," Tommy starts talkin' so fast I can barely understand him, and all while he is sparring me at the same time. "Stand up. Hands high, dat's right. Now slide back wit' ye front foot while steppin' back with the back foot. No, no, like dis here. Slide'n step. Yeah yeah, bhoy, left widda jab right widda hook. Swivel dere. Swing here fer fecks sake. When ye go chest to chest wid 'em, don't give an inch. He clatters ye, don' slash yerself and don' say nuttin' just keepa goin' like she's a job. Just remember we fight 'cause we're men and we'll do it."

"We fight because we are men and we will do it."

"True 'nough."

Over the next ten minutes, Tommy gives me pointers while the others in the room watch and throw in their opinions. Even Lumpy notices something and turns round all surprised.

"Bounce, bounce," Vincent yells at me.

Tommy slaps me a good one across the face, "Wake up, ye feckin' sausage. Ye ready for da yoke to try'n hert ye? Are ye? Ye'll wake up den, won't ye? Ye like yer mudder, don't ye? Don't ye wish ye could live under'er skirt again, don't ye?"

The others laugh.

"Duck out the way den here comes a right cross."

I drop my hands while my eyes pop out and I rush from the way of it.

"Don't drop 'em, Sally. . . . Ye wanna be a poet, do ye?"

The men laugh again, louder this time.

"What is it Ragtime call ye d'udder day? Eddie Allen Poet? Dat's his name?" Tommy asks the others as he moves around and swats down my fists.

"Poe," Dinny says.

"Yeah Poe," Tommy says. "Ye wanna name fer yerself? Yer a poet warrior are ye? The man here's name is Poe

Garrity in his corner ready to die fer his country sure of himself as he is. Killin' 'em wit' the werds, does he. But a man can't have a name widout neck. Ye got neck, bhoy? Do ye? Well ye'll go'n prove it then. Earn yerself den and if yer a sausage don't come back."

"Let me see ya fists," Dinny says, standing from his desk, and we stop our bouncing and sparring.

He takes my hands in his. Dwarfing them with his muscular thumbs and big round fingers, wide palms. He then turns my hands round and opens them, feels the calluses and closes his eyes.

"Ya haven't worked for a few days," Dinny says, then looks in my eyes. "Killed a man though."

The room goes silent.

"Ya can forget anything anybody told ya in this room for the last while," Dinny says, closer to my face now than ever before, then whispers. "Don' forget this. Only remember this. Most important thing I'll ever tell ya. Ya lookin' at me?"

"I am," I say, focusing in on his green eyes.

"This . . . as long as ya alive . . . don' quit."

The men again mumble in agreement.

"He hurts ya, get back in for more. No one can beat the man outta ya. If he does, and you quit?" Dinny says, then nodding toward Tommy Tuohey. "Like he says, don' come back."

"Today ya make ya name," Tommy says. "A real poet don't sit in rooms. He's out in the world fightin' it."

"Has nothin' to do wit' Petey Behan," Dinny says walking back toward his desk. "But if ya quit, don' come back here. You'll never make it. And we won' have ya."

I look over to Cinders Connolly who has always been so kind to me, but his face is strong and hard and looking away. Vincent is staring at me in a demanding smirk ready to uproot the friendship he and I have too. Waves of distress ripple through my body. And when I think about going back to Mr. Lynch if I couldn't stomach this fight, I remember being blocked by Dinny's claiming him. Which means, of course, there's nowhere for me to go.

"Jimmy," Dinny says to The Swede as he sits at his desk. "Lumpy holds the money, tell Chisel no holder's fee. He's only there to fan the odds, introductions and whatnot. I'll give 'em a bite afterward."

The Swede confirms as Dinny looks over to me, "Good luck, kid. G'on now, lead the way. Vincent, you stay wit' me up here. You stay up here too, Tanner, yeah?"

Tanner nods.

"Every man has a day to prove 'mself," Tommy says to me. "The world demands it."

Vincent unlocks the door and opens it for me. Down the stairs I walk, The Swede, Tommy Tuohey, Cinders Connolly, and Lumpy Gilchrist behind me. The first person I see is Paddy Keenan behind the bar as I enter the saloon below. He looks to me, tosses a towel in front of him at the bar where Ragtime Howard looks back over his shoulder. Beat McGarry, remembering things for future stories, as he loves to do, is smiling slyly as he sees the four of us descending. Like three broad-shouldered moose sipping from the river, Red Donnelly, Gibney The Lark, and Big Dick Morrissey look back too and so does the flat-faced Philip Large whose mouth is open in wonder.

Fear and anger rushing through me, I shoulder through a few immigrants and stand over the table that holds the beers of Petey Behan, Martin, Quilty, Harms, and their leader Richie Lonergan, who looks at me coldly as I stop.

"Behan," says I.

He looks up from the side of his face as the men following me come to a stop above, Tommy's hand on my shoulder.

"Meet me outside."

Chisel MaGuire appears of a sudden between us and blurts, "Finish ya drinks, boyos. We gotta challenge."

"Hey hey," I hear a whooping.

"Them kids?"

Behan looks away from me and picks up his beer, downs it. Stands up close to my face as tall as he can make himself and turns his back to me, walks to the door.

"Yeah. Yeah," the men shout.

As we shuffle toward the rear room door in the traffic, I hear men speaking in languages excitedly. Outside, Richie pushes people out of the way so he can stand with the rest of us, though he hobbles and leans on Harms. It is drizzling, though the cold has mostly subsided from the snap that came round the day The White Hand took back control of the docks from the ILA and the Italians and the New York Dock Co. There is a freedom in the air that I hadn't felt since getting soused that night. A feeling that we had cleared the way and any disagreements now between us are no more than the faction fighting or the coming up of a man. It is our time and I can feel it and how we make things is our business—all the rest can watch and get out from the way.

I am surprisingly at ease and at the ready. Pushed up by the courage in my youth. I feel a comfort in it even, for I am not the only man throughout time that has his day of test. I am only one among many who seek dignity. Because although we bring our ways to the world, we lose them too. But were it not for men like Dinny Meehan, those old ways would not stand so tall above us, a hand on our shoulder. I feel myself gaining. I feel a power within me ascending to the fore. The child in me to the aft. And like the brave men of Dublin whose words cut open hearts . . . the men who write in blood as they stand proud against death just this week, I too stand with them ready to give my blood to sacrifice my childhood and walk among the other seers, the tribe of auguries and the unkempt visionaries that stride upon dirt paths with glinting weapons, protecting their families. A man among the sodality of men. Making survival out of this life that is after throwing difficulties in the path of us.

"When Lilacs Last in the Dooryard Bloom'd," I mumble under my breath, still not knowing in the slightest who it was that wrote such wonderful words. Something so ancient and stirring, yet here I stand inside the fighter's circle with cobblestones beneath my feet, buildings above me in place of Ireland's green floor and trundling hills. I take off my coat and my tie and push back my hair, close my fists.

"We have here a challenge!" Chisel stands on a chair in the alley and points toward Petey as the onlookers lower their voices, the underpass of the Manhattan Bridge to our left, the rail yard at the end of Bridge Street in the foreground with Manhattan looking down to us. "One youngster who come up with the Lonergan crew, a Brooklyn-born boyo . . ."

The Swede kicks the chair from underneath Chisel, "We ain' barkin' t'day, get up'n fan the odds and shut ya hole."

I see Richie Lonergan pointing and trying to speak with Lumpy, though The Swede has turned and is in the way, holding him back with one large paw on Richie's chest. I can't really hear him, but I believe Richie is claiming a percentage of the take if Petey wins. Harms is using his shoulders to press The Swede and offers supporting comments for Richie's claim. And Bill Lovett is casually peeling off bills with his legs open and speaking to Petey's ear, then handing a wad to Lumpy. Meanwhile, The Lark and Big Dick along with Red Donnelly, Cinders Connolly, and Philip Large have their arms spread out with their backs against the circle of yelping men to keep it wide enough for the two boys to fight.

"Back up."

"Poe," Tommy Tuohey yells in my ear. "Dis boyo'd like to get in close on ye, giver teek, mora less. Needa keep distance with long jabs from ye, hear it?"

"I do."

"If'n when he gets in on ye close like, ye gotta puck yer way out, hear it?"

"I do."

"Don' tangle too long on the inside. Dat's his game. Yer to keep a distance and pick off the fact he's got the short arms like."

I look up and see Dinny and Tanner and Vincent in the shutter windows looking down on us. Vincent waves a fist at me and smiles as Dinny and Tanner stand behind him with their arms crossed, watching me.

From above I hear Vincent clapping and yelling and a few others as well are on my side, including Cinders Connolly, who yells and smiles at me while struggling to hold back men and next thing I know, Petey is walking toward me with his fists up, as I hadn't heard a bell or anything announcing our beginning. Closer he gets. Closer still until I can see the meat in his shoulders and his wide face. He tries cornering me, but I slip away, ducking from one of his swings. I lose my balance a bit and hear Tommy Tuohey yell something, but I can't hear it clearly.

I feel in me that I don't want to swing at him. That I don't have the anger in me to attack, so I bounce like I was taught and go from side to side, avoiding him as he bears down. His aggression makes me feel hunted and he yells something out to the fact that I was the one that challenged him and why am I running now? And then finally Petey puts his hands down and comes directly at me. As I jump out of the way, he grabs my shirt and yanks me back toward him and as my left shoulder bumps against his body, he swings up with a left and twice with sweeping right hands that catch me on the knuckles covering my face. The crowd roars and I see the veins in Lovett's neck pull up as he yells, Frankie Byrne and the Lonergan crew standing at his side.

My knuckles burn and I feel a small lump grow on the top of my head where he somehow clipped me as I back away, and before I can think about it much, someone from behind pushes me toward Petey, who is surprised and takes a wild swing that is partially blocked by my hands again.

"Stay away from 'em," I hear Tuohey yell to me. "Jab jab."

As Petey moves in again, I straighten my left arm as long as it will go and duck my head at the same time as the punch lands on his forehead. He quickly swings back again, but his arms aren't long enough to connect. I do it again and the onlookers jump up in excitement. One more time with the left jab and I follow it with a straight right that goes over his shoulder, and with all of my weight heading toward him and missing, he swings three and four times from my stomach to my chest and up to my mouth where his last one lands before I move away from him.

And that is what I need. The anger wells up when I realize yet again he had punched me in the mouth. He had kicked me by taking my coat last year during winter. Wore it as a prize for taking my honor and continues pushing me and pushing me until he had punched me in the mouth that very morning. My fists tighten.

"Yeah." I hear Vincent yell from above.

"Dere he is! Get 'em, Poe."

We close in on each other and I measure his head, leading with a right hand that must have missed. I chase after him until we meet in the center, chest to chest, swings on swings, some going over shoulders, others landing in ribs and still more popping on an ear and dotting an eye until I find myself on the ground looking up as the crowd jumps and pushes Red Donnelly aside above me. The Swede then attacks them, pushing them back.

"Get back."

I feel a great winding in me that seems to suck all of my energy away. I can't catch my breath and struggle to my feet, panting and hurt, though I don't realize my nose is bleeding until it itches strangely and when I rub along the nostrils, find it wet and not in its normal shape. I feel death in me. Or a terrible fear. Defeat now taking the weight away from my anger, I now feel as though I stand against death and take one more deep breath and jump over Richie Lonergan's shoulder to get at Petey and grab ahold of his shirt collar and won't let go no matter how much Richie pulls at my hand.

"That's right, Liam." I hear Vincent.

"Get 'em, boyo." Tommy encourages. "Don' leggo o' dat feelin'."

And with many men joining in the affray, I finally wheel Petey out of his celebration and sling him across the fighter's circle, tackle him while he is on one knee trying to get up. I punch and punch, but I am picked up high by The Swede and put on the other side of the circle while the others help Petey up.

"Fight like it's a fight, kid," The Swede points and yells in my face. "A fight, not a tacklin' match."

Again, I am overcome with wind in me and put my hands on my knees as The Swede tells me to go back at it. As Petey closes in, I keep my hands upon knees and watch him. He swings at me and I duck and the both of us tumble to the ground with my face in his chest and arms wrapped close around him so he can't get a clear punch to my face. Still though, I am so winded that I feel the quit in me. My muscles are strained to the limit and I shake in a strange, hungry feeling that comes over me, stealing away my courage.

Again The Swede is breaking us up and I can feel the paving stones scraping the skin off my left arm and shoulder, my head rolling on the ground too.

"Let go, kid," The Swede yells, yanking at my arms.

"Let 'em go, kiddo," I hear Tommy, at which time I immediately release my grip, then kick up my legs to push him away before he gets a free shot in.

"Stand up."

My mouth by now is wide open, trying to catch my breath, while I feel my nose is plugged from the inside of it. The bottom part of my face entirely covered with blood. More of it dripping from my nose to the back of my throat, I spit a glob of it on the pavement and see for the first time my own blood in the mud, mixed with the rain water and the Belgian bricks and the yelling voices and the struggle of life on my shoulders. My thoughts pulse in an intensity with this realization, and so I put my fists above my face and walk to the center again as the crowd cheers on seeing the quit in me had not won over.

I remember again my length being a weapon and the moment Petey gets close, I snap his neck back with a quick left. Then again, while backing up into the mesh of men being held in check by the dockbosses. I know I can't do it again, so I wait for him to come closer again and hold my right hand in wait this time. When he fakes a swing, I throw the right as hard as I can, emptying out my energy, but I miss and as I stumble to gain my balance, I can feel the incredible shaking in my legs. Petey punches me across the cheek with an off-balance left and I let go of my own fists and grab at his shirt again, throwing him away from me, though he doesn't fall. Any break I get from his onslaught is a moment in heaven as gaining my breath becomes the most important thing. I find myself on the ground again with muffled cheers, sitting on my duff and looking up.

"Get up, Liam." I hear someone yell.

"Get back in there."

As I roll to one side to get myself up, I spit again and the blood I see with my eyes, mixed with the blood I taste again gives me some sort of energy that is not at all phys-ical, but only the grind of emotion in a body completely evacuated of strength.

I swing weakly at Petey as he catches me in the ribs, then again on the top of my head as I try to duck. I push him away, but again he paws at me with a smacking sound to my lips and yet another thud comes to my head as I fall into the crowd, caught by Cinders Connolly with one hand before my face smacks into the cobbles.

From what I am told, I got up from the ground two more times after that only to get sat again. I did not lose consciousness entirely, though I can't quite recall all that happened afterward. Slowly coming back into reality, the men all have their arms around me as I sit at one of the immigrants' tables inside the Dock Loaders' Club. Even Chisel MaGuire shakes my hand with Tommy at one side, Cinders on the other and a tableful of whiskey shots bought for to celebrate a man's coming up.

"Looky dat nose on ye," Paddy Keenan says. "All lamped up like."

"Look like a monkey's bollocks," Tommy smiles. "The brutality of it."

"Gargle this down then," Paddy says, handing me another shot. "No slap-arse farmer now, eh, kid?"

"He'll buck 'emself up and we'll keep werkin' on his scrap skills."

After quite a bit more celebrating and drinking, Petey comes up and stands over me with Richie and Abe Harms and Matty and Timmy behind him.

"Good fight, Liam," Petey says sternly, puts a hand out for shaking.

I reach up and shake it as hard as my beat muscles allow. My nose broken and I lost the fight, but my dignity intact. I feel a petting across the top of my head, then a pat on my shoulder. I look up and see Dinny Meehan there. At least I think it is Dinny. But it is not. It's Harry Reynolds instead, who, in the face looks quite a bit similar to Dinny.

"Ya comin' up," Harry says. "It's the smart thing to do, considerin' the circumstances. Ya gotta be pragmatic in these hard times. Ya doin' well."

"Harry? Did you see it? The fight? I thought you'd left."

"I'm here. I saw it," he says.

I squint at him, focus, but then change my mind again. It actually is Dinny Meehan. Not Harry after all.

"Dinny?" I say, wiping the blur from my eyes.

But Tommy and Paddy and Richie and Petey and everyone else look at me with castigating glances, half-smiling smirks, "Who's that?"

"Harry and Dinny," I say under my breath, shaking my head in a befuddled state, falling backward in the chair. "Harry and Dinny and . . ."

CHAPTER 5

Abattoir and Exodus

"SADIE!" DINNY YELLS FROM A BACK room of the Meehan brownstone on Warren Street, then stands in front of her and I; wearing an undershirt, his broad arms and heavy chest block my view of Sadie.

"Yes?" she asks.

"Nevermind. . . . Ya remember each stop, yeah?" Dinny asks me while putting three envelopes on my chest.

"I do."

"Make sure ya tell her she's pretty and . . ."

"The young man knows what to say," Sadie says, moving in front of him with a smile. "But the most important fing is to listen, William. Always listen to a gal, if nuffink else. Ask questions, then listen and show that yu like the person she is—'at's more important. Now come 'ere so I can finish up on the sides."

Sadie pulls my ear down and I can feel the cold scissors on the side of my head. She was the one that nursed me back to health after my uncle left me for the streets last year. She was the one that gave me life again and also who stepped up in my mother's absence. Good Sadie. Sadie Leighton, cousin of Pickles, and Darby, who'd come to Brooklyn as youngsters before she had arrived from the

Irish enclaves of East London, eventually allowing herself
to be won over by Dinny Meehan, becoming his wife.
Bearer of her husband's many secrets, many sins, and his
son too, L'il Dinny. She looks at me and smiles, then runs
water over her hand from the sink, which is always colder
in the mornings, then mixes the cool water with petroleum
jelly and runs her fingers through the top of my head.

"Yu gonna look so much be'a after this, William," she
says, concentrating on my hair. "Got a bit scruffy, yu did."

"Do you think me good-looking?" I ask.

"O' course," she smiles. "And wif 'is new 'air style, yu'll
knock 'er down. More important than looks is personali'y,
yu know. Gals like a man wif personali'y more'n they like
'is looks."

I feel my nose, which is bent and painful.

"Still a bit swollen," Sadie says looking at it with my head
in her hands. "It'll get be'uh, just give it some time. This cut
though, in yu eyebrow 'ere. It's a deep one. 'At'll be a scar
no doubtin' it. Look 'ere, Dinny got yu a coat for today, put
it on, eh? And 'ere's some flowers for the lucky lass too."

I stand in front of the foggy mirror in the kitchen with
my puttied hair, shaved on the sides and the back, bruised
face, new coat, and a fistful of lilacs and dandelions and
carnations and lily of the valley for decoration.

"A real gentleman wif a New Yoork 'aircut too."

"But I don't know if I like Anna Lonergan," I whisper
to Sadie.

She stands next to me in the mirror, adjusts my tie. She
blows some hair off my shoulder and gives an awkward smile.
I can tell she does not agree about this matching either, but
won't say it. Though she knows that I can see it on her. Gives
me her thoughts by the look on her face, purposely.

I look to her, "Did you used to care for Vincent like you
do me?"

Sadie laughs, "Vincent didn't need much lovin'. Full o'
vinegar, 'at one. Carryin' on like 'e knew sumfin'. Prancin'

like a roosta' in the coup, cursin' an' all. 'E never needed much from me. Just a mum for a bit 'til 'e grew ou'a needin' one."

I was third in line, Vincent being just ahead of me. It'd become a tradition: Dinny finding street gamins, bringing them to his home to raise, turning them into his family with Sadie's nurturing. All three of us were so different though, myself being consumed with the idea of bringing my mother and sisters to New York. Vincent intent on sacking as many girls as he could and . . . I turn to Sadie again, "What was Harry like when he was brought in. He was first right?"

"Ma," L'il Dinny interrupts, tugging on her in front of the mirror.

"Oh look," she says sarcastically. "The rattlin' in 'is belly begins and 'at's when 'e comes to realize 'ow much 'e looves 'is mum, eh?"

She bends down and picks him up and as I watch them doting over each other, I eventually come to understand that she is not going to answer the question on Harry, instead quickly changing the topic.

"Did yu know Dinny's got two sista's in Albany?"

"Uh, no I didn't know . . ."

"We're not movin' to Albany," Dinny interrupts from the bathroom.

"Just a visit's all I ask for, Dennis . . ."

"Let's go," Dinny appears in the kitchen, waving me out.

Outside in the predawn shade, Vincent looks up from the stoops as Dinny hands me one more envelope, though this one is empty. "Listen. Ya listenin'? I need ya to go to the corner o' Bridge'n Tillary before the bike shop, yeah? Take the streetcar to the stop at Adams, walk east on Tillary but don't go south o' there, that's Camorra, south o' there."

"All right."

"When ya get to the Tillary Street Abattoir, ask for Feinberg. David Feinberg, and give'm that envelope. Just tell 'em it comes from Bridge Street and he's got one mont' to pay. He'll know who's sendin' ya. One mont', that's all ya gotta say," Dinny explains, holding up one finger. "Then go to the bike shop wit' the flowers, got it?"

"I do, but it's empty," I say holding the envelope.

"S'posed to be, a'right? A'right, ya look good. Everythin's good," he says. "Ya feel good?"

"I think so."

Vincent chimes in, "A bull don' go runnin' after one cow, remember that. He walks down and gets 'em all."

"He just means relax, is all," Dinny says, then pulls out a piece of plumber piping and opens up the new coat I am wearing, fits it into a newly stitched area that holds it perfectly. "Ya won' need it, but just in case. Ya got quite a bit o' dime on ya."

"Nice hair," Vincent says, smiling. "Now ya look like one o' us."

"Big day, let's see what ya can do," Dinny says. "What I tell ya about things?"

"What?"

"What I tell ya?"

I search, "Don' quit?"

"Right," Vincent agrees. "Don' fookin' quit, that's all ya gotta know. Show up everyday. Do it. . . . I been there. Where you are now? I been there. Ya just gotta fight through shit. Ya wanna quit, ya don't. Keep goin'."

Next thing, all I see are their wide shoulders walking away. Through darkness beneath the washing halo light of the low lampposts, turning collars to the damp and cold and dropping down onto the narrow cobbles, they walk toward the water again as most of the city is deep at sleep.

It is May and the rains begin to descend from the cement gray sky and down onto New York kicking up city dirt in the morning and coal dust, opening the cakes of crusty mold between walls and windows and summons the scent of street oils with the river's brine churning too, lumping up in the nostrils. A smell I'd never had back home. A smothering thing for the first few minutes of a downpour as it stirs in the sinuses and in the mouth. But as I come to Bridge and Tillary, a different odor comes on me. A great smell of carrion rot and the iron in blood from a fresh kill. Here there is a small field with fenced pens and a long, wooden, one-story edifice darkened by the rain. The abattoir is on a raised plain of ground and below pink streaks run from it through the street where the rainwater and the sanguinary viscera mix together, descending as if the slaughterhouse itself is bleeding or weeping ruddy tears. Low-hunched dogs circle the structure with eyes of great suspicion, nosing the air for the blood in it. With flowers in hand, purple and yellow and white bulbs that offer color to the dusky grays and the blacks in my view, the wind and rain falling on my new haircut, I tilt my head to keep the drops from my eyes and jump over pink and red puddles. Hitting a pocket of air thick with the smell of death, I stop in the street and gag uncontrollably from the belly up. Though nothing comes of it, my mouth waters with sputum and the horrible taste in the air.

I look up and see a man wearing boots to his thighs and a cutlass in his hand. He is at his work as thoughtlessly as any other man of labor, and he holds a sheep from behind, between his knees, raises its head, and slices open the neck. Held up by the fleece atop its head, the animal wiggles uselessly until it is flung in a pile of others for immigrants that consume hogget and mutton. The gaggle of live sheep watch the man at his work, baaing mawkishly and seeing their brethren slain, and still willingly step forth for their own turn. Ready to die or ignorant of it, I can't tell. But the look in their eyes angers me and I think of the words of one of those dead rebelpoets in Dublin who himself so happily gave his own blood to stir that of the many, "the old heart of the earth needed to be warmed by the red wine of the battlefield." His sacrifice inspiring an entire generation of men and women, fathers and mothers, and even myself as I'd have willingly given my blood too had I not been blockaded. But these animals die for nothing. Don't care either, and I hate them for it, as it scares me deeper than anything else in the world— dying for nothing at all. Just dying like they don't mean anything, like a child dying with no mother or father to cry for them, bury and honor them.

The sad-eyed beeves of cattle and the fretful instinct in the face of the fowls and swine lead me to the notion of death being everywhere around me. I can smell it and feel it as it calls for me, for all of us. I stand there in the street with the staggers, this hell and all the thoughts of death surrounding me.

"What ya lookin' for?" says the butcher in his long boots.

"Feinberg," I say, walking up to the pen with my flowers.

He looks me over until I say, "Bridge Street."

He tells me to wait, slops through the deep red puddles and disappears inside the flooded house. Up close, I see piles of viscera to one side, offal on the other. A loose-necked sheep hangs upside down and is peeled from hind to head by another man who looks sideways at me; he is Hebraic in his features, with a great skepticism in the eye that no foreday rain could purify by ablution.

The blood-slaked ground here on Tillary Street warms the cold heart of Brooklyn too, for everywhere people fight and kill for their place so that they can feel the pride of victory in the comfort of kin meeting ends. Dignity. New clothes. Good neighborhood. Status among other men. Food in stomachs, and through organizations—legitimate or not, split most often along ethnic lines—we war against each other for sway and command in a place that can't support the many of us. Particularly so on border neighborhoods there are violent paroxysms, such as this neighborhood where the Irish in the north and west meet the Jew from the east and the Italian of the south in a city still dominated by the governance of the old Anglo-Saxon ascendency above us all.

Eventually a smallish, balding man of some sixty years emerges from the fetor of the body's blood in the showery breeze.

"Feinberg?"

"Who's asking?"

"I think you know who it is," I say, certain he recognizes my dialect. From my back pocket I hand the envelope to him over the paling and chicken wire, "One month."

As I walk away, he raises his voice at me and says the words he knows he shouldn't. "Dinny Meehan."

I turn round.

"You tell Dinny Meehan he'll have to come find me in prison. Twenty-five thousand dollars a year I pay to the inspectors of the State Board of Health. Then I have to pay you, then I have to pay those Geppetto Italians and don't forget I have to pay my own too. And the union. It's not worth it. Go fuck yourself, Dinny Meehan. Tell him that, why don't you?" He throws the white envelope into a rain-dimpled puddle, holds ten shaking fingers up to me angrily. "That's how many butchers have been arrested in the past two weeks for paying bribes to inspectors. I'll be next. Any day now will be the warrant issued by the commissioner. So you tell him, 'Fuck you Dinny Meehan.' Now get off my property, you bastard child you."

The man with the cutlass of a sudden comes toward me from within the pen and I jump backward. Losing my balance, I put one hand to the ground to stop myself from falling while the other holds tight on the flowers. Quickly I wipe my wet hand on the back of my trousers and reach into my coat pocket for the piping, look back over my shoulder as I run out of the blood and mud down toward Tillary Street. He does not follow me, however, and from this house of death do I take leg bail north on Bridge Street, happy I'm unharmed.

On Sands Street at the bicycle shop I look at myself in the glass. I have no idea what any girl would see in me. I have nothing to offer, my face is mangled, and I'm a parentless child. On top of it all, I've just had my intestines scared out of me at the Tillary death house. I see no point in courtship. And I don't see that I have the personality that Sadie says I need so to impress a girl. I push my hair back with wet fingers.

"How are things, Mrs. Lonergan?"

"They're good, child," she says with Mr. Lonergan behind, many children running inside. "Come in, come in."

"Can I speak with Anna?"

"About what?"

"Well . . ." I try to avoid stating the obvious and also to avoid looking at her maimed face.

"The man," she says, referring to Dinny. "He'd like ye to spake with Anna, is it?"

"He would."

"Oh," she says, turning her head to reveal the burns and scars, waving Anna over.

"Here, I got these for you," I say to Anna as she walks up.

Taking the flowers, she looks at me. Her face is beautiful, I can't deny it, and somehow, even without makeup or even a shapely dress or hat, she still appears like she was made for pictures. Like her mother, her hair is bunned atop the head and her neckline showing the softest skin without a cent of jewelry on her. There is a bit of the tomboy in her that's left over from a Brooklyn childhood, but at some point she could no longer deny the beauty that rose up and out of her, changed her. Likewise, the contrast of the soft pouting bottom lip on her contradicts the stern upper lip that eventually wins over, "Why are you giving me these?"

"Because I think you're pretty and . . ."

"Ya full of it," she says, thrusting the flowers into my chest. "Give'm back to Dinny Meehan, we ain't gypsies here."

"I don't know anyone by that name," I say.

"The hell ya don't."

Mr. Lonergan laughs at me as the children sing songs while dancing in circles, which I feel is a mockery of my shame-faced stance there in the entrance of the bicycle shop. Before I can think of asking her some question so that I can listen to her answer, like Sadie explained, Mrs. Lonergan comes back and stands in front of me, waiting.

I look over her shoulder at Mr. Lonergan, then ask her, "Can we talk, you and me?"

"Sure ye can, bhoy," she says, looking back at her husband in triumph. "Anna? Help yer fadder take care o' dese childers will ye now?"

"Sure, Ma."

"What is it, bhoy?" she says outside with the white noise mumbling in the background.

"The man tells me to give this to you and not to the mister," I say handing her an envelope. "It's two months' rent."

"Good, good, tell the man many t'anks, yeah? It'll go straight fer the rent here at the bikecycle shop, t'will. What is this all over it?" she says, noticing a red smear.

"Oh," I say, realizing it is blood. "I wiped my hand on it by accident, I'm sorry."

"No matther," she says turning back.

"One more thing."

"What is it?"

"Has Bill Lovett been seen round here, Mrs. Lonergan? Does he come by? Does he speak with your son and his fellows?"

She looks away, then back at me, "Well I've not seen Mr. Lovett in quite some time. Since before all that stirring up in the Red Hook last month, I'd say. Don't werry though, we know who the man is round here."

"Has he come here to the shop looking for you to pay him tribute?" I ask, remembering Dinny's directions.

"Absolutely not," Mrs. Lonergan says in shock. "My son knows who the king is round here too and wouldn't allow it. Besides, he never even works with Lovett any longer.

Dinny's got Richie's whole crew up in the Navy Yard werking for Red Donnelly and with Cinders Connolly under the bridges everyday," she explains with logic. "Like they never even see Bill Lovett like."

"All right, thank you. I'll let the man know."

"Good lad, many t'anks. And tell him we're doin' rather well here on Bridge Street, and with Richie and his boys werkin' regular work now'days maybe, if God allows it, maybe we can move to a better neighborhood that has more money. I mean to say, we love Irishtown an' all. To the core of us, but in Crown Heights or Prospect Park there's moneyed people who ride on the weekends for the pleasure in it and spend more coin than anyone here in Irishtown an' it's a legitimate business proposal I have here."

"Prospect Park? That's a nice area, I hear."

"Oh t'is child, t'is," she says in a loud and happy tone. "And trees to fill yer eyes all the days. Will ye tell 'em?"

"I will."

"I mean we're not unhappy about the man's kindness in helping, no no. But with a family an' all, ye know, with a family like ours, best to move to the better schoolin' areas and cleaner churches with the smarter people. I mean look at this bhoy. Tommy? Tommy, c'mere, child."

One of her young sons comes walking out the door and with only a pair of talking shoes on him where the sole of it flops at each step.

"Look at him," Mary says to me. "They call him Tiny Thomas 'cause he's small fer his age. He's six but looks four, does he not?"

I don't know if I should agree, but simply nod.

"He needs a good school," she demands. "Prospect Park's like a heaven to us on Johnson Street. A heaven. We deserve a legitimate business and to live with the good people. The gentlelife."

"The gentlelife, yes," I agree wholeheartedly with the sound of that description. "I'll tell him."

"Oh yer a sweet child," she says and cups her hand on my jaw. "And yer face looks better too. Yer eyes 'specially, not blackened t'all any longer."

"Thank you," I say, wishing I could say the same about her own face.

"But the nose looks atrocious," she finishes, tilting her head back to look down at me.

And before I can respond, she closes the door to the bicycle shop with her envelope at her breast and off to the next stop I go.

Standing in front of the tenement on Bridge and York, I throw the flowers to the sidewalk and enter, up the stairs I go and knock on the third floor.

The youngest daughter opens the door and I ask her, "Is Mrs. McGowan here?"

"She'll be back in just a moment," says the daughter.

"Oh," I say, unsure of what to do next.

"What's your name," she asks openly.

"Uh, Patrick . . ."

She smiles, "No it's not."

I look away, but she holds a stare on me, "I remember you from my brother's wake."

I nod my head.

"You've gotten bigger since then."

"Have I?"

"And I like your haircut, it looks nice on you."

I smile and again look away, "My nose looks like a blooming mushroom though."

"It'll heal," she says kindly, laughing at my accent.

"What is your name?"

"Emma."

"How old are you?"

"Fifteen."

"Me too," I say and look up at her sweet and genuine face. "Wait here."

"What?"

I run down the stairwell in the dark, jump over the stoops, and grab the flowers from the sidewalk and sprint up the stairs.

"Here, these are for you."

"Oh," she smiles, smells them. "You didn't get these for me though."

"Now I did," I say, out of breath. "You deserve them. You're nice and I think you're pretty and I mean it too. Not just saying it. I mean it. I remember when Vincent was talking to you on the sofa at the wake. I thought you were pretty then, but . . . uh . . . I had a lot on my mind, I suppose."

She smiled at me in a wondrously uninhibited way.

"Do you go to school still?"

"Yes, I do. At PS 5," she says.

"That is over by McLaughlin Park?"

"Yes."

"I wish I could go to school again," I say.

"You could come to my school, they would take you in."

"Really?"

"They're always trying to get the kids to stay in school, but so many leave to get jobs."

"I'm saving money to bring my family here, so I guess it's best that I work."

"Well, I think that's good of you. That you care about your family."

I could see that she was thinking about people who don't care about their family. Maybe even that her father was on her mind, who I'd never met or heard anything about.

"There are a lot of us that care about your family," I say.

"I know, your friends have been good to us since before I was even born. When my Ma was pregnant with me, my brother and, uh . . . your friend," she stuttered, not wanting to say Dinny Meehan's name. "They were best friends. Just kids really, but they made their way. Before that, we were not doing well. Working together, those two got us a place to live and everything. Your friend has always been there for us."

The humility of the girl. Her youthful beauty and the genuine things she says, understating that her family was homeless and desperate. All of these things make me very happy. It is amazing to me that through all of these hardships, hard work, and hard living in Brooklyn that I can feel something so delicate in me. So warm and colorful that makes my stomach turn in happiness. There is an immediate attraction between the two of us, but being so young, neither one of us knows what to do with it. But on every moment we have together in the hallway do we hang. Hoping it won't end. Fools for feelings, the two of us.

Downstairs we hear the door open and without looking I know it is Mrs. McGowan.

"Emma," I whisper.

"Yes?"

"My name is William Garrity. Just don't tell anyone, all right?"

She smiles at me. That smile where a secret between her and I is held. That trust which comes from a place where distrust is the standard. A bit of happiness twinkling far off in our minds yet matured but still endowed and aroused and savory like the meat of the lamb. I smile back at her marble-white face and bright lips amongst the tenement wood-grays and rush down to help Mrs. McGowan carry up her groceries.

"Such a nice child," she says.

"How are things, Mrs. McGowan?"

"They're good, child. Send t'anks to the man from me, will ye?" she says, wearing the same shawl I saw her wearing months earlier.

"I will," I say as we reach the third floor.

And from the doorway I look to see the fatherless daughter holding tight on her grandmother's dress and thigh, looking up at me through her thin blond hair and big gnome eyes. Behind her is a toddler about L'il Dinny's age, who looks up at me distrustingly as does his mother, the widow McGowan.

"You know he still talks of your son, Mrs. McGowan. Everyone does too. We have his strength with us. A lot of stories come from that man's life, and I'll make sure they'll be told for a long time. They got him when he was ripe, they say. Should be here with us now."

"He's with me everyday, child, and we'll be leavin' Brooklyn, if God above allows it. The jobbers ye bhoys got me an' me daughters downtown are helpin' us save. We want to go to the West. Or maybe Rochester where I've a cousin. Far away at the least of it. But the man, well . . ." she trails off.

I look at Mrs. McGowan's face when she speaks of leaving Brooklyn and notice that she longs for it. Only the reference to Dinny Meehan stopping her from continuing to speak of it. I scratch my head and look past Mrs. McGowan at Emma, who has by now hidden the flowers I gave her.

"For you," I say handing Mrs. McGowan a bloody envelope.

"Thanks so much. Come in for some tae?"

"I can't, but thank you," I say, then nod toward Emma, who smiles at me.

* * *

WALKING DOWN THE HILL ON BRIDGE Street toward the Dock Loaders' Club, I think that there is nothing in the world that is more beautiful and intriguing than Emma McGowan. I don't have feelings for Anna Lonergan. I can see why Dinny would want us betrothed, since the Lonergan family has so many boys in it, along with the teenagers that follow Richie. It's the future Dinny is concerned for, but what about what I want? I want to be with someone who makes me feel the way Emma does, but with all this talk of leaving Brooklyn or moving—Sadie, Mrs. Lonergan, Mrs. McGowan. . . . Why they all want to leave is no surprise, of course, but I hope only that Emma does not go just yet. But the way she hid those flowers from her mother leads me to think that she does not want her mother to know she is being courted by one of Dinny's boys.

Reporting back to the Dock Loaders' Club, all the men I know as I remember them are there: it's Tommy Tuohey at the stairwell looking out for the men upstairs, and Paddy Keenan and James Hart unloading the automobile truck back behind the rear room in the morning, because it's in the morning when we get most of the day's work done anyway. Rain or not. But even though it's morning, Beat McGarry and Ragtime Howard sit in the same spots as they always do in the afternoon and in the evening; at the end of the bar not far from the stairwell and the rear room never once lifting a finger to help.

"And it was all a hoax," Beat finishes a story while everyone tries not to listen, for they've heard it many times. "The man never jumped off the Brooklyn Bridge at all, but still became famous. Some people say that's what made him smart. Can ya imagine that, kiddo? A lie as proof of a man's intelligence? If that's what the future looks like, count me out. I'll just stay safe and sound right here. . . . Where'd ya get that, William?" He notices me fiddling with the pencil I keep in my pocket.

"I . . ."

"Ya stole it. Do ya know how to use it?"

"I do."

"Hmm," Beat says. "Keep it to ya'self. People round here don' like writin' things down, ya know. But that reminds me, I found out about them words on the picture o' President Lincoln over there about the dooryard."

"When Lilacs Last in the Dooryard Bloom'd?" I ask, looking over toward the lone picture of Lincoln on the wall behind us with those words underneath it.

"That's it. It's from a poem, ya know. A poem about Lincoln, in fact. Someone musta hung it on the wall years ago. Been there since I can remember."

"I knew it," I say. "Had to be poetry."

"Guy named Walter Whitman wrote it. Not Poe after all." Ragtime grunted.

"No one said it was Poe anyway," I tell him.

"No? I thought Ragtime was monikerin' ya Poe 'cause he wrote Poe-ems," he said, laughing at his own joke.

I don't laugh much at Beat McGarry's jokes, but that's all right because no one really does anyway. "What was Walter Whitman like?"

"He was a newspaperman and a poet, wrote a big book o' poetry, and that's the title o' one o' his poems there," he said pointing at the picture.

"Where did you hear all of this about the poem by Mr. Whitman?" I ask Beat.

"The Gas Drip Bard. He was a lifer at the Union Gas Company, now he just tells stories. He's what they call a shanachie."

" I know what a shanachie is," I say. "I want to meet him."

"We'll do that someday."

"Let's go," James Hart says slapping his hand on the bar as I remember still having one more envelope to deliver to the widow Gilligan.

We jump in Hart's automobile truck out back and before long he is chaffing about it. "Great day for a move," says he, holding the wheel and wiping the outside of the window with a dirty rag, bumping over the rough streets, dodging potholes and horse-drays and trolleys down Flatbush.

"They say Mick Gilligan shat himself before Vincent, Richie, and Abe killt 'em last April," Beat yells over the engine, bouncing in his seat.

"Well I don't know about that," Hart says. "But I was there when he came runnin' outta the Dock Loaders' Club scareder'n I ever seen a man. That Jew German boy o' Lonergan's shoved a gun in his face before he scampered away with that kid'n Vincent Maher on his tail."

"That right?" Beat asks, always the story gatherer. "True they shot at him as he was jumpin' the fence?"

"Got 'em too, in back o' the leg. I seen it."

"That right?" Beat confirms, notching another piece of the puzzle together for future stories as he is known to. "Vincent told me he shat himself right before they tossed him in a soap silo."

"Heard that myself," Hart said. "But I wasn't there for it."

"All right then."

Old man Beat McGarry has stories about everyone, but about Vincent Maher he has many.

"Oh they love 'em down at the Adonis Social Club," Beat tells me as we drive along, bouncing in the seat of the automobile truck. "It's there women are paid to give pleasure. But this guy? Maher? I heard they don' charge 'em because he's got the length of a horse, so they say. If ya know what I'm referrin' to. Like they wanna take turns on him, right? Not to mention, he'll talk a lassie's ear off, which makes them hot and ready, talkin' does. A dirty talker. A real masher, that one. Once he hurt one of the owner's top girls from the insides, ya know? Like he went too deep in her and she was out of commission for a week. Jack and Sixto Stabile, the owners of the Adonis confronted him, demandin' to know what he did to their top-earnin' whore. Well Maher, ya know what he did? He unbuttoned his pants, dropped 'em right then and there to show 'em his middle leg and holding it up with one hand, smilin' like a mischievous boy he says, 'She asked me to go to the hilt.' And what do the Stabile's do to him? They laugh and buy him drinks."

"Really?" I ask after getting out of the truck.

"It's true," he says assuredly as we enter a building and walk up a stairwell, then qualifies himself. "That's what I've been told at least. The I-talians think highly of 'em 'cause he's like an Adonis himself."

We knock on a second-floor tenement where through a hallway window behind us we watch outside as the Myrtle Avenue Elevated rumbles by over the street at eye level—the truck parked below it where Bridge Street crosses as deep into Brooklyn as I'd ever been. A woman answers with two children under her dress.

"Hello, Mrs. Gilligan," Beat says, as we all take off our caps. "We're here to help. Are ya ready?"

"Where is what I was promised?"

I step between the two large men and ask if we can have a word alone.

"Come in, child," she says and leads me to a room that has clothes and bed sheets stuffed into paper bags and other meager belongings packed and ready. "What happened to your nose?"

"Uh . . . how are things, Mrs. Gilligan?"

"Fine."

"Uh . . . the man says he is very sorry for your loss."

"And?"

"He wants to help you get started in a nice safe place out where your mother and father live in Grays Fairy."

"Grays Ferry it's called. I know that already child, what else?"

"By St. . . ."

"St. Gabriel's Church, yes."

"And to get started with a nice place, I have this . . ."

"How much is it?" she asks, grabbing the envelope from me. "What is this all over the envelope?"

"Uh . . ."

"Is this blood'r somethin'?"

"I don't know how much is in it."

She takes a deep breath, "This is . . . it's generous, please tell Din— Um, please tell the man that it is very kind."

"I apologize for your loss."

"Don't. It's the best thing that coulda happened to us. I shoulda never agreed to leave Philadelphia for that idiot and this shithole in the first place," she says. "Let's get this junk loaded and get the hell outta Brooklyn."

"Yay!" yell the children as they run through the bagged-up apartment.

CHAPTER 6

Black Tom's

IN THE EAST, A DAYBREAK HINT of amber sun rises behind us at the Fulton Ferry Landing, beyond the bridges. An empty Finnish steamer awaits our loading there, five hundred barrels of corn syrup made in the neighborhood to be sent out to the world. All the men are in place, eighty-five laborers standing together to answer the morning whistle and the flag, handpicked by Dinny Meehan with Cinders Connolly, the dockboss, whispering in his ear, confirming selections with a nod. The Swede in his dangling height and Vincent Maher with a tilted cap stare into the crowd of men—those what await work and those too that grumble for not being picked. They look into each man's eyes as Dinny is pressed into multiple conversations with Connolly, then Lumpy Gilchrist, and the stevedoring company's representatives concerning wages and hours.

Climbing down from the steamer is both myself and Tommy Tuohey from the stern's rope ladder. The ship captain stands cross-armed in the pilothouse above. His crew, too, stand open-legged looking down at the longshoremen. The steam winch engine turns over with a rousing and the drum-end man cranks the boom of the crane round to the pier with ragged gloves covering his hands. Connolly reaches up to the hook as it is lowered toward the barrels that had already been unloaded from a freight bay early in the morn, stacked and organized on the pier planks in a great massing by the old Fulton Ferry house where the elevated train terminates.

"Take the hook off that burton fall," Dinny says to Connolly. "Hand it to me."

Connolly does as told and with his long, shouldery arms he unlatches the hook from the chain, holds it heavy at his side and walks with it. Walks toward Dinny Meehan standing in front of his men and eighty-five laborers in the shape of a horseshoe facing the steamer, separated by gangs of hold men, hatch men, pier men, and deck men.

"Ain' the listenin' type 'parently," Tuohey explains in his Pavee tongue, speaking of the captain. "Say he don' favor to be bulled."

I look at Dinny Meehan from the side of him. The thick brown hair felled back over the top of the head, shaved short above his small ears, which look like a fighting dog's that are cut short. The thick shoulders on him are of an age-old farming man many moons in siring. Eyes of a strong and verdant color, I watch him at work. His face looks up and into the pilothouse where this captain awaits. Taking hold of the winch hook, Dinny turns round to the band of laborers behind him who of a sudden become quiet. Their long faces gaunt without dinner. Or breakfast. Willing to work. Hoping for it, they move their heads about to see the face of Dinny Meehan among the crowd and the words what he is ready to speak.

"Men," he yells, now with his back to the ship, though he points toward it with the heavy hook. "This ship denies you work. And they'll have us waitin' out in the heat, too, for all their concern."

The men grumble.

"They say they can make a better profit if they load these barrels with their own winch chain and cranks and engines. That they can do it themselves. Don' need muscle. Don' need us to stack it for the sea journey the way it should be stacked in the hull like we know how."

The men turn their eyes from Meehan's words up to where the captain in his navy blue coat is still standing cross-armed in the pilot room estranged to their caste. And we look up too to where his fifteen sailing men stand on the deck waiting.

"No matter that we unloaded and sheafed this load and got them ready for the sling. That makin' a profit for some company far away is more important than the meal for your family. What's to be done here? I ask you."

"Burn it." A man bellows out as Cinders Connolly smiles a toothy grin.

"Take their money."

"Send 'em back to Europe empty as they come."

"Now let's be judicious," says one of the men from the stevedore's table with a straight-sounding, Anglo-American accent. "Can't we work something out here?"

Dinny yells in response, "Yes. Yes. Good point. May I have your attention, men? Listen, It'd be easy to force them to our terms, would it not be?"

The men all agree.

"In good faith, I offer the crew of this rig two kegs of beer and five bottles o' whiskey not to work." Dinny then turns round and points, repeats to the men on the deck. "Two kegs of beer and five bottles o' whiskey. An offer not to work today. After we load ya, come over to 25 Bridge Street, though I do ask that ya tip the tender. His name's Paddy and he don' serve for free. Is that fair? Is it?"

The crew, tired from their journeys and waiting in the low sun, talk amongst themselves. Point to the captain above them and send three men up to speak with him. After a few more minutes, this captain comes out of his perch and casts slurs across the bow at Dinny Meehan and the crew of men behind him.

"Better dealing with unions than you boys," the captain admits defeat. "At least they respect authority and don't undermine it."

"Well, sir," Dinny says as the planks drop down from the ship. "Ya think you'll get a fair deal workin' wit' King Joe'n the ILA, have at it. But he's already fat with his luxuries. These men're hungry for work."

Lumpy, who has his eyes at the sky in his concentration, whispers into Dinny's ear some numbers after calculating the cost to the stevedoring company for the men, the hours it would take to load the cargo, the percentage the gang would earn and the loss from the two kegs of beer, five bottles of whiskey, and paying Cinders his portion of the tribute.

"Maybe we can keep some o' these barrels," Vincent offers.

"The fook we gonna do wit' barrels o' corn syrup?" The Swede admonishes.

The steam winch engine has been cut off, replaced with brawn. Cinders Connolly has put back the hook on the burton fall, and five men on the deck, including Philip Large, begin yanking on the rope with their hands and their arms and their backs. Tearing downward in concert, the rope is run through the deadeyes and roved through the timber mast above. Wrenching down again and again, the rope is then quickly curled in a perfect circle on the deck behind, next to the sailors.

On the pier, the lanyard sling lifts upward. Ten barrels inside are swung above the pier gang. The burton fall is reeled in by the deck gang and strewn up and over the ship's deck. The sling is then steered toward the combings by the hatch gang who call down in warning below, into the echo. The hull gang clambers with the dropping casks and then stack them in such a way that the Atlantic Ocean may not maim them in the ships pitching fore and aft.

Smiling at us, the sailors stand on the deck as happy as sailors can be. And in time with the yanking of the rope by muscle, sing an old song that's particular to them.

King Louis was the king of France, before the revolution.
Way haul away, we'll haul away Joe, up.
And then he got his head chopped off, it spoiled his constitution.
Way haul away, we'll haul away Joe, up.
When first I met a Yankee girl, well she was fat and lazy.
Way haul away, we'll haul away Joe, up.
And then I met an Irish girl, she damn near drove me crazy.
Way haul away, we're bound for better weather.
Away haul away, we'll haul away Joe, up.

But all I can think of is what the captain said while Tommy and myself were up with him. That his ship has three stops in Europe, first of which is Queenstown, Ireland. And as Tommy and I leave for the next ship to work the details with another captain, all it is I am chewing on is of stowing away on this Finnish steamer. Escaping with the barrels of corn syrup to where my family waits silently for me out East on the Atlantic.

That night after the divvy the Dock Loaders' Club is filled with songs and revelry as they always are on Saturdays, for on Sundays not a man among us on the docks of Brooklyn show for work. Tommy Tuohey mans the front door, Paddy Keenan the tap, Chisel MaGuire in his outdated stovepipe hat and dusty tails awaits the occasional affray to break out for his flim-flamming a few dimes from the action, Needles Ferry wanders in and out with glassy eyes and bony fingers poking out from his unbuttoned sleeves, and the old timers drink steadily with the bucks of the local terminals, Cinders Connolly, Red Donnelly, Gibney The Lark, and their right hands like the hefty Big Dick Morrissey, dark-skinned Dance Gillen, flat-faced Philip Large, and Dago Tom too.

I am one for the drink this night and the Lonergan crew no longer stares at me seeing the weakness I once had, but instead see hard drinks in my hand and hard friends too. Lanterns sway on the beams when the door opens and candles flatten as the giant belly of the bridge above us rumbles and thunders when trains pass overhead.

"Bat'n a ball," I say to Paddy and soon he slides across the rye whiskey and ale chaser. I hit them hard too and ball up my fists as they go down. "A man with his drink and cleansing his worries," I say as Ragtime Howard hears and nods with me in agreement.

The Scandinavian sailors drink mightily and speak of a place called the Somme, which is much in the news these days for so many soldiers are wounded and killed that it's said the French river will for one hundred years have the tint of human blood. It isn't long before the two kegs and five bottles had been downed that they start again with their drinking hymns, arms round our like. And among them are two Irishmen who know a good song of their own too. One of them was what they called the shantyman who leads in their sea songs and who confides in me that he's tempted to stay in Brooklyn and forget his family back home. I look at him out of the corner of my eye hard-like, for I am cold with missing my family, unlike himself, and offer to switch places, as I know of their stopping next in Queenstown.

"Oh well," he says. "I s'pose I don't really mean it in any case."

"Me neither."

"One fer the boyos back home then? An auld one?" He asks me and raps on the mahogany for as much silence as he can command, then begins a ballad solo standing right next me.

> It hung above the kitchen fire.
> It's barrel long and brown
> And one day with a boy's desire,
> I climbed and took it down
> My father's eyes in anger flashed.
> He cried, "What have ye done?"
> I wish ye'd left it where t'was,
> That's my old Fenian gun.

But the song only makes me sadder and angrier as I wish it's me too taking down my ol' Da's gun, though it seems never to be.

"Another round, Paddy," I say.

And the night is hearty and the night is fun and soon enough Big Dick Morrissey carries me upon his shoulders as we walk south along the piers and I hold his black hair like it's the mane of a gypsy cob and I as free as a tinker who owns nothing but the wind and the grass and the horse hairs in his grip. And somewhere, sometime, someone says that a man is never happier with the drink than when he is at his saddest. So here I am then, filled with the drink and the sadness and happiness all motley in me. Thinking of my hopeless mother and my missing father, and anything that could become of them is up to my imagination as there's a war between us that is spreading and worsening each and every day.

"Hey, you fellers gonna unload us tomorrow or should we have another drink?" Popped out a couple of heads from a saloon where sailors know to visit off Clark Street when they dock their ships late in the day.

"Anyone unloads a ship tomorrow in these neighbor-hoods, they'll be dead by Monday," The Lark yells passing by.

In Camney's Saloon off Atlantic Avenue we drink more and the hour is late, but most of the men remain awaiting Dinny to arrive as planned. After a bit and without anyone noticing, Dinny and The Swede appear in the saloon and before I know it, they are bought a round of drinks. And as was usual for the time, it doesn't take any longer than five minutes for a drunkard to challenge Dinny to a fight because with the drink, all the men of Brooklyn convince themselves of their being king of Kings County.

"Tell 'em to ask me again in a little while," Dinny says to The Swede.

The Swede turns round and tells the man and his culchies. And as he does so, Tommy Tuohey and Vincent

Maher separate them from behind, shouldering through them with cruel glances dyed in the wool of their hard-postured faces. There are not four men in Brooklyn more feared than this group. And Bill Lovett included would make five. After some while, Tuohey takes the challenge of the man who requested Dinny and before even making it outside, bloodies and fells him, quieting the challenger.

I am watching Dinny from a wall where I lean opposite the bar as Eddie Hughes and Freddie Cuneen talk excitedly amongst others. Happy Maloney and Johnny Mullen exchange words about France, the war, and the Democrat Wilson.

"He'll keep us from the war," they say.

"Didn't help save Casement though," Dinny turns round and tells them. "Won't help free Ireland. Presbyterian from the north counties, his like. It's in his blood to care nothin' for Catholics, hear me?"

"Yeah," Maloney and Mullen agree. "You want the Republicans to win?"

"Both sides are of the same spawn, the American gov'ment's as Anglo-Saxon as England. Good'n all of 'em, too. Even them that claim Irish or Catholic, they get high enough in the castle and they gotta prove they're as dried up as them Puritans or else they'll be out on their ears. This Wilson feller? Just wants ya vote. Do anythin' for ya to vote his way, then he'll send ya to France for battle sausage. Mark it."

Maloney and Mullen are respectful as Dinny turns and faces the tender, who shakes his hand while The Swede and Tommy Tuohey have their backs to him, facing the crowd. He then leans back and says something to Tuohey, who yells toward The Lark. Within seconds, The Lark is leaning on the bar with his one good hand wrapped around the other that has but two digits left on it—pinky and ring, like some odd forepaw. They talk only the two of them, under a low ceiling at the end of the bar. Dinny puts his hand on The Lark's shoulder, who immediately begins looking apologetic until he is calmed and sent back to the crowd.

"Ye're next," Tuohey thumbs toward me. "Let's go."

I smile and shoulder through him and The Swede for the honor to stand at the bar with Dinny. He shakes my hand before staring ahead with elbows on the bar, "How you?"

"I'm doing well, thanks."

"Drinks tonight, eh?"

"Maybe too much," I say.

"Things?"

"About what exactly?"

"Anythin' I need to know?"

"Don't think so."

"Heard about that Feinberg feller?"

"What about him?"

"Took him down. He was sellin' diseased meat all along to local butchers. Payin' the State Board o' Health to look the other way. People in Brooklyn been shittin' their intestines out 'cause o' him. Now they closed the abattoir."

"Oh."

"Heard from Petey?"

"Eh, no."

"Not even a smirk, right?"

"Nothing."

"They been whisperin' things, Lovett'n them," Dinny says under his breath. "You seen Darby Leighton around?"

"Darby Leighton? I haven't at all."

"Ya ever see that one, ya let us know. He's been banished for good, all right?"

"Alright."

Dinny nods at my agreement, then returns to the topic of Lovett, pushing hair off his temple, "That's the one thing I never expect from Bill and them. The silence. Silence an' whispers from that group o' larrikins? Nah."

"They got somethin' brewin'," The Swede mumbles over his shoulder to us, then turns back to the crowd.

"Nothin' from Wolcott? Silverman?"

"No, uh . . . Silverman is Wolcott's guy, right? Silverman and Wisniewski?"

"Right," Dinny agrees. "My cousin Mickey's seen Silverman hangin' around the Imlay docks lately. . . . Stormy down there, Red Hook."

"Not lately," The Swede mumbles again over his shoulder. "All them guineas and Dock Company schemers and Lovett and his rowdies, and now they're all mum like mice?"

"What about union boys, you seen any movement? ILA? Wobblies?" Dinny asks.

"I haven't."

"Heard anythin' about Thos Carmody?"

"Tanner Smith took care of that situation, from what I remember."

"Thos Carmody better be dead," The Swede says.

"No body's been found though," Dinny mumbles.

"Thos Carmody better be dead," The Swede asserts again.

Dinny and I both have our elbows on the bar next to each other looking forward and covered by Tommy, Vincent, and The Swede. Dinny looks at me, "Heard ya gave them flowers to the McGowan girl."

Feeling the drink and dizziness in it, I look away.

"Hard keepin' things together. Ya don' see it much . . . difficult though, keepin' it all together."

I nod.

"I don' want ya to give up on Anna, a'right? It'd be a good thing, bringin' us all together. Lonergan fam'ly's got eight boys in it, young bucks. Be good to bring us like one family, don' ya think?"

"It would, sure."

"So why not do it?" The Swede says. "Think it's easy keepin' it all together? Easy for you. Just show up and ya get all the benefits, but ya don' want nothin' to do with helpin' out. We all got fam'lies, ya know, y'ain't the only one. They're closin' in on us. All of 'em. We need to get bigger. Ready for 'em when they close in."

"A'right," Dinny says to The Swede.

"True. They wanna take us down, I can feel it . . ."

"Who?" I ask.

"They all do, look around," The Swede says whispering, though his eyes are blown open and face shaking.

Vincent tries changing the direction with a smirk, "I'll take ya down to the Adonis Social Club before ya take the plunge wit' Anna or the McGowan colleen. Get a taste, yeah? Ya gotta know what ya gettin' into before ya get in it, ya know? The Adonis? It's like a fookin' buffet o' skin . . ."

The Swede interrupts, "Ya want us to help ya, ya gotta help us too. Y'ain' gonna marry no McGowan girl, don' listen to Vincent. Listen to me . . ."

"Hold on," Dinny says, turning me back toward the bar, away from the others. "Lovett's got his idears. We gotta think 'bout things. How they're gonna play out. What about him cuttin' a deal wit' the ILA? If they want sway here in Brooklyn and they offer him things? What about Wolcott and the Dock Company? Red Hook's important and Lovett knows it. He could make a deal wit' them if he wanted to, right?"

"You don't trust him," I say, hitting the whiskey glass.

"Nah, not at all. He's mannin' a border on two fronts— Red Hook wit' the I-talians, and the Lonergan fam'ly. If he wins over the Lonergans, then he's got all five o' Richie's followers and a bunch o' young bucks in his younger brothers, plus anyone else among us that might see Lovett offerin' up opportunities. Then what? Ya gotta war. If we win over the Lonergans, Lovett's weakened and we can avoid trouble."

I don't say anything, wanting not to commit. I understand the logic, but what he is asking me to do is weighty.

Dinny leans back into me, "Least tell Mrs. McGowan what ya intentions wit' her daughter are, yeah?"

I nod at that, and look at Dinny's face. He seems to have conceded defeat in my marrying Anna. How he plans on winning the Lonergans over though, I do not know. The Swede growls and grits his teeth, turns away from me.

"Tomorrow ya work wit' Tommy. Ya need some more time wit' him. Man can fight. Ya saw here tonight? Did ya?"

"I did."

"Tomorrow then."

"What time?"

"Morning time. Meanwhile, I found a place for ya ma an' sisters," he says out of a sudden.

"You found a place for them?" I ask, slurring heavily and feeling myself losing balance.

"Over by Prospect Park, on this side of it. Eighth Avenue, nice neighborhood. The place gotta be cleaned up, but. . . . Needs some work, true. Rent's paid for a year. After that, you can pay the rent yourself. But when your family gets here, they'll have a home."

I look at Dinny and my first instinct is to thank him, but all I can give is a half-hearted smile because of what he has asked of me. To kill a man. To marry someone I do not love. In return I have benefited, it is true. But these are dire demands, and it's widely known that a favor from Dinny Meehan means an oath of loyalty. The price of this gift, then, a home for my family is, well, an amount I'm not so sure I can pay. I know that it is considered disrespectful and selfish and unappreciative, but the only thing I can say to Dinny in return, through my blurring vision and slurring of words, "I'll not kill another man as long as I live."

"Get 'em a place for his ma and that's his thanks," The Swede says.

Dinny looks away, then back at me. Unaffected by what I've just said to him, he drinks a drink.

"Ya like fireworks?" he says casually, eyes green in the enveloped saloon light of amber and black. A child's eyes. An ancient's eyes. Sometimes I wonder if he ever really did exist, Dinny Meehan. I even doubt it at times, it was so long ago that all this passed. But there he is in my thoughts, sitting here now with nothing left but memories to feed my old mind. So many memories and passing faces, but some faces stick forever. Can't be forgotten, like Dinny's. His eyes too, that saw right through me, for a man who does not believe in time is a man sees straight to the soul of us. A cross. A fire. Water, sin. He smiles at me from the bar. Hand on my shoulder impressing upon me his understanding, foreknowledge. Even precognition, as if he were some seer. The gold glazing light of the mutton-fat flame shining generously on his beautiful, august face and autumnal-brown mane. The light oscillating along his features with the spectral drafts in the air. A bard of acts, not of recounting, but of creating and fashioning. Shaping our surroundings at his order like some artificer.

And from there I can't remember much. I don't know if even I thanked him. I don't know even what his reaction was. For the rest of that night there are only images.

Looking away, I see into darkness. Camney's Saloon is as full of the old-world shade as any place where the water meets rotting wooden piers in Brooklyn. The light is sparse and I can see the embers of a pipe, darting red-flare trails through the wetted, wooden night. A candle's flame lights little circular areas between the tender and his patrons, but their faces quickly fall back as they move in and out. Faces embraced by the moving shades of black shadows and where men's accents take over because of my limited vision. I drink from the harsh liquid that burns in my mouth and down through the throat, spreading like a coat of thin lava through the innards.

"We're all lost here," I say to Dinny, though I don't remember his reaction, whether it was a smile or a nod.

Drunk and dreaming of better days, am I. Latching onto the unlikeliness of love and Emma McGowan. In hope I stretch myself to believe in it, even as I don't have the ability to understand what love is in my young years. But we have our dreams. Dreams of living the gentlelife where there is not so much struggling, but stuck in this wilderness of freighters and dock sheds and one-room tenements where mothers lose their children to insanity and pain, fathers dissolve into the night one way or another. Living in a time when we'll not share our stories of struggle for the fact that we commit horrible things to get by. That our children, and their children will only guess as to what we did to put food on our tables, for we'll lie about what harm we done. Cover it in darkness and silence and it's at this moment, sitting in Camney's Saloon on a Saturday night that the idea of my telling this story could only be allowed the light after my own passing. After I've gone on because of the shame of my state. Of our state. But as they say, it's a late day for regrets. Just as we don't know the stories of the families of the Great Hunger, you won't know much on the stories of the Brooklyn waterfront of the Great War. Not until I'm dead will I allow my story come up, at least.

And as I go down, holding on to a man's shirt and the bar for balance, drunk and undone as I am, I look up. Look up to see cruel eyes. A face from a gallery. As if it were down a dark hall. Deranged and irrational eyes I see beyond the shoulders of Vincent Maher, Tommy Tuohey, and The Swede. Eyes that move from Dinny's back down to where I now reside among the peanut shells and boots. I see him. I watch him side his glinting weapon. Shining in the old-world shade before it's sheathed in the grommet of his trousers. He then turns away, gone into the black. It was the face of Garry Barry, though I can't speak for I am so mangled by the drink. A killer looking to alter the fate of time to his will. Though no one notices Barry in the black, Dinny is covered by his loyal guard and the assassin is unable to penetrate them to slay our king. And me in no state to caution him.

"Too fookin' young to be drinkin' that hard," The Swede muses.

"Oop we go, bhoy," Tommy Tuohey laughs, pulling me up by the arms, my shirt collecting around the shoulders, exposing the lank of my torso.

But I can't stop thinking about the eyes I saw in the darkness. The meanness in them. The deprived reason in them. The horror in them that outlines the face. I had heard about Garry Barry from Beat. That when Barry was a baby a tenement collapsed on him off Court Street. Seven people died, but the child was found in the debris bleeding from the skull and ears. Beat said it was that injury what made him sick in the head, since he always thought of himself differently than others saw him. Since the beginning he felt he should be the leader of the gang, yet no one else felt that way. Still, he was ready to risk everything to become leader. Only thought of one thing, ever. To be a leader of men, regardless of how absurd it was to the reasonable mind. Fixated on the one thing only—illogically fixated. When Dinny took over in 1913, Barry claimed to be the leader of the Red Onion Gang, a smalltime clan that sometimes won the right to charge tribute off the Baltic and Atlantic terminals. But four other young men claimed to be the leader too, none of them accepting the others' leadership. Making deals, Dinny ate up all the old gangs along the waterfront under The White Hand's name and Barry was mentioned as a possible dockboss. But instead, Barry challenged Dinny to fight for leadership of The White Hand—a nonsensical claim. Of course Dinny wiped him up and Barry lost his chance at becoming a dockboss. He was banished to the fringes of day labor, always trying to win back his rightful demand of heading the gang—a mindless insistence altogether.

"Instead, Dinny made Harry Reynolds dockboss of the Atlantic Terminal after . . ." Beat trailed off.

"After what?" I asked.

"After somethin' happened between Dinny and Harry Reynolds. Anyway, Garry fookin' Barry is a guy ya need to stay away from. Fookin' dicey, that guy."

And I feel Beat's words to be true in this case, seeing Barry's eyes here at Camney's Saloon. Scaring me wordless. Puts a fear in me so deep and so overwhelming that I feel myself begin to vomit. The watering in my mouth again and the seizing in my stomach. The shot of heat emitting from me like a yellow fever jumping out. Every moment I see those eyes and the shaded face that hold them, yet those eyes are not particular to Garry Barry, but in all men of my time. Disturbed to the depth of me, those eyes can be found in myself as well. That horror that resides in all men is in me too. And I know it.

An explosion far away shakes the bar bottles and the windows in their frames. A second explosion shakes the place again as men begin pushing to get outside to see what is occurring out there.

"We're under attack," a man yells.

Dinny smiles, then orders another drink before looking over to me as I hold a spittoon in my grasp to vomit in. Smiling only, Dinny is. Knowingly.

The saloon is all but empty within moments and yet still more shells burst out in the water, zipping and screeching in the night. Tailing off in spiraling whistles. Tommy and Vincent pick me up under the arms again and behind us are Dinny and The Swede. We come down the block toward the water where everyone else is heading through the maze of puddled alleyways between pier houses and docks, and we jump up onto a train platform, one after another in our suits and ties and boots. Out through a doorless opening for a wooden stairwell and down to a pier where I can see through watery eyes an orange blaze beyond the Buttermilk Channel and Governor's Island. I am unable to fix a gaze on it for too long without my need to retch, but here and there I can see hundreds of miniature shots going off before three, then four loud ones that blow long flames of red and orange in every direction against the night sky above Jersey City, out across the way. Even engulfing Lady Liberty in smoke, whizzing shrapnel.

Pinging off her body after a splitting concussion. Harbor
lights blink open and crank sirens fill their lungs as spotlights
feel through the clouds and firebells clank off the water. When
another explosion lights up the sky, black smoke can be seen
billowed upward, the burst of orange light coming up through
the black, burnishing the west. The night has come alive, but I
can only see it through wet eyes that make the orange and
amber comets smear across the dimming penumbra.

Cinders Connolly watches in amazement, his hands wide
open at his thighs and his high, broad shoulders erect, yet
all the words he can summon are, "That shit's amazing."

"I don't see any warships," one man says.

"Who's attacking us?" another questions.

"That's a munitions island," states an older man. "I
dragged a barge there two days ago in the tug to the depot
there on Black Tom's Island. Coulda been the Hun set fire
to it. Fenian maybe."

Dinny comes up from behind with his men round him.

"Coulda been an accident," The Swede says.

"Yep," Dinny looks at me as Cinders laughs.

For the next hour or so, all of us watch across the water
toward Jersey City where the fireworks blast out in all directions. Not even Lady Liberty's reaching arm is visible, smothered by gloomy smog of fires in the earth and explosive
strikes that light the night, streaked with bullet sparklers.
Blooming open from the heat like popcorn in a pan.
Streaming through the darkness like hope flashing its yellow
teeth, and yet still what can come just as easily from the darkness is not just hope and light, but a cruelty of whimsical
genius. The most important thing I remember from that
night was that I'd never look into those eyes again. Whether
they're Garry Barry's, or they're my own. And I won't go to
the place Dinny buys me to keep me under his controlling,
for I'll never take an order to kill a man again. No.

CHAPTER 7

Mother of Caution

OUTSIDE THE LONERGAN BICYCLE SHOP ON Bridge Street are panhandlers and rain-soaked bootblacks and snuffling mares pulling junk drays and old-timers shuffling about. The great abutment to the Manhattan Bridge a block and a half away climbs slowly skyward and to the north as seen from the corner of Front and Bridge Streets out the shop window. The children who rent the bicycles have increasingly stayed away from here due to the stories of Richie Lonergan and his crew, who blacken eyes and abuse those who don't return the bikes on time, which had been stolen in the first place. It is also widely known that an Italian boy from Navy Street who attempted to bull Richie into selling drugs out of the shop was found in a garbage-strewn courtyard with his face and head swollen beyond his own mother's ability to identify him. Two knife wounds were found on the boy as well, one puncturing the heart and the other slicing at the throat.

Mary, mother of fifteen, stands behind the counter inside, a worried look on her disfigured face. With Tiny Thomas playing on the floor behind her, she wipes wisps of hair off her forehead as she sees Richie and Anna coming in the front door. Taking a deep breath, she knows that she is up against her own children who are able now to think and act on their own without her controlling them. Oftentimes their actions are purposely contrary to what she demands.

"Please, Lord, give me the strength to stay humble," she crosses herself silently, forehead to chest, shoulder to shoulder, her face forever scarred. Forever scarring her thoughts too, for she is known as Mary Lonergan, wife of drunk John and bearer of his brutality, whether it be the violence that mutilated her, or the many children he's damned her with. "Please, Lord, help me," she continues as her two eldest walk toward her.

Richie's tie is bedraggled and his gray-blue eyes and wide shoulders, wild blond hair give him the look of some war-torn, weather-beaten teenage foundling. His sister, graced with natural beauty but wearing a sack dress with a torn sleeve stands next to him four inches shorter, her sprouting curves the topic of many conversations in the neighborhood.

"Richie?" Mother Mary says carefully.

"Yeah."

"We need to talk."

"About what? You can't send Anna to come and get me . . ."

"I can, and I already did."

"I'm workin', Ma, ya can't send her to the docks no more . . ."

"I ain' scared o' no one over there," Anna says sternly to him.

"It ain't that," Richie says, discouraged that he can't express his thoughts. "It's just that . . ."

"Richie," Mary says, coming around the counter and standing in front of him. "Have ye or the boys said anyt'in' to anybody about what Bill told us?"

"He said to keep quiet about it."

"And yez have?"

"Yeah."

"All right then."

"Is that all?"

"Ye bhoys're workin' with Connolly at the Fulton Ferry Landin' an' Donnelly in the Navy Yard?"

"And sometimes down with The Lark an' Big Dick at the Baltic Terminal too."

"And yez just do as yer told? No words on Bill'r nothin'?"

"Nothin'."

"Anybody talk about Non Connors? That he was set up?"

"No."

"Dinny's cousin, the golden-haired one, replacin' Connors as Bill's righthand?"

"Mickey Kane? No one talks about it," Richie says, looking at his mother sharply and searching for words. "I don' . . . you're not . . . don' tell me what to do . . ."

Mary ignores Richie's attempts to confront her, looks at Anna, and speaks over him, "Dinny sent a bhoy over here with flowers fer Anna."

Richie blinks, "Who was it?"

"That bhoy from Clare, Garrity."

Anna looks up to her brother to see his reaction, her mouth half open.

"Don' do a t'ing, Richie," Mary says. "Be smart. Dinny and Bill're fightin' over ye. It's obvious. They both want yer loyalty. Ye've gotta stay prudent here. Let 'em fight it out, those two, but goin' after that Garrity bhoy again will only make t'ings worse. Petey already gave it to 'em good, no sense in doublin' back now. Dinny made 'em come here with flowers fer yer sister, we could see it on his face that it wasn't his own idea. Just let Bill'n Dinny fight it out among themselves . . ."

"Let 'em fight it out?" Anna interrupts. "No, Bill is the only one for us, Ma. We've known him since day one. His family lived in the same building as us when we was young. We need to help Bill. He'll be the man one day, everyone knows it, Dinny Meehan's just keepin his seat warm is all . . ."

"Anna," Mary says calmly, though her voice is shaking. "Dinny put up the rent for this bikecycle shop . . ."

"Richie earned that on his own when he beat Red Donnelly in a fight," Anna raises her voice. "Look what he done to the Leighton fam'ly, Ma. Look what he done to Non Connors. He's an animal."

"Still, it was Dinny's money," Mary yells over her daughter, then turns to her son. "What I'm sayin' is it's too early to choose sides, Richie. What if Dinny kills Bill? Everyone says Mickey Kane's bein' groomed fer takin' over Red Hook. What if that? Ye listen to yer sister'n ye'll be out on yer arse, ye will."

Richie does not answer.

"I know," Mary says looking away. "No response from ye. Ye don' listen to yer poor ol' Ma, but ye'll listen to that Jew bhoy, Abe Harms. That's fine, he's got a voice o' reason, I s'pose. What's he tellin' ye to do then?"

Again Richie does not answer.

"All right, that's fine," Mary says, still shaking. "Ye don' listen to yer fam'ly. Certainly not to a woman. Ye listen to yer friends. Ye listen to men only. I understand it. Just be smart, Richie, is all I'm arskin'. If ye take one side over the other, ye might find this bikecycle shop burnt to the ground one day when them two men finally have it out. And they will have it out, mark it. The two toughest always do. Ye t'ink I haven't seen all this before? Yer father and me brother, yer uncle Yake Brady and his bhoys back in our day? One day yer father's a peacock, but when Yake Brady left the gang, yer da was no more than a feather duster. Left out, and we had no choice but to leave the Lower East Side for Brooklyn or else he'd get killt. Don' put all yer eggs on one man over the other's all I'm sayin', Richie. Does that make sense to ye?"

Richie looks toward Tiny Thomas on the floor, "Why ain' he at school today?"

"He's sick," Anna says.

"Again?" Richie says, as Tiny Thomas looks up to his eldest brother without realizing they are talking about him.

Mary walks round the counter again, turning her back to her children. Richie, Anna, and Tiny Thomas all watch her. Pensively, she places her palms on the counter and looks up, "All I ask fer is a healthy fam'ly, fed children, and the chance to move up and out of this place, yet I have the scars of a woman whose been t'rough terrible battles. Look at my face. Look at it. Is this the face a mother deserves? I was once beautiful like yer sister is. Men wanted me as they want her now. They fought over me and look how we've turned out. Anna?"

"What?"

"Ye listen to me an' ye listen now," Mary says angrily. "Ye tell Richie to go with Bill over Dinny and yer puttin' us all at risk. The whole fam'ly. Ye t'ink Dinny won't kill Richie? Look what he done to that Gilligan fella, would ye?"

Richie looks away, shifts his weight off the wooden leg.

"That's right," Mary says to Richie. "They say ye did it yerself. Killt the Gilligan fella with Abe and that Maher man at the soap factory under the order o' Dinny Meehan. Is it true?"

Anna looks at Richie, then to her mother, "And what if he did do it, Ma? So what?"

"Well," Mary says looking in her son's eyes as Anna folds her arms indignantly. "Then ye did what the king said ye should and not some upstart. Good on ye then. Bill becomes king one day? Ye do what he says."

CHAPTER 8

Miscarried Betrothal

"DINNY," SADIE SAYS TO HER SON. "Come over 'ere now, we're almost done."

L'il Dinny has to use two hands to pick up an apple that he dropped on the grocer floor and when he stands, he hits his head on the cart inside the shop, begins crying.

"Oh no," Sadie says with a smile and picks him up. "Lemme rub it for yu and it'll be gone."

"Cute kid," says a voice from behind them. "Wish I had the chance to get to know 'em."

Sadie turns round and sees a figure in the dark, then grabs at L'il Dinny's hand and pulls him up from under his armpits, "Da'by?"

With a wet cough, Darby Leighton smirks and walks closer to Sadie and the boy, "Ye call 'em Dinny, eh?"

"'At's his fava's name," Sadie says with an apprehensive smile.

"That right?" Darby says, looking at the child suspiciously.

Sadie glances toward Mr. Cohnheim behind the butcher's counter, a small and elderly man who does not recognize the fear in her face. She then looks back to her cousin and begins saying something, but stops.

"Do I scare ya?" Darby says, his face pallid and bony.

"No," she says, holding L'il Dinny closer to her chest.

"For what ya done to ya cousins?"

"I didn't . . ."

"Ya know, when me an' Pickles first came to Brooklyn, we used to live under a pier together wit' Dinny Meehan while ya was still in London. Guy named Coohoo Cosgrave was the leader o' our gang back then. He was crazy, Coohoo, but he saw Dinny as like the next big thing even though me'n Pickles had been around for mont's. Pickles didn' like Dinny. Didn' listen to Dinny, an' look what happened to Pickles."

"I don' know a fing 'bout all that . . ."

"Sure ya do."

"Da'by?"

"Yeah?"

"Are yu sick? Can I get yu some food to eat? Yu look 'ungry . . ."

Darby looks at his cousin with a self-conscious glare, "That ain' ya problem to fix no more. You chose to ignore us, so don' play like ya care."

L'il Dinny's squirming in Sadie's arms takes away from her feeling sad about what her cousin had just said to her.

"I wanted to go wit' Dinny," Darby says. "But I couldn't. I got eighty-sixt instead when you'n him got married after the trial. Wasn't my fault Pickles an' Dinny hated each other."

"Dinny wanted bof o' yu to join in. Dinny . . . Dinny said 'e looved me. Dinny courted after me, paid for us to get outta 'at rattrap we lived in and promised 'e would join our families togeva, but Pickles . . . Pickles just wouldn't listen. Pickles has a mind o' 'is own so 'e didn't wanna listen . . . I'm sorry Da'by. I know it was you'n Pickles 'at saved all 'at money to get me outta East London, bring me an' Frank 'ere. I'm so fankful and I'm so sorry fings've turned out the way they 'ave . . ."

"Don't be," Darby says, his face gaunt and somber. "I see my older brother Frank's in good wit' Dinny. Got that job for 'em over in the soap factory. But I'm just lumped in wit' Pickles ain' I?"

Sadie looks at her cousin, "I'm sorry."

"Stop bein' sorry for things that don' matter," Darby says angrily. "Ya chose Dinny Meehan over ya fam'ly, but that don' seem to bother ya, does it?"

"Da'by . . ."

"Are ya gonna tell 'em I came to see ya so he can send The Swede after me again?"

Sadie puts L'il Dinny on the ground, but holds his hand tightly.

"Ya know," Darby stands closer to her. "One day Bill Lovett's gonna kill ya husband. And I'm gonna know about it ahead o' time. Maybe I'll say somethin' to ya. Warn ya. But maybe I won't, either. There's a lotta people out there want him dead. Cops an' unions an' businessmen an' I-talians an' ghosts all in between 'em too. All them guys? They know he's real. They know what he does and who follows 'em. They'll get 'em, one day. Until then, I'll be out there. Driftin' around, probably. Can't work in Red Hook wit' Bill. Can't work for Dinny on the north docks. . . . Can't talk to my own cousin unless I sneak up on her."

Sadie and Mr. Cohnheim watch as Darby turns round and walks toward the faded light of the front windows. L'il Dinny pulls on her arm to get away, but she holds his hand tighter and brings him close to her long dress and leg. Pushing away, he begins wincing and squirming uncomfortably.

"No yu don't," she says with a tear on her face. "Yu'll not be gettin' 'way from me."

CHAPTER 9

The Dead Coming

October, 1916

Before yet the blinking of dawn does Thos Carmody come. He stands on the deck of a coasting lighter-barge as if floating. Disembarked and pulled by two harbor tugs off Manhattan's Chelsea docks, then traveling south of Battery Park he now coasts toward Brooklyn's Navy Yard. Up and rising in the quiet reaches of the black morn like a ghost come upon the living to reckon some mortal transgression done him, for as far as anyone knows in Brooklyn Thos Carmody is dead since April. But here he is. Alive and amongst the great churning traffic of the New York Harbor before even the sun can emerge from the east. The propellers of the port tugs up ahead of him bubbling under the water, yanking the slack. He drags from a hand-rolled cigarette and exhales into the East River fog.

Much colder up in Buffalo where he hid over the past months, he is not bit by New York City's October morning chill. Up there, Carmody met with his boss T. V. O'Connor, President of the International Longshoremen's Association. O'Connor was on his way west to patch up his losses from the summer's ill-fated general strike on Puget Sound and the Pacific Northwest. Against Carmody's wish, O'Connor sent him back to Brooklyn. Carmody feared

Brooklyn. Feared what was coming to it. Wanted instead to go out west with his boss, far from New York. Does not want to come back to Brooklyn where there is sure to be another war for power and sway over the racket of labor. But back here again he is, where the cost of human life is always cheapest.

* * *

IN APRIL, WOLCOTT OF THE NEW York Dock Company— the union's biggest enemy in Brooklyn—had caught wind of Carmody and Joseph Garrity recruiting his Red Hook employees into the ILA. Wolcott hired Dinny Meehan as a starker to kill Carmody for five hundred dollars. Meehan then hired his trusted childhood friend, Tanner Smith, to do the job. Smith, a lowly Greenwich Village ex-gangster-turned-dockboss had then paid Carmody to disappear. Carmody's life had been spared, so he took the "fifty dime" Smith gave him and planned on never returning to the city.

Tanner Smith had played his hand well. Or so he believed. Instead of killing Carmody, Smith used the opportunity to try and muscle himself into the union's upper folds. Smith pocketed most of the money his old friend Meehan gave him and told Carmody to tell King Joe and T. V. O'Connor of the ILA that he'd saved Carmody's life.

"I can turn all o' the longshoremen on the Brooklyn waterfront to ILA," Smith told Carmody, handing him the bullet he should have killed him with. "If only I was a ILA man, of course."

"Fuck Tanner Smith," Carmody says under his breath as he drags and exhales again, floating on the deck of the Brooklyn-bound lighter and looking up to the shadows of the two bridges that connect Brooklyn to Manhattan. Striking a match and cupping it in his hand, Thos pulls out the bullet Tanner Smith gave him and turns it in his fingers. "I'm gonna put this in your back, Tanner."

* * *

UP IN BUFFALO, CARMODY HAD PUT in a formal request to O'Connor to accompany him to the west coast.

"I can't go back to the city," Carmody had explained. "I can't go. King Joe don' care if I live or die and Brooklyn's run by the Irish on the north docks, the I-talians in the south. With the New York Dock Company between 'em there's no way we can bring them together under the ILA flag. It's just a tangled mess."

"What happened with the Irishman ye were werkin' with in Brooklyn?" O'Connor asked. "What was the man's name?"

"Joseph Garrity."

"Joe Garrity, that's right. Where's he?"

"Uh . . ." Carmody scratched his chin. "I heard his nephew and a few other Whitehanders got 'em, burnt 'em alive in McAlpine's Saloon, Red Hook."

"Jaysus," O'Connor said, noticeably angered. "What else?"

Carrying some of O'Connor's bags toward a car, Carmody continued, "Bunch o' I-talian ILA men were killt, beaten up, and a guy named Non Connors was the only one charged."

"Non?"

"Yeah."

"Who is he?"

"He was Lovett's right-hand man in Red Hook."

"That right?"

"Yeah."

"That's an interesting t'ing, t'is," O'Connor said, looking up in thought. "And Tanner Smith says he can turn Brooklyn to ILA?"

"That's what he says."

"Ye t'ink he can do it?"

Carmody saw his chances of going out west dwindling by his telling the truth. "No, Tanner Smith can't turn Brooklyn to ILA. More importantly, the ILA can't hire Tanner Smith. The newspapers already say the International

Longshoremen's Association is made up of a bunch o'
ex-cons and thugs. Smith was best friends with Owney
Madden before they sent him up to the stir. And he's close
to Dinny Meehan to this very day. Best chance we have in
turning them is to make a deal wit' Lovett and make them
two fight—Lovett an' Meehan. Which'll weaken the gang."

"No better man to do that than yerself," O'Connor said,
looking at him, then giving his order. "Go back to Brooklyn
and make a deal with Bill Lovett. We were able to bring
the south Brooklyn I-talians into the ILA by makin' Paul
Vaccarelli a vice president in New Yark. Offer the same
to Lovett."

"Meehan will expect us to be goin' to Lovett."

"And?" O'Connor said, picking up his own bags. "When
Meehan finds out ye're still alive, he'll go after Tanner
Smith fer not killin' ye. In the meantime we'll be comin'
up from the south with I-talians t'rough Lovett's Red Hook.
Yer job is to make a deal with Lovett against Meehan. If
what they say about Lovett's true, he'll want to take the
gang over one day. He hates Meehan, is that right?"

"Yeah."

"Perfect. Lovett'll be lookin' fer ways to strengthen his
forces. We've got the whole o' the ILA behind us. Make a
deal with Lovett," O'Connor points at Carmody. "Get him
and all his men to join the ILA and we'll help him take
down Meehan. That's yer job. Eventually we'll get all o'
them Brooklyn bhoys to turn."

"And if that don' work?" Carmody sneered.

"T'will," O'Connor said.

"Might not. Lovett hates I-talians."

"Look, man," O'Connor said, putting a hand on Carmody's
shoulder. "Yer the man fer the job. There's no other. Ye get
Brooklyn in better shape and I'll make ye King Joe's right-
hand man, treasurer of New Yark. Ye'll be rich with the handouts, ye know it. I know ye want to come with me out west, but
it's King Joe who'll take this over in a few years. Until that day

comes, I need him watched. He'll kill me if he gets his way, King Joe will. I need someone I can trust to watch that man, and ye'll do. Yer a good man, Thos. Now what happens if Lovett don't come our way? What will ye do then?"

Carmody bowed his head in both humility and concern, "It won't turn easy, Brooklyn."

"We got half already with the I-talians. If it was easy, I'd ask someone else. What'll ye do?"

"If it don' work, I got inroads wit' one o' Meehan's men. Vincent Maher is the fella's name. He secretly goes down to the Adonis Social Club south o' the Gowanus Canal for the prostitutes. It's owned by Jack Stabile and his son Sixto, and Jack and Sixto Stabile are in Frankie Yale's pocket. Frankie Yale is in Paul Vaccarelli's pocket. Paul Vaccarelli is in our pocket."

O'Connor nodded in respect to Carmody's sharp mind, "What do ye plan on doin' with this Vincent Maher feller?"

"If I can't make a deal wit' Lovett, I'll have to make a deal wit' Meehan."

"Meehan?" O'Connor asked, tilting his head and seeing clearly Carmody's astute and cunning way, as it was Meehan who sent Smith to kill him from the start. Carmody had moved up in the ILA for his ability to turn the Irish of West Manhattan and the Italians of Southern Brooklyn to ILA by using the same strategy of "division and rule."

"And why would Dinny Meehan choose to join the ILA?"

"He'd only do so if he has no other choice. Everyone's against 'em. Even some o' his own guys. Every day he becomes weaker. How long can a gang run out in the open in New York? Openly controlling labor? He'll be forced to make alliances, and when that day comes, I'll be there. In the meantime, Lovett's the guy. Either way, it's gonna get ugly," Carmody said, running his hands through his hair, as O'Connor got into the backseat of a car and rolled down the window to speak to him.

"Ye'll report to King Joe in New Yark, but I want to hear from ye every week. Understand it?"

"Right," Carmody said, as he watched the car pull away without him in it.

* * *

NOW, ON THE DECK OF A lighter-barge in the waters cutting through New York City, Thos Carmody drags on the hand-rolled again as he enters Brooklyn through the cover of darkness. Death hanging over him, he decides on his own that before going to Red Hook and dealing with Bill Lovett on this day, he'll go to the Navy Yard to see a guy named Henry Browne—an ILA man who has the ear of Red Donnelly, one of Dinny's dockbosses.

Thos Carmody shakes his head in disbelief. He is sup-posed to be dead already. Yet here he is haunting into Brooklyn and knowing that when his presence is found, it will spook the old gang from Irishtown. Scare the life out of superstitious and furious men like The Swede, who is closest to Dinny Meehan. If there's anything those wild boys believe in, it's ghosts of the past. And of course the intentions of this ghost of a man is to split the gang in two. Lovett on one side. Meehan on the other.

But his being alive will truly affect one man more than any other: Tanner Smith, who will be exposed for betraying his childhood friend, Dinny Meehan. So it's best Carmody makes his presence felt so as to cause chaos within the gang. Spooking them from afar. Having them take care of Smith so that he does not have to do it himself. But if Tanner Smith is not done in by Meehan's men, Carmody will be forced to get Smith before Smith gets him.

As the lighter-barge that carries Thos Carmody enters Wallabout Bay by the Navy Yard, two gigantic warships are dry-docked on each side of him as if entering through the portcullis of a haunted industrial sea-city informed by the past and its dead, resistant of the future. He flicks his cigarette over the deck rails, one of many red, yellow, and orange flares that hiss when touching the water, as men with strange face-helmets and lead suits spray flames into the wounds of the warships at his left and right, healing them with fire like some devilish gargoyles at the gates of hell. Healing them so that they may go back to war in Europe and rip more lives from this earth.

"Fuck," he says under his breath, knowing his return is that of a specter. But Thos Carmody might just rather be dead than back on the waterfront of Brooklyn, for he is unsure he'll survive what is coming. There is no way he can control all the angles, but when the time comes he might just disappear himself again, depending on how harried things get. The newspapers are reporting on the possibility of a draft if the United States enters the fracas over there. He might just have to volunteer as a soldier in the Great War to get out of the way of all the little wars in New York City.

CHAPTER 10

A Mute Fury

"LIAM, GET YER ARSE UP, BHOY. Places to go fer us," Tommy Touhey says to me in the doorway, Sadie behind him.

I barely understand a thing he says with his accent and his speed.

"Where's Dinny?" I say.

"Left oo'ready," Sadie answers. I look over to L'il Dinny across from me, sleeping away with his miniature barrel chest and the pure white skin of his face.

I sit at the edge of the bed and feel the cold coming back. It's one year I'm here. I rub my eyes. Still no word from my mother. There are Irish papers in America that speak of British retribution in the countryside and everywhere in Ireland they are choosing sides, like the preparations for a terrible fight. Some rebels are raiding country constabularies for arms and in English prisons others languish, plot a future of freedom from behind bars, as symbolism goes. They are all poets, I see. Writing a sonnet in blood, and with hearts of stone they are troubling the living stream. Truly is a terrible beauty that now is upon Ireland. Warrior poets, rebelpoets, my father and brother among them. Myself so far away. The American president seems to have no wish on helping my small nation become free like the many others he says Germany and Austria-Hungary oppress. Too close to England, is America. Dinny was right.

Between him and I, though, there is a silence. A silence initiated by myself. A lingering thing where I have set aside any real decision. A festering silence where ulcers can flourish. A limbo where I am afraid to commit to his gifts, or sever ties. No longer am I the gentle child accepting all that is sent me. But neither am I an independent man.

I look to the floor at the boots by the bed. They are open at the mouth like a dying old man, tongue dropped out in front. I never knew McGowan, though I've lived in his shoes all this time. Heard many stories of him before The White Hand walked with the prowess and sway they own after I came. Back when all the gangs fought against each other, dock for dock at the turn of the century like packs of faction-fighting families. Back when Dinny and McGowan were inseparable as children-warriors. When Dinny first began his work as an artificer and craftsman of dockside thugs with the Irish milk still fresh in them. Roaming the dock neighborhoods and piers in their purest years, homeless and hungry and desperate, as I myself know all too well. From the lowest low they came. The root of The White Hand, those two, Beat McGarry told me. But I am growing out of these shoes. My toes curl at the end of them and the laces have snapped, eye-holes ripped open. I am some twenty pounds heavier than when I arrived, and I've learned much of fighting from Tommy Tuohey.

"I think yu must grow in yu sleep, William," Sadie says, looking up at me, and as I head down the stairwell of the Warren Street brownstone, she whispers, "Come back for lunch, William."

"I will."

"It's to Red Hook wid us t'day, Poe."

"Is it?"

"'Tis."

My stomach turns. For close on three months Tommy and I had parted paths when ships land at the Red Hook slips. The Italians that live in the tenements surrounding it, the ILA and wobblies staking their claims, the New York Dock Company and their owning the property, and Bill Lovett, whose silence makes The Swede insane. I'm not ready. I'm certain of that, at least. I don't even seem to know who I am and neither does anyone else, as they have many names for me, whether it be Liam or William or Poe or kid or child or bhoy.

"Wouldn't mind a squarin' off wid'm, Bill Lovett," Tommy says in his speedy speak, holding out his big right fist in my face as we walk south. "A fair one me'n him. Man to man, ye know? I ain't afeared o' him."

"He fights dirty, I hear."

"I heared it too, but I swear on me mudder I'll kill 'em with the fists. A proper man fights and that's how he wins and when it comes to it we'll fight and we'll do it."

"I don't think that's a good idea."

"I don't give a shite 'bout any man," Tommy stops and yells, pointing in my face.

"Well I didn't mean . . ."

"I'll fight any man anywhere," he yells over me on the sidewalk. "I'm the best in the feckin' werld an' don' give a feck 'bout him nor any man. My breed's pure t'rough and t'rough me, 'tis. Me da was a Tuohey like his da, but I got McDonough blood too. And Butler and I also got McDermott and uh . . ."

"I really . . ."

"Shut up a moment then, eh. . . . Kelly too. I'll take me coat off fer any man and I'll fight 'em," he says with his eyes ablaze and his shoulders back like a ready rooster. "On a dock. In a ring. The roadside, no matther. Any man. Swear on me mudder's life I would. You see that?" he says, pointing to the harbor. "Dat's what the world's made of. Water. And it's made o' dirt and I'll bury any yoke in either one that crosses me. Or I'll beat him so bad I'll leave'm a hospital case at the least of it. . . . I love ye, Liam, I do. I swear to God above. Hope it don't happen, o' course, but I swear to

God dere, up dere: ye died tomorrow straight to heaven ye'd go, Poe. Ye're a damn good lad but fer feck's sake, bhoy, ye gotta open yer eyes up, ye feckin' sausage."

Before I can react, he starts in again.

"Ye don't accept a man's gift, it's a war yer arskin' fer. I know Dinny got ye that place over there and I know ye won't live in it. Ignore it, that's what ye do. The man gets yer family a place fer to live and ye ignore 'em. Ignorin's worse than a challenge, bhoy. Do ye not know it? Ye're a feckin' child an' I'll bend yer arse over an' spank ye if ye don't open them damn yokes up."

"I don't want to kill a man ever again, Tommy. And he won't say that he won't order me to do so."

"Whole werld knows ye'd rather be back home, we know it. But ye're not goin', bhoy. So there's plans fer ye here den. People who care fer ye too and ye ignore'm. Now here's what ye're gonna do. Ye're gonna go to the man and tell 'em thanks and that ye'll move from his wife's house to yer new place in the marnin' tomorrow."

"I want to know that he'll not order me to kill another man, is all."

"He won't."

"You speak for Dinny now?"

"I do. He loves me 'cause I'm a real man and I'll tell 'em tonight, too. Ye know that man's a man o' his word, ye know it?"

"I do."

"He knows I am too and he knows that yer no killer but ye gotta open yer eyes, bhoy. Ye're not goin' back Ireland-way. Brooklyn's yer home."

"And you? You're never going home?"

"Ain't got a home. It's not the life fer me. I was born in a mansion on wheels under the big blue sky wit' the wind and the weather but I'm gettin' on now. Twenty-seven-year auld now'r twenty-eight, I t'ink. Time fer me to start breedin' some sons so maybe when their war's over I'll go back, dat's what I'm t'inkin'. Dinny knows I can't be tied down. And maybe after their war yerself can come too, but fer now we gotta stay here."

"I just wish I could answer the call."

"Maybe there's other ways, bhoy, we'll see. 'Til den I'll keep trainin' ye like yer me own, now put 'em up, c'mon."

I put my hands over my face and my left foot forward, sliding with it, then stepping back with my right foot.

"Dat's it, lean back when I swing at ye. Here goes," and he swings as hard as he can at my face, which I lean back and out away from.

"Dere ye go, here comes a hard left jab, move to yer right," and I duck to the right, away from the jab, and throw a straight right toward his face in return.

"No ye don't. T'rowin' yokes at me like he does. I trained ye proper, bhoy. Ye're like me own bhoy ye are, ye son of a bitch ye."

"Why doesn't Dinny trust Lovett?" I ask him as he puts his arm around me, feeling close.

"Well Dinny's our king, we know dat, but Lovett don't seem to know it. He t'inks he knows better, don't he? Dem two just need a contest for king o' Brooklyn to the winner."

"No gloves either."

"Hell no, dey just kill yer clout, gloves do," he says still with his arm wrapped tight around me, unlike what most Irishmen would ever do. But Tommy Tuohey's not like most Irish men—he's Pavee and he's got no problem telling me he loves me.

"I do love ye," he says, then presses his fist against my nose. "But I swear to God up dere and me mudder I'll break yer sniffer to straighten it out if ye don't open them feckin' eyes o' yers and look round wid 'em."

When we arrive there is a tug-towed barge at the wait where quickly Tommy and I climb it by the rope ladder. Entering the bridge and helm, we shake a firm shake with the captain, an Argentine who knows little English.

"Whadda ye got in here?" Tommy says.

I look down at Bill Lovett, who is surrounded by a throng of men waiting for work, though there is not a single Italian among them, even though they're everywhere else in Red Hook. He wears the cloth cap of the dockworker, though his ears flay out childishly and his cheeks are reddened in the October air. The papers like to say things about him as if he were born a pure Kerryman with the apple cheeks, the baby face, the rosy lips, and whose temperament is matched to the Irish county's rocky slieves—flagstone disposition and gloomy weather—yet a Brooklyner through and through, always at the ready for an affray and damned by the albatross round his neck that is his working-class constitution.

I can see hate in him that he has to look up at us on the ship. A fury that he keeps close to himself. Hate that he is below his enemy. I count the seconds it takes to finish this conversation with the captain, who so maddeningly does not seem to be in the hurry that I hope for. He and Tommy go over silly details, barely understanding each other. I interrupt angrily to translate Tommy's rare English for him. Then the Argentinian looks at me as if he can barely understand myself either, the fool.

I look down again, but I only know a few faces that stand by Lovett, like Frankie Byrne and his old gang's followers, Jidge Seaman and Sean Healy. Well into his forties, Richie's father John Lonergan is there too, standing with his arms crossed and proud to be back in the game. And then there's Dinny's cousin Mickey Kane, who avoids my stare, though I believe it's because he's not wanting to be associated much with Dinny, for whom Tommy and I are known as being close cronies. But men talk just as much—if not more than—women and the rumor is that Lovett secretly talks among Frankie Byrne and them, referring to Kane as a tout. A dangerous thing, even in rumors.

Up here though, the little captain in his big hat is in no hurry, so I press into his little coat, "We're up against time here, let's get moving."

He looks up at me, tilting his head.

"Hurry up, got it?"

"Poe, wait outside with yerself," Tommy says, then turns back to the captain who stares me down and I stare him back.

Finally, we climb down and Tommy speaks with Lovett. I hide behind Tommy's shoulder with my hands dug deep in my pant pockets, as the wind rushes over my face. Everyone knows that Lovett carries a .45 in his coat and as I think of this, he looks around Tommy at me. Looks into my indignant eyes and as he does so, I think of the pipe in my coat and look around. A bad combination is in the air, I think, as Tommy and Lovett converse. Lovett's dumb will and coarse pride against Tommy's keen sense to sniff out dishonor, disrespect. The slightest insolence from Lovett could spark Tommy's seeing it as a challenge, which to the end of the oceans would never be ignored by him. Regardless of our standing among his own men in his own territory, Tommy's fearlessness and boastful, blaguarding nature could explode in an instant's summoning.

"Ye got 'nough men den, yeah?"

Lovett looks away without answer.

"Got 'nough men'r ye need me to get some from The Lark up Baltic way'r what?"

"Nah, we'll do it wit' less," Lovett answers casually with Byrne and the rest behind him.

"We can get more men . . ."

"I said I don' need more men, we got enough here wit' us now, right?" Lovett says, his teeth gnashing and his fists clenched at his hips.

"Right man, ye're on then," Tommy says, then adds, "I'll let Dinny know . . . Poe?"

"I'm here."

"Job's done, we're off."

I am only worried about going through Lovett and his men who are in the horseshoe shape of longshoremen gangs. I can't let myself feel the relief just yet and every step seems a slow one. Ahead of me I see Tommy, standing erect and proud, nod toward Mickey Kane, though I ignore him. Keep my head down through the shoulders and the staring eyes.

"Yeah," I can hear Lovett say as our backs are turned and almost through the rabble of labormen. "Ya let 'em know too that I'll be fast up there under the Manhattan Bridge to pay tribute to the king o' the pikeys. Ya let 'em know that, eh?"

Now it's well known that Tommy Tuohey is a gypsyman from Ireland, but it's mostly just British that call them "pikeys." Which you don't want to do. You don't. There are a flood of reasons why and I'll not begin categorizing them, but right here and now I feel the fear that I am going to die. Forget my mother and father and sisters and brother, lost somewhere in the motherland. Forget all of the things I have been worrying about for months on end—my demise is going to be a worthless one right here in the asshole of Brooklyn. I think of running, but if so, I might as well keep running all the way to California as I'd never again be held with any semblance of honor or regard in Brooklyn.

Tommy Tuohey stops ahead of me when he hears this, still amongst fifty laborers. He stops, with Lovett still behind us. I don't say a thing and nor does anyone else. He thinks, though I can't see his face. He thinks more. About what I can't say. Maybe about his wanting to start his own family, his own son one day as he mentioned. About getting out of Brooklyn like so many others long to do. Or maybe about killing Lovett.

Like an old bear I hear him grumble deep in his chest, then he keeps walking without a response. Through the crowd we go north, back toward our territory. Silently, him and I.

Up the road, I speak to him as we walk quickly through the tenement neighborhoods, back toward Baltic Street. "He'd never fight clean."

"I'm off to tell Dinny that you'll not again go to Red Hook with me," he responds solemnly. "I'll kill the man next time and it'll be a bloodbath afterward."

"So why doesn't Dinny come down here for each ship with Lumpy, The Swede, and Vincent and his men like he does all the other territories?"

"Lovett's filled with the pride. He wants to be treated special like. Like better than other dockbosses. Only t'ing happens when ye treat a man special is he wants more. Nature o' men, 'tis. But dere's only so much Dinny'll allow, so he sends me fer talking with captains as I'm good at, and den the job's done. But dat feckin' Lovett, he'd love to glom himself the reigns o' dis gang. But he's in no position fer it, is he?"

"I wouldn't think so."

"I'll tell Dinny o' yer plight with the place fer yer mudder," he mumbles while staring ahead. "I'm a man o' me word—ye know it, don't ye?"

"I do."

"Not just a man o' me word but I love ye, Poe, I really do. God knows ye'll go to yer heaven up there when the time comes. Not to werry, I'll not allow Dinny to bring ye down with me to the Red Hook again."

"Not to werry," he says, just like Mam had said to me one year ago with the tears in her eyes when I left her. "Not to werry," it is again, but it's worry I see on the face of my friend Tommy Tuohey walking next to me. The first time ever I'd seen it on him. Sure there was fury on his face, but bedfellows are fury and fear, as I know. And as I see Tommy Tuohey with fear it brings a turning in my stomach.

I do not argue with him on this point, though, but keep my mouth shut to it. And for the rest of the morning we meet other ships at Harry Reynolds's Atlantic Avenue and Baltic Street with The Lark and Big Dick until lunch when I begin the long walk back to Warren Street and Sadie, happy to be alive. Happy for another day. I feel the Saint Christopher in my pocket that my mother gave me. It feels familiar there and I rub it with my thumb, holding the back of it with my index finger as I walk. It isn't much, this charm, but it's the feeling it gives me that means more.

"William!"

I hear a woman's voice as I come round the block at the layers of stoops along the Warren Street sidewalks.

"William!"

I look up to the yelling of my name and I can see Sadie. She is waving her arm out the third floor window with Vincent at the bottom of the stoops looking up at her.

"William!" Sadie yells one more time. "Yu got a letter from Ireland."

My ears pop open and I take to the wind. Running as fast as I can. Past children playing in the street. Past Boru, Mr. Campbell's horse and past Vincent, who leans against the metal railing with his cap tilted over an eye. Up the stairs I am, three at a time.

Sadie quickly hands it over inside the parlor and L'il Dinny stares with his mouth open as I run through the door.

"Weeyum," he tries saying my name as his mother does, then asks me a question with his palms open.

"I was goin' to send Vincent wif the letter, but it was already late in the day," Sadie explains.

"No worries," says I, as I take it from her. "It's already been opened?"

"Came like 'at, William."

I sit down on a chair in the parlor and read as fast as I can.

"What's it say, William?"

I keep reading.

"Is yu da alive?"

"She doesn't know for sure where he is," I say. "My brother Timothy is back home on the farm, though. Da went into hiding."

"Is yu muva safe?"

"She seems to be," I say, then look up to Sadie. "But my da told my brother to tell her that she needs to go to New York with me as soon as she can, with my sisters. That maybe one day she can come back but things are only to get worse before better."

"Oh no," Sadie says. "There's war comin' to Ireland?"

"Doesn't say," I respond, thinking about things. "If the British are opening the mail. . . . Wait, this says July 1916 on it. Four months old."

"It'll all be fine," Sadie says. "We just need to wait for the war to give way for 'em to come to New Yoork is all. Ya gotta keep savin' money, William. And maybe now's a time to fix up 'at place over off Prospect Park, eh?"

"No," I say, putting the letter down. "There aren't many commuter ships, if there are any, crossing the Atlantic, and there won't be for a long while. High risk of being sunk, so she can't come anytime soon."

Sadie looks down.

"The British have been to the farm," I say, putting the letter down, my fury muted in the company of Sadie.

Concerned, Sadie looks away, over toward L'il Dinny, "And?" she asks.

"She just says that they took Timothy away for a few days and when he came back the doctor told him to get rest and that he would heal up soon enough and that my Mam just had a few bruises and they took some livestock and a horse."

"Oh my." Sadie puts her hand over her mouth.

"They'll be back too, she says."

"William, they'll be all right, d'yu understand me? D'yu? William? Yu 'ave to keep at it 'ere where yu can make money for'm, William. When the day comes, yu'll be ready. Yu'll 'ave a place for'm to stay, the whole lot of 'em, the whole fam'ly,

William. I'll make sure they's comfortable, I will too. They'll lov'it 'ere, they will. I promise yu, William," she begins crying, then tries to stop but then L'il Dinny starts crying too when he sees his mother and next thing I know, my eyes are like sacks of salt water until I grunt them away, squeeze my fists.

I pull the tears from my eyes and whip them onto the floor. Standing up, I reach into my pocket and grab for the pencil next to the Saint Christopher. Into my room, I close the door behind me and write a letter to my mother that I'll not share with Sadie. That I'm on my way to Ireland, stowing on an Atlantic crosser as soon as I can and that I'll bring enough guns and ammunition with me to take down England by myself. Gritting as I write, the lead snaps and I crumple the paper, throw it against the wall. Pacing about, I pick up the paper and open the window where I see Vincent below, looking up. With matches I burn the letter and throw it into the air.

"William?" Sadie knocks gently. "Do yu wanna talk, William?"

I don't answer.

"Yu spoke wif Emma recently?"

But I don't want to talk and I don't want to think of Emma McGowan either. It's been three months since I saw her and a guilty feeling comes up to me every time I think of her. That I should have at least tried to keep in touch, but I didn't and now she probably thinks me just like any other male—a big void. Like all the other men in her life, dead or disappeared.

Sitting with my head in my hands, I think for a bit. Lie down and look at the ceiling until the anger passes and changes and finally turns. Whittling the pencil down with a knife, I bring a point to the lead again and write to my mother to tell her that I love her and I've a home for us here in Brooklyn one block from Prospect Park.

CHAPTER 11

The Old Wall

I AM CHOSEN AMONG FIFTEEN OTHER men of the bar to follow Dinny and Red Donnelly. Looking at me as if he does not know me, The Swede pats my coat to make sure my pipe is in it. The Lark and Big Dick are chosen as well, and pushing off the mahogany with us, we all come out the front door of the Dock Loaders' Club in a cluster, armed. Crossing John Street, Tommy Tuohey horseplays with Vincent by messing up his dark brown mane. Like children, we are. Walking through the old rowdy neighborhood, clowning like we do. Throwing rocks into the water as we walk down the bulkhead through the main rail yard of the Jay Street Terminal, we call out. Yelling like boys. And among the waterfront masts and derricks of shore-head boats, scows, and steam lighters, Cinders Connolly and Philip Large wave at us as we pass. Between us and the ships moored in the slips are chains of loco-motive-pulled, covered hopper cars being filled with grain and raw sugar for the refineries close by. And there are also giant open hopper cars for transporting coal and ore. Slowly sliding through the angular waterfront yard that is lined with crisscrossing and curving rail ties, the rail cars connect to the floating bridges hauling them into the terminal across the waterway. The rail tracks travel out of the windy train yard along the East River and into the Belgian brick streets among tenements and storehouses and over sidewalks.

As we stride in our great bunches, we see school children walking in single-file lines toward Mass at St. Ann's for the Feast of Teresa of Ávila of the Discalced Carmelites. Among the children are the older boys and girls.

"There she is," Vincent says pointing with one hand into the crowd of kids, the other hand on my shoulder. "See her?"

And I do. I see Emma McGowan smiling at me and quaintly, among the other girls, she waves at me excitedly.

"Oh my beautyful colleen," The Lark sings out in a silly voice, holding his heart with his two-fingered hand. "I wanna roll around the purple heather wit' ya. Will ya roll around wit' me, lassie? Will ya go?"

The girls scream in laughter as I push The Lark away from me. I smile at her too, though, as she looks back over her shoulder entering St. Ann's.

We then pass the Jay Street Terminal freight house and the Kings County Electric Light and Power Company building and finally the succession of Atlantic White Lead Company buildings on both sides of the street with their blind brick façades squared off and windowless. A long stairwell reaching up to a single, half-opened door has a man watching us contemptuously from on high. Above him is a succession of smokestacks that seem to stand guard over the old, rough-cobbled neighborhood of east Irishtown like medieval sentinels. I always felt there was something majestic about the old neighborhood with its row houses barely distinguishable from its factories. And as I'm looking up at the sentinel smokestacks, thinking, I run into Big Dick.

"Pay attention, ya muck," he says, grabbing me by the head happily, then letting me go as I push him away. "Look how stout he is, the kid—hard-bitten to the core."

Others laugh at me, and with Dago Tom, Johnny Mullen, and Happy Maloney next to me, we look up as Dinny turns round, a water tower atop another painted masonry building behind him. Down the way are five blocks long of seven-foot-high brick wall between us and the Navy Yard beyond.

"Sometime ago," Dinny says as we stop our pranking to listen. "When the neighborhood and the gov'ment was at strong odds, they posted snipers for the boys that climbed this wall. They were lookouts, them kids. But they were much more. They were survivors. And we are their offspring. The offspring of children that survived a great, great hunger the likes o' which the world'll never come to understand. Or care to. Who somehow came away still alive, barely, after a famine came to the countryside, which our enemy wielded against us, and summoned their god and their laws alongside, like weapons to kill us, to send us into exile on ships that were more like pine-box coffins, understand?" Dinny looks at each of us.

I look round as well at the faces of these men I stand with here in the street. Notice their strict attention to Dinny Meehan and the dignity he inspires.

"From our own home, by foreigners. And if these children hadn't made the trip themselves across the ocean, then they were the sons of an exiled child. Or daughters. The marines . . . they used to march outta the Navy Yard here. That's why there were lookouts posted on the wall here. Even in New York, they couldn't get our people to live by their law—still can't. Here in Irishtown they never talked. If there was a dispute, the gangs enforced the neighborhood's way. No one went to the police. But if someone was arrested? The whole neighborhood surrounded the patrolman screamin' at him, peltin' him, ran alongside his wagon and stood outside the police station for days chantin' and chantin' until he was let out. They couldn't get Irishtown to abide by their law here in America, and no wonder. The foreigner's law never served 'em back home, or here. Only starved and sent 'em away.

Ignored 'em when their babies and mothers withered and died. Starved. Evicted in the winter, a pauper's death. And here it was more o' the same. Called 'em animals, savages. It's no wonder the people o' Irishtown ignored their law here, but the soldiers and their officers o' the Navy Yard and the law they enforced hadn't a care what our people'd been t'rough. . . . Still deny it," Dinny looks down, then back up at us. "We don' want no problems today. Red just wants to show us somethin' in there. We don' want no fights, but the men in there gotta remember who we are. Remember who they are. So instead o' goin' t'rough the gatehouse, we'll make our own entrance then. From our neighborhood, into theirs."

He turns his back to us and walks across the russet-yellow paving stones of Little Street. Takes off his cap and throws it over the Navy Yard wall.

Dance Gillen smiles and looks at me, "No second thoughts now."

Cinders Connolly and The Swede boost Philip Large up and others for they are tall enough to reach the lip on their own and one by one we scale it like invaders, stand atop.

"Like a city on its own," I say, looking inside the Navy Yard as we jump down on the other side.

Along the dry docks, levels upon levels of scaffolds reach as high as the smokestacks and surround multiple vessels that are raised above the water level. The underbelly of the warships exposed awkwardly, whole steel panels removed and open below the ship with many men working on them secretly like midwives prepping for childbirth. To our right is a large building, which, from the smell of the smoke coming from it, must be a coal plant where energy is stored for the plenty of steam engines in the yards. There are some six piers jutting into the horseshoe basin where cranes reach deep into the tramp steamers and lighters and barges, delivering war materials into them to be sent Europe-way. For England and for France. Floating piers with chains of train cars are being pulled by tugs with their noses in the air, propellers churning deep in the water behind them.

Jumping down one by one, the tint of hand-held hammers and the pound of steam-powered hammers upon rivets into ten-inch-thick sheet metal echoes in our ears. Puddles rippling at each blow, we walk across freight tracks where dump cars swivel and drop loads into rivet castles, which are next to triangular sand piles tall as three men. We come by many shops and smitheries for pipe and copper, foundries for brass and iron, a rigger and flag shed, and a machine shop. From muddy corners come three and four rats from slushy pools of dirt and sawdust. Next to the long lumber stacks, debarked and naked of their natural color is the Navy Yard's own firehouse with a pump-well inside the stable doors and the naval prison behind where men hold onto the bars above and stare disheveled and mourn-faced at us below.

"There's a revolution happenin' here," Red Donnelly yells toward Dinny as he leads the way. "Ain' got nothin' to do wit' rivets either. What no one wants is rivets, damnit," he says smiling. "We don't need no rivets to patch holes in the warships. There's cases and cases of 'em here. Piles of 'em. Not needed. Thing o' the past, rivets. Or soon will be. C'mon."

Men above on their scaffolds stop working, look down to us. Talk amongst themselves of us as we pass in the mud and tracks below. At the head is Dinny and his enforcers, the dockbosses and the rest of us following.

"It's right over here at this dry dock," Red motions, excited to show Dinny. "Here, look at this."

We see a man sitting on a stool in the dirt with orange and yellow sparks bursting around him. He is pointing something at a transport ship called the SS *Tyninghame*. Some sort of blast had ripped a large hole in it, opened the side of her, and clearly visible to us is the boiler room within. The man is holding some sort of concoction that has a flame coming out of it, causing the flares to blow in all directions, hissing out in the mud and elsewhere. He is wearing a mask and helmet and his entire body is covered with some alien suit.

Risking burning, Red goes up and touches the man on the shoulder, who pulls up the mask. When we see the person who is causing such ruckus we are kicked by the oddity.

"Fookin' woman," Dance says.

"Ya remember when the *Rochambeau* and the *Ancona* were sabotaged by the Hun?" Red yells toward Dinny, pointing at the woman. "They was fixed right here in the Navy Yard with this machine. It's called a welding machine, right? The *Craigside* had five fires in the hold. Fixed in record time and back out on the water. The screw steamer *Assuncion de Larrinaga* was afire at sea, patched and gone. The *Samland* too. All of 'em. A small bomb blew out the boiler and hull, then welded back together faster than any sheets and rivets could ever be replaced. Sent back to the war. And cheaper too. It's technology like this place has never seen. And so easy a woman can do it."

Dinny's face is stone still, though he has questions, "Cheaper for who?"

"Well . . ."

"Cheaper labor?"

"Yeah, that. Cheaper for the gov'ment to fix, too."

Dinny nods.

"Problem is," Red continued. "These men . . . and women. They know what they got. They got somethin' that's valuable. That's really needed."

A worker in overalls and sage eyes surrounded by some twenty others walks up to us. The leader reaches for Dinny's hand, takes his hat off.

"This's Henry Browne," Red introduces.

"Just want ya to know we wanna work wit' ya," Browne says to Dinny.

"Me?"

"Well, you yeah. Together."

"Who am I?"

The man looks at Red, who nods.

"I don't know ya name," he says with humility. "No, sir. But I want ya to know that we're willin' to be open to workin' together. I mean, we're workers and we can take care o' ourselves and whatnot, but ya know. . . . We need power. A union needs to be able to back its threats, ya know? We need yous. Thos Carmody says that if we all . . ."

"Who?" The Swede interrupts. "Who'd you say said somethin'?"

"Carmody?" Browne says, again looking at Red.

"I told ya," Red says to Dinny.

"Whad this guy just say? Thos fookin' Carmody?" The Swede demands.

Browne is confused at the reaction, especially when he looks at Dinny's face, who does not show surprise.

"You seen Thos Carmody lately?" The Swede asks the Orphan.

"Yeah," he shrugs.

"Like lately? The last couple few weeks o' somethin'?"

The man is concerned. "I saw'r 'em yesterday."

"Goddamned fookin' asshole . . ." The Swede says, his face red and his hands pulling at his own hair.

"Jimmy," Dinny says to The Swede, calming him.

"Hey, get back to work, Henry," a man yells toward our two groups. "You and ya men. Back to work now."

A crank siren starts its blaring and ten men come jogging out from the marine barracks, ten more out of their quarters next to the naval prison with rifles.

"Where in the hayell did these guys come from?" says a uniformed man with an accent I've never heard. "I mean to tell ya, they ain' come from no gatehouse, did they? I reckon not. You men need to cl'are out from this premises im-mediately, this here's fed'ral property and you is trespassing . . ."

With a look at us, Dinny tells us not to fight back.

"We'll give ya'll one chance before bullets will fly," the disciplined man continues yelling into the air without locking eyes with any of us. "We'll escort ya through the gatehouse or to the brig—ya'll can make that decision on your own, but that there's your two choices."

"Henry," Dinny says, shaking the man's hand again. "Thanks for ya time and comin' over to meet wit' us."

Quietly, we allow the marines to walk us through the newly paved concrete and the mud, over the freight rails. There are armed men ahead, behind and on both sides walking in perfect stride and with all sorts of colorful accents from different parts of the country, yet bellowing out in unison, "Left, left, left . . ." and staring in some deep distance as if their minds had been cleansed. Somehow we had managed to be herded into filed lines, though Big Dick jokingly pushes The Lark from behind, who almost falls.

From shutter windows and open doors and scaffolds above, the workers watch closely. Watch us to see what we're like, what we'll do. The many of them immigrants themselves who live in the neighborhoods. Quite a few of them connected to Red and Dinny, but most have been brought on within the last couple years, business being good with the war as hungry as it is.

"Look at 'em, boys," Dinny says. "Just look at 'em. Don' let 'em forget. Show 'em who we are."

Wanting us to give the workers something to remember, Dinny too stares up at them flinty and obdurate. His eyes focusing in on theirs as we are frogmarched. Centering in to remind them of the cruelty of last April when we fire-bombed the holdings of the New York Dock Company down in Red Hook. That we've no fear of uniforms nor long guns of federal troops nor ILA harriers, for that matter. Telling them to watch us. Telling them to stare at us. Telling them that the government may have their deeds and their rights to the property, but would always be within the clutch of The White Hand butted against the old neighborhoods. Within the threat of the gang's tactics and its demiurgic leader whose name they do not know. Whether it be marines or labor syndicates, no walls will hold us out, as our like comes from within the hearts of all working-class men and women. Hard and pure forevermore.

But instead of looking up at the Navy Yard men, I watch Dinny. Up at the head of us. And I can't help but to see him a bit differently. The man for whom I trust so much of my own life and my family's. Watching him scale old walls when maybe he doesn't see the new ones surrounding us.

CHAPTER 12

Always Closing In

NOVEMBER, 1916

HARRY REYNOLDS ALWAYS KEPT TO THE distance. He was smart that way. Noncommittal. There was nothing about him that stood out. The only thing remarkable about him was his resemblance in the face with Dinny Meehan. A strong resemblance, although Harry was not quite as muscular as Dinny. But what he lacked in matching Dinny's great strength and dominant personality, he made up for in pragmatism and subtlety.

Never once do I remember Harry drinking with us at the Dock Loaders' Club or socializing outside of the longshore work he so admirably accomplished day-in, day-out. After getting his envelope upstairs at the end of the day, he simply disappeared. Into the distance again.

Beat McGarry once told me that Harry was an orphan at the St. John's School for Boys. The only other thing I knew about his past was that he was a prodigy when it came to picking locks and thievery. His inherent pragmatism and independence made him a natural sneak. Beat also told me Harry was in the newspapers one time, although he had lied about his name.

"What did he say his name was?"

"Patrick Kelly, of course. But the newspapers loved him,

they called him," Beat opened his hands as if showing me a large headline, "'The Coal Hole Robber.'"

"Really? Why?"

"He snuck through coal holes into the basement of tenements and picked the locks and quietly went into rooms taking canned goods."

"Canned goods?"

"Hungry, ya know? But he took valuables too and sold them at pawns for nickels on the dime."

From the beginning I noticed there was something odd between Dinny and Harry though. Harry seemed far too intelligent to only be a dockboss. I wondered from the beginning why Harry wasn't closer to the ear of Dinny upstairs at 25 Bridge Street. But no one talked about it. Even when I asked big-mouthed Beat McGarry, he buttoned up.

"I dunno," he said, turning away from me.

But Harry Reynolds is by far the most respected dockboss Dinny has. At the Atlantic Terminal, Harry never kept a true right-hand man. He has different men work with him, such as Dance Gillen or Whitey and Baron Simpson or Quiet Higgins or even Eddie and Freddie—fringe members, the most of them. Yet somehow, the Atlantic Terminal runs smoother than any of the others.

I work with him at times. And although he doesn't say much, what he does take the time to enunciate is always valuable information.

"Do you think they will ever let Pickles Leighton and Non Connors out of Sing Sing?" I asked him one time as we worked.

He didn't answer, of course.

"What was Pickles Leighton like? And why was he sent up to the stir in 1913?"

No answer.

"Do you think it strange that Dinny married a girl who has two cousins, one in prison, the other banished from the docks?"

Silence.

"Why does The Swede hate Non Connors so much? Was Non Connors set up because The Swede talked Dinny into doing it?"

Harry just watched the hatch gangs at their work guiding the nets into the belly of the barge tied up at the pier. Slowly dropping the loads into the hands of the hull gangs below.

"Is it true they're all going to come after us through Lovett and Red Hook?"

Harry takes a deep breath, "Ya got a lotta questions. A kid known for stealin' pencils and askin' questions? What happens if ya don' get all the answers? What? Nothin'. In fact, ya'd be better off."

I'm not sure why I want to know everything, but I just keep asking and asking. Lifting sixty-pound crates all day and walking them toward the nets, I look at my hands. They are bleeding in the palms, and my shoulders and lower back ache, legs wobbly. Dropping my hands I see Harry in front of me again. He whispers to a man walking by him and the man nods. Harry always seems to speak to men on a deeper level than most. And men respect him greatly for it. I suppose we all have things we are gifted with, though many people are never given the opportunity to use them. There's nothing that can stop me from asking questions, surely, but just like Tommy Tuohey helps me learn to fight and be aggressive, Harry Reynolds helps me to survive with subtlety and pragmatism. And with bleeding palms I lift another crate. Walk it down the pier in line with the other laborers along the belly of the barge.

Later. Upstairs at the Dock Loaders' Club, The Swede lets Harry and I in.

"Where's Vincent?" I ask, but The Swede shooshes me.

Our boots clomping and the floor creaking in the silent room, Harry sits down in the chair in front of Dinny's desk, me in the chair behind him. The Swede walks around us, stands next to Dinny. All is quiet.

I had never seen Dinny sleep before. I had doubted it ever happened. Coming home late every night. Up earlier than anyone. I never even saw him yawn. Here he sits at his desk, eyes closed. The room silent, the world goes on as usual outside. The shutter windows pried open, the cool November air mingling freely among us. Stretching out behind him is the skyline of Manhattan Island and the millions that reside on it. The distance of the constant city sounds move in our ears. A flat sound almost like the rain. Imperceptible and obvious. Downstairs a lone immigrant sings a song amongst the chatting and tapping of feet to the beat. When the song ends, men clap and glasses touch off against each other.

In his wooden chair, at his empty desk, he sits like some ascetic attaining his oneness, yet he is no more than the man I know in front of me with his eyes closed. Lumpy in the corner with his numbers, The Swede standing at his side, and Harry in front of me, we wait. And we wait longer. I wonder if he practices this as some sort of test to ensure everyone in the room understands that it is him that we all recognize as leader. That we need him. Depend on him, though he is not that type. Simply enough, he sits. What goes on in his mind, I cannot know. But I can see how the strain would get to him. I am no more than a minor member of this crew. A youngster, yet my relationship with him and the burden I bring is complicated. With so many other things to balance, so many enemies that want us felled, I am sure that he must take moments to feel a union with the realities he faces. And certainly, he faces them almost exclusively, for none of us have the ability he does to direct and orchestrate such an act. Then, if that weren't enough, producing reactions that benefit us, our existence an anomaly in and of itself, for so many gangs have by this time been eradicated or made unnecessary. To make a material world, create a space for us in this ever-modernizing place, I can see that he must take time to come back in his mind to a state of blankness. Of perfection. Where the swirling problems that surround us are juggled in his head. Then made even. Flattened, so that he can reorganize them. Categorize a hierarchical structure through the eyes of an unbiased mind. So here he sits. Simply enough. Sits. Becoming unity. Ceasing to exist.

He opens his eyes and looks at Harry and I. "You seen Vincent?"

Harry looks behind to me, then back to Dinny, "Nah."

The Swede runs his hand through his hair and grits, walks behind us to the door, "We think he's workin' wit' the I-talians."

"We don' think that," Dinny says. "You do."

The Swede points to Harry and I, "You fellers know . . . him and a few others go down to that fleshpot Adonis Social Club . . ."

"Calm the hell down wit' the accusations, Jimmy," Dinny says to The Swede, then turns his attention to us. "You two see 'em, just lemme know, yeah?"

We both agree but can feel The Swede chewing on ideas behind us. Pacing back and forth by the door, then walking over to stand to the right of Dinny. A moment later he sprints toward the door again and puts his ear on it.

"Stop wit' that shit," Dinny says.

"I thought I heard Tommy say somethin'."

Harry is looking in Dinny's face and back to The Swede as I do the same. Finally The Swede comes to stand next to Dinny and relaxes a bit.

"Two barges today?" Dinny asks.

"Yep," Harry says.

"How's the kid?"

Harry looks back toward me again, then looks up. "He's gonna jump ship to Queenstown, Ireland."

"What? I didn't say any of that," I say, angered that my torment between going home to Ireland and staying here in Brooklyn is exposed in front of Dinny.

"Ya thinkin' it though," Harry says, looking down and back.

"Let 'em go then," The Swede says, exploding from his spot by the windows and pointing at me. "Jesus H. Christ almighty, he ain't worth a shit anyway, for fuck's sake. Everyone's jumpin' ship here. The whole fookin' world's goin' . . ."

"You're an asshole, Harry," I say.

"Did ya think Harry'n me are enemies, William?" Dinny asks, looking hard at me.

"No but . . ."

"Keep secrets?"

"I don't know what the deal is between you two. I don't even understand most of what Harry says anyway."

"Among us," Dinny says, waving his hand between himself and Harry. "No secrets. To the rest o' the word though, not their business. If Harry'n I got issues, we resolve it between ourselves, but we're always honest. You though, ya not so honest."

"Damn right, he ain' honest," The Swede jumps in.

"Your family is not in the position mine is," I say. "Stuck in the countryside where the fucking Brits don't have to abide by any rules. With no man at home, just a woman, two young sisters, and my brother."

"My fam'ly's dead," Dinny says, then spreading his arms wide. "This is my fam'ly. And this fam'ly offers your fam'ly lodgings. You remember what that means? Ya told me once that ya father used to allow strangers to stay wit' ya in exchange for work on the farm."

I look away.

"It's part o' who we are. For some, the hunger and fear undermines our communal ways. Our instincts and our need to be among our own. That's our lament. To be divided is to be conquered. But, when we come to the aid of our fam'ly an' neighbors when they're in need is to be united again. To never say a bad thing o' the poor and the destitute. Our hearts filled with sympathy. Empathy too, 'cause we been there. Overflowin' wit' it, and when one o' us comes into some luck," he says, again opening his arms, "is something we then share. It's our way, William. Ya remember ya home? Ya humility? Ya people?"

"I know about it."

"We all have choices that we gotta suffer t'rough. We have somethin' here that's real. But because it's real, everyone else in the world wants to take it down 'cause we don't play by their rules. By their invisible laws, no. We don't. When we make decisions, we make them as a whole. I don't make them. We all do. Because we're all involved. All o' us here, we all decided ya uncle needed to go away after he took over recruitin' in Brooklyn from Thos Carmody. But that was because we all decided it. Not me. And why? Because they planned on making us extinct entirely. Like what they've done to the others in Manhattan. Look at Tanner Smith. The man was set to take things over in his neighborhood 'til the unions and police and the Jews an' the I-talians and the stevedorin' an' shippin' comp'nies and them temperance people and more . . . all decided gangs're a thing o' the past. That the Irish ain' gonna run things on the docks no more. So now he's just a dockboss tryin' to survive. Nowadays, if ya don't have a legitimate business where ya can run ya illegitimate business? They shut ya down. But not here. Ain' gonna happen here," he points into his desk, then leans across it. "Not'n Brooklyn. . . . The old way, Liam. Our way. Ya father's way. And those that choose death or imprisonment over subjugation. Because our way is more important to us than their way. Did ya uncle believe in doing things our way? Or the Anglo's way?"

"A different way," I say obstinately.

Dinny laughs, "That's why ya one o' us, Liam. Because

you too refuse to live on someone else's terms. . . . Only one thing a man can do in his life: be bold. Always bold. Always. If ya ain't got patience when a man's bein' bold? Y'ain't got patience for bein' a man. We give ya a choice, this way or that way, and ya choose neither. Ya choose y'own way, and that's why ya one o' us. And together we survive."

Then there is quiet for a moment, until Dinny calls out, "Jimmy?"

"Yeah?" The Swede answers.

"How comfortable ya feel sendin' this guy to kill someone? Like if we depended on it?"

"Wouldn't."

"Harry?"

"Nah."

"For what it matters," Dinny says. "I wouldn't think it a good idea either. So as soon as ya can learn that ya can stay who y'are and that we respect what ya offer, then ya don' have to worry about ever again killin' a man."

"Red Hook?" I ask.

"I don't think that's a good idea either. Dangerous down there. Tommy can handle himself when the ships dock. Ya bring another thing to the table for us, William. Ya can read."

"I can."

"Write too, no?"

"I can."

"Know math?"

"I do."

"And people like ya," Dinny counts on his fingers. "Everyone here likes ya. Except Petey Behan. Now here's ya next decision that ya gotta suffer t'rough. . . . I want ya outta my home. Tonight. Ya gotta place to stay. Rent's paid for a while. If ya show up tomorrow mornin', I'll see ya then. If ya don't, I'll never see ya again and you'll be done wit' us. But one thing I can say to ya, if ya decide not to come back. Don' come back. Get outta Brooklyn, especially our neighborhoods. Eighty-sixt like Darby Leighton.

Done. Forever. Go proselytize like a fookin' dried up Puritan in Kansas'r Missouri'r Texas'r wherever they hatchet saloons, got it?"

"I do."

"Ya wit' us, then ya wit' us. Today's the day ya make a decision, understand?"

"I said I do."

"Good, who's next?" Dinny looks to The Swede at his right.

But before there is an answer, we hear a great bellowing downstairs. Then the throwing of chairs and more bellowing, followed by stomping up the stairwell toward the office.

"Jimmy," Dinny says, as The Swede pulls out a cudgel and hides behind the door.

Harry immediately has a knife held by his right ear. Me with the pipe in my right hand. Dinny himself now has a revolver and holds it on its side on top of his desk as he sits up, though Lumpy is still fast at his world of numbers and unaware.

A knock to the door and Tommy Tuohey's accent comes through, "Tunics here."

"Fookin' tunics here again," The Swede says.

"How many?" Dinny asks.

"Two, Brosnan'n his boyo," comes the voice from behind the door.

"Let 'em in," Dinny says to The Swede.

And through the open door comes Brosnan with his long tunic and copper buttons, peeking round the threshold, his son-in-law Culkin supporting him. Blackjacks in hand and making a big show of it.

"Dinny Meehan," says he.

"Say it again," The Swede dares him.

Brosnan looks over to The Swede and back toward Dinny. "Ye love the fight as much as I do, man. But in this world there's more o' the maneuverin' than there's the fightin'. Regrettable as t'is."

"Point, Brosnan?"

"Ye know that stipend ye've been givin' me? Ye'll now be givin' it to him," he says pointing to Culkin. "Double it fer meself. And if ye don' like them terms, I'll be happy to give these newspapermen that keep knockin' on me door a word about ye—all o' ye."

"Thought ya was made detective, ain't they pay more?" The Swede says.

"Well t'is an opportunity of which . . ."

"That's a word," Dinny interrupts. "Means weakness, nothin' else."

"Ye bowsies are makin' it hard fer us, ye know. They thought yer ways were over when we locked up Connors as the leader."

"Why'd they think that, eh?"

"Listen, the risk we're under is a greater one now. Times'r changin', but ye tinkers are not changin' wit' 'em. Ye stand out like niggers in the bright o' day when they see ye, all o' ye. Ye'll take me down with ye when ye go. I know that." Pointing again to Culkin, Brosnan goes on. "This young man's wife is my daughter and though I know ye don' give a shite fer us, we have our own family to care fer. When the big fight comes, we'll either die with ye, or be shamed away. Ye know it like I do, man. Yer like passed from this great state o' New Yark a decade or more ago. From where yer ideas come there's a bad thing followin', be sure. Stand up to the Anglo-Saxon and ye'll be butchered in the onslaught like swine at the fair. Eaten fer the pleasure in it. And here we are standin' right next ye in their sights."

"Who ya talkin' about?" The Swede winces.

"Ways," Brosnan says. "It's a battle o' ways, ain't it? Yers an' theirs. Ye don't know 'em like I do, ye don't."

"Who?"

"Them," Brosnan says in a gravelly timbre, raising his head back and looking down his nose at us and speaking more like a Mennonite evangelical than the Catholic he is.

But before he continues, he pulls a tin cigar holder from his tunic and lights a Na-Bocklish. "Ye can try an' break it down by class'r gender'r color o' skin, what have ye. Don't matter, that. The great many of us live and believe the ways like vast subjects to a crowned king or God's children to the altar. The great masses of us. Each an' all of us lookin' to rise up from the doom like Lazarus o' Bethany, don't we? Oh they're comin'. Them. Them up there pullin' our strings. Them. Up there tellin' us lowly peasants what's right'n wrong. Jailin' us fer what's wrong, promotin' us for what we do right. Oh no, they're no different than ye, Dinny Meehan. They demand loyalty. Demand it. No different really than ye and how ye treat yer followers. Defy 'em, an' they'll come fer ye. They're comin' now, just slow. Slow an' sure. Gatherin' up like a giant swell they'll swallow ye like the great suck o' the ocean and leave ye bathin' in a welter o' yer own blood and bones, all o' ye. Oh they're comin', sure enough. Slow and sure of 'emselves."

"Jesus wept," The Swede says, spooked to the depth of him.

"Eddie, give 'em what they ask," Dinny says, then turns to Brosnan. "You're on. Anythin' I need to know about, ya talk to me."

"We will," Brosnan nods with two morose eyes looking at Dinny as The Swede looks away, fear smeared across his startled face.

Sitting in front of me, I can only see the back of Harry's head, but we both look toward Dinny at his desk, the city over his shoulders. His defiance unchanged by Brosnan's words and warnings. Always unchanged, is Dinny Meehan. Always who he is and nothing different.

"One thing," Dinny says pointing toward me. "Give this kid ten percent what I'm givin' ya. Every week."

"Fer what reason would we do such a t'ing?"

"We're related, you'n me. By blood and by money," Dinny says.

"I'll not do it . . ."

"He's from Ireland, remember that place?" Dinny cuts
the man off.

"I know it very well. Better than yerself."

"Well, they're fightin' to be free o' the British and the
kid's got family there. I'd like ya to do your part and give
for the cause, like the rest o' us. He's treasurer," Dinny
points at me again.

I look at Dinny sideways for he had only minutes earlier
offered me a way out of the gang.

Holding the bills Lumpy just handed him, Brosnan yells
toward Dinny, "Those men of Easter and their sorry little
failed rebellion, that what yer referrin' to? They caught the
pisspots o' Dubliners, so they did. The damned Fenian fools.
T'was Dubliners spat on them in the streets too. Then caught
the bullets of law, an' ye want me to give to their like? And
what of all them Irish soldiers fightin' in France as we spake,
what of 'em? Are they nothin' to ye? They're Irishmen too."

"Proof only that they're as desperate as ever an' willin'
to take a mere soldier's pay from his enemy so that he can
feed his fam'ly before he's killed. We know you're a souper,
Brosnan, but if you two walk away from here wit'out payin'
ya ten percent for Ireland, I'll tell my men to kill ya both
right here and now. Bury ya in the East River, copper'n all."
Spit flying from his gnashing mouth. "We'll deal wit' what
happens afterward, but ya walk in our home wearing the
monkey's tuxedo of a law that don' benefit our neighborhoods in the slightest, shake us down for a bite at our people's table, and not give back to our cause, and we'll fookin'
flay ya both and pike ya up in them tunics as a warnin' at
the gates o' Irishtown."

The Swede with his cudgel, Harry with his knife, Tommy's
fists, and Dinny's gun surrounding them, Brosnan wipes
his face with the back of his sleeve.

"Seems ye can't never take the cottier out of a man, even
a generation later," Brosnan grunts back. "The mind of a

tenant farmer and half-blooded raggle-taggle gypsy is the whole rake o' ye."

Calmly, Brosnan and Culkin peel a portion of their earnings and hand me it and walk out with Tommy, and as the door opens we see Vincent at the top of the dark stairwell. Brosnan looks at Vincent's shame-filled face and lowers his own head without greetings, descends the stairs with his son-in-law in tow.

"The fuck you been?" The Swede says.

"Dinny?" Vincent looks up.

"Yeah."

"First off, uh . . . I was at the Adonis again."

"For fuck's sake," The Swede barbs.

"Honesty is good," Dinny says. "You found things, though?"

And he had, sitting down where Harry sat he goes on to tell us that he was locked in a room naked and forced to lie on a bed. The whore sent away. Thos Carmody himself had done this to him, Vincent explained, along with the owner of the Adonis Social Club—a man named Jack Stabile and his eldest son, Sixto. That they work with Frankie Yale of The Black Hand.

"What's that?" The Swede says.

"Yeah, Frankie Yale."

"Workin' wit' the ILA down there? At the Bush Terminal?"

"Bigger than that," Vincent says. "Yale's got guys that're gonna support the ILA when they go on strike, see? So, Carmody's Irish, right? So Carmody went to Lovett and an offer was given to work together, I-talians'n the ILA'n Lovett's guys."

"Ya fookin' kiddin' me?" The Swede says.

"But Lovett spit on the offer, says he don' work wit' wops an' told Carmody to go back an' work wit' white men."

Dinny holds his chin, piecing it all together in his mind.

"Listen, though," Vincent says. "That ain't all. Lovett's workin' wit' Wolcott an' Silverman o' the New York Dock Company now."

"For chrissake," The Swede drops his arms.

"But these guys? Yale, the Stabiles, an' Carmody? They wanna do business wit' ya, Din," he explains, facing the man at the desk. "I-talians an' the ILA. They're businessmen, don't care about Irish'r Italian. Means nothing to 'em. They're young turks and say you'n them together can squeeze Lovett from the north an' the south. Squeeze 'em. But the Stabile men, father'n son, they call 'em Pulcinella, Lovett. I don' know, that's what they call 'em, like a Pulcinella is some sorta clown'r somethin' like, 'cause Lovett looks like a clown, right?

"And?"

"The Stabiles say you owe 'em for killin' their guys back in April and . . . and I-talians live in the neighborhood o' Red Hook too, but can't work the docks there. That it ain't fair to them, but they'll work together wit' ya, Dinny. Offer ya a hand for shaking, they just don' want ya to spit on 'em, like Lovett did."

"And?"

"Offered me a job in Chicago if you say no," Vincent says.

"They got lots o' offers, don't they?" The Swede says.

Vincent looks from The Swede toward Dinny, "And that Garry fookin' Barry went to them to kill you for a price as a starker."

The Swede speaks out again, "Like what's he thinkin'? Barry? He's got one follower, Cleary. The fuck's wrong wit'at guy? Garry fookin' Barry, Jesus. He still thinks he should be the leader. No fookin' reasonin' wit' that fool."

Dinny thinks, turns his chair round and looks out the window behind him.

"Everybody's pickin' sides, Din," Vincent says as humbly as he can.

"They're closin' in on us again, Dinny," The Swede says, blathering on and on. "Always closin' in on us. We shoulda never trusted Lovett. The man wants to take things over."

"That's enough," Dinny says.

"They're fookin' closin' in on us, man," The Swede says, withdrawing into his own head. Holding it in his hands and pulling his own hair out with straining fists, clump after clump. "They want us dead. Bathin' in a welter o' blood and bones. Dead. Dead . . ."

I sit up in my seat and look over to Harry. Watching The Swede lose his sanity unsettles me deeply. I look over to Dinny, who lowers his hands to calm him, but The Swede just paces, his own hair in his fists.

"Jimmy . . ." Dinny tries again, but The Swede erases any words by simply screaming over him, the long face and open mouth like some gaunt wraith of a man panicked by a horror.

"Jimmy, I ain' gonna tell ya again . . ." Dinny says.

Falling to his knees in front of us, The Swede shakes and wrings and twists, clenching his fingers. Breathing hard and grunting, he slinks his long shoulders, contorting and bending his great frame so that with the flat of his fists, he beats on the floor like a child. He whispers something unheard to himself. Just speaking out from somewhere in him. Somewhere far away. Lurching and twitching from some invisible implosion in his soul and rupturing heart, his elongated limbs waving like live wires flopping in the street from downed electric poles.

I had never seen him nor any other man act in such a way. And for less than a second he looks at me, then looks away muttering again. From that look I draw an ominous feeling and stand from my chair as if it were a primitive, rote response to the look in his eyes. We all stand. And as we do, The Swede looks up, jumps from his knees, and grabs Vincent by the coat and pulls him to the ground as I watch without movement. A moment later he appears above him with Vincent's gun in his hand. He turns it around awkwardly and holds the trigger with a thumb at his own chest. He pulls back the hammer, face red with long tears streaming down the cheeks. Backs away.

"I ain't goin' t'rough this no more," he says, still backing away, then seemingly arguing with something that is not there, he turns his head angrily and mutters. "I'm coming, I'm coming."

In anticipation he yawps in the air and pinches his face as he pulls the trigger and just as I hear the clap of the gun, Harry jumps and pushes The Swede's hand upward. The bullet then comes out of the back of his shoulder knocking against a wall flaccidly and landing on the floor next to Lumpy, spinning. The Swede falls to his back on the ground and quickly there is a puddle behind him, the room filled with the heavy scent of iron in the blood and gun smoke.

Dinny jumps from his desk as Harry rips the gun out from The Swede's loosened grip. Dinny pulling him up, then pulls down The Swede's tie and shirt and looks to see where the bullet passed through. A small red dot appears just under the clavicle, and gently coming up through it is blood that seemingly defies gravity. The blood is wiped from the hole and again there is only a dot slowly being obscured by the flooding blood again.

Lumpy picks up the damaged bullet and tries to hand it to Dinny, but he is ignored.

"Is he gonna die?" Vincent asks, shaken.

"Needs a doctor," Harry says.

"No," The Swede pleads. "No hospital. No, no, no. I won't go to no hospital. No doctors. Just take me to my sister, Helen. She'll take care o' me like I know she can. Helen can take care o' me just like she did last time. Dinny? Dinny?"

"Yeah?"

"I'm sorry, Din," The Swede says, his eyes glassy.

"Don' worry 'bout it, Jimmy. We'll take ya to Helen so ya can get better and be close to ya fam'ly."

"No hospital," The Swede begs from the floor.

"Jaysus," Tommy mutters.

"No hospital," Dinny assures.

Picking up the gargantuan, crumpled spider by the limbs and torso, Dinny along with Vincent, Tommy, Harry, and even Lumpy go out the door and negotiate the steps in the dark stairwell and are enveloped by the voices of drinkers who find out who caught the shot of a gun upstairs.

And I don't know why, but I do not follow them. I stay. Away from them. For the next hour, I stay in the second-floor room by myself. The empty office. Standing with my hands in my pockets, I look out the shutter windows over the water. The quiet. I hear the city swooshing mildly in the distance, the stable permanence of sound, the invisible human fracas that babbles gently in the background. But in here I feel the quiet. Try and let all of our problems flatten out for a moment, I sit in Dinny's chair. At his desk and close my eyes. Close them.

CHAPTER 13

Scalpeen Memories

JANUARY, 1917

JANUARY AND THE BITE IS MURDEROUS. The whipping wind whistles off the water where under the bridges we huddle, hands covering ears. The sky is as hard looking as the cement under our feet, and the same color too. Broken only by the Brooklyn Bridge above us, that sky over the city is as mean and thoughtless as some of the men that show hungry on the docks looking for a day's wage. Same look in the gray eyes of them.

From inside the tenement walls come skirling flue pipes wheezing in the gales, and glims of light flash through crevices as if the tenements, whelmed with many families, were out to sea rudderless. Children bunch in front of the coal fire and the potbelly stove, if they have it. In memories, and the bones of our memories where reside the unconscious thoughts and recognitions in the marrow, is a feeling where remembrances are signaled when our bellies rattle with the hunger and when the weather attacks the skin.

It is a silent song that voices rarely dare to share, and no one cares to disturb the silence of it, for it is no more than a cognizance in our blood. But we all knew it as it truly is: the past speaking to us. Coming out in our eyes and our need for fight. We know, even as most stories were withheld us due to the shame of our caste, we know of and are haunted in the mind's eye of our fathers and our mothers and theirs, the elements hard on our bodies and the hollow yearn for alimentation. Evicted from the land. Evicted from our community and the closeness for which our people so long had found strength. Remember in us the scalps dug in the onset of winter under some stray hill a few miles from the icy Shannon. And the scalps and lean-tos of the shanty emigrants of Jackson Hollow south of the Navy Yard here in Brooklyn. And those shoeless and gaunt in Darby's Patch before Warren Street was ever paved and before Dinny Meehan had come to it. The seasons of cholera and yellow fever that swept through Irishtown from the human cargo dumped on the shoreline, amassed there.

Unsaid. Simply known, we work in the wintry conditions and the empty air that strips the body to a barrenness where survival is top of the mind. Just how we like it. With two bailhooks, I dig into the work. Piercing wheat sacks. Picking them up with my back and legs and thrusting them up into a train car shadowed by the long torso of a transport steamer. Dinny working right alongside us, watching over us and reminding us that in this work we live. Down here. Below the Anglo ascendency and his laws, forever. Forever reminding us where we come from. Forever living by the underbellies of ships, outside in the weather, with memories remembered only in the distance of our blood.

* * *

AFTER A WORD WITH DINNY, TOMMY Tuohey heads south alone. A man of any and all weather, Tommy strides down Columbia Street. Down Furman Street where to the right is the shit-green New York Harbor, and left is the bluff that separates the Brooklyn waterfront from the old Dutch and English mansions of another time, now divided and subdivided for the peasants and the newly arrived. He passes the old Penny Bridge on Montague Street that now brings the workingmen from the street grade above to the warehouse and pier house roofs below to the blacked-out area where the ships let off and the gangs that take to their ways there.

Of course, Tommy knows nothing of such histories, for he lives only in the felt memories of his own blood and in the weather on his own skin too. A free man who lives in the love of the company of others and in the contests of will and individual struggle, ignorant by nature and by choice of the constructs of the settled people, and seeks only work for his next meal and drink and talk.

Tommy turns on Imlay Street in the morning air, an emissary for The White Hand. A late-night drizzle had turned much of the sidewalks to sheets of ice, and men walk gingerly with their hands on wood fences and brick walls for balance as they make their way along the big buildings owned by the New York Dock Company. Not many of the men in Red Hook own gloves or winter-wear in general and instead stand round donning the same coats they wore at summer, but with long underwear underneath and vest and hat, hopping in place. The breath that comes out of their mass gives them the appearance of ranging cattle and heads of beef. Awaiting the line to be called for to pick men to unload, they stand shoulder to shoulder patting down their upper arms.

Walking through their gaggle, Tommy Tuohey looks up and points at the barge just dragged up off the Imlay bulkhead, "Who dat spakin' widda captain?"

"Darby Leighton," says a man Tommy doesn't recognize.

A tug driver and his son look to Tommy, then turn their backs. The father rushing his son back onboard with a hand under his elbow and quick he is to the throttle and the river.

"Dat right?" Tommy says.

"Ya scared?" says another man.

"Scared o' what?"

"Scared? Are ya scared?"

"I'm not scared of a damn thing. Kinda question's this, ye feckin' sausage?"

"Hey," yells Joey Behan, Petey's older brother. "Tommy? That you? What are you doin' down here?"

"The fook kinda question's that?" Tommy says again. "Joey Behan? Ya not s'posed be down here s'marnin'. Ya s'posed to be up Baltic way. Dinny know ye here?"

"Nah," Behan says walking toward him. "Ya gonna tell on me, are ya? Ya fookin' tout. We're takin' over now. Ya can go'n tell ya pikey king that, ya fookin' weaklink."

"Ye call me a weaklink, Behan? I'll kill ye with me fists I . . ."

"Shaddup," Bill Lovett says, walking toward the commotion with five or six men round him following in the cold smoke. "'Less ya wanna fight over it. Ya wanna fight over it?"

"I'll fight any man with the fists . . ."

"Then stand up to it then, here I am," Lovett says, looking up to Tuohey as a crowd gathers round.

"Richie?" Tommy notices Richie Lonergan coming up behind Lovett. "The feck ye doin' down here, eh? And all yer bhoys wid ye? Dis a t'ing yer all doin'? Is it?"

Tommy looks around and sees the golden-haired Mickey Kane who is wearing a fearful gaze on his face, "Mick? What goes here?"

"I challenged ya to a fight, man," Lovett says as Darby and the captain watch from the deck above, smoke coming out of their own mouths up there too. "Are ya fookin' soft?"

"Fair fight 'tween me'n yerself and ye'd find out what'll happen, but ye got all yer boyos here," Tommy looks up. "Who da feck's dat tall feckin' gorilla bastard?"

"Who, him?" Lovett says. "That's Wisniewski. And the guy next to him's our new business partner, Silverman. Ya got somethin' against 'em?"

"Silverman's the name o' him? From the Dock Company?" Tommy says. "Ye takin' over? Dat what yer after, Bill? Anyt'in' fer the power is it, Bill? And dis here? James Quilty, fer feck's sake? Ye t'ink ye'll get away wid'is do ye? Ye'll not . . ."

And without listening to another word, Lovett comes up close to Tuohey and swings a right fist that Tommy ducks away from. But it's a man behind him that pushes him back toward Lovett, and Tuohey finds himself within the fighter's circle in the cold.

"C'mon, Tommy," Lovett says. "You'n me. Right now. One on one. That's what ya want, right? One on one, man to man?"

"Well dis don't seem . . ." Tommy begins, face reddened. "If t'were only you'n me . . ."

"C'mon, fookin' pikey scum," Lovett yells at Tommy up close, then pushes him with both hands by the neck and face as they both square off.

"With me bare hands, ye know I will, Bill . . ."

"Then let's do it. C'mon."

And the men of the circle laugh except for the Lonergan kid and his right-hand Harms, who have a sullen look on their mugs. Of them all, Wisniewski is the biggest with a chest on him like a bull ape, though he is dressed in a fine suit with a kerchief out of the coat pocket. And Silverman, who is almost as tall and even better dressed with shiny hair on a hatless head and a long elegant coat.

Lovett pushes a left jab toward Tommy who moves to his right to get away from him, as he once taught myself to do. Looking at all the faces and moving round the edge of the circle, Tommy takes his time. He is adept at skipping sideways like a trained fistfighter and avoids Lovett until Frankie Byrne punches him in the ear from outside the circle. Lovett then makes a move, swings a mighty right though it barely touches the side of Tommy's head, who juts out of the way of it, then lands a quick left to the side of Lovett's face. More of a push than a punch. The circle shrinks more, crowding the two fighters into each other.

"Back the feck up, ye fecks," Tommy yells. "I'll kill the masses of ye one by one . . ."

And just as he is challenging the entire circle, John Lonergan punches him from behind in the kidney, Joey Behan grabs him by the neck, while Frankie Byrne kicks a leg from under him.

"Take'm down," Matty Martin yells as Richie Lonergan uppercuts Tommy in the face as the older Behan holds him.

Somehow Tommy breaks free and tries to run through the crowd, punching anything that gets in his way. One man goes down on his ass with his arms spread out, trying to hold himself up by the bodies of others. Petey Behan grabs hold of Tommy's coat from behind, which begins to tear and others tackle him, kneeing him in the nose three and four times so hard that his head and hair jump at each blow.

Jidge Seaman brings the heel of his boot down onto the back of Tommy's head and Sean Healy too winds his leg behind four and five times into his back and neck until Tommy is no longer moving and all laugh as he has begun wheezing and snuffling at each deep breath, smoke billowing, and blood plopping out of his mouth in freezing chunks.

"Great time for a nap, ya stoopit fookin' tinker," Petey Behan says.

"Shaddup," Lovett demands, pushing people from his way, then kicking Tommy over onto his back so they can see his face.

"Oh Jesus," says one man, shocked at the unconscious staring of Tommy Tuohey below.

Looking over their work, Lovett pulls out his .45 and holds it at his hip, "This is what happens when a guy from outside comes into our territory. This is ours. No one else's. Ours. No more do we pay Dinny and them and no more will any of you report to 25 Bridge again. Ya report to me. And that's the end of it. All o' ya's. Anybody comes down here that you don't know about, take 'em to the ground and ask questions later."

And as Lovett is quiet for a moment, the silence of the men appears still, even as the rest of the world keeps going. The ship captain lifts the hatch as he descends inside the barge and with a clang does it drop. Darby Leighton climbs down a rope ladder at that moment too while the moaning of ships of all sizes and stripes roam out on the harbor in the morning cut.

"Richie?"

"Yeah?" Richie responds.

"C'mere," Lovett turns his gun round and pushes the handle to him. "You and yours are wit' me now. For good."

"Right."

"Finish it," Lovett says.

Lonergan pulls back the hammer and shoots twice into Tommy's abdomen, who grunts and turns onto his side, waking up for the pain. Lonergan then limps closer, within the circle, points the barrel at the back of Tommy's head and explodes half of it open like a dropped watermelon.

"Mickey Kane?" Lovett yells.

"Yeah?"

Lovett looks behind him with anger in his eyes as Lonergan puts the gun on Lovett's chest, "C'mere."

* * *

"Man?" Brosnan yells for Dinny across the pier amidst the falling snow. "Hello, man."

Dinny emerges above on deck.

"There's dead down Red Hook way. Yer's, I t'ink."

Peering down at Brosnan, I see Dinny's face and with this news I see nothing. Nothing at all. Nothing different than ever I'd seen on his face, as if he knew it was coming all along. Knew it.

"Well there ya have it," Cinders says coming up from behind. "That's where them Lonergan kids went and the rest of 'em. We gonna hit back now, Din? What?"

Fifteen, twenty men stop working and look up to Dinny when they hear the news. Fifty more as it spreads round. At that moment, Harry Reynolds runs up to the pier and stands next to myself and Brosnan, looking up at Dinny.

"Man," Brosnan yells up. "I can't guarantee what'll be ordered if there's another bloodbath down Red Hook, do ye hear me? The papers'll run wid it. District Attorney'll have to react."

"Shaddup, Brosnan," Vincent yells. "Ya got no say here."

"Where's The Swede?" Brosnan asks.

Dinny's face just looks hard and distant, like he's not listening up there on the deck where I watch him. Like he's not there at all.

"God please don' let it be Mickey Kane dead," I hear Cinders mumble under his breath.

CHAPTER 14

Hope for Summer

HARRY IS STONE-FACED LOOKING AT THE third-floor room as next to him I stand in shock at the shape of the place.

"Well my mam and sisters can't live here."

"He said it needs work."

"He did say that, but there's a huge hole in the floor," I say, looking down to the second floor kitchen where three dirty-smiled toddlers look back up at me, an older child slumped in another chair. "Broken window over here and the walls look like the inside of a whale."

Harry turns on the faucet but only a brackish sludge comes out. "Can't see how they're flushin' the jake in this buildin'. Pipes're rusted out."

"This place is a horror. Fireplace is blocked up and I can hear rats up there."

"One block from the park, though," Harry says, nodding out the kitchen window. "Can see the treetops from here. Look at 'em all."

I look, but only see branches frozen and swaying hungrily in the winter-gray backdrop. Brown ice and muddy snow accumulate at the edge of rooftops and cornices, but just beyond I can see the tops of the trees, their beauty distant and only made true by imagining them. Hibernating in the darkness of now with nothing but hope and flights of fancy to make them real. Better days ahead, but stuck in the present, I doubt them. Feel that they're not to come and yet wonder at the idea that what makes people keep drudging through the muck of now is the chance at better times ahead. Drudging and drudging and most times dying before ever able to reach that summer day when the trees are blooming with color and the heaven we all hope for shines on our loved one's faces, warm and generous. If it hadn't been for so much winter that I see and the impotent struggles of bettering ourselves, then I wouldn't be so filled with the doubt. So much of it. The real truth of things is that hope is always in the distance. In the future. Forever in the distance and many times we never reach it, like Tommy Tuohey. He wanted a family. He wanted a wife and sons and he died unknown.

I take a deep breath. Exhale outward as Harry looks at me, "It's just work's all," he said. "Work is everythin'."

When I look back on it now I'm a bit unsure how I survived at all. A miserable adolescence of course it was. Your happy adolescence hardly being worth your while. I sit back from the typewriter for a moment. Push the pen and paper to the side. An old man with nothing left to him now but prayers for forgiveness, another form of hope for the future. I hold my head in my hands. There were things we had to do to survive. Hard and pragmatic decisions. Good and normal people in bad predicaments, we were. Our art was not based on rejecting our parents' way of life or born out of spare time—no, our art was that of need. Need to survive. I tell myself this and hold my beads, pray. I wasn't ready to make the sort of decisions demanded of me back then in my adolescence. But they had to be made.

To this day I still think of auld Tommy Tuohey standing up to anyone, ready to fight the whole world and getting himself butchered for his bravery. He taught me to fight with my fists, Tommy did. A valuable thing in those days. And he taught me to be strong, too. Dinny sent him to me for a reason, but I'd be incomplete if it was only Tommy that taught me about life. It is at this point in the story when things begin to turn. With Tommy Tuohey gone, Harry Reynolds steps in. Begins watching over me. Influencing me too, under Dinny's watchful eye. Always in his vision.

"Ya ready?" Harry asks as he walks past me and toward a broken-glassed window.

Standing there in that wretched hole of a room, I haven't a choice but to talk myself out of quitting it all. From just running away. Just going away with myself. "Don' quit," Dinny's words ring in my head. "No one can beat the man outta ya."

I want terribly to feel bad for myself, but I just grumble toward Harry, "The people around here in this neighborhood seem humble and kind at least."

On one knee by the hole in the floor, Harry starts listing off things, "We gotta go to the lumberyard for four-inch-wide slabs, two inches thick. And studs to support the flooring, some plywood for the walls and ceiling. Then to the plumber. We gotta get measurements of them pipes, fittings, new jake for the lavatory, sink in the kitchen, sand the floors, paint the walls. . . . I got wood glue and a saw, hammers and things," Harry says looking up to me. "Then when it's all done, we go to the furniture store."

I rub my hand across my face and hair, "I need a mattress."

"You can stay wit' me off Atlantic Avenue 'til we get this place sealed up."

I thank him with a lowered head.

"We'll need access to their place to fix their ceiling too," Harry says, looking down through the hole. "Do a little bit every Sunday. You still don' know when they're comin'? Ya ma an' sisters?"

"No idea," I say. "Did Dinny tell you to help me?"

Harry doesn't answer that, " Y'ever done work like this?"

"Repairs? A little on the farm."

"We can get Dance to help us out here and there, and James Hart'll let us use the automobile truck to load up supplies. When ya mother an' sisters get here, it'll be like new. I mean," Harry says, still kneeling down to the hole in the flooring and looking up to me. "I'd like to help, if ya want it. Get it ready for 'em an' all. I never had a fam'ly o' my own. Don't even know what it's like, but . . ."

"Dinny says we are a family."

"Yeah, not a real fam'ly though. If we had our own fam'ly, we probably wouldn't be in a gang, right?"

"Well, that's not really true . . ."

"Ya know what I mean, William," Harry says, standing up and walking toward the kitchen window. "I don' even know if I'm Irish. Ya know my last name? Reynolds? That's not mine. It's the name of the nun that adopted me."

"Well you can be a part of my family. I uh . . . I just don't want anyone knowing about this room that doesn't need to know about it. I don't want it getting around where I live. . . . If Lovett and the Lonergan crew find out . . ."

"No worries. No one knows anything right now except Dinny an' Sadie an' the inner circle, but you can trust 'em."

"Vincent?"

"He'll never say nothin' to nobody."

"Lumpy?"

"Nah, I don' think he even knows who you are," Harry says with a slight smiling. "He can't keep up wit' nothin' except numbers, anyway. And he knows. He knows never to say nothin' to nobody anyhow."

And looking out the window to the barren treetops, I give in entirely. To the treasure of hope, and imagine my own mother living here like it's a dream. The safety and the calm it might bring. Far from that war and the Brits.

Out back at the bottom level there is a small courtyard where children could play, if it wasn't so cold. And although my two younger sisters Abby and Brigid are getting too old for games, I know that they'll enjoy the other children from this and adjoining buildings. There is also a stable house about a half block away where four or five horses reside, steam coming from their long heads leaning over the sidewalk. I can't wait to see what the park will be like during summer. Left to imagine it only. Left to overcome doubt. Hope lands in the summer and if we're lucky, my mother and sisters will land here too.

I look to Harry, "I just want you to know how much this . . ."

"Don' worry 'bout it," he interrupts. But there is much to be thinking on. So much in the way of their arrival.

* * *

IT IS LATE JANUARY WHEN HARRY and I start spending Sundays in the Prospect Park room and the months drag on. Dinny Meehan—the man that has pulled us all up out of the darkness and given us our lives—is himself dying inside. Without The Swede, who is slowly recovering under his sister Helen's care, Dinny slowly fades into silence. But worse yet is the silence on his face. The blank look. The distance in him. Something had been taken from him, yet no one knows exactly which thing it is that's drained him of his color and vigor that so defines him. Some days he sleeps in, even. When he doesn't show in the morning under the elevated tracks to meet myself and the dock-bosses, we are forced to make our own plans for the day. In these days I gravitate more toward Harry Reynolds, who carries on with things and is so generous to me. And he pays me extra too, which is a great help as I spend much of my time planning for the future.

Red Hook, though, it has gone from Dinny's territory to seceding entirely. It is gone and no one speaks of it. Least of all Dinny. Here we had for so long fought against the Italians who people the neighborhood tenements down there. Fought against the unions too, and right from under us our own man slips away with it. Lovett and his crew had bided their time well, kept quiet and made their move. At the Dock Loaders' Club whispers are sent from ear to ear, things like, "Dinny's always been too good to some" and "He was soft on Bill and it came back on 'em."

But I don't know of any man in our midst that could've handled Lovett better than Dinny. Some things are inevitable, and although Lovett is a powerful dockboss that deserves respect for the number of men he can rally and for the dangerous environment he took over, it is no doubting now that his betrayal is complete.

I know that every man leaning on the bar hopes for revenge, but nothing is said beyond the whisper. And we try to move on, quietly. As always, under the shade of the Manhattan Bridge with the sun setting beyond its overpass, Paddy Keenan drops drinks in front of the men who've earned a spot at the Dock Loaders' Club mahogany trough. Connolly, Donnelly, Gibney, Morissey and Howard and McGarry at one end of bar by the stairwell; Dance Gillen and Philip Large taking the seat of the missing Lovett and his crew by the crook in the bar. Maher, too, sitting with them now, as Dinny wants to be left alone upstairs. Many are missing due to the treasonous act by Lovett and those that follow him. Always strong due to our numbers, this makes us concerned as well. Knowing too that Tanner Smith's actions weaken us, there are grumblings from Gibney and Morissey, "He ain' even Irish American, really."

"Dinny'd give Tanner the gun to shoot him wit'," Cinders says soberly, interrupting them. "The man's loyal to the marrow for those that helped him when he was in need. Better dig that right an' now, boyos, 'cause that ain' gonna change just 'cause Tanner stiffed 'em. Ain' gonna change. Tanner helped Dinny and his father get out o' Greenwich Village years ago. That means a lot to 'em."

* * *

THE MONTHS ROLL ON THOUGH, INTO the spring. The best news is that Mickey Kane will live. Shot twice, but mere flesh wounds. They tried to break his spirit and send him back to Dinny a whimpering pup, but Kane comes round practically unchanged.

Though Dinny has changed. And the look on his face tells us of his down-turned thoughts. February into March and then April and still Dinny doesn't speak to us. Stares away out into the distance where Manhattan stands above, across the river and out the window of his second-floor office. Sitting at his empty desk and listening with glazed eyes as dockbosses complain of the problems in their terminals with nary a suggestion from him.

"Can't we send someone down to the Baltic, Dinny? We need help," Gibney The Lark says with Big Dick sitting behind him. "Like we can't keep havin' these Polacks show up drunk in the mornin', even though they got a few dollars to shine their way into a job, when they can't do a damn thing if they're passed out in the pier house at noon."

"Ya can't run ya area, ask Harry what he does," Dinny says, then turns his chair round to look out the window.

Gibney holds his hands on his knees with one hand missing three fingers. He turns red in anger, yet keeps his tongue to himself.

"C'mon, Lark," Big Dick says standing up and slapping Gibney with the back of his hand. "We'll take care of it."

Vincent and I look at each other from across the room. He shrugs at me, opens the door for Gibney and Morissey. It is quiet in the office. I look over to Lumpy, but there is never eye contact with him, and as usual, he is fast in his computations of the day's earnings but after a few more moments, he turns dumbly to Dinny, "Lovett's not coming anymore, right? Because I don't have his . . ."

"Right," Dinny interrupts.

Pushing his glasses up, Lumpy then rests his arm on the desk with his job completed.

"Well we're making about twenty-three percent less

without the Red Hook section . . ."

"He ain' comin' back, I said." Staring out the window, then turns and looks to Vincent and I as if to make sure we'll not share that information with others.

"Dinny?" Lumpy asks.

"Don' fookin' ask me nothin'," he responds.

Looking out the window again, he says nothing more. Nothing. Not a word. I think maybe he is looking over to the right for The Swede because that's where The Swede usually leans, but his eyes stay on the Manhattan Bridge in the foreground and the city beyond it, stretching long across the shutter windows.

What he is thinking, I can't know. All I know is what's missing. I blame myself, of course. Blame myself for using him like so many of us do. And maybe that's why he is so quiet. As punishment, since he doesn't seem capable of doing anything to those he loves. Knowing how to fight. Knowing how to kill too, but not knowing how to hold us to account when we take him for granted. The people close to him. The people he loves. Instead, his silence and distance is there to make us think on things. Like maybe if I would have been grateful for the place he paid for with his own money for my family, then maybe he wouldn't be so cold to me. And maybe he was doing that to all of us too for not seeing him for what he is, instead of seeing him for what we can get from him.

But I don't believe that explains it all, and as Lumpy and I leave the room, he sends Vincent away with us too, again. Up there alone now, is he. Staring. Wondering who he is and what his place in the world could be. It's been said before that at twenty-seven years of age, if we haven't already figured our way, then we find ourselves on a precipice. On a wire. Deciding whether to jump or to stick to what we know and try and survive by using the tools we know we possess. Leaving behind the hopes that we held for ourselves in youth and accepting what we already understand we can and cannot do. Like anyone, Dinny had dreams for himself. Though he never talked about them to us. And many of those dreams were wrought with years ahead of him still. Time was there for those ideas to come to fruition. But at twenty-seven, dreams become hardened. Realities take their shape, then shape you in their wake.

"First Coohoo Cosgrave, now The Swede," Beat McGarry whispers to me downstairs, his droopy eyes and face looking like a melted candle.

"What happened to Coohoo Cosgrave?" I ask.

He shakes his head slowly, lowering his eye to me and drinks a long drink, "Then there's what happened to McGowan . . . and Tommy Tuohey now?"

"What about them?"

"Tanner Smith?"

"What are you saying, Beat?"

"Lovett and those that followed him too? What if you was Dinny? How'd you be about all this? And now the income is way down."

"Aye," Paddy agrees, listening in.

"It's gettin' bad," Beat continues. "So bad, Needles Ferry went up to see Dinny offerin' him to spread drugs around the neighborhood for a profit."

"But Dinny wouldn't have it," Paddy finishes the sentence.

"And Chisel Maguire, too, pitchin' Dinny that we should open a policy wheel an' faro joint the gang can manage and protect."

"Wouldn't have gamblin' either," Paddy says.

"Nor would he entertain Vincent's notion of a bawdy-house up here in Irishtown."

"No way."

"Dinny'd be no different than the man he took down to get control over the gang if he went with any combination of those three offers. He's stickin' to labor an' that's the end of it. He's no Christie Maroney. He'll never sell Irishtown out."

"No he won't."

"What do you think he'll do?" I ask.

"Dinny's t'inkin' about t'ings is all, William," Paddy says.

"You're saying that he is having doubts? Like, what could he be doubting? He provides for people. For us. For all of us. And even more in the neighborhoods. I meet people all the time that he sends food to, pays their rent entirely. What'll happen to them if we fold up? How will I get my mam here?"

Paddy and Beat listen without comment while the dock-bosses lean on the bar, their righthanders and others standing behind them. Many others too, standing in the cramped and crowded saloon blathering away. I look round to them, hats held low with cigarettes and pipes hanging from their dirty faces. The toothy grins and untrusting eyes and when the door opens we all look to see who it is. To make sure it's no enemy. And so it must be doubt that haunts Dinny here. Doubt that all he does—all that we do as a group—is for the best. Doubt that he'll ever make it to the summer of his life where the trees are green and the sun splashes on his face.

I drink my drink down and look upstairs through the darkness. Drop my glass next to Beat and Ragtime, in front of Paddy and elbow my way through the crowd. Put my hand on the banister looking up. They all look at me quietly as I start to walk up, and after a few steps, I start running. Up the stairs by the twos and pound on Dinny's door, then walk in.

He is standing with his back to me looking out the window. Unresponsive, as if he's given up entirely, which angers me. That I'd for so long followed this man was a fact that hitched me to his honor, among others. Now, here he stands with his back to us. Well, I won't have it. And the fact I am still young yet, only in my teens, gives me the opportunity to confront him without fear of his full wit and strength.

"How long are you going to feel sorry for yourself?"

No answer.

"I'd more or less find my own way in this world if you're not in it," I say. "Been three months since all that went down. You . . . you think The Swede'd put up with your sitting hind on hands?"

Nothing from him, other than quietly placing his hands in his pockets and looking across the East River toward the Manhattan Bridge from his perch.

"I'm sorry. I'm sorry that I didn't trust you about the place you got for me. I'm very grateful for it. Harry helped me understand it and so did . . . so did Tommy," I say, giving myself a quick cross for his memory. "I was wrong and I know that now. I'm sorry for not appreciating what you do. You've done so much for me and I haven't been appreciative. I can't make everybody else say that. Or even notice what you do for them, but I know that they need you. Things on the docks are falling apart, Dinny. Cinders and Philip Large keep dealing with Austrians that don't know how the system works and Red's area in the Navy Yard is almost all union now, with that man Henry Browne leading the way and asking about you every damn day. Harry and Gibney have had to work together to fight off outsiders and that imbecile Garry fucking Barry keeps talking about how he is going to take the gang over. You know that? You know he says he talks with Thos Carmody and King Joe from the ILA? Like they're backing him. Is that true? No one believes it, but do you know if it's true, Dinny?"

Still nothing but his back.

I hold my fist in my hand and look back to the door and reach for the handle. As I do so, he partially turns to me with his head bowed.

"Got a lot on my mind. More than you know, really. But uh . . . it's against all I know, turnin' Tanner out. He was there for me and my fam'ly when we needed it. He helped us," Dinny said.

Downcast, he slowly reaches into his desk and places a book on top of it. "I know ya birthday was a couple weeks ago, but this was for you."

I walk over to him, as he turns back to the window again without ever looking at me. Picking up the thick book, it has no words on the hard, dark blue cover. I open it to the first few pages and it says, *Leaves of Grass*.

"Whitman," Dinny says toward the windows.

"How did you know I would have wanted this? Thanks," I say, holding the book open, turning to page 176 where I find the poem "When Lilacs Last in the Dooryard Bloom'd." The poem that I only knew by title from the old broken-glassed frame on the wall downstairs.

It's gotten dark outside and even darker inside. Dinny drops a box of matches in front of me as I sit in the chair opposite his desk to read. I pop a match and hold it to a candle and point to the first line in the poem, read it slowly and with purpose. Spend the next couple minutes reading it, then start to read it again and although I know it is Lincoln that the poem is about, I can't help but think of Dinny Meehan. As if the poem is about him, not Lincoln. A great man, even though Dinny is a killer and sends people to jail, pays off the police and commits any and all sins to be sinned. I don't care. For me, Dinny is a good man in a bad place with little to no choice. He helps people who need it and does bad things in order to do so. I close the book.

"Thanks for thinking of me," I say.

"Sure, sure."

"I know that all you want is to have us all be together. Most people . . . they don't understand why you always tried for Lovett. I think I do though. Has he always been this way? Lovett? Why won't he just see that we're best as a group and the real enemies are others? Why does he act the traitor and go to Wolcott and Silverman and Wisniewski?"

Dinny is looking down and shrugs his shoulders, "Is there any avoidin' it?"

"I suppose there isn't."

Looking back toward me Dinny asks, "Ya know much on hist'ry?"

"A bit."

He grumbles and looks away, "Ya ever think it's true what they say about a man who overthrows another man eventually becomes the man he overthrew?"

"I don't know much about that."

"Ya will one day, right now ya just green. Ya need to read some, ya know that?"

"I do."

"I know ya wanna get an education. An' ya will someday, I know ya will. Just don't forget us when ya do."

"I won't."

"We'll all be dead one day and you'll be alive still, but ya can't forget. It's because o' the life I lead that they come after me. I don't go by their rules, right? But . . . they can never kill me off. Ya know? We'll always exist. Always, as long as they do."

I look at him with my head tilted.

"Ya know, uh . . . Sadie. . . . We've been tryin' to have more kids, ya know? I mean she's always wanted a big fam'ly. Been a while since my son was born and we been tryin' but . . . I don't know what's wrong."

"She's never mentioned that to me."

"I love my wife more'n anythin' I've ever loved and I can't seem to give her what she wants most."

"Well, you can't give everyone . . ."

"But children? I need fam'ly. Just like you, ya know? Need fam'ly. My blood. Carry our name . . . everythin' that's important's wrapped up in fam'ly, and someone up there . . . someone—whoever it is'r whatever it is—just don' want me to have fam'ly. Right from the start we were thrown off the land . . . sent away to New York. Then to

Brooklyn, like I'm nothin'. Like I'm a nothin' in this world.
Still takin' fam'ly away from me to this very day."

"Don't you have two sisters up in Albany?"

"No, they're dead," he said. "They forgot about me.
They're dead to me. Abandoned us, those two. They just
want their lace curtains and their English tea and their
property-grubbin' husbands. Landowners, ya know? They
always wanted to become exactly what's held us down for
so long. Ya can't explain it to someone without it soundin'
absurd by all measurements. Respectability among the
subjects. You're too young to know about it, William. But
that's all they think about. They're ashamed o' me. Now
they have their own fam'lies and pretend like I died too.
They always said I acted like my uncle Seamus. Always
complained my older brothers'n my uncle Red Shay and
. . . and about our father's knowing things, like Irish words
and ways. When they got married, they lost the Meehan
name and took the name of some other. Wanted nothin'
more than to forget about the past," he says shaking his
head. "All of it. Just wanted it all to go 'way."

"Well at least you have Mickey."

He nods his head in agreement, though I can see he feels
I don't quite understand, "Yeah, least I got him. Ya right."

"You really mean a lot to me, Dinny," I say, swallowing.

He nods heavily, "You uh . . . talked to the McGowan
girl lately?"

"I haven't. Like I'm not sure what to do with my feelings at
all about her since I'm so incomplete. I don't feel like I can
concentrate on her without knowing about my own family's
safety. I'd love to give myself to her, but I don't know myself,
really. I don't even know her, other than a chance meeting."

"I got ya."

"I mean, I'm attracted to Emma. She's beautiful. Truly
is. And a good person, it seems. Very good person. But uh
. . . they wanna leave Brooklyn anyway and I'm still tryin'
to get my fam'ly here in the first place. So . . ."

"Mrs. McGowan likes ya," Dinny said looking over to me. "She tol' me she thinks ya'll be a good man one day. She can see it in ya."

"That's nice of her to say."

"She understands what ya goin' through. So does Emma."

"Is that true? They're not upset with me?"

"Nah, they understand. The McGowans are good people. I'm friends with that family for many years, ya know. I met them when they were homeless, huddled in some stairwell corner of a courtyard," he stops and looks at me. "Empty ya pockets."

"What?"

"Empty 'em."

I do as he says, empty them onto the desk. He fingers through the dollar bills and the coins and lint, investigating as if he does not trust me, and finds the Saint Christopher, picks it up.

"My mother gave me that," I say.

He looks at it by the candle as if it were some foreign, strange object, "For good travels, right?"

"Yes."

The candle in the darkness lights half his face; the cold night-wind ringing up through the open-shuttered windows moves his earthen brown hair. I shiver looking at him. A dangerous and gentle man.

He needles through the rest and finds half a pencil, picks it up, and looks at me, "Ya stole this."

I don't answer because I know he does not want any record of what we do lying around for the law to come and use against us. He looks at the pencil and then at me again and says, "Don' forget about us."

In the darkness upstairs we stand with hands in pockets, candle between us. Over his shoulder through the big windows are the city lights against the starless matte above. Forever over him, as his heart was shaped by the city that leans on him now, and it's in the city that he'll always be remembered.

"Let's uh . . ." he says. "Let's have a meetin'."

"All right."

"Sunday, after church."

"What are we going to talk about?"

"The dockbosses, you, Vincent, Gillen, Mickey . . . and The Swede'll be back by then, too. Sunday . . . we'll talk about everythin'. I gotta go get a head start though, talk to some people first. . . . Tell the guys downstairs, would ya?"

"I will."

"We'll talk about everythin' and we'll figure it out, but I gotta go do this first. Then we'll be ready."

"All right."

"Do me favor, William?"

"Sure."

"Send up Vincent, yeah?"

And I am happy when I see the light in his eyes again. Ideas sparking. The time has come. We will attack Bill Lovett and his followers in Red Hook. A war will be on. A war within The White Hand. But as I am telling Vincent that Dinny has summoned him back upstairs, I see a smile on Vincent's face. A smile. A smile that tells me that maybe Dinny will not plan a full attack on Lovett, but will instead manipulate the earth and the waterfront winds against him. Turn everybody against Lovett, or at least everybody that Dinny summons. And in order to do that, Dinny will have to make deals with other gangs. But Dinny has always been known to make deals with other gangs to bring them into the fold, as he did in 1913 with the Red Onion Gang, the Swamp Angels, the Jay Street Gang and many others, and eventually the Lonergan Crew too. Into the fold. Under the umbrella of The White Hand. But the gangs of today are different than the gangs of 1913 in Brooklyn. They are unions and Italians and business gangs and such. Up the stairwell goes Vincent smiling. Smiling to himself.

CHAPTER 15

The Black Bottle

April, 1917

At Tillary and Bridge Streets where hounds still circle the abandoned abattoir for the faint visceral smell, Tiny Thomas Lonergan crosses the cobbles. The dogs are bold in their hunger and prancing, stalking. Surly in the eyes and desperate. What once was a great subsistence along the fencing now is left only the scent of rotting sheep heads within. Blind pups chase their mothers' swaying teats while gaunt males maul each other for scraps found curbside in metal cans. As the boy reaches Flatbush, they lick at their rabid, toothy grins, bump chests and thrash at each other. Trying to keep up, Tiny Thomas can hear their horrible mouths popping and throats gnarled with low growls. He yells ahead toward his older brother Willie, "Wait up!"

His voice shrill and panicked, the five-year-old appears to be limping, though the uneven gait is due to his wearing a lone boot, his other foot bare entirely, "Willie."

It is early April when the wind does not have as much pinch to it and the boys are answering the yaps of other children. Yelping off, for the winter was a long one. Now playing up Bridge Street a few blocks off the Lonergan first-floor Johnson Street room. Looking to the sidewalk ahead of his path for glass shards, passing across the brick facing of factory walls and ground-floor windows, busy with his worrying of being left alone, the blond-haired boy cries forward, "Jeez."

Up ahead, Willie disappears in the wreckage of a pre-Civil War clapboard building that had fallen amongst itself sometime over the winter. Into the sidewalk and the cobblestones has the debris spilled, a young boy at the top of the rubble with his hands in the air yawping his victorious war cries. Four and five others scrambling up the remains to challenge him. When Tiny Thomas finally reaches his brother's height, he looks down where he sees three children in a close circle.

"They're playin' stink finger down there," Willie says.

"Stink finger?"

"Yeah."

Tiny Thomas wipes the snot from his upper lip with the back of his hand, "What's stink fing—"

"Never mind it," Willie says, slowly climbing down.

"When are we gonna get the carrots and the beans for Ma?"

"Let's play for a while first, then we'll go."

"Uhright."

Over a couple of hours, Willie and Tiny Thomas play with the others, becoming knowledgeable of the catacombs in the rubble. Tunnels remaining where hallways had been on the first floor. There is even a hatch door access to the cellar, but Tiny Thomas is too scared to go down. The threshold too much to cross into such a dark mysticism. He refuses it, even as he knows it exists. Disbelieves it, he does. Disbelieves ten-year-old Jimmy Wojtowicz with his brown teeth and awful smile that there is candy below.

"If ya go in dere wit' me fa five minutes," Wojtowicz says, he with the diminutive head and the billowy belly of a forty-year-old man, "Ethel'll show ya her privates."

"No I won't!" Ethel screams.

"I'll make her do it, don't worry," Wojtowicz confides to Tiny Thomas, smiling.

Tiny Thomas looks round.

"And I'll buy ya two candy bars and two sweets too. Come wit' me," Jimmy convinces, then grabs Tiny Thomas by the shirtsleeve.

"Wait," Tiny Thomas yelps, pulling his shirt away and leaning back. "I don't wanna go in there. Not even for nothin'. Lemme go. . . . Willie!"

"Here," Wojtowicz says, handing him a chocolate bar yet to be unwrapped. "Take this. It's yours. Just come wit' me in there."

"Why do you want me to go in there wit' ya? I'm gonna tell my brother."

"Ya brotha's nowhe'e to be found. Let's go, c'mon."

"I'll tell my brother, Pegleg."

"Pegleg's ya brotha?"

"Yeah. I'm a Lonergan. He'll kill ya."

"He don' even live around here no more—he's been down wit' Lovett since the gang split in two . . ."

"Lemme go. . . . Willie!" he yells toward his missing brother. "Lemme go."

And Tiny Thomas breaks free, runs up the wreckage as fast he can. Crawling out from the hole that led to the hallway and the cellar, he skitters upward like a wee spider toward the summit of the heap.

"Ow!" he cries. Stops at the top, sits down, and bends his shoeless foot up to his eyes to look at the bottom of it. He's stepped on a five-inch nail, three inches of which have entered his foot.

"Ow, ow, ow, ow!" he cries, tossing his fingers around and covering his eyes with his palms so that maybe it will all stop and go away.

"Thomas," he hears on the other side of the rubble.

"Anna?" he recognizes his sister's voice. "C'mere, I gotta ouchy."

"I can't come up there, you come down here. Why haven't ya been to the store? Where's ya brother?"

"Dat really Anna Lone'gan?" Wojtowicz says excitedly and runs up the pile himself to get a look at her, stopping next to Tiny Thomas. "Wow, she's sumpin' special. That's ya sista?"

"Anna," Tiny Thomas cries.

"I'll help 'em down," Wojtowicz tells Anna.

Tears tumbling down his cheeks, Tiny Thomas leans on Wojtowicz so he doesn't have to put his naked, pierced foot down.

"Oh my," Anna says. "We have to take it out."

Wojtowicz stares at Anna's face. Her lips are so perfect and although some of her strawberry blond hair has fallen out of the bun, it seems to drape perfectly over her shoulder. Angelically. Her skin too, so gentle it looks like a pool of milk or white marble and her small nose and long eyelashes bring a bit of heaven to this ugly earth.

"How do we take it out? Just pull it out?" Anna asked.

"Uh . . . I'll do it," Wojtowicz says, offering himself as a man.

He puts his thumb and finger around the nail as Tiny Thomas, sitting on his big sister's lap, grits his teeth, mouth crumpled in a cry.

"Count to t'ree, uhright?" Wojtowicz warns.

"Uhright."

"One," and he pulls it out quickly.

"Ahhhh!" the child yelps, hugging his sister with his thin arms, pulling himself closer to her in his deep pain, digging his fingers into her back.

"It's bleedin'," Anna says, and takes out a used kerchief from her pocket and wraps it around the hole where blood bubbles up, leaving red droplets on the pavement. "That was in deep. Look how long that nail is."

"Maybe 'e should see a doctor," Wojtowicz says.

"No," Anna says defensively, then holds the child closer. "No hospitals. When we get home Ma'll put some butter on it and it'll all be better."

Wojtowicz looks at Anna with an amused, confounded look.

She looks back at him, gritting, "It's there they'll give 'em the black bottle."

CHAPTER 16

Two White Men

"Giancarlo!" a trebly, deafening screech comes from a window above Union Street in Red Hook.

"Jesus, God . . ." Thos Carmody looks directly above him at the woman with the shrieking voice that pierces the street traffic, splits his ears.

"*Stai attento. Ci sono uomini bianchi nascosti,*" and looks down at Carmody looking up at her.

"*Eh? Va bene, mio amore, ok, ok,*" the man named Giancarlo says, then moves off the street while others look around them, move themselves from the area as well.

A trolley passes in front of Carmody's view and he looks at his watch. Across the street, Vincent Maher stops in front of a tailor and looks at Thos, winks at him, then looks west down Union toward the Red Hook waterfront. An extremely short Italian man emerges from the shop. He is so small that when he shakes Vincent's hand in the doorway he must extend it to its full length. In Brooklyn's Little Italy, the tiny Italian man's business is famous by word of mouth for his quality of fabrics and colorful silks and top-grain leather shoes. He smiles happily though and pulls on Vincent's tight pants, then opens his arms as if to say he is in great need of a change of clothing, then touches his small chest and again opens his arms to their length as if saying that he is the best tailor in all of Brooklyn. Together they walk inside. Thos reaches in his coat to touch the .38, but pulls out a rolled cigarette and lights it. He looks above him again, but the woman has disappeared from her window.

From across the street Thos watches as a tall, well-dressed man comes from the opposite direction as had Vincent Maher. Silverman is wearing a tan suit with no hat and his hair has been combed flat on top, the features of his face seemingly pushing outward at a peripheral view.

"Right on time, Silverman," Thos says looking at his watch, then glances down the street for the next trolley, which is still some blocks away. He notices that there are no longer people walking on Union Street. It has emptied. Again he looks up where the woman had yelled. Bites his lip in concern.

When the trolley is only three blocks away, he walks across the street, jumps over the tracks without touching either one, and opens the door to the tailor.

On one knee, the tailor is measuring Vincent Maher's legs and looks over to Carmody entering. Tilting his head, the tailor thinks it strange that yet another white man enters his shop.

"*Sir, benvenuto*," he says, struggling to stand from his knee and walking toward Carmody with a big smile.

"Unarmed," Vincent says to Carmody without looking at him, instead keeping a mean stare on Silverman.

Carmody pulls out the .38 and points it over the head of the small man walking toward him. Points it at the towering Silverman. Looking back at Maher, then recognizing Thos Carmody's face, Silverman runs toward the fitting room behind the counter.

"*Calmati, non fare un suono*, don't make a fookin' sound," Vincent Maher instructs the small man with the extent of his knowledge of the Italian language. "*Calmati.*"

"*Quello che sta succedendo qui?*"

"*Calmati,*" Vincent says again, not understanding the tailor's question.

"*Cosa hai detto?*"

"*Non fare un suono,* shaddup," Vincent leans down toward the man's face. Speaking very clearly now in a flat-American accent, then repeats himself, "*Non fare un suono.*"

Thos Carmody walks between them, the small Italian man watching with his eyes as Carmody holds the .38 out in front of him while entering the back room.

Without a rear exit, Silverman is cornered. He stands on a raised area of the fitting room with a three-way mirror behind him. His hands out in front of his face as if to stop a bullet from hitting him.

"Thos," Silverman says. "I'll talk to Wolcott and I'll tell 'em what we're gonna do, Thos. I'll tell 'em what you guys want."

Thos stands still and stares with the .38 outstretched, pointing toward Silverman who rambles, "We'll make a deal. You guys can have Lovett. I swear ya can. I'll set it up so ya can get 'em. I know exactly how to get 'em for ya, Thos. Exactly. C'mon, this ain' right. I can make it work . . ."

Thos continues to stand still, holding Silverman at gunpoint while Vincent and the little Italian man wait quietly in the front room.

Outside, the trolley rumbles toward the tailor shop.

"Ya really thought Vincent Maher'd backstab his boss and take money from you to kill Dinny Meehan?" Thos says, squinting toward Silverman. "Ya really thought that'd happen? Ya underestimate the kinship o' the Irish, ya know."

"No, I didn't . . ."

"Ya see that?" Thos holds a single bullet between his finger and thumb. "That's what was supposed to kill me. Paid for by ya boss, Wolcott. But I'm holdin' it now. Still alive here, now. Ain't I?"

"Thos?" Silverman says, but his voice trails away. As the sound of the passing trolley outside hits its loudest point, Carmody shoots through Silverman's hand, which enters his face and brain. The back of his head smacks against the middle mirror and breaks it. Large shards come down on the body that lies with one leg stuck underneath it, eyes swelling and blood trails branching down from the ears and staining the collar of his tan suit.

Carmody hears the Italian man scream and weep in the front room, "Keep 'em quiet."

To make sure Silverman is dead, Carmody places a coat from a hanger over the body's face and shoots one more time, then pulls the coat back and throws it on the ground behind him as the trolley rolls down the street, out of earshot. Reaching inside the pocket of the dead man, Carmody pulls out a large wad of bills. Finally, he spits on Silverman, on his cheek and lips. He then walks out toward the front room where the small Italian man is shivering, sitting on a chair by the front door. Carmody hands Vincent Maher the warm .38. Vincent checks it over and feels its smoldering heat, then puts it back into its empty holster inside his own coat.

"*Grazie*," says Carmody, also with an American accent, handing the large wad of money to the Italian man, then putting a finger over his lips for shushing and using the same finger to give the signal of cutting the throat. "*Grazie da Frankie Yale e Jack e Sixto Stabile.*"

Together, Vincent Maher and Thos Carmody leave the store with caps pulled from back pockets. Run toward the trolley down Union Street.

CHAPTER 17

Four Guys, One Black

TILTING HIS HEAD IN PAIN, THE Swede walks down the stairwell from above the Dock Loaders' Club and comes among the drinking men lined along the bar, three and four deep. On his face is the aching in his clavicle above the heart, the pain throbbing through him. Strands of deep pangs pulsing in his shoulder and neck and a fever still rings in his left ear. He is not a man to rest in comforts, and so he asks to come along on a task he was long known for leading.

At the bottom of the stairwell he stands with his right hand resting on the banister and refuses to allow others see his pain. Left arm hanging motionless and head to the side in a disdainful stare, he nods toward a dockboss, Gibney The Lark, who walks toward him.

"What's doin'?"

"Gonna borrow your man Big Dick for that gimmick you'n Dinny talked about," The Swede says without looking at him. "It's all right?"

"Yeah yeah," The Lark says. "You want him over here wit' ya?"

"Can ya tell 'em just get Dance and a couple more fellers and make a fookin' clearin' in here so I can get through wit'out touching nobody?"

The Lark quickly recognizes The Swede's meaning, "Sure, yeah, gotcha."

Standing still, The Swede keeps at his staring ahead, attempting with all of his strength not to allow the eyes on him to change his stance. He can hear them mumbling and he can feel their eyes, but the whispers about The Swede's personal life have recently become topics of regular conversation.

"Good havin' ya back, Swede," old man Beat McGarry says from the bar.

The Swede does not react. He only watches as Big Dick stands from the bar pointing across it to dark-skinned Dance Gillen, then dropping his big hands on the shoulders of two others, Eddie Hughes and Freddie Cuneen. The four of them push their way back toward the stairwell and the darkness and surround The Swede, then begin pushing their way to the front door around him.

"The fook out the way," Big Dick booms with his voice, pushing three and four bony laborers from the path. "Step aside."

Dance and the other two follow suit, creating a passageway through which The Swede walks as some crude general of an indigent battalion, men being tossed from his weary direction. Faces look at him and know his secrets and those that don't know the extent of them quickly learn through whisper and through remembrances from stories told. The saloon has gone mostly quiet as the tall, shouldery man with white hair carefully crosses through. Silence being what it is, the sure way to know that rumors abound and with Lovett having broken off with many others and Meehan without reaction, a weakness stunk the air like foaming blood in salt water.

He can sense it too, The Swede. As he senses many things. He can feel them question him and he can taste the disruption in trust and fear that has always accompanied their leadership. Stepping gently but with a wintry face, he knows that they wonder about his feeling the need to shoot himself down like he done. Wonder what guilt brings a man to it. And so old rumors of him are summoned again, in his weakened state. That The Swede had made a child with his own sister behind the closed doors of the home they keep. And that his mother, stricken with insanity herself, did nothing. Could do nothing, for she lies in bed day and night, staring into a fear that exists in her, wholly dependent on her son's providing, daughter's changing and feeding her. Some deny it, though.

"Was Non Connors started that," Cinders said, tucking a thick strand of light-brown hair behind a shorn ear, then turns back talking to the fool-mute Philip Large.

But the men only look at each other and know that not even Cinders Connolly can be sure. But Beat McGarry tells me the truth of it in a whisper.

"Helen Finnigan. The Swede's sister Helen got kidnapped by The Black Hand a few years back, true thing," he assures. "Down Red Hook where The Swede had a few followers before The White Hand took power. Dinny appeared out from Irishtown and offered The Swede to come into the fold o' The White Hand if he paid the ransom, which he did. Afterward, Dinny and The Swede and a few of us raided a place owned by The Black Hand and stole all the money back. In their own fookin' neighborhood too. A guy got killed, but ya know? That's what happens. But The Swede? Reunited wit' his sister, a love grew between the two that was as unholy as it was genuine. The girl hadn't been seen in many months after Dinny an' us got her back until one Sunday morning she showed up at St. Ann's wit' a newborn. And there ya have it."

"The Swede's the father?"

Beat looks at me from the side of his face, "Seems that way, uh? The Swede loves his family. Maybe loves it too much, ya know? The man's heart is all twisted up like a vine, thorny and beatin' blood. Never knew a man so mad and full o' love too. He'd do anythin' to make sure food's on the table, rent paid. Any fookin' thing. Ain' no different than yourself, really."

"Jesus," I say. A man so furious about family. To the point of perversion even, is The Swede. I see him now for the first time edging through the crowd and our eyes. They can say what they will about The Swede, but there is not a man more loyal to Dinny Meehan than himself. No man as loyal to his family either. That is The Swede.

Outside, Big Dick holds the door open for the man with all the eyes on him to pass through. Across the street The Swede can smell the dung and sweat of horses mixed with the grainy scent of hay. Above, the giant Manhattan Bridge pushes through the sky its vigorous metallic channeling of sound over the water as if the air is being sucked through a chamber of reverberations.

"I'm goin' wit'," The Swede says to Big Dick, who nods as the five begin walking toward the Sands Street Elevated Station.

Slowly The Swede walks with a gentle stride unlike the others as they ascend the long stairwell outside, walk past two platforms and finally board the Fulton Street Elevated, which takes them south through the neighborhood. Wobbling along slowly through the façades of tenements and factories, they look into the windows of second and third floors as the train moves along the buildings only a few feet away from the tracks where the poorest live close to the elevated rails.

The Swede's long frame and limbs are not made to be stuffed into a mass transit passenger car and Big Dick too, in his width and size, is crammed into close quarters. When people walking by can't get through due to the massive frames of them, The Swede refuses to move and instead the passersby are told to go back. The youthful men are recognized as the old Irish maulers from the docks that everyone hears of but don't know much about.

The Swede's long, gaunt face seems stretched to the point of irregularity to them. His white hair and white eyebrows too, ghoulish even. Large, muscly hands spread wide across his torn trousers and the onlookers, too, see the windswept faces of them, the shining blue, silver, and glim-green eyes wild and pursuant.

At Boerum Place, dusk takes on the day as they look down street level. Below, blooming street lamps are aroused and blink and twinkle to the surface as the four surround The Swede, who walks carefully, consciously avoiding any contact. At the end of the stairwell he stops the others with his sullen, pained eyes, "I'll stay here. I'm no help t'day."

Big Dick gives him a black cigar and matches, "I'll go wit' 'em and it'll be done, like done."

The Swede slowly bounces his head in agreement and trust, "You gotta pistol?"

"Yeah, a .38," Dance says.

"Don't use it 'less ya have to."

And within a few seconds, the four disappear in the crowd walking the two blocks to Hoyt Street, where once the Red Onion Gang ruled before being brought under The White Hand umbrella.

The sound of their train pulling away and the screeching of brakes from another elevated train stopping at Elm and Duffield Streets ring in the background. Ignoring them and anyone else, a man drapes a rug from his window above, airing it out. When the four reach the makeshift saloon at the corner at Hoyt Street beneath a brick tenement, all four walk in casually. Big Dick looks through the smoke and population to see if there is a back exit, though there is none. Quickly, Dance motions to the others and points to Garry Barry's back, sitting at the bar with a thin girl at his left side and his right-hand man to the right.

Big Dick touches Eddie and Freddie and whispers down into their ears. Without hesitating, he then pushes his way through the crowd and wraps his bulky arm around Barry's neck, pulling him from behind and toward the door like a big cat drags away its prey. When the thin girl notices what is happening, she announces it into the air with a scream.

Barry's right-hander jumps to attention but is quickly pushed off balance and clapped by a looping fist and a quick left sent by Dance Gillen, both landing squarely.

"Fookin' nigger can't stand among us and . . ." a man yells until Eddie and Freddie throw him to the side, boot him in the back and head for good measure.

Barry is dragged outside backwards kicking and holding onto the door frame in a panic, breaks a small window with his hand hoping beyond all hope that someone will help him. Anyone. Unable to scream since Big Dick's hold is so powerful, he spits into the air to get as much attention as he can possibly muster out of mere desperation. A few seconds later and Dance comes running through the doorway onto the sidewalk and kicking Barry in the kidney and thighs. Eddie and Freddie follow, rushing through the doorway with fists loaded and swinging through.

"Hold 'em up, hold 'em," yells Dance.

Crashing a right cross over Barry's left cheek, he catches his balance. Big Dick's hold is so tight that Barry's head doesn't even move as it is struck with clubbing fists.

"Drop 'em," Dance yells.

As Barry is felled, saloon patrons make for the exit frantically. Emerge from the Hoyt Street saloon onto crackling glass at the entrance outside, the weak knocked to the ground and holding onto the doorframe, sprinting in many directions outside. Slipping. Running. Faces flushed they rush past the four that clout the screaming man on the pavement. Up above, multiple heads pop out of tenement windows to see what the calls for help are about. Five or six children watching the large adults brawl, looking to see if their father is among them.

Big Dick jumps on Barry and Dance among the grappling. Barry's pant leg being held, he jumps up and pulls to free himself. Ducks under Big Dick's tackle and scampers out to the street where all can see the half-black man run him down only seconds from breaking away.

"Garrett," the thin girl howls after tumbling into a pile of glass on the pavement, trampled by knees as others trip over her and sprawl to the sidewalk.

"Oh my God," another woman yells from across the street with a baby swaddled between her and its grandfather.

Eddie and Freddie each hold the sleeves of Barry's coat, tearing it while he hysterically tries getting away. Big Dick bowls into him, driving him to the ground as onlookers cross the dirty street aloof, their conversation only stemmed for a moment.

Another woman looks away after seeing Barry's head bounce off the cobbles, eyes rolling back.

For the next few seconds, the four men stand over Barry and kick him in the face and back and stomach until he can no longer move. Taking off his hat, Dance Gillen jumps in the air, feet high, and lands on the face and stomach simultaneously. Struggling to get his balance after the impact, dancing as he's known to, he takes to the air for another. As Big Dick, Eddie, and Freddie start running toward the Boerum Place Station, they both look back to Dance.

"Let's go. Let's go."

Looking up, Dance notices he's been left alone with Barry, looks down one last time and instead of pointing the .38, aims his boot for Barry's nose.

"Red Onion Gang, eh? Garry fookin' Barry? G'night," Dance says.

The swinging boot not only breaks Barry's nose, it breaks three bones in his face and sinus cavity. Dance then jumps over him and catches the others down the dark street, lit only by the halos of gaslight lamps over the cobblestones as the day is divided by night.

The thin girl, who just moments before was drinking with Barry, sits down next to him after the others have run off. Her palms cut by glass, dress spreading wide along the pavement, her scent is of alcohol and cigarette smoke.

"Oh no, no, no . . . no," she cries as blood runs from his mouth and nose onto the cement. "Why would they do such a thing to you, Garrett? Why? What did you do?"

Garry Barry's breathing is irregular. Snorting desperately through the ringing concussion, one dead eye open and staring. Snorting every few seconds out of sheer instinct. Snorting as blood and bones bubble and rattle through the sinuses.

CHAPTER 18

Against All I Know

DINNY MEEHAN AND HIS COUSIN MICKEY Kane walk into
the Marginal Club, home of Tanner Smith's small gang.
Lefty, guarding the door, looks up from a table and
before he can stand, is punched in the ear from the side,
then in the ribs from behind with a low right hook that is
brought up for a third blow under his jaw, dropping him
to the floor.

Mickey opens Lefty's coat and takes out the gun, hands
it to Dinny who holds it in his left hand, then reaches into
his own coat and takes out a second gun and walks upstairs
slowly. Mickey following him, watching behind with his
own weapon hanging at his hip. Dinny opens the door on
the second floor. Tanner looks up from the table, "Din?"

"Sit down, Tanner."

"What's the deal wid 'is?"

Dinny walks over and rests one gun on Tanner's nose,
puts the other into his belt. Mickey reaches into Tanner's
coat and takes out the Nagant seven-shooter.

"King Joe says he don' wanna hire ya, Tanner," Dinny
says. "Seems as though Thos Carmody don' really like ya
much. And since Thos has the king's ear, ya're out."

"What are ya . . ."

Dinny unscrews the rod on the gun, rotates it to the side,
then pulls it toward the nose. Pushing the brass-encased

bullet through the loading gate, he stands it upright on the table in front of Tanner.

"Only way back in's through me, and since ya can't be trusted, ya're out. We're square now, you'n me. Ya helped me get to Brooklyn back when I was a kid. Now I just saved ya life because ya should be right now dead."

Tanner looks up at the two, "I known ya since ya was a bug. You too, Mickey. We're fam'ly. . . ."

"Ya go to the wrong side an' we'll kill ya," Dinny says. "I see ya gettin' comfy wit' the Cunard people or the Silver Star or police or anybody I don' like, I'll send Mickey alone next time. And don' try an' get back at Carmody either— us'n him are yoked up now. We're goin' on strike soon, but you? Ya're out. Ya got a problem wit' that, ya take it up wit' Thos Carmody."

"I think I will," Smith says.

Mickey Kane puts his gun away, reaches across the table with a tight-fisted swing at Tanner's mouth, and kicks him in the ass after he is felled, then throws the table across the room and the chair as the two leave.

With a pained look on his face, Dinny looks back at Tanner Smith on the ground by the overturned table and bites his lip, shakes his head in disbelief.

CHAPTER 19

The Ritual

UNDER THE TENEMENT AWNING OF LOW-RISE, wood-framed houses pushed against each other over by where the bridges reach deep into the neighborhoods and where elevated trains pass every fourteen minutes off Johnson Street comes a terrifying sound from 113. A woman's screeching from within one of the open, empty windows. Walking by, some stop in wonder. An old man with a cane has stopped his shuffling and tilts his ear to the air. The screaming endures. Mothers from each tenement stop their washboard laundering within their homes to hear. Stop their rocking chairs. Stop their hungry husbands from making love to them in the April mid-morning. Stop their window-smoking and shoosh children from their questions for to listen to the banshee inflections, as they know it themselves like some horrid ritual in this place where the peasants have settled from countries that flung them of their borders.

It comes down the stairwell, too, as the draft horses puff their necks high, snuffling and stamping at it. Three energetic, wagging dogs have come to a halt and look in the hole where the wretched song comes from the black of the doorway. Cheering children look behind them, over their shoulders and drop the rock that has outlined on the sidewalk their game-playing and men in their window chairs pull from their facial hairs, look out over Johnson Street.

"*Mikä se on?*" says a long-bearded man.

"*почему она кричит?*" asks a bulbous-armed woman.

And finally after some long minutes of the ancient maternal lilt from within the stared-upon building emerges another mother in her peasant gray housedress—this one Irish. This one screaming as they all do. As if it's the first child ever died in the world. Holding its distant body close to her chest as its limbs flail in her desperate strides.

"Thomas," Mrs. Lonergan tries to wake him.

Young Anna, following her mother and seeing it all, holds her own face and stops on the sidewalk, bends down to her knees. Bends to the god of death. The cruel god and taker of innocents.

Mrs. Lonergan in her stride falls with the boy held to her, plunges into the cobbled street, scraping her knees and elbows bloody. Bloodying the skin on her shoulder. Her sack dress hiked high, up to her torso and her legs are open in the air wagging for all who've stopped to see her. They see underneath her. Where that child, dead in her hands now, had emerged alive six years ago. His shoeless foot swollen and gangrenous. His open-mouthed stare evacuated of all the stirring of life. Gentle now, his smile is without the guile and treachery this city offered him.

CHAPTER 20

Save Our Souls

May, 1917

Alone, Darby Leighton has his back to the Atlantic Basin as he stands on the bulkhead of Commercial Wharf among the dock's warehouses. Ahead of him on Imlay Street are the twin, six-floor masonry block-and-mortar structures of the New York Dock Company. His sallow cheeks a sign of malnutrition and with bright eyes, a pale broth of color in the skin and a great concern for his surroundings, Darby Leighton has the look of a lost soldier.

Through the wind in his ear, he can hear men speaking. He looks to the north where two jump-formed annex silos above four wood-cribbed bins and grain depots have only a few men there. They are deep in thought of their work under the clanking chains of the grain elevator, ignoring him. On the other side of Imlay is Van Brunt Street where just beyond to the east is the great contiguous crush of immigrant tenements. Italians bearing down on the South Brooklyn levee. Massing in endless enclaves, sections and wards only put to an end where the land meets water. Pushing them closer and closer. Closer still as they multiply and reduplicate in immense breeding surges, still hungrier children who see the waterfront hard-strung riches with resentment and lustful craving. Won and run by white men in their neighborhood.

A cluster of dogs trot the pavement back and forth, weaving amongst each other, tails in the air happily. Red Hook a terror to defend from incursion or raid, the three north–south streets curve east into Brooklyn, providing multiple entrances and exits for enemy forays. Behind Darby Leighton, five ships await their unloading in the basin and yet Red Hook's northern terminal is empty of all labor men. Not one longshoreman has shown on this morning. Not even has an unwelcome Italian surfaced, as they regularly do from Union, Sackett, and Degraw Streets. The pier house supers are missing too. The stevedoring company left without notice and there are none of the warehousemen Wolcott and the New York Dock Company had redirected to the docks over the last few weeks.

The terminal is empty of the boisterous men that work here. Abandoned of all its life like shore-water sucked out to sea ahead of a disastrous flooding. Like the work of some terrible creator or pagan artisan. Darby Leighton, like anyone would, saw in this the work of Dinny Meehan, the man who lives in the silence of things. Perpetually waylaid. In the void where everyone knows his name, yet no one knows his name. With many men following him as if he is more a driving force behind a certain behavior than a man of blood and skin. Darby shakes his head, exhales out the nose.

"What're we waitin' for?" screams a hand from the deck of a barge. "You got men're what?"

Ahead of Darby there are at least eight entrances to Truck's Row where the multitude of automobiles are lined up for loading the ship cargo. Teamsters stand on the running boards with the doors open, staring at him, waving their hands at the ships that need unburdening, yet it is only he who stands between the vessels heavy with cargo and the empty automobile trucks.

Darby Leighton's eyes remain calm. As men yell from both sides, still his eyes are calm. Calm as they've always remained. As calm as when he arrived from East London five years old with his older brother, Pickles, and fatherless. Calm as when he watched Pickles push a knife in a man's stomach so deep that the hilt came back bloody. Calm even when he lived under a pier in Brooklyn with Coohoo Cosgrave and Dinny Meehan himself, and McGowan. Calm as when he watched Coohoo, The White Hand Gang's first leader, lose the plot, screaming over and over, "My soul is pure, a cloud in a mountain shroud. My soul is pure, a cloud in a mountain shroud," and ran into an engine repair shop and drank from a five-sixton jug of oxalic acid, eating out his insides in front of Darby's serene, unaffected eyes.

With a great resemblance in the face to his cousin Sadie, he looks behind him at the ships at dock alongside the pier houses and the sailors awaiting the berth to no avail. Then looks down to his hands in his pockets. Down to his shoes.

"Jesus, man," yells a truck driver. "Are ya gonna just stand there? Where's your men? Where's anybody round here?"

Placid eyes Darby turns to the driver. Behind the trucks he sees a youngster walking his way. One of Richie Lonergan's. Matty Martin, coming closer.

"Bill's on a tear wit' his buddy Flynn and ol' man Lonergan," Martin says. "You gotta run things 'til he comes back around."

"Come on. We're still waitin' here," screams a deckhand from one of the barges behind Darby. "You bringin' men're what, kid?"

In a monotone voice, Darby points over his shoulder to the ships, "You guys gonna help wit' this?"

"Richie wants me back watchin' over Bill."

"There's ten o' ya watchin' over 'em. Can't you guys at least come an' help?"

"Sorry," Martin said. "Richie's younger brother died this morning so . . . ya know? I gotta be there for Anna . . . an' her ma."

Darby nods his head, looks at Martin, "Bill know about Wolcott?"

"Yeah, he quit," Martin says walking away. "It's in the papers. Don' look good for us, I think."

"You seen Wisniewski an' his boys?" Darby yells out to Martin's back.

"Nah, Wisniewski went wit' Wolcott though, right?" Turning away the wind causes the stripling Martin to hold his hat and walk sideways, one hand in a pocket as he turns up Imlay Street and gone.

"He's leavin'? The kid's leavin'?" a man yells from a truck. "Is he goin' for men?"

Darby looks toward Truck Row. Does not answer the man. He looks down as the gusts winnow the dirt and sand along the stretch of pavement at his feet. Separates the grains in a natural way into piles. Shaped by the wind. A funnel no larger than a man forms on a long sidewalk and steps down into the street sucking loose garbage and city debris into the air before feebly coming apart in front of Darby's eyes.

* * *

TWO WEEKS AGO, WHEN BILL LOVETT learned Silverman had been murdered in a tailor shop, he'd gone into a frenzy. Darby Leighton did not know how to calm him. Lovett posted Joey Behan, James Quilty, and Frankie Byrne's boys at the myriad entrances around Truck's Row with weapons. Wisniewski had come with five warehousemen at Wolcott's order too, and as much as could be accomplished, Red Hook had been shut down of any and all outsiders—including the throngs of Italians not allowed to work the docks.

"No I-talians either," Lovett said to his men while striding across their posts. "They can go down to the Bush Terminal. . . . No fookin' ginzos ever."

Red Hook was sealed all the way down to the Erie Basin. Down to the Gowanus Canal, an impossible extension of waterfront terrain to defend consistently with the number of men at Lovett's hand. But for the moment at least, anyone seeking passage through the streets were scrutinized, patted down, and their vehicle inspected at checkpoints. Still, it was the endless possibilities of invasion that drove Lovett's excitement. If Meehan wanted to send killers for him, there were twelve entranceways to the northern terminal alone, not to mention the dozens of corridors and entryways along the tip of the hook and the streets leading to the canal. Then there was always the possibility that Meehan could hide one hundred men in the hull of a ship. Right in through the basin and bulkhead. This possibility drove Lovett to take great measures and every ship that threw a rope toward the Red Hook cleats and bollards was searched at gunpoint. Then there were the trucks.

"How many men could hide in one truck?" Lovett asked Leighton and Lonergan. "In five trucks?"

Before Darby could configure it, Lovett had gone off.

At Lovett's demand, Wolcott sent a couple Italian-speaking factory workers to the tailor shop on Union Street to find out who killed Silverman. They reported back that it was no more than "two white men." The diminutive Italian tailor had kept silent under the questioning of his countrymen. But Lovett did not trust the Italians Wolcott sent. Did not believe they cared much for extracting information from a tailor who turned the questioning of him into a sales pitch for his wares.

Within the boundaries, Lovett talked to every man on the perimeter six and seven times each and every morning. He checked his own gun even more, ensuring it was fully loaded and ready for war. Richie Lonergan limped behind Lovett everywhere he went with his right hand held deep in his pocket, holding his own piece. Darby Leighton there, too. Up to the ship captain to find out what was to be unloaded and how many men he would need, asking Abe Harms to check again the rest of the Lonergan crew to make sure they were keeping aware, meeting each man at his post and reminding them of the two white men that had shot Silverman in the face. Losing sleep himself, Lovett kept a round-the-clock notice and began showing fatigue in his red eyes.

* * *

ONE WEEK AGO LOVETT WAS TOLD that Garry Barry had been hospitalized and was expected to die. He found out from Maureen Egan off Hoyt Street that it was "four guys, one black."

"Gillen," Lovett said to Darby. "Dance Gillen. Whitehanders. Killed Garry fookin' Barry too? Shit."

Darby nodded, "He offered to kill Meehan so . . ."

"I know the fookin' reason why, for chrissake," Lovett yelled at Darby's face in front of the Egan girl. "We gotta double-down, got it?"

"Yeah . . ."

"Then let's do it then," Lovett screamed and started running back toward Red Hook to the south as Lonergan tried keeping up.

Darby stood still watching them with a stoic stare, then turned to Maureen Egan, "Thank you."

Afterward, more men were taken from longshoremen and loading duties and posted on top of pier houses, in windows of empty tenement rooms and in the back of trucks with holes cut through the fabric. Wolcott provided more guns and more men and Wisniewski, Wolcott's lone underling, had become entirely dedicated to protecting Red Hook from a similar donnybrook that had passed one year previous. Petey Behan and Timothy Quilty were given guns, which they shot into the choppy channel for giggles. Matty Martin, too, who accidentally shot down his own pant leg and took a flesh wound to the thigh.

"Dimwits, fookin' all o' ya," Lovett called them.

It was taking twice as long to unload at the piers, which left ships at their anchor for hours at a time in the Basin. Clogged to the Buttermilk Channel even. Stacking to the north, the mouth of the East River was backed with steamers and barges along the anchorage, yet Lovett was hysterical about his war with Meehan. Fanatical in speculating on the next move of his opponent.

"Why won' he fookin' hit us already?" Lovett would stamp about the Red Hook Terminal.

"He might've made a deal wit' the I-talians," Darby said, but Bill had traipsed away.

* * *

FIVE DAYS AGO, DARBY LEIGHTON COULD smell alcohol on Bill Lovett's breath in the morning. After hearing Darby explain what happened to Tanner Smith, Lovett was not able to think clearly and asked, "Why did that happen to Tanner? Thought they was close, them two."

"Tanner went to the ILA with the money Wolcott gave to Dinny to kill Carmody for a job wit' 'em," Darby said.

Bill dug the crook of his hand into his eye, then looked Darby in the face, "If Non Connors was here, he'd help me. You. What the fook're you? The better o' you Leightons is up in Sing Sing wit' Connors right now. Both put away by Dinny's hand an' you can't even gimme a straight answer." Then walked away and sat down at a table with Joseph Flynn, a childhood friend from Catherine Street, and poured a fresh beer from the keg that had been set up inside the Red Hook pier house. Lying next to him were three dogs that Lovett fed and cared for. Darby looked at the dogs as one of them lifted its leg and licked it's own grommet intently.

Darby then looked at Richie Lonergan, then to Frankie Byrne. Between the three it was generally agreed, without a word exchanged, that Lovett was distancing himself.

When a runner had come later in the day from Johnson Street about Tiny Thomas, Richie and his father left without telling anyone. Abe Harms followed as Lovett watched.

* * *

NOW, WITH HIS BACK TO THE Atlantic Basin, Darby Leighton watches the perimeter from Commercial Wharf where not even one man is posted. Lovett's dogs trotting and smiling and wagging. Alone, he scans the empty entrances between the screaming of ship captains behind him and the screaming of automobile truck drivers ahead. Not even one Italian has shown for work in four straight days. For years they had shown every morning and every year more came and demanded work on the docks only to be run off.

"An' suddenly they don' come?" Darby says aloud.

Bill Lovett, too, had not been seen in Red Hook for two days.

"Are you people gonna unload this shit or what?" says a man with a Greek accent walking toward Darby from the dock.

By the end of the day, two of the five ships have moved north toward the Atlantic and Baltic terminals. Two more south toward the Bush Terminal while one waits for the next morning to see if anyone will show, as it has cargo that needs to be stored in a Red Hook warehouse.

That night Darby sleeps on the dusty pier house floor next to an empty keg and table with two chairs. He is awoken by the voice of Bill Lovett and five others.

"The fook ya doin', Darby? Y'ain' even watchin' the entrances. . . . Richie?"

"Richie ain' here, Bill," James Quilty says.

"Oh yeah . . . Frankie?"

"Yeah, Bill?" Byrne answered.

"Man the posts, we gotta unload this ship out here."

Confused, Byrne looks at Darby, then leaves.

"Let's go Darby, for fuck's sake," Bill slurs.

Walking out with Bill, Darby notices some twenty laborers lined up ready for work, but does not ask where they came from. Keeps his tongue. He immediately finds that a few of them look Italian, points at them, "Wops."

"Wha?" Bill says, turns round. "Never fookin' learn, do yaz? Never learn, no fookin' wops in Red Hook," Lovett screams in the face of one man, then pushes another.

On the deck of the ship above, a lone captain is looking down at the assembly of laborers. Counts the number of them with a finger.

The Italian man that has just been screamed at looks down the line to his left, then nods. Looks down the line to his right, winks.

"*Il mio nome è Sammy de Angelo*," he says with a boasting, confident stare while pointing at his own chest. "Dis is our neighba'hood, so says Dinny Mee'an. *Ora si muore.*"

Sammy de Angelo's bubbly lips curl as he pulls from his coat a pistol and points it at Bill Lovett's face, fires. Smoke plumes out from the gun as Lovett falls to the ground holding his head, blood leaking over his knuckles and inside the arm of his coat.

Sammy de Angelo walks with a swagger and a proud, downturned mouth toward Lovett for another bullet to the brain. He is cocksure amidst the chaos as two other Italians jump out of the line with clubs and knives and beat upon Frankie Byrne's crew and Joey Behan. All the rest scamper away, wanting nothing to do with the violence.

"Ga'bye, Pulcinella," de Angelo says to Lovett, but is tackled by Darby Leighton.

Another shot and a plume of smoke comes from the brawling group below the ship captain on his deck. He watches the laborers struggle from his belly now, cannot know the difference between them. Who is good and who is bad, wrong and right he would not know.

From the ground and the scuffling, Bill Lovett stands. The right side of his face and head immersed in blood. Stands quickly, his lips red, cheeks blossomed in a natural rouge, one floppy ear covered in a thick, maroon fluid. He wipes his mouth and spits within the struggle and jumps on the outstretched arm of Sammy de Angelo with his knees. Jumps on the arm that is holding the gun. Ripping it from the fingers, Bill shoots one of the Italians clubbing Joey Behan. Shoots him in the ribs from a very close range. The man looks at Bill gravely and begins running sideways toward Union Street, holding his lower trunk. By the time Bill has turned to the other side, another Italian is running off in a different direction toward the perimeter and the safety of tenements. Lovett throws the gun to the ground behind him and pulls out his own .45.

Sammy de Angelo looks up to see his Pulcinella standing over him, blood running down the clown's face and arm, teeth gritting and a terrific stare in his eye. Held by four men, de Angelo is then shown the .45 that is to rip the life out of him. With only seconds, Sammy lips his lone request in a soft whisper, "Save our souls."

Darby Leighton hears a deep crack in the air by his ear. Holding de Angelo down by the neck he watches, blinks his eyes as the head bursts. He feels the tension in the body of the man suddenly depart and go loose. He stands, almost losing his balance and looking at the stained pavement where once there was a face. Looks to Bill Lovett who is speaking to him, but he cannot hear a thing.

CHAPTER 21

Lonergans' Tumult

MAY, 1917

IT'S A SUNDAY AT THE DOCK Loaders' Club. Filled to overflowing, yet it's a muffled crowd. And when the conversations move past the whispering, they are hushed by Paddy Keenan and others. Stilled to respect the occasion for grieving.

Every man claimed by The White Hand has dressed himself in his cleanest togs on this day, if he has it. The regulars have a place on the bar while the rest spill outside onto the sidewalk and the street, though every man's movements are gentle, somber. On their faces reside the promise of no faction fighting on this day, yet by the end of it that promise will wane. But for the moment they are shoulder to shoulder with their voices low. Soft sips of beer are pressed to lips in the morning's mourning, for it's at Dinny's order the whiskey and home brew are under lock and key. I'd never seen the saloon so packed with sorrowful men, but with the war here now I'd see many more wakes and rites and processions. The passing of a child, though— it brings the heart out of us.

The United States government has committed itself to the war in Europe, and so it needs to whip up support, fill the ranks. In the Navy Yard and outer neighborhoods we can hear the patriotic banding through the streets. Hovering over us, it seems. The age-old summoning. Even as we are busy at our ways. Gangs of firemen in their sashes and scepters and banners and brassy, out-of-tune horns and their puffed chests stamping a few blocks away in militant files, with elderly Civil War veterans egging them on. In the background we hear their soldiering with their snares *a-rowdy-dow-dowing* and their bass drums round the necks *a-ploppety-plop-plopping*. Though they mostly avoid our neighborhoods for fear of being pelted with stone confetti from the open-windowed mothers above warning them away from their little ones. Patrolmen, too, singing along and joined by army men to stick posters of recruitment on light posts, gluing them to brick walls, the old slogans and the glories of war.

The papers can't get enough of the frenzy of going "over there" and with all of it, even some of our own disappear off the docks without notice, enlisting quietly of their own will and slipping on Navy white or Army gray. And off they go to forever, as it's to be a war that chews up the poor in great bunches yet again. Johnny gets his gun to go and kill the Hun in France for America at England's gain while the quiet in Irishtown keeps, as long as Dinny Meehan is in charge.

Next to The Lark and Big Dick at the bar, Red Donnelly looks at his union card, shaking his head. Henry Browne from the Navy Yard ILA at his side, holding his own.

"My father was killed by a union man," Red says. "Now look at me."

The Lark and Cinders Connolly consoling him from two sides.

It is on the lips of every man in the murmurs of this Sunday morning. Banding with the ILA and making a deal with Italians to establish a border. Partitioning Red Hook; north for us, south for them. Some say it is a contract exchanging the soul of us. That letting them cross the

Gowanus Canal is a sign. An indication. Don't see how we are to benefit from it, the gain for us too difficult to wrap heads around or ingest. Some even go on to say that it was the New York Dock Company and Wolcott's plan all along, dividing our territory.

"Five short years ago, pushin' The Black Hand off the Red Hook brought us all together," I hear one man whisper. "Now this."

"Sold us out," another whispers. "Red Hook was always ours."

I sip from my beer, listening to the men.

"Hoosh now," Paddy tells them.

And as the voices lower, I can hear in the distance the whining of bagpipes a few blocks off. Asking for us. Asking more of us. Providing a pedestal for our lonely souls to stand on and be cheered. And to take a bullet for America and England. And then the distant bands and *run-tumming* and *thum-thumping* drums are drowned out by a passing train above, *ca-click ca-click ca-click* and the rolling, thunderous swooshing acoustics over the East River we live with.

"Hoosh hoosh, I say," Paddy says to the rising voices as he pushes five or six froth-topped glasses across the mahogany. "A child's passed fer Godsakes."

From the ceiling we hear the creaking of steps. The slow, ominous creaking of footsteps for which every single one of us turns our heads to look upward. We watch Dinny coming, boots first and surrounded by men on the stairwell. Among them are the faces of three I've never seen, and if I'm to heed the voices around me, then they are the witnesses the District Attorney will be calling on for the trial of Bill Lovett, who is charged with murdering Sammy de Angelo. One of the men looks moon-faced and from rumor I gather that there's another witness recovering from a bullet in the ribs.

Dinny's contract binding him to death is slung across his face by a look. It was always like that, of course, his face knowing death. But when you see it coming for yourself it makes a look. And he had it.

If he never wanted his story told he wouldn't've kept me around. He preached silence but kept a kid who was known to steal pencils next to him. A future writer. He knew what was coming. Nobody could really follow Dinny's mind, so it was all a secret. And that's part of what always kept him ahead of others. Keeping himself stronger than us, harder and smarter. But that all came natural. So much so that we never recognized the ancient face he began taking with him in those spring days, 1917. Eventually someone would kill him. Not cancer or sickness or old age or some injury. Men taking him down. And at foolish reasoning too.

Allowing part of one of your territories to secede gives words to a revolt, it is said of Dinny who relinquished half of Red Hook to outsiders. His job now is to stanch or at least stave blood, but eventually someone will come for him with knives to cleave the skin of his frame or guns to clap open his brain. Eventually.

He stands on the steps and waits for everyone to stop talking, Paddy Keenan snapping his towel at them. Standing amid the men myself, I look up to hear what he says too. Hoping him to contradict the mumbles these men begin daring to whisper of him. Waiting for us, Dinny shows no concern for mumbles or death and even looks more content and at ease than I'd seen him in some long time. As a man who is taken with challengers would be, I suppose. In love with those that protest him even, I'd say. With his eyes taking the voices down more and more by the second, I see this melancholic little objection the men have is no more than a test to him—as a woman tests her lover's love for her to see what he is willing to put up with, drawing him out of his masculine cover. But Dinny won't be drawn out. I smile knowing that he is solid for such a test and those who mumble are ready to consent . . . for now.

"It's a sad day. Let us be humble for the Lonergan family and offer our humility as a gift. We provided them wit' a respectable grave at Calvary Cemetery for the child, and there'll be Mass afterward at St. Ann's, as his mother requested," his eyes alert, mouth almost smiling with agility. "I believe that in honor o' Tiny Thomas, we should also take steps to never again allow children to run round our neighborhoods without a pair o' shoes on their feet, and a second pair for the closet."

Standing next to Cinders Connolly, a father himself to young ones, I hear him sniffle and see his eyes going watery at these words as he looks down to his folded hands.

"Let us be respectful of the Lonergan family on this day," Dinny says, knowing full well that the Lonergan family is seen as among the lowest of classes. Some even call them traitors for committing to Lovett, which gives even more words to the whispers that Dinny is losing his grip. Slowly he comes down the steps as men finish their beers, wipe it from their clean-shaven faces and head toward the door in low mutterings that are no longer objections. Their hods and hooks and hammers, trowels and tape measures and chisels, and all the tools we've shaped for the work we do, that shape us too, are left in the corner.

We go up the long hill of Bridge Street. South, two hundred and fifty strong. Sullen in our climbing the pavement and spread across the old cobble road yellowed with time and uneven and burrowed with dark cavities like the mouth of an old seafaring swain.

The brightness of spring is on our necks and at the head of us is Dinny Meehan walking gently. And he walks with a great shyness and servility in him, though all know him a powerful man. A man of a greatness that harkens, within all of us, to the old times in Irishtown when the rest of the world was kept away by a great tradition of silence. And by great leaders mostly mythical in their span, the embellishments of Irish storytelling being as traditional as the drink in our hands. Leaders who became great and mythical by their acts of defiance against the Goliath of law—not unlike Dinny. Flouting their dominance boldly, openly. Then persevering after its retribution, and coming out greater in popularity from it all. Greater still after death. These men of myth and all those that followed them, kept the Anglo-American law out of Irishtown, and kept Irishtown Brehon in culture and tradition. Their names though, still to this very day even, are unarticulated. Don't exist for you and I. Only in the oral fashion had they been spoken of by Irishtown's shanachies, who called them, of course, Patrick Kelly.

Up in the windows as we pass are children that see in us a greatness they'll never attain, but won't stop the trying for it all the same. Behind them is the shame in their mother's eyes. A woman's derision put on men who are tasked with ensuring meals for his family by violence for which he is forced to use. That she does not agree with his methods and his damned patriarchy. Yet it seems her feelings change just moments later and with a sudden rush in her of the pride and understanding of a man's doom and fortune in their time, the men are then seen in a truer light. That they defend her love, at the least of it. For nowhere in the world does a mother's spite toward the freedom men exercise in violence at her family's defense become end and all. That it is an ugly business for them, making meals where meals are hard-won. And where many go hungry and without work, these men fight for space. And succeed too.

I feel happy to be among them and look round me in cheer, even as we are quiet and refuse the slightest remark, for in each man is the cause and the dignity to mourn one of our children's passing. We stride through Bridge Street heads down, yet The Swede and Mickey Kane, closest to Dinny now, peer upward for enemies. As we pass the

Lonergan bicycle shop, Vincent Maher and Harry Reynolds walk amongst the dockbosses. I am now sixteen and my voice is thickening and I hold with a stronger grip the pipe under my coat, ready at any calling for my people. That they are now my family and knowing that I love them and knowing they love me too, as men can. But when we pass McLaughlin Park where the children of PS 5 play, I watch and wonder as there are quite a few kids my age there. Emma McGowan is there somewhere, sheltered and behind fences, me out in the wind and the streets. But at least I am with my people, I think to myself. Though I can't help but wish for an education and swear to myself I'll read the book by Walter Whitman when I get a chance.

When we come to Johnson Street, we go right in our masses and as fate would have it, the Lonergan home is directly between Dinny's Bridge Street and where Bill Lovett's Jay Street gang once headquartered, until The White Hand gripped them and pulled them in like all the other gangs. On the first floor is the wake where we stand outside, a rough lot. As we wait, a shoeless child pulls on my coat sleeve and blurts a request. Though I don't hear him, I look down and press my finger over my lips and give him a coin. It isn't until later that I learn he is one of the Lonergan children running unwatched, dressed in the funeral uniform Dinny bought, though he'd taken the shoes off. A man leaning on his cane as he slowly comes to us is treated with dignity, and we make a path in our crowding the street for him to get through. On the sidewalk, a large-shouldered Russian woman with a flowery, dirty hat tilted to the side har-rumphs at our numbers and our ways, and many others watch from tenements above in their window chairs and elbows leaning on the frames.

There is only the sound of the city in the distance as we shuffle in queue outside the Lonergan home. We are very quiet now. In front of me is the fidgety Needles Ferry holding his hat at his side—the skinniest man I've ever met. Behind me is old Beat McGarry, normally with a mouth full of words, it is now closed and his eyes are to the ground in front him, hands behind.

Cinders Connolly emerges from the tenement and finds me in the line, whispers in my ear, "Come wit' me. Give condolences to Anna . . . respectful an' humble."

I nod to him as we cut in the line ahead and soon enough men are coming out the same door we are attempting to go in. Inside we lean against the hallway stairwell for them to pass in the opposite direction and eventually I come to the room where the miniature casket, opened for all to look in, is flush against the wall and under a window. On another wall is a clock that was stopped at ten twenty-four, the moment the wee one was found.

To the casket I come and look down into the frozen face and give a little smile at the tot's new coat and tie—the first suit ever he wore. A cross is held in his tiny fingers folded so naturally that I forget for a moment that he is gone, and behind his head and above is a small whittled-wooden statue of a weeping and handsome Christ, with his thorny crown and naked breast, looking up in his agony as if he knew the child too.

I cross myself and move to the left, where wearing her mourning weeds, Mrs. Lonergan sits staring into the candle that she holds in her lap secured by a gaudily orna-mented, rusted-green candlestick with a finger hole. To her left is Father Larkin holding her wrist with one hand, his beads in the other. Two women at her left sing strange, spontaneous songs and hymns, reminding me of the coun-tryside of my youth. Mrs. Lonergan slowly rocks to the loose rhythm in them and seems far away in thought and overcome with the seemingly spurious grief that is over-whelming her.

"May your boy rejoice in His kingdom where all our tears are wiped away," I offer.

"Oh," she says awkwardly, and looks up. "What a kind t'ing to say. May God be with you too, William."

I bow and move on but I can't help but feel so proud of myself for touching her, and the humility in it and pride in myself mix together and make me feel so wonderful that I almost cry too, if it wouldn't be so selfish to do so. But quickly I am taken away from my own feelings of greatness, for when I see Anna the first time on this day I am shocked by the blackening of her eyes and swollen nose. Behind her is the shamed father leaning his elbows on his knees in a chair pointed toward a side wall. Some say that Anna's father punched her for not taking Tiny Thomas to the hospital, but most know that when John Lonergan found out about the boy's death he drank himself violent, as he often does. I can see that Anna is forced to breathe through her mouth and it is only afterward that I notice her wearing a new dress. She is not as sad as her mother, though, and instead carries an air of forthright responsibility to her.

"My most heartfelt condolences to you and yours," I say to her.

"Thanks, Liam," she says while looking past me to the person behind with a sternness I don't expect.

In the kitchen are the young males quietly peopling the table on the other side of the parlor wall. Abe Harms and Richie Lonergan look up at me distrustfully as I walk by, and as I notice Petey Behan, who is looking away angrily, I feel Vincent Maher pull me from the line to where, standing on the other side of the kitchen, are the men of The White Hand huddled closely together. I can see as well as the others that the Lonergan band across the small kitchen are a disconcerted bunch. Frankie Byrne and his men stand behind them, along with the older brothers Behan and Quilty. That they feel bitter on our having a claim on the family by our reaching out to them— providing casket, flowers, dresses, and little suits for all, and a grave. Showing up in our great numbers too, while Lovett sits in a cell at our benefit. Richie himself is the most egregious looking of the bunch, shooting his eyes away and cracking his knuckles and wrists on the table nervously. As I mix in with The Swede, Maher, Harry Reynolds, and others, Dinny approaches the sulky table of youthful males with hat in hand and his cousin at his side, Mickey Kane. A round of handshakes is accomplished, though the boys do not stand at Dinny's reaching out to them. They are whispering to each other and with the plaintive, keening women at their singing, I cannot hear a thing said but I know it is of business that they speak. With Dinny and Mickey's back to us, I see Richie's eyes look around them toward me, then look away.

The line of inquisitive visitants peering in on the dead child continues to move slowly, eerily. Blessing child and mother as a matter of routine. Their humility related more to the shame of curiosity than sorrow for the family's loss, and it is Anna that seems most put out by it. Her hair off and over her shoulders is a silky, strawberry-yellow swirl so lucid that it seems to be from another place, certainly not from this dark den where so many malnourished children flop in a two-room flat a block away from the old slaughter-house on Tillary Street and the elevated trains. With her hair up, the skin of her neckline is revealed as a deep, unsullied milky hue and with a new dress on her, she is a beauty of uncommon genius, if not for the blackened eyes. And although she seems the picture of youthful elegance with her small shoulders and slight overbite and an upper lip that is full and bright, there is disgust churning in her as she sees us manning the kitchen. She moves from her place in the grieving line and holds Dinny's arm firmly, looking up to his head.

"Ya can all go now," she says with a flinty and lowered voice that threatens a break into screams. "I thank yaz all very much for what ya offered. We all thank ya, but it's our home and our grievin' and we have the right to do it the way we wish ourselves to do it. In our fashion."

"Anna?" Mary yells toward her. "Let the men stay, oh. Oh Lord above us. Why all this . . ."

"We'll go," Dinny says humbly, turning his attention away from Richie. "I'm sorry to offend."

"It's fine," Anna breaks in with Mary wailing loudly, drowning everyone else's voice in her tears. "We'll see ya at Mass afterward . . . and thank you. . . . Shut up, Ma!"

Mary howls louder still at this affront from her own daughter, as Anna turns red in the face, then screeches to Dinny, who is bowing away humbly, "Yeah, and if ya so concerned, Dennis Meehan, then why not tell ya witnesses to go away then? Yeah? That's how ya can help our fam'ly . . ."

"Anna," Mary yells.

"I'll never consider this child as a proper man for me," Anna says pointing at me, her face red and shaking. "Let Bill go—he's a real friend of our fam'ly. Get out. Out."

Dinny nods calmly and we leave the kitchen, entering the line toward the door and the hallway. Behind us we can hear Anna raising her voice over her slouching mother who stares into the candle, "We've got our pride, Mother, and we'll keep it. Upon all of us there still lies the curse of Cromwell for as long as we are under that Dinny Meehan!"

"For the pity of Jesus on his cross, not so cruel, Anna," Mrs. Lonergan whines, heaving and sobbing to the tune of the old women's keening at her side.

As we come outside I look back and see Richie and Abe and Petey and Matty Martin and Tim Quilty standing in the doorway looking on us. The older brothers and Frankie Byrne's boys behind them. And in the air we can hear a block or two away, even out here on Johnson Street, the dull *farumping* of bass drums, the tint pulses of snares, and the patriotic trills of half-keyed bugles among some claps and muted roars of happy Americans. Though we don't respond to the boys staring us down, The Swede says, "Can't let

Lovett go, ever." But the only thing I see on Dinny's face is loss. Although we have Lovett, it does not seem we have the future, for it's in those boys where his plan resides.

A few hours afterward, Richie began yelling at Anna by the casket as mother Mary ran through the house. Richie then floored his father before bolting south with his followers helter-skelter, where they went drinking down on Union Street, which confused the locals who thought a deal had been struck. Confused by the slurs of the young Irish boys that upbraided and abused men on the street. The ginzo-hunting spree left some fifteen innocent Italians with broken teeth and arms. For their efforts, all were taken to the Fifth Street Jail where Lovett was being held for murder.

CHAPTER 22

Work 'til Holes Are Filled

JULY, 1917

AND THEN SOMETHING HAPPENED THAT I'D never experienced before. Believing in God, I certainly feel as though there are things in this life that are bigger than myself. That I can't control. In my youth, however, I only half-believed in these larger powers. But as it is in this life, you only hear about these types of things after the fact. And at our level down in the bottom, as usual, we are the last to know about big changes. The reverberations of great decisions in New York City starting at the top, eventually make it down to the flesh of the lowly, where we dwell. The arrangements made by the rich and the aims and conclusions reached will affect our lives mostly, yet of course, we were never queried as to our thoughts. Instead we find out by the great big and impersonal, untouchable manner of the secondhand.

Since Beat McGarry does not know how, I read the newspaper aloud to him and Ragtime Howard and Paddy Keenan at the Dock Loaders' Club.

From on high, among the clouds above Wall Street in Manhattan, looking down at us and across the East River as if soaring, or like God commanding his flock, is Jonathan G. Wolcott among his own class. The last we had heard, he resigned from his position at the New York Dock Company as Vice President of Wage & Labor. Having had his strongman Silverman murdered, his confederate on the Red Hook docks Bill Lovett arrested, and being left only with the lump Wisniewski at his side, Wolcott had lost to Dinny Meehan and the International Longshoremen's Association. Without a plan to win back dock labor, we saw his resignation as his ruin. But that was not the case at all, at all. Born and raised among the Anglo owning class, his resurrection is not quite as humble as that of Jesus of Nazareth, but resurrected he is. Brought back to the top without question of his failing, as if failing weren't a measure he is held to in the first place. He's held high no matter of standards or merit, for their standards of merit have nothing to do with success or failure as we know it.

"A Waterfront Assembly has been formed on Wall Street to oversee all future building contracts on the Brooklyn waterfront," I read aloud.

The board of directors is a collection of landowners in Brooklyn, executives of big businesses, the waterfront commissioner, and a few select Brooklyn politicians. All the shipping companies and dock and warehouse and factory owners, box companies, coffee and tobacco companies, and local weapons manufacturers, and tenement landlords are on the board. Utilities too—like the gas works, industrial rail, trolley, and electric companies. Even Hanan Shoes. If it is big business, it has a representative on the board of the Waterfront Assembly. With Wall Street as its home, up there in the clouds above us, looking down as if we are ants, its plan is to make the Brooklyn waterfront bow to the gods of efficiency.

"In the past," the newspaper quoted from a press release. "Companies on the Brooklyn waterfront grabbed up land as needed and made whatever they wanted, wherever they wanted without consideration of the big picture. What we propose to do is to replace the old plan of pell-mell, helter-skelter construction and oversee a larger plan for industrial growth. The future is coming, and we must prepare. New York is the biggest port in the world, but Brooklyn, one of the main points of exchange of sea-going goods, is increasingly inefficient, slow and clogged, which creates long wait times for ships that load locally manufactured goods and unload goods from abroad there, costing millions of dollars. The Waterfront Assembly's goal is to modernize Brooklyn's port terminals with stronger lines of communication between major stakeholders in the area and come to agreements on how all future construction can create a more efficient workspace. The board is funded by local businesses for the future of a new Brooklyn waterfront."

And of course, this press release was signed by the fat, monocled man Jonathan G. Wolcott himself, who was voted by the board to be president of this newly created Waterfront Assembly.

It seems an innocuous quotation and plan, on the face of it. But knowing Wolcott as we all do down on the docks of Brooklyn gives us to thinking that the future of our neighborhoods is now in the hands of the one man who hates us more than any other. I only met the man once in his office above the Buttermilk Channel in Red Hook, but remember him I do. The man who called Dinny Meehan a "Luddite." Who feigned an English accent. Who compared us and our ways to thieving monkeys. Who snorted and sarcastically referenced our being Roman Catholic. Who made fun of The Swede without his understanding it. Who boasted of his direct male lineage to that of the original Puritan ships that came from England in the 1600s. Who hinted at making a deal with the Italians in the south, then did make a deal with Bill Lovett. And who paid Dinny to kill the ILA recruiter Thos Carmody. Of course Carmody was never killed, but most importantly, and one of the biggest reasons Wolcott resigned was because Dinny had made a deal with both the Italians and the ILA against him. This is the man that is in charge of future contracts in our neighborhoods.

"Ya think he won't have a say on labor?" Beat asks. "Think about it. All these business-minded men, and they're only thinkin' about contracts? Nah, that's how they do. They say one thing, but mean another. Their main goal is to break up organized labor. Ya can read, William, sure, that's fine, but read between them words and what do ya hear?"

"It's true what he says," Paddy agrees.

In our world down here, when a man quits he never shows his face again, for his honor is stained forever. But in the world of business, apparently, there is no place for honor or sincerity, as we know it. The New York Dock Company—Wolcott's former employer—that owns more land than any other waterfront corporation in Brooklyn, is a member of the Waterfront Assembly, of course. So we can only assume the company is complicit in Wolcott's becoming an even larger figure in Brooklyn than he was as their vice president. But overlooking us now from the safety of Wall Street in Manhattan, forty floors up. His Anglo-American absenteeism and control reigning from above. His idea of Americanism, temperance, sedition, corporate efficiency, and anti-labor gathering strength, yet beyond reach. I'd only seen the man once before, as mentioned, but I'd never see him again. He'll reign from above, unseen. Our greatest enemy from this point forward, yet his throne resides in a safe distance across a body of water, up high where the future will be orchestrated. I can see in the eyes of Paddy and Beat and Ragtime that the history we know is again repeating itself in the now. As it always does. Like Williamites or English civil servants or colonial administrators of the past, our fate will be decided by an untouchable enemy.

I put the paper down after reading it a second time. The candles on the bar turn sideways and hiss when the front door of the Dock Loaders' Club opens, the clamoring *cha-chum, cha-chum, cha-chum* of the Manhattan Bridge above us ringing out until the door is shut. I'd secretly hoped that with Bill Lovett under lock and key, we'd be left alone to live our lives on the waterfront the way we want it. That a great abeyance would come upon us. That all we would do is work hard in the wind and in the morning, the soldiers of the dawn. To make our money, even though we don't need a lot of it. But to share it with the families that need help, and move on peacefully. But I begin to see the larger powers that are collecting against us. Things we can't challenge or fight, like time. Things we can't even see or completely understand, like change.

In his office, Dinny knows all of this. He sees it and understands it better than any of us. That from above they attack. Their misleading, dispassionate, and banal declarations about contracts on the docks are like a predator's hiding in the bright of the sun as it swoops from the air. Our history speaking to us, to the depths of us, we see Wolcott from the fear of our stories of men who, with an incredible indifference for humanity, starve us. Starve us and send us off the land for our not bowing to their ways. Ignore the evidence against their cleansing, exterminating us, and simply continue piling up dead mothers and children by the thousands while continuing to strictly adhere to their economic policies. Bending law to their demands. Bending law so far that its strength is that only of the will of those who live in the detached distance, beyond sight and high above us, unaccountable.

In his own way, Dinny decides to fight back by going directly to the people that love him. Dinny Meehan has proven to me many times that he is a great leader and knows how to clear the way for us. That he has a keen sense of how to fashion and maintain our power. In April of 1916, when it was a day for legends that we fought off the many that sought our seat at the head of Brooklyn labor, it was Dinny that came up with an ingenious plan. Then a year later in the spring of 1917 after losing Red Hook, again Dinny Meehan came out on top, even if he was forced to cut a deal with the ILA and allow the Italian to cross the Gowanus. Over and over, he proves himself a leader against absurd odds. And now, seeing a new enemy, he gives his next order. Which comes in the form of boots.

Harry Reynolds and myself are waiting on Atlantic Avenue in the middle of the night when an automobile truck driven by James Hart pulls up. He looks at us and smiles, and from the passenger seat we hear Dinny, whose face pops out, "Let's go."

Harry and I jump in the back where the Simpson brothers, Baron and Whitey, as well as The Lark and Big Dick are sitting with growlers in their fists and big smiles on their faces. We pick up Chisel MaGuire and Dance Gillen too, then meet up with two other trucks filled with our like and head north as the grinding of gears and the squeaking fan belts ricochet off the night's barren tenement streets. We drive all the way up just a block and a half from our headquarters to a building I'd seen many times on the corner of Bridge and Water Streets.

"Hanan & Son," Harry whispers to me.

"I don't want to get caught," I whisper back.

"We won't."

"If a patrolman happens by, what are we saying? What is it we are doing, thirty men in three trucks?"

"Won't happen."

"I need to keep working and saving money, Harry. What good is fixing up the place by Prospect Park if I'm in jail? And what if the war ends and my mom and sisters can come and . . ."

"The guys o' Poplar Street already know. Brosnan'n Culkin're keepin' watch, uhright?"

"How do we know they aren't double dipping and plan to arrest us? Didn't you read about Wolcott and the Waterfront Assembly?"

"That's a good point," someone says.

"We can still trust them," Harry says. "They won't turn on us, yet."

"Yet," I repeat.

An old man is waiting outside the shoe factory, and when he hears us, he twirls an about-face and pushes up a bay door, waves us in. He is the night security at Hanan & Son and when I see his face I recognize it as the Corkonian who regularly visits the Dock Loaders' Club on Saturdays, sitting between Beat McGarry and Ragtime Howard and is friendly with Paddy Keenan too.

As we stuff the trucks, slinging pairs of boots tied together by their laces, the old man pulls on his pipe and gives a turn.

"Heared about that Lovett," he says in his Cork burr. "Heared he made a deal widat Dishtrict Attorney to g'off to war with time served as his penalty. Up wit' the 77th Infantry Division, ye know he went. And that he wants ol' Non Connors goin' wid' 'em too. Wasn'til later, after signin' the deal that the DA finds out Connors is up in the shtir, Sing Sing way, so the judge turns angrily and says to Lovett, 'Well why don'che bend me over an' call me Mary, why don'che?'"

"That's not true, is it?" I ask.

"Beat told me it jush t'day," the man swears with a high pitch.

"Is that what really happened?" I ask Dinny.

Dinny looks back to me as he is slinging boots and boxes, though he does not seem all that happy about the deal sending Lovett to the war.

"Say ga'bye to Bill fookin' Lovett," The Lark turns his hat goofy and salutes with the hand that has only two fingers left on it.

"Fookin' asshole that one," Big Dick mumbles.

Within an hour all three trucks are packed so tightly that we have to run alongside them in the middle of the night east on Flushing Avenue past the Navy Yard in south

Williamsburg. At a restaurant, Lumpy Gilchrist is outside standing dumbly as a man next to him directs us to an alley where we unload the shoes into the basement through a storm door. Lumpy's brother, the owner, wipes a hand through his hair in frustration until Dinny walks up to him, reminding him of why such a thing occurred. Lumpy, though, the poor fellow, has no idea what is happening. Only gifted in life to do one thing, he is without clue on any other topic. As we unload the trucks, Lumpy stands awkwardly in our path and counts the shoes with a finger in front of his face, stopping only to push his glasses up.

"Watch out," Big Dick says, bumping him out of our way, though Lumpy never loses count.

Regardless of what happens to him, he never loses concentration. Dinny stops and helps him to his feet, "Up ya go, Eddie," but Lumpy does not thank or even take notice. Just counts with a bent finger in front of his glasses and an open, muttering gob.

A few days after that, everyone in Irishtown and beyond has new pairs of boots with the Hanan & Sons emblem embroidered on the sides of them and the newspapers go batty over it, for no one in the neighborhoods know where they came from, even though everyone knows.

"I couldn't say from where they come," said Mrs. Lonergan in the morning edition a couple days later. "But they're Heaven-sent, surely. Whoever t'was t'ought of us after the passing of Tiny Thomas, my poor child of only six years, is certainly the most t'oughtful o' gentlemen, even if they are stolen from that fact'ry who couldn't t'ink of givin' alms themselfs."

Dinny had asked Mrs. Lonergan not to speak with the newspapermen that showed up on Johnson Street, but she couldn't resist the attention. Even if the papers mocked her accent, made fun of her ignorance. But in any case, the brilliance of the orchestrated move simply added to Dinny Meehan's legend, even though he didn't really exist in the first place, as far as anyone would admit. And Mrs. Lonergan's publicly shaming the highly profitable factory succeeded in stifling any notion of its demanding the stolen property back. The death of a shoeless child in the neighborhood where they manufacture shoes effectively suffocating any legal action against the thousands of dollars' worth of their stolen product covering the feet of tenement children.

And for myself, I was finally able to retire McGowan's boots. There was a certain connection I had with those boots, however. I had gone to McGowan's wake and watched as the dead man's boots were taken off him within his pine coffin in Mrs. McGowan's tenement room. My first day out of Sadie's nest and into the world of the Brooklyn docks, Dinny gave me those boots and I'd been wearing them ever since. Wearing them proudly, as Dinny and McGowan had been such close friends for so many years before I'd arrived.

"Looky 'ere," Sadie says laughing, pulling up her dress enough to show me the boots on her while L'il Dinny falls on the rug trying to carry a pair.

But from the great beyond comes another demand on us. It is not of Wolcott's doing, but it seems as though from up high, well past our ability to control and fight against is yet more bidding for our loyalty. The Great War is everywhere in Brooklyn now, and the weapons needed are soldered and welded in Irishtown factories. Iron forged in Navy Yard foundries for ships and vehicles. Bombs and torpedoes manufactured by the E. W. Bliss Company under the Manhattan Bridge between John and Plymouth Streets and soldiers plucked from our many households and sent right along with the war goods to the French trenches and an assured death. Men must either accept their drafting or be deemed seditious. There really aren't many other options, and so they go, and both Simpson brothers taken from us and never again to be heard from—dead and gone the both of them. Happy Maloney too is drafted. And Johnny Mullen, as well as Fred Honeybeck and Gimpy Kafferty and Lovett's drinking buddy from Manhattan, Joseph Flynn. And just as we are getting to know him, Thos Carmody is taken from the ILA and sent to Europe. And only a week after he'd been officially named King Joe's treasurer of New York City, a promotion earned for his work bringing us into the ILA fold. I remember Vincent Maher shaking the man's hand, for the two of them had killed together already. A mighty thing that brings upon fellows a great and lasting bond.

"We'll work together again some day," Vincent says to a parting Carmody, though he doesn't believe it. "At least Tanner Smith can't get ya way over there."

And many others are drafted or recruited or swayed into volunteering by the bands and the propaganda—many of whom I simply don't have the memory to name. Our ranks diminishing again.

But others step up, like Mickey Kane, who has grown right in front of us and is named the new dockboss in Red Hook, with Dance Gillen at his side. He'd been groomed all along without our realizing it, and even though he is Dinny's cousin, Kane had done well for him by sticking next to Lovett and reporting everything from within. Taking a ripe beating in the process. He'd earned the promotion, though, and his reputation as a brawler is known throughout, as any time his name is ever mentioned it's immediately followed with "ready scrapper, brisk fighter."

It must have been Dinny's plan from the start, making Mickey Kane the dockboss of Red Hook. Mickey is Dinny's last surviving family member loyal to him. Tall and powerfully built in the shoulders and upper body with a big head of blond hair, Mickey follows Dinny's orders closely and has no issue with the Italian ILA men taking over the south terminal in Red Hook. I can see by the way Dinny speaks to his cousin how proud he is. Like a son he sees him, even.

The two had grown up in Greenwich Village but were separated when Dinny's side of the family was decimated
around the turning of the century. With his dying father,
Dinny left for Brooklyn until he took control of the longshoreman gangs and summoned his younger cousin to his
side. And Mickey Kane did not let him down. He worked
hard. Went undercover and paid his dues, earned his scars
and made Dinny proud. I admit to feeling a bit jealous of
Mickey Kane because the attention Dinny gives him is
unlike what he gives the rest of us. Mickey Kane is blood.
He is from his mother's blood, and many of us feel as
though one day he will replace The Swede at his right side.
His most-trusted. Dinny had raised many of us—Vincent
Maher, myself, and he took in Harry Reynolds too, along
with everyone else. But Mickey Kane was different. Mickey
Kane would one day inherit Dinny's waterfront.

With Kane in charge, I am welcome to run messages in
Red Hook again, and for that I am happy. Even if just south
the Italians, of whom I was once so afraid, now are able to
work there. It's a fair shake they got and relations between
us and the Italian are at an all-time high.

As I turn the corner on Imlay Street one summer afternoon in 1917, I see Darby Leighton running past me at a
terrible and desperate pace.

"Why didn't you trip 'em?" Kane asks as he runs by me,
The Swede holding his shoulder as he runs by with Dance
ahead of him.

"Sorry," I yell after them and join the chase.

All the others are banished too. "Eighty-sixt," as they
say. Joey Behan and his best friend James Quilty, older
brothers of the Lonergan crew, volunteered for some Army
infantry division, we heard. Having been a part of the gang
for quite a few years, Frankie Byrne and his followers were
sent away too and certainly they'd never get hired on the
Italian docks. Where they went, we couldn't know. Maybe
to the war, maybe to the Jersey shore. As long as they don't

show their faces in our territories, they won't get demolished. We never told them that, but they knew it still.

Eventually Richie Lonergan and his boys are released after spending a few weeks' time at Elmira's Reformatory after their ginzo-hunting affair. Dinny helps get them released early by hiring Dead Reilly to represent them, even though no one died.

Thankful to Dinny for his reaching out to her eldest son and his followers, Mrs. Lonergan shows her appreciation by bowing to him like a peasant anytime she sees him.

"Oh, to the Lord above do I t'ank ye, Mr. Meehan," she supplicates herself in front of him.

"Stop it, Ma!" Anna scolds her mother.

Mrs. Lonergan also thinks Dead Reilly, our attorney, is the second coming, for the man always has shiny shoes and shiny hair and pinstriped suits with a pinstripe mustache while speaking words she thinks both elegant and mysterious, though is simple legalese. Eventually though, she has her way with Richie.

"There's no future wit' Lovett, as much as I love the man," she tells him. "Why not help the man's helped us so? Ye can't go on cutpursin' at the Sands Street Station now that yer out. Too big fer it'n Dinny won't allow it. All o' yez're grown childers now. Time to be smart and take what's offered ye."

"Ma," Anna says, arms crossed. "Ya got no loyalty."

"And ye'll do the same when ye've got little ones, Anna, so shut yer gob. Every mont' the man pays our rent at the bikecycle shop. What's Bill Lovett doin' fer us now? What?"

Richie eventually decides to help disperse the boots throughout the neighborhoods with us and I find myself handing them out right next to Petey Behan himself.

"I've got three girls," a woman says to Petey and I. "I'm s'posed to put boots on 'em?"

"Free gifts and this one's complainin'," Petey says to me as I smile back.

At the Dock Loaders' Club, I've become quite the bother with my hat in front of men at the end of each workday.

"Why not give a few coins' worth, boyos?" I say to the dockbosses at the mahogany trough.

"Here ye are, Poe," Paddy Keenan offers me a small wad. "Tell 'em this comes from Kilkenny by way o' New Yark."

Ragtime pulls out some coins too, nods as he drops them in the hat. Cinders Connolly and Red Donnelly, they give their bits as well. The Lark happily offers a few of his own and Big Dick and Chisel and Dance and Needles Ferry with a coin or two and Eddie and Freddie and Quiet Higgins and Dago Tom and many immigrants who feel the pressure in it, give what they can so as to warm themselves up to Dinny and his boys. Upstairs I run and Vincent and The Swede and Mickey Kane and even Lumpy Gilchrist, who has no connection to Ireland at all, give their own too.

"A small fortune we have here, Dinny," I say, planting the overflowing hat on his desk.

It is during that summer the sun shines more than it ever has in Brooklyn and everything seems to slow down. Every Sunday Harry and I borrow Hart's truck with plumbing pipes, a new bear-claw bathtub that weighs near two hundred pounds, or a load of ceiling studs to replace the old rotted ones. Hours are spent, the two of us, and I am amazed at how gentle Harry is with his hands.

"Never much of a need to twist it hard, Liam," he says to me while lining up the long pipes with the fittings. "As long as they're lined up, a simple turn will do. Musclin' it don' help. You'll strip the threads that way."

And that seems to apply to everything he does. I learn from Harry things that young men need to learn. The lessons all fathers are wont to teach their sons, that patience and taking the time to prepare and plan ahead of time is much more important than anything else. I learn that I have to take my time and make sure the work is done right. That getting it done well is the most important aspect of a man's job and that completing it quickly but without accuracy is the worst thing a man can do.

It takes the two of us to carry the kitchen sink up three flights of stairs. Having to stop halfway up to rest my back and my hands and fingers which were stuck in place, I mention that I had no idea how heavy a sink was.

"When ya ready," Harry simply says, and we push our way up, sweating and straining all the way, step by step, higher and higher.

When we get it inside, we heave it up under the window where the new cabinetry is that we'd only just completed. There is a large hole in it for the sink to be dropped in, but when we do so, we notice something.

"It doesn't fit," Harry says.

I look at it, "Pretty close."

"Half-inch off."

"Well, let's cut out a larger hole."

"With what?"

"Handsaw?"

Harry looks in the hole where the sink is stuck in the air, "We're gonna have to get the other size that we passed up on."

"What? I'm not taking this back. . . . Carry this all the way down, then carry another one all the way up?"

"Doesn't fit."

"We can make it fit."

Harry looks up at me, "Won't ever be right and I don't want my name on it. We made a mistake and . . ."

"Half inch," I plead, wiping sweat from my forehead.

"We won't be as careless next time. Let's take it down."

"Jaysus," I complain, rolling my eyes. "Isn't there another way?"

And Harry simply turns away, as he is done with the conversation, and back to the store we go. I am truly put out by it, and when we stop for a rest halfway down the stairwell, I throw my hat to the ground floor. And when we get back in the truck, I slam the passenger door. But in the end I have no choice but to admit being wrong. The sink we eventually install fits perfectly and although I take it upon myself to show humility and say openly that I was wrong, Harry only looks at me and says, "Don' embarrass ya'self. Just do it right."

And I feel like it's fine that Harry says it like that, because some men might say worse. Or use it as a way to show they are always right about things. In fact, since he doesn't really say much, it allows me to fill in the blanks. Allows me to recognize on my own that a man is measured by his work: a lesson not enough sixteen-year-olds are taught, or willing to see.

Yet we have more holes to fill; the one in the kitchen flooring is still there. Looking down it, I see one of the children in the second-floor room sitting at the table in an oddly slumped manner. He is an older child, maybe eight, but he does not seem to move much, and when he does move, it seems shaky and awkward. I see a belt wrapped around his chest that is secured to the chair, the chair secured to the wall. His wrists are bent and contorted, fingers knotted up, and his feet are splayed, and when he looks to the side I can see that his bottom lip sticks out and there is a distance in his eyes.

"Let's go," Harry says. "We'll start on the floor next week."

"Sadie would take interest in the family below," I say to Harry as we climb down the steps in the darkness.

"She'd what?"

"The Burkes below us, she'd likely take an interest in them."

He doesn't answer.

"Harry?"

"Yeah."

"Sadie wanted me to ask you if it would be all right if she helps decorate the place. She wanted me to ask you."

We keep at our pace down the stairwell. Further and further we go and still no answer from him. At the bottom he turns half round and speaks without looking directly at me, "When I'm not here."

CHAPTER 23

Long Shadows

SOME THINGS ARE TOO SHARP TO speak of. So is the case with Harry and Sadie, I find.

"Don' ask me about that," Beat McGarry says. "Leave me out of it entirely, ya fookin' hear me?"

"I do."

"Good then."

Harry's room is a mean dwelling where only a bachelor can be comfortable. A one-window room, with one chair, one plate, one set of utensils, and no running water. On one side there is a small bed for him and a cot for me on the other, and between us is an automobile engine on the floor that he takes apart, then puts back together again for the exercise in it. There is also an entire block of tree trunk on the floor with the shape of a horse's head carefully sculpted and sanded out of it, though it is yet undone and lays there like some wooden statue frozen in time.

"Who is that for? Is that going to be a hobbyhorse?" I ask, though I get no answer.

As I read from Mr. Whitman's poetry, Harry pulls a candle from a table and holds it over the mechanical heart in the middle of the room and reaches into it with one hand like a surgeon, wiping its black blood on a soiled towel, eyes fixed on some wonder within. Outside, a train slowly passes like a big rusty wobbling and moaning iron dragon every eighteen minutes or so during the day, every thirty minutes at night and weekends. In some parts of the wall you can see straight through to the studs and when a pink-nosed creature appears sniffing round in its own minor business, Harry is quick to his shiv and sticks it in the neck where it lets loose of its own life, gently relaxing without time for a single squeak even and me there holding my pencil with mouth agape at his speed.

I don't complain about the room though, even as we live right above the Long Island Railroad Depot and where the Fifth Avenue and Fulton Street elevated lines cross as well as a couple Atlantic Avenue trolley lines.

One morning I leave Harry's place and as I walk out of the building I sense a change in the weather. The air has become crisp and the shadows seem longer, or at least at a different angle or shape. Breathing in through my nose, I can feel the change. Sense it. The excitement in the onset of autumn brings out a feeling that the constant movement of life is, well, constantly moving. The air beautifully unsettled by the current-like winds, I fasten a coat button and dig my hands into my trousers, which are getting tighter as I keep growing with a thickening in my thighs and in my chest and shoulders too.

And I think, if everything is changing and growing all the time, then where I'm headed seems a good place, because everywhere I look there are people that care about me, which is important because without people who care for you in a place like Brooklyn then surely you'll have difficulties. Even if I am with men like Dinny and Harry, who love nothing more than to live on the edge of life and brawl their way through it as opposed to giving into what the city throws at them. Like their demand upon life, their love is stronger than most and with it, I am able to save more money than I could by living a more docile, pliant existence. I learn to fend for myself with them, and so I have come to walk with a more self-assured gait on these streets. But reading Mr. Whitman, I believe, helps me to better understand the love men can issue, for it seems he loves a man's heart through to its soul.

I climb the stairwell outside at the Fifth Avenue Elevated and take it north toward the Bridge District, our home front. Reading my book about Brooklyn before it was so industrialized, I smile when it talks about "the hues" of autumn. And with the pencil I stole, I underline passages such as, *I walk with delinquents with passionate love, I feel I am of them—I belong to those convicts. . . . And henceforth I will not deny them—for how can I deny myself?*

On the train I look below at the passing school amidst the brick factories and storehouses and the huge, round fuel cauldrons across the street and turn back to my book ever more determined to study and educate myself. Taught by Mr. Whitman, though he gives lessons not on arithmetic or economics or English history, but on empathy and compassion, which I know deep inside of me to be good and to be right.

At the three-level Sands Street Station I come down the long stairwell with my hands still dug into my pockets, book under my arm and smiling inside. Going east on Sands underneath the gigantic pillars of the Manhattan Bridge between Jay and Bridge Streets that support the anchorages of the suspension superstructure, I go left toward the north. I sneak unseen past the Lonergan bicycle shop where this early in the morning Anna and Mary and a few of the children are quietly behind the glass, waiting for buyers. Coming closer to the water, on the left is the huge Hanon & Sons brick building and I smile and look down to my feet that are happy inside my boots, bright and new against the drab gray of my attire.

The weather on my skin amidst the great mammoth feet of bridge stanchions and pylons and buttresses and trains

going in all directions with the wind on my face and life
pulsing and screaming out every iron-shuttered window,
poetry in my mind . . . I know I'm alive. Know now that
Brooklyn is my home. Accept it entirely. That Ireland is my
heart, but I am now and will for the rest of my life be
anchored in Brooklyn.

At the Dock Loaders' Club, Paddy Keenan is cleaning
up from the night before and when he sees me he says,
"Word from Ireland," and passes me a letter. "Dinny gave it
over to me s'marnin' fer ye to have."

Again the letter has been opened then shoddily taped
back together. Mam writes that there is still no sign of my
father's whereabouts, but a family friend saw his name on a
prison ship's manifest. He'd spent many months in a place
called Frongoch. Since then, though, he's been released
but they haven't heard from him at all. Mam says she only
hears from the locals to stay strong, hold out. She says
there's almost no hope securing passage as long as the war
is on and that she prays it'll be done with soon. In the letter
she asks if they are drafting eighteen-year-olds in America.

"No, only twenty-one-year-olds for now," I say aloud.

"What's that?" Paddy asks.

"Sorry, I was just talking aloud."

The next sentences in the letter are confusing to me, but
I realize that because her letters are read by British authori-
ties, she must use coded language and not tell the truth of
things altogether. She explains that Timothy has taken over
the farm and has proven himself worthy as a farmer, but
that British soldiers often "visit" the farm and surrounding
areas. This makes me nervous, for we all know they have an
appetite for younger girls and Abby and Brigid are now
entering their fifteenth and fourteenth years, respectively.
Her last reference in the letter is to Timothy and the failed
request of Irish nationalists to drop requirement of
Ireland's boys into conscription for British services.

"That would mean the girls will be left alone," I say.

"Get ye a drop, Poe?" Paddy asks with a bit of an echo as it's only the two of us in the place. "I heared their convention might result in another half-arsed Home Rule with the payback of Irish conscription in the war. How old is yer brother?"

"Fighting age."

"Hmm, well anyway, ye can only do what ye can when faced with t'ings that're much bigger than ye."

And that's Paddy for you, always summing things up in a sentence. "Things that're much bigger than ye," he says. That's what I seem fixated on. That the world is against me maybe. Against us as a whole, whether it be in Brooklyn or Ireland.

Just as Paddy says this, Dinny comes down, and I can see on his face that he is wearing down. Tired even, though he fights through it. Ever since he was so quiet about Lovett killing Tuohey and breaking off, The Swede trying to kill himself, and Tanner Smith backstabbing him, he's not had the sharpness in his eyes that I knew him for having.

Behind him is the manager of the Kirkman Soap Factory, Frank, the eldest Leighton brother, and I can see on his face that Dinny gave him the big "so long." A few mumbles from Leighton and down the hatch goes a whiskey. Shaking hands with Dinny and Paddy and myself, he says his goodbyes and puts on his hat as he slouches toward the door, shuffling outward.

"Can't ask a man to choose family over job," Dinny says.

I look at him, then at Paddy.

"Paddy don' talk," Dinny assures me. "But he knows everything. And tells me more than I tell him even."

"Well he's the Minister of Education," I say without a smile.

"Just too harried now," Dinny says, pointing over his shoulder with a thumb toward the man that just left. "Them Leighton boys're just too wild and even though Pickles is in Sing Sing, Darby eighty-sixt, never know what could happen. . . . Darby'd been seen at the soap factory, but it wasn't Frank that told me. He apologized, but that's the end o' him at Kirkman's."

"Why'd you marry into that family if they're so wild?"

Dinny looks at me, then looks away, unhappy of my asking such a question, "There once was a day when marryin' into a family brought factions together."

I nod, thinking of his ideas on me and Anna Lonergan.

"Them days gone," Paddy mumbles.

Mickey Kane then comes up behind Dinny, tall and blond-haired and handsome. In the face he is very young looking, but in the chest and shoulders he is thick, and with big hands, it seems he still has more growing to do. Looking behind, Dinny smiles at him and they shake hands with a woody sandpaper and cupping sound. Kane is probably the most handsome man I've ever seen and Dinny is more than proud of rearing him. His jaw alone is thick and wide and his blue eyes set apart broad, hair flayed back and shorn over the ears. And although he is bigger than most men, he is also faster and more athletic too.

"Goin' back down to Red Hook," he tells Dinny, who nods.

The two of them are like statues in my mind. Men more able-bodied than any I'd ever know. Mickey had become the last connection to Dinny's mother's side, I could see. The last connection to anyone that had his blood, really. And that connection is a powerful one. Still, though, there is a pit in my stomach about Harry Reynolds. And the way Beat McGarry shut the conversation down so quickly, I know there is something deadly about Harry and Sadie and Dinny. What, I do not know. Somehow, though, I will find out. Some day.

But although Mickey Kane is given special favor and run to the top of us quicker than the rest, he takes what Dinny teaches him with a great humility, and with Dinny in Irishtown and Kane in Red Hook, there is a feeling at the Dock Loaders' Club that all is well. All is right, even now that The Swede is not what he once was. Even as Wolcott slowly assembles against us, for the time being, at least, we are good for the fight. Right and able.

Dinny looks out the window as Kane walks across it, then back at me, "Let's go to Manhattan for a meet. Ya got the hat money?"

"I do."

Paddy smiles at me because he knows like I do that we'll go and see Mr. Lynch, which means I can send some letters back to my mother and sisters through the people he knows in Clare back home.

"Give it to Eddie," Dinny says looking toward the stairwell where we can hear Vincent's voice coming down as The Swede and Lumpy are doing all they can to ignore him. Through the front door comes Big Dick, Philip Large, Dance Gillen, Henry Browne, Eddie Hughes, Freddie Cuneen, Dago Tom, Chisel MaGuire, and many more to support us, leaving the dockbosses on their own at the terminals.

We come to a neighborhood north of Greenwich Village on the West Side called Chelsea and walking down Fourteenth Street in our large numbers, Vincent whispers to me smiling, "See that?" he says looking ahead of us at three girls in heels and hats and curvy dresses. "Ya fookin' kiddin' me? Some people say the cradle o' civilization is Africa. I say, nah, it's the hips of a woman's the cradle o' civilization, true thing! Nothin' more beautyful than it. Watch it move, kid. Amazin', ain' it? At the Adonis they got girls just like that except they'll love ya an' treat ya king-like. Guys like you'n me got the dime that makes 'em happy too. Ya come wit' me sometime, yeah? I'll meet ya up wit' the owners today."

"They're Italian?"

"Sure they are, so what?"

We go into a clubhouse where the lobby is filled with cigar-toting men. Democrats of many stripes and ethnicities. Most connected to Tammany Hall. Even I know that.

Union fellows too. And Italians. I meet many of them who are mostly known by monikers like my own, "Poe."

"Poe," Dinny says. "This is Silent Charlie'n Red Mike."

"Poe," says Vincent proudly. "This is the Prince o' Pals. And this here's Jack and his son Sixto, say hello, kid. Guys from the Adonis like I told ya about."

"Hello," I say and can't help but notice the one named Sixto, the son of the owner. He is probably twenty-three years old. And with a big smile across his moon-shaped face, he plays like he is the most mannerly and polite man the world has ever held. Graciously nodding when he meets me and others, he puts our nicknames to memory and true enough, he doesn't forget a single one of us.

"Poe," Dinny again says, introducing me to a big dog-faced man with black hair. "This is King Joe."

"Poe," Vincent says again. "This is Paul Vaccarelli."

The Italians call themselves businessmen, though they have a strange sense of wealth and are gaudily adorned in summery suits, tight and beige. With pinky rings, pink kerchiefs, and curly coiffed hair, they look nothing like ourselves. One man is wearing a tiny bowler cap tilted to one side gallantly and with glinting, pointy slippers on him. He is the Vaccarelli fellow, the crudest, scariest-looking man I've yet come across in all of New York, for although he is dressed as the gentlest of gentlemen—overdressed, in my estimation—he has the scars of a pugilist and a cruel set of black eyes. Of all the shadows leaning over Brooklyn, Manhattan's men who've turned from streetwise murderers and pimps to supposedly legitimate businessmen bring the coolest shade over our lifestyle back in Irishtown. The message, though, from the Italians to Dinny and The Swede is that ethnicity is becoming less important.

"Business brings us togetha," Vaccarelli says with half-lowered eyes like some profligate salesman. "And Cat'olicism, too, right?"

But Dinny is not buying, and every once in a while he looks over to me, the sense of obligation and restraint on his face. Looks at me as if he'd rather be down by the docks working in the wind and the weather by the belly of a steamship. Fighting off others.

"Things is changin'," Vaccarelli says happily. "Glad to see all o' us can come togetha wit' our similarities instead o' our diff'rences. We got big plans, right? Lotta money to be made an' ya know what? We'll hit soon. Hit 'em ha'd. Shut t'ings down in the New York Ha'bor. Then they'll listen to you'n me, won't they? Won't they?"

Dinny nods.

When we leave and head south, I look to Dinny, "Are we going to be all right, Dinny?"

He smiles cautiously, then looks over to me, "You'll be all right, especially when we get ya ma an' sisters over here."

On the corner of Barrow and Hudson, as we are entering Mr. Lynch's saloon, a man with a great jowly beard surrounded by five other men are together walking out.

"Hello, sir," Dinny takes off his cap to the man, who grumpily looks up.

"What can I do fer ye?" says the old man.

"This is William Garrihy," Dinny introduces me. "He's a Clareman."

"Well, that's no surprise," says the man.

"We're here to make our donation, from Brooklyn."

"Well," the man stammers, looks around at us all. "We do appreciate it. We're in it together though, aren't we?"

Then he walks off with his men and in we go where Mr. Lynch comes from behind the bar to greet Dinny with a big handshake. Mr. Lynch is so tall that he almost meets The Swede in height, who grimaces every time he has to shake someone's hand.

"How are ye, bhoy?" Mr. Lynch says to me. "I see ye got yer wits back."

"I'm fine," I say. "I have another letter for my mother."

"Well lemme have'r, bhoy and we'll send 'er right off then. Good seein' ye, man," he says to Dinny, avoiding his name. "Heard about Tanner."

Dinny shrugs.

"Ye saw the man as he was leaving?" Mr. Lynch says, pointing toward the door.

"Yes," Dinny said.

"The bhoy get to meet 'em?"

"Yeah, he did."

"Who was that man?" I ask.

"Well, bhoy," Mr. Lynch booms, then bends down for a whisper. "None other than John Devoy in the flesh. Old-time Fenian and head o' Clan na Gael himself!"

"The legend himself?" I say, looking out the window.

"Yer fadder ever speak o' the man, did he?" Mr. Lynch asks.

"As if he were alongside Brigid, Columba, and the Twelve Apostles," I say quickly.

Mr. Lynch laughs and crosses himself jovially, his wife Honora and young boy James smiling from the doorway adjacent the bar.

CHAPTER 24

Dinosaurs and Fire

WINTER, 1917–1918

I DIDN'T KNOW IT, BUT THE long shadows that brought in the autumn of 1917 were to be an omen. A sign to us before a great calamity, like a terrible mist seen coming over a mountain bringing famine on the crops, disease. Again we were attacked by an abstract force that can't be challenged. Can't be beaten back or outmaneuvered. The winter that followed would last a year and a half, or so it seemed. I'd been so excited by those shadows when they first came, but had no idea the change they brought would have such devastating ways about it.

October and November of 1917 quickly bring below-freezing weather, and the cobalt skies shake out sugar snows of powdered ice shimmering down to our lowly Brooklyn. Beat McGarry and other old timers pull up memories of the blizzard of 1888 and all the children lost to it. The winds that yank south off the water and into Bridge Street knock hats off heads, careening and tumbling uphill past Plymouth and Water Streets. The icy, aching belly of the great Manhattan Bridge above us groaning to its ore in the stinging air.

Everything is in short supply and we can't blame anything but the war and the winter, which aren't really enemies we can take on. Although we can't fix our anger upon any one group for the shortages, we can see that the invisible hand of the owning classes suddenly becomes protective of its own survival. Food prices since the war began went up, but nowhere near as high as they've gone recently. The price of fruit has doubled and vegetables are almost completely absent from the grocers' shelves. Chicken is so expensive, rich folk in Crown Heights and other wealthy neighborhoods have it shipped directly to their homes, undermining the market. Flour is in short supply too—a staple for cheap bread. But the government is able to buy up large supplies at regular prices as they're first in line, and with that right they send great amounts of it to Europe to feed that insatiable war machine.

The worst of it is coal. Absent from many New York City rooms altogether as it hasn't been absent since before the turn of the century. When in December a ship was accidentally rammed by a tugboat, 40,000 tons of it was given to the East River to have. Much of that coal, however, was bound for the Navy Yard behind its great wall, guarded by armed soldiers with bayonets round the clock.

A couple years earlier, farmers had been invited down to the city to sell their goods directly to the people, cutting out the grocers' profit. These markets were wildly popular in Irishtown and harkened back to the old days. But in the winter of 1917 and early 1918, it is too cold for traveling from upstate and there isn't enough yield anyhow. In any case, bankers and the powerful use this as an example that the market itself must fix pricing issues, which is their official way of excluding the needy. As often happens, since the beginning of time, it's the poorest and the hungriest and the coldest suffer the most when the resources dry up. And the enemies of the owning class too, which is most certainly the gangs that live by their own codes along the neighborhoods abutted by piers and docks.

When a newspaper boy in the neighborhood has to have the tip of his nose cut off due to standing outside too long, everyone in our neighborhood demands to know what is going to be done about the lack of coal and food. Over many months, the weakest of us succumb to the elements. Newborns are born to malnourished mothers and soon enough they both perish in their freezing beds. The old, too, found dead and stiff in their heatless rooms. And when the government and the rich turn their backs to the poor, the poor turn to the likes of Dinny Meehan.

But as is always the case, there is great danger in assuming the role of helping the poor and needy. One morning at the The Lark and Big Dick's terminal at the end of Baltic Street, Dinny and Vincent and Lumpy walk through the labor line picking men when three shots are sent into the air. Again Dinny has survived an attempt on him. With nothing more than a flesh wound through his underarm and back, Dinny never seeks medical attention whatsoever. The two men that shot at him are dragged away and it is thought they are starkers hired by the New York Dock Company or a shipping company or something, but that is not the case. It is found the two would-be murderers had been recently paroled from Sing Sing and knew Pickles Leighton. Sometime later one of the men is found in a lot between buildings on York Street dead three days at least and stuck to the grass with grub worms and maggots and larva inching out from his eyeballs and the open wound in his neck. I never heard what happened to the other.

With a lack of food and warmth, people become more and more desperate. For an entire month Harry Reynolds is held in the Poplar Street Jail after he was fingered for stabbing a man in the kidney at the Atlantic Terminal. The man was unaware of how things were run on the Brooklyn docks and assumed he could take control of the laborers on his own, charge them tribute for his own gain. After getting poked with a shiv, the man was given directions to the Long Island College Hospital a few blocks away by a group of laughing longshoremen. It was there he told Brosnan and Culkin that it was Reynolds did it, but by the time the hearing comes around the man has disappeared. Or been disappeared by something. Dead Reilly just shrugging toward the magistrate as twenty of us sit in the court gallery sneering with moue mouths in the dim light and woody pews of law.

One morning after getting the signal from the Chelsea Hotel where King Joe of the ILA resides, Dinny tells us that we aren't going to work in Brooklyn today and instead, we're going to the waterfront to make sure no one works at all. For three days we stand around with our smoking breath and talk to ship captains and crew, trying to keep warm by barrel and bonfires. When a group of scabs supported by the police, among other brutes, show up on the waterfront to work, it's our job to run them off with cudgels and pipes. This is a job we are very good at, of course, and within twenty minutes over one hundred men are dispersed, clutching their heads and elbows in pain.

"Is it almost over?" I remember a captain asking us about the strike.

"One dollar an' twenny cents raise per hour, and it'll all be over," Dinny says, repeating the slogan of the ILA as if he only half-believes it.

Within the week an agreement is made and every longshoreman in Brooklyn and those we struck with in Manhattan and New Jersey get their raise. The production of war materials is just too important and although Wolcott and the Waterfront Assembly got involved, even they knew it was not their day. Even in their minds, the American war industry needs to continue unabated and the port of New York being of such great importance in supplying it, concessions have to be made to the workers. World economic power is shifting from the old world to the new world, with every bomb paid for by England and

France's coffers happily pocketed by American industry. But Wolcott and the Waterfront Assembly would not forget what we'd done. The Anglo-American ascendency would never forgive it either.

With the victory, the International Longshoremen's Association has officially claimed leadership of New York's port union, and the communist wobblies are put aside. The ship owners lost. T. V. O'Connor, president of the ILA, and King Joe, who runs New York City, are household names now, whether you think them heroes of the working man, or seditious anti-American exploiters of war. Board members of the Waterfront Assembly and the editorial pages are filled with opinions about the waterfront strike and the Irish longshoremen "that'd be happier if Germany won the war against England." But only the most liberal of people ever associate the strike with the destitution of the poor, as it would only conjure up "support for the red factions."

In reality, none of us know much about the revolution in Russia at all, but the rich certainly do. And they use it to create an ever-greater divide between them and us. Rich and poor. They see it as a challenge to their way of life and everywhere around them they point to signs of their being overthrown by the communist savages. Even though we are not communists, and have no capability of overthrowing the rich, they press their fears upon us in the newspapers. All the while King Joe constantly berates and speaks out against communism; no matter, he's painted with a sweeping brush as "a socialist red at heart," by none other than Jonathan G. Wolcott, who is given lots of space in the newspapers for his ideas.

We didn't know it at the time, but what we were really fighting for was the creation of a middle class. Or at least that's what it mostly turned out to be. A semblance of security, food, and warmth, instead of dependence on an untouchable, invisible, plutocratic elite above. Our battling to reach the middle and have security is something to this very day that I am so very proud of. Yet again, though, our fight is not appreciated in textbooks and the court of general opinion, as hardly anyone associates the unions and their courageous battle against power as fighting the good fight.

I didn't even know The Swede could read, but there he is right in front of me, sitting at the window ledge by Dinny's desk with a newspaper covering his face.

"People start believin' this shit the more they hear it," The Swede says aloud, reading a quote from a ship owner, a board member of Wolcott's Waterfront Assembly. "Listen to this . . . 'Those unions and the gangs that support them in the New York ports are going to go the way of the dinosaurs. I'll make sure of it. You can't hold the country hostage when we're at war with evil. Are those boys supporters of the Central Powers or just plain Bolsheviks? Take your pick.'"

Dinny listens, then asks which company that ship owner is from.

"Everybody's readin' this shit," The Swede says.

That night, over at the Fulton Ferry Landing, Cinders Connolly, and a few others board a ship with three barrels of gasoline. We pull up heavy hawsers from the mooring bollards and throw them into the water, where a tug drags it out to the center of the East River as it slowly catches ablaze for all to see, cargo included.

"Look how beautyful it is," Cinders says, fire in his eyes. With the Brooklyn Bridge towers to the right and stretching toward the great city skyline in the background, and with the frigid city folk attracted to fire like flies to light, the blaze is there for all to witness. Like an old portrait, the ship twists in the water from its internal injuries and tilts sideways as embers crackle in the night and vaporize with a serpent's hiss into smoke when enveloped by the water. Turning and turning portside into death and left as soot and cinders floating downriver. When gone, and again the brumal night takes its place dark and humming in the distance, and the smell of fire-burned winter all round us, we turn back into our neighborhoods. But for as long as we rule the waterfront, never again do we read a quote like that from a ship owner, no.

It is a bitter holiday season that year, and Harry and I spend much of Christmas day on the second floor below my future room, patching up the gaping hole in the flooring. The Burke family lives below me, and the father is a small fellow named Thomas, maybe twenty-five years of age.

"Not been a thing in that fireplace all winter," he says, looking up to Harry standing on a wooden ladder as I hand him slabs of wood to repair the ceiling above, which is also my floor. "Except for the dining table an' chairs, that is."

I look round their kitchen and remember the table the eldest child used to sit at, though it's now missing. The child is stricken with some sort of debilitation and sits now in the lone chair in the parlor while all the others stand.

"Do you think he's gonna raise the rent?" Burke asks. "Fix somethin' in here and that's what they do."

"He raises it, we'll talk wit' 'em," Harry says.

"He'll raise it all right."

"Yeah? What's the landlord's name?"

"You don' know it?"

Harry looks down to me, but I shrug.

"Nah."

"Vandeleurs, but I've never seen 'em. He lives somewhere else—Connecticut, I think. Two big guys show up on the first o' the month, inspect the place, and take the rent. When they see that ceiling . . ." Burke trails off.

"You workin'?" Harry asks without looking down to him.

"I can do anythin' asked," Burke says, reeling off his experience as if he were in an interview.

"I was just wonderin'," Harry says.

"Well, if you have any inroads, I'd appreciate it. Can't find steady work in any place," Burke says.

Harry looks down toward the parlor where the boy stares and groans, his mother speaking to him in warm, sweet tones even as we can see her cold breath in the room. But he does not respond like a normal boy. He stares into the distance and smacks his lips while his mother rubs her hand up and down his arms to keep the cold off him. She kisses him and holds his head, then looks toward Harry and I.

"Come down to the Atlantic Terminal tomorrow, 5 a.m., we'll see if ya can work."

Burke smiles, and sure enough he shows thirty minutes early next morn with a big grin on him. A few days later I run some messages to the Atlantic Terminal.

"Hello, neighbor," Burke says to me, hand extended.

"Hello."

"I wanted to thank you for the opportunity—best thing that's happened to us in a long time."

"Well it's Harry that you should thank."

He smiles and back to work he goes in the tightness of the freezing weather.

Having descended on the city as if a blessing to our enemy, the constant cold wears us down. Into the bones and joints of our hips and shoulders, as if turning us to glass on the inside while they, looking down from above, sit in their warmth and watch us slowly deteriorate by the forces they see as being sent by god to teach us a lesson. A calamity which Wolcott and all those landowners and executives in Brooklyn of the Waterfront Assembly have every capability of mitigating, but instead we get their wrath. The wrath of them is, of course, as always, to ignore the suffering. Ignore. The harshness being a callous disregard for humanity. Overlooking the needy. Rejecting not by overt action, but by evasion. Forgetfulness, even. That is their wrath. The deliberate dragging of feet in assistance, if assistance is given at all. Creating a vacuum between help given and help received by a great and extensive bureaucratic blockade. And although we all know that the pitiful assistance offered to us cannot help even a small amount of people, it is still considered assistance and therefore frees up the owning classes from a thorough criticism of true neglect.

Though Dinny waves it off, "We don' need their help."

But we do. We really do, as there are more and more stories of babies and the aged becoming sick, even dying from maladies related to the freezing temperatures.

As has become our only way of hearing the words of our enemies, it is to the newspapers that we turn.

"This long and apparent deadly winter, as it's termed, is proving to be an effective mechanism in reducing the surplus of workers who've grown slothful and inefficient," Wolcott says in one editorial. "This overgrowth of inefficiency causes the working man to grow weary of his employer, whereas he once was happy to have his job. With so much time on his hands, the working man takes to his saloon and drinks himself useless. A curse for disobedience and fecklessness, I'd say with this deadly winter, at least, less time is spent in the gin mills, more on their work."

CHAPTER 25

Gale Day and the Grippe

THE WORST OF IT IS YET to come, but some good news still makes it through all the bad.

"Bill Lovett's dead, I heared," Paddy Keenan whispers one afternoon.

"Really?" I say.

"That's what they're sayin'. Uniformed man entered the Lovett home yesterday with a letter, hat in hand."

"Are you sure he's dead?"

But within a few hours Richie Lonergan and Abe Harms are upstairs with Dinny, then come down with Vincent Maher, grab Dago Tom, shoulder through the saloon, and leave together, all four.

"Where are they going?" I ask.

Beat McGarry watches them move across the front window south on Bridge Street. "Prove themselves again. Their loyalty."

A few days later Richie and Abe are in the City Workhouse, charged in the death of some Italian, but from Beat I hear that the dead man is an enemy of Yale and the Stabiles down at the Adonis Social Club. Of course Dead Reilly appears on their behalf and soon they are let out. Free to work with The White Hand again.

Out the front window I see Mrs. McGowan and her three daughters on the windy sidewalk. The four of them fighting against the cold and shivering, but still standing as if waiting.

I open the door, "Hello, Mrs. McGowan, how are you?"

"I apologize son, I truly do . . ." her teeth chattering.

"Don't apologize, Mrs. McGowan. How are the little ones and your son's widow?

"She's fine," she waves her hand. "I mean they're fine, the lot of 'em. T'ank ye so much fer arskin'."

"What can we do for you, Mrs. McGowan?"

"Eh . . ." Mrs. McGowan turns. "Emma, do ye remember the man William here?"

"I do, Ma."

"Good then," Mrs. McGowan says, a bit rattled. "Eh . . . we've a problem with our room. It's been cold for so long, and without any coal, there's not been a moment's warmth. First a window broke, but we covered it in cardboard, so that's fine but . . . eh . . . then part of the ceiling fell in and there's an awful draft. We're on the third floor, so . . ."

"Why not ask the landlord to fix it?"

"Well there's the problem in it," she says, now a bit perturbed. "The man says we made the damages and we need to pay to have them fixed, so he says. But we've been werkin' and savin' every dime up at the Clock Tower where Dinny got us those jobbers an' . . ."

"So he won't do normal maintenance? What's his name?"

"Oh, I never see the landlord, only his agents. But I think the man's name is Vandeleurs."

"Of course it is."

"Eh?"

"Let me talk to Dinny about it and we'll see what can be done."

"I don't think there's any way of getting in touch with the man . . ."

"Dinny will do anything in his power for you, Mrs. McGowan, you know that."

"I do," she says solemnly, as if renewing the vow that had married her to the ways that had both pulled her family out of homelessness and taken her only son. And I look at her. And though I hadn't realized it fully yet, I begin to see her as what my mother could be. Married to our violent ways, a woman without a say in it. Wed to that which could take my mother's son too: myself. Standing out on the sidewalk I watch Mrs. McGowan, sad and slumped and showing her age. And even as she is only in her forties, it seems she's much older. Worn and tired, just as I'm sure my own mother is.

"Let me talk to him and I'll come and see you about it," I say.

As they are walking up Bridge Street I see Emma smile as she whispers to her older sister, then sneak a look back at me. A tight and cold wind washes across the woman and girls and in unison their long dresses extend and flay to one side like ship sails as they hold their hats with one hand while their Hanan boots are revealed below. I turn to the side and dig my hands in my pockets against the wind's assault, but at that moment I am full of myself and run back up to them on the sidewalk in front of the Pfeiffer Color Works factory. "Mrs. McGowan?"

"Yes, William?" she shuffles to a stop and slowly turns her stiff neck toward me, a rhythmic hand-hammer pounding on hot steel every few seconds within the Plymouth Street foundry across the cobbles.

"I was wondering if you would allow me to see your daughter sometime," looking through the wind to her and stumbling with my words. "I know that I made a mistake in not speaking to you or her for so long and I, uh . . . I'm sorry. . . . But if you would allow that to me, I would be very grateful. I mean, I'll still talk to Dinny . . . I . . . uh . . . I didn't mean like I'd talk to Dinny only if you allow me to see Emma . . ."

"No, no, I understand," Mrs. McGowan says. "I think it's a wonderful idea. You may see the girl, yes."

Emma looks at me with her mouth half-open, then looks away. Almost angrily.

"I'm sorry, Emma, I was wrong."

"It's all right," she says, embarrassed, but her older sisters look at her happily.

And I am proud to humble myself to her because she is a good person. She deserves people to humble themselves to her because she has humbled herself in this life too. Going to school during the day, babysitting her nieces at night, working at the Clock Tower building on the weekends—this is all she ever does. Even if she doesn't like me, I don't care because she is the type of person I would always be proud to be with, for not only does she have the humility that I appreciate, but she is more beautiful every time I see her. And when I do see her, I study her thin waist and bust. Her slender neckline and full lower lip and hazel eyes and the natural curl to her chestnut hair and her overall shape so I remember what she looks like since we spend so much time apart.

When I tell Dinny about the cold McGowan home, the window, and the ceiling, he quickly dispatches Harry to fill the holes. I offer to help, and when Harry says it may not be needed, I offer to run for the new piece of glass and the materials needed for the ceiling.

"Well that'd be helpful," he says.

"Good then, I'll go now."

"You don't have the measurements."

"Oh yeah, all right, let's go get the measurements then."

Harry glances at me sideways, but there is nothing in the world that I want more than to see Emma McGowan again, and to be around her generally.

* * *

"Hello, Emma, how are you?" I say as Harry and I walk in their room.

"I'm fine," she says with a half-smile, though I notice that her nose is red and her eyes are a little heavy looking. She holds a handkerchief over her face and turns away, sneezing.

"I haven't been inside here for like three years," I say looking around, then up to the fallen ceiling. "We're going to fix this place up a bit."

She smiles awkwardly, "It's been so cold in here."

"Please, don't hesitate if there's anything you need. Harry and Dinny and I are happy to help. There's no reason for any of you to suffer when we can easily take care of these things."

"That's true," Harry says in the background.

Getting to work, Harry and I begin taking the rubbish from the ceiling that had fallen to the floor and carrying it downstairs in armloads. Emma brings us tea and within moments there is soot and dust in mine. I drink it anyhow as Emma retires to the kitchen where Mrs. McGowan and the sisters stay, whispering. One of the older sisters seems to take interest in Harry, though he doesn't notice. He just keeps working.

"Isn't she beautiful," I whisper to Harry.

He hears me but doesn't answer.

"Do you think she likes me?" I ask him.

He continues working until a few moments later when he turns to me and whispers in my ear, "You need to tell her how you feel. She doesn't know how you feel about her. She wants you to be honest and forthright. Do it."

I look at him with my mouth open, "I will."

Just as I resolve to speak with her, a runner from 25 Bridge Street appears and Dinny sends me to do another job elsewhere, unwittingly taking me away from her.

As I am leaving, she clasps her hands in her lap as she stands in her doorway upstairs. Smiling at each other as we had the first time we spoke in this same doorway when I gave her flowers some two years earlier, I try to speak, but nothing comes out.

There are a thousand things I want to say to her right now, though I can't organize anything in my mind well enough to articulate my feelings for her. I am overcome with nerves and on the verge of bursting, yet all I do is smile at her. I wish to kiss her on the cheek, or at least shake her hand, but we do not touch at all. I simply nod my head and smile again before walking down the stairwell. Sensing my excitement for her, she smiles back and slowly closes the door.

"Idiot," I say to myself and vow that next time I see her I will tell her just how I feel about her, as Harry advised. That I don't want anyone else in my life but Emma McGowan, and maybe one day when we are older we can be married and move away from the city to start a family together. Her and I. But all of this is childish dreaming, I know, but I do dream it as I walk down the stairwell alone in the dark toward the gray sunlight streaming out of the tenement windows below. I do dream, like all of us in our day. For the summer of life when need and necessity is not our only calling. Striving for the gentlelife that keeps us waking early in the morn, fighting through today's gravelly, arduous existence for a better life. I do dream like all Americans, and I'm ready to work hard for it, and to share it with my family. And hopefully, with Emma McGowan, too.

What Dinny wants me to do is find out what I can of the Vandeleurs man, which I do. He tells me to follow the two agents that travel to fourteen buildings in Brooklyn. They are large men and they don't look very kind either. After going to my building last on Eighth Avenue in Prospect Park, they take the trolley back to the Bridge District and over the Manhattan Bridge they go and into a clubhouse a few blocks south of Cooper Square.

"Did they see you following them?" Dinny asks.

"I don't think so, but," I say raising a finger, "they told the Burkes that they'll need to pay ten dollars more next month."

Dinny nods, but I continue, "Listen Dinny, while researching this landlord Vandeleurs in the city directory and the newspapers, I found out that he is a member of the Waterfront Assembly. Vandeleurs is a small-time player in it. He's not a major landowner but he's involved."

Dinny looks at me from his desk with a look on his face. I recognize that look from the look he had when Anna and the Lonergan crew kicked us out of Tiny Thomas's wake. The same look on his face when he didn't speak to anybody for four months.

Dinny looks at me again. "Good work. Real good, but let's go after this Vandeleurs guy."

"Oh there's no finding that fellow in Brooklyn," I say. "He is well protected, Vandeleurs is."

"Well," Dinny says. "We'll talk to his guys then, about this raisin' the rent."

The conversation ends there, but it makes me think. About Wolcott, the WASPs that keep banging the drum about a prohibition on alcohol, the Waterfront Assembly taking control and turning our territory into their property, Italians wanting to act like businessmen instead of the thugs they truly are. And it's not until that moment that I recognize how true The Swede's words really were just before shooting himself. They truly are closing in on us.

A month later, though, ten of us are waiting a few houses down from my Eighth Avenue building.

"Ya gonna live around here, William?" Dago Tom says to me.

"I am."

"So many trees," Mickey Kane says with Richie and Abe behind him. "And the park's just a block away, looky that."

"There were a lot more trees before this long winter came about. Firewood, you know?"

We are leaning against automobiles that we don't own and drays too, but nobody says anything to us. Up and down the streets are long sidewalks and stoops that protrude from buildings. Of course, it's cold. Again with the cold weather and again shivering outside. It never seems to end, regardless of it being day or night. Cold. Always cold and windy.

Dinny and I are among them, but when we see the two agents enter my building, he and I duck out of sight, as we don't want to be identified by them. Each of our men have weapons in his belt or coat, and as Dinny and I turn the corner, we watch the eight of them enter the building to confront the agents.

An hour after, Dinny and I walk upstairs at the Dock Loaders' Club, we hear the banging of boots on the stairwell and the carrying on of Vincent Maher and the rest of the boys. They walk in the door and drop three huge wads of money wrapped in rubber bands.

"Wow," I say.

"No shots right?" Dinny asks them.

"Nah," Vincent says. "We just gave 'em a little show so as they don' forget never to raise the rent no more, right? They was real professionals, though—got work ID cards an' all. Look."

"Joseph Roston, 22 Baxter Street," Dinny says aloud, picks up the second one. "Michael Benner, 43 Mott Street."

"That neighborhood?" Vincent says. "They prolly work for Vaccarelli."

"Eddie?" Dinny says. "Take out twenty percent of this and split it between the all of us. William, you start backtracking and hand the money back to all the tenants these two guys stole this money from. Tell 'em that it's for repairs and whatnot. Don't tell 'em anythin' else."

"Got it." I take the wads from Lumpy and start running down the stairs. I can't wait to get to the McGowan home and give back the family their month's rent. Or at least the majority of it. Emma will really be proud of me then and I can have that talk with her.

* * *

"Sorry, William, she's not available at the moment."

"Where is she?"

"She's not available, I'm sorry."

"She doesn't want to see me, does she?"

"No, no, that's not it, son," Mrs. McGowan assures. "Really, she likes ye. She really does, but she's just eh . . . indisposed at the moment."

I don't feel as though Mrs. McGowan is telling me the whole truth and so I sulk away. I think that maybe with the grippe going around, Mrs. McGowan doesn't want me to give it to her since I'm always outside and around people who've caught it. I want to believe that, but I just don't know for sure. Brings me down because I think that if she doesn't like me, maybe it would be hard for Mrs. McGowan to say it. So I'm down, and even handing the money back to people for their rent does not cheer me up, but when I come back to the Dock Loaders' Club, I am shocked by what I see.

"Johnny Mullen?" I say, shocked to see the old gang member back in the club. "I thought you were in the war?"

But Mumbling Johnny Mullen does not look good. In fact, he has lost weight and his eyes are blood red. He'd survived three wounds to his chest and abdomen and now walks with a terrible stoop, clothes hanging off him, and a wet cough. He is given a whiskey that ten men argue over paying for and someone else runs around the corner to get him a sandwich, but with the gentlest sip he winces and gags. Within three days of returning from the Great War, Johnny Mullen is dead from the grippe.

There isn't a lot about it in the papers, but there is much talk and everyone who shows signs of it are immediately avoided. Over the next few months, many people show up at 25 Bridge Street to ask for help with burials. Stories of dead relatives and friends turn worse as they make the rounds, and Death himself seems to live in Brooklyn. But it's not just Brooklyn that Death is visiting—it's all over the

Northeast. And then I hear stories of it in Ohio from James Hart and New Orleans and California, too, and everyone says it's the Great Plague all over again. But still the newspapers are mostly silent and the government even more quiet, which leaves the rumors up to the common folk and their myths.

Lore of the Great Grippe during the Great War is mostly lost to time now, but out of the many of the stories came one that grew legs and was picked up by physicians and medical researchers. That was of a visitor to Brooklyn from Albany in the winter of 1918. It was an uncle in the Sullivan family that had come to the city to visit a newborn niece. Mary Regina was the child's name, and this uncle infected the baby with the grippe without his knowing it, and within hours of his journey back upstate did the uncle die. Little Mary Regina took deathly ill too and could barely breathe with her tiny lungs bubbling in fluid, and gasping and wheezing did wee Mary Regina go until her parents had no choice but to make plans for a miniature coffin. But just as suddenly, the baby recovered and for the rest of her very long life she never again got sick. Not a-once. Even as she worked as a nurse for more than forty years, caring for people with the most contagious diseases the port of New York could throw at her. She lived deep into her nineties, in fact, stronger than any man. Immune to all flus and colds and survived long enough to tell her great-grandchildren what it was like growing up in old Brooklyn.

Such stories give hope, but with the government and businesses doing all they can to avoid panic, the topic is mostly ignored, as usual. But we don't have time to point fingers at them anymore. We already know they'll not help us, even as they say they are doing all they can. They let us starve and freeze, as usual. And as usual we see the past repeating itself forever in the present. It is us at the bottom that see the worst of it, the longshoremen families of the New York Harbor and the city's poor. Every morning when ships come to the Brooklyn anchorage, we look for the Yellow Jack on them. This flag signifies that the ship is contaminated, but we always take them in anyhow. Some ships are quarantined, though, and sent to the Atlantic Basin in Red Hook or Wallabout Bay, left for the cargo to rot like the old British prison ships during the Revolutionary War.

One day I admit to The Lark and Big Dick down at the Baltic Terminal that I feel a bit of a fever and fatigue, and out of their coats they pull bottles of potato vodka, "Swish it around the mouth, kid. Spit it over there. Wash yer hands wid it."

I've never seen them act so serious and I feel that at any second they are going to tell me the vodka is actually made out of urine or something. When I try to give the bottle back to them, they pass and tell me to keep it.

"Go home for the day, kid."

I have nothing to do, so instead of going back to Harry's room on Atlantic Avenue, I go to my place on Eighth and, climbing the stairs to the third floor, sneezing and wheezing, bottle of vodka in my hand, I enter and see the black floors. The hole in the kitchen is covered and has new wood slats contrasting with the old black ones, making the place look undone altogether. I can't take off my coat because I feel so cold, but on my hands and knees I begin sanding from the far corner of the girls' room with nothing but my bare hands and a few pieces of sandpaper. I am coughing and swishing out my mouth and rinsing my hands in the new sink and getting more and more nervous because I feel I am getting worse. And on top of it, I am alone. I have to gather energy to stand up and open the windows because my nose is getting filled with sawdust and I am dizzy from the vodka and the fever and my sinuses feel tender and swollen and my eyes are heavy and after two hours I am so exhausted I fall asleep in the doorway between the girls' room and the kitchen on the floor.

* * *

"Hello?" I hear the door open with a woman's voice. "Anybody in here?"

"Hello there, Mrs. Burke," I say, coming to an elbow.

"Are you sick?"

I look away. She crosses herself, "Can you tell the man that you are always with that we are very thankful and that we feel safe in his care?"

"I will," I say, knowing that she is speaking of Harry.

She quickly closes the door behind her and I lie on my back and look to the ceiling, palm on my forehead. Within seconds I am back asleep still in the doorway and I don't wake until the next morning, but when I do I have to pee so badly that I run to the lavatory in the hallway and moan in relief loud enough that I'm sure everyone on the third floor hears me.

When I come out, Harry Reynolds is there. "You sick?"

"Uh . . . "

He puts his hand on my forehead. "Feverish. C'mon."

"Where are we going?"

"Hospital."

"I thought we don't go to hospitals?"

"Only the ignorant don't. You ignorant?"

"No."

"Let's go."

* * *

I AM LEFT IN A LARGE room with many sick men, yet I am isolated by a partition. It is at Long Island College Hospital a couple blocks from Harry's room on Atlantic Avenue that I'm interned. They keep me here. They are very strict about my not leaving too and ask me to stay in bed, but I love to sit on the ledge of the large open window and look out onto the water.

They have books, too. Lots of them. In one long day and night I read the entire book called *Treasure Island*. I'll never forget Jim Hawkins's description of a buccaneer picking his teeth with a huge knife on the beach. And there's *Gulliver's Travels* too, which I love so much I read it twice. And there are translations of *The Count of Monte Cristo* and *The Hunchback of Notre Dame*. I read them so fast that the nurses bring in their own books for me to devour.

"Well he'll be caught up in no time," one says.

But sometimes I don't feel well and sleep for many hours during the day. Then at night I lie awake, unable to sleep and sit on the big window ledge overlooking the East River and the Hudson River darting west of Manhattan. Again Lady Liberty standing proud, holding her torch. I can see the Atlantic Terminal, too, though it is covered with one large warehousing structure after another and pier houses and dock sheds and train depots and overhangs and so many different edifices that all contribute in sending goods out from the manufacturers' factories here in the neighborhoods and in to New York from abroad. The shorefront being a place of great exchanging, I see it differently from on high here. The longshoremen and laborers seemingly moving in peace among each other like ants below, maneuvering existentially from one place to another on the piers and on the decks, in hulls and docks. The tumult and turbulence of life on the waterfront doesn't exist up here, and I can see why the newspapers and the men of the Waterfront Assembly would think us all a bunch of wild men who love nothing more than the drink and the fight.

The nurses are quite often nuns, and with their headdresses, long white garments, and masks covering their mouths and noses, I feel like I am certain to die. They never come too close, but when they do they look at me with only their eyes visible, I believe I see pity in them, but I can't be sure. When they cross themselves and curtsy before leaving me, I can't help but to think they're planning last rites. I feel we are treated well enough here, but in my memory are the old stories, told to me when I was a child, of the workhouses in Ireland of my grandfather's time. Erected under the auspice of the poor and desperate gaining work after the great blight and famine came, in actuality they became a place to die for hundreds of thousands stricken with the diseases that come with starvation and malnutrition on a mass scale.

Many men are taken to another floor where the sickest are sent never to be seen or heard again. To pass on. What they do with all the bodies is up to my imagination only, but there are rumors of a crematory in the basement. Better than mass graves in the hospital's courtyard, I suppose.

Despite this, it is maybe the most peaceful time in all of my younger days with the bleached-white sheets and the breeze. With no docks, no fighting, no cold weather, and no need to defend myself, I am left to my imagination and at night I think of Emma McGowan. And in the morning, too. Then in the afternoon I close my eyes and I think of the two of us walking down a suburban street with children following us and she is so proud of me, because I'm a man who thinks about his wife and his family, and our children will grow up to be city councilmen in small towns where there is peace and where the wind wisps through the trees in our backyard and we drink tea on Saturdays and her mother, Mrs. McGowan, sits in a rocking chair on the back porch smiling in her golden years, fat and happy. The gentlelife. Dreaming of the gentlelife. But that is not all that I think of. Emma and I spend a lot of time alone together, in my imagination. She shares everything with me and allows my hands to wash over her hips and to kiss her neck. I can smell the passion in her breath as she breathes into my mouth and together we hide from the world to enjoy each other's bodies. I already know about masturbation, but with so much time alone I become an expert. I am not the only one, of course, at night behind my partition the air is full with the symphony of the pleasurable moanings of men followed by the timbre of snores.

One morning while lying in bed, I tilt my head when I read an article in the newspaper: *Police Corruption in Brooklyn at its Height.* Detective William Brosnan is mentioned in the article, but both the police chief and the district attorney come to his defense. In the article below that, I read what makes my stomach turn completely: *Temperance Leaders and Waterfront Assembly to Meet with Bishops of Local Roman Catholic Churches.*

I put the paper down and the first thing that comes to my mind is the look on Dinny's face when I spoke to him last about the Waterfront Assembly. How he avoided the conversation when I asked what we could do about them. Now this. "Oh they're comin'," Brosnan had told us. "Like the great suck'd o' the ocean and leave ye bathin' in a welter o' yer own blood and bones, all o' ye."

Just then a man stands over my bed with his chart and his airs. I can see that he grew up in a rich household by the way he demands things from the nurses. His white coat is pristine in its cleanliness, and I can also see he takes great pride in never getting his hands dirty—always giving orders and never taking them.

"You can go," he says without ever looking at me, then signs my chart at the end of the bed, walks away without the slightest concern of anyone's ideas other than his own.

I grab my clothes and put them on as fast as I can, tie my Hanan boots in a flash. I have never been more sure of anything in the world, and as I walk out the hospital doors, I take to the wind toward the McGowan home. I stop only for flowers and with the wind and everything in life all new again, exciting and different and strange and yet familiar, I sprint down the street and run up the stairwell to knock on the door.

Mrs. McGowan again answers. Slowly opens the door on the third floor.

"Good morning," I smile, filled with excitement and energy.

"William?" she looks up surprised, as if I'm supposed to be dead.

I smile, "Do you think it'll be all right if I take Emma . . ."

"William, William," she interrupts, her face turning color, then looking away from me. She shakes her head no while looking up and hides behind the door, then slowly closes it while crossing herself, leaving me and my flowers outside.

Then quickly the door is back open and Mrs. McGowan is angered, "Ye tell Dinny—that's right, I say his name! Ye tell 'em if he wants to help us, then let us go. Let us leave Brooklyn and stop enslavin' us to it. That's right, bhoy, it's fer him we can't leave and it's fer him my daughter's dead now. An' me son too. Who'll be next? Is it yerself then? G'on then, tell 'em."

The door slams in my face. I drop the flowers at my arm's length. I'd never known anyone to be angry with Dinny like Mrs. McGowan is. And . . . Emma is dead. Emma.

I walk down the stairwell slowly, my head tingling. I lose my breath for a moment and stop and lean against the banister. My chest heaving and heaving until I see spots and sit down, cold sweats raking through my body like shock waves. I just want to ask questions, I think to myself. I just want someone to answer all my questions. I have so many, I just wish there was someone to help me with them. But orphans don't have what is most needed: the mother. The father. The grandparents. The siblings. The cousins. The infrastructure for a child's mind.

Thinking back on it now as I stand from the typewriter and my pencil and paper, looking out through the window onto the New York Harbor, I know that not having my family close to me for those years set me back. For a long time, I was behind others who'd grown up with the support structure that a family gives a developing mind. I'm an old man now and certainly I've caught up, but for so much of my life had I been behind those of my own age.

I had a family, true. I had Dinny Meehan and Harry Reynolds and Sadie and others. It's true, I had them, but there's nothing replaces a mother. A father too, but it's the mother that makes us who we are. And why she couldn't be there to answer my questions was, well, yet another question I wanted answered.

For a moment I thought I might have a new family. The McGowan family that has loads of women in it. But it wasn't to be. Instead, I got a slammed door in the face. I walk outside and curse the cold weather. The godforsaken wind that never stops. Curse all that I can't control. It's everything in the world I can't control that ruins me. I fight back tears, even though I long to feel sorry for myself.

But when I do, I think of Emma. Died in her blooming years.

She'll always be beautiful.

CHAPTER 26

Lace Curtains

ON THE ELEVENTH DAY OF THE eleventh month at the eleventh hour of 1918, an armistice is called in France. The Great War is over. The world is changing, but in our neighborhoods most things stay the same. The wind, ships, bridges above us and death always there. A week or so before the war ends, a train derails on the other side of Prospect Park from my Eighth Avenue room by Ebbets Field—almost one hundred souls scrubbed clean from the dirty earth in seconds.

In the West Village of Manhattan, Harry waits for me with a hat over his eyes and his hands in his pockets at a waterfront ticket box as I finally book passage for my mother and sisters. I take the receipt and place it in my wallet. Harry pushes off the wall he'd been leaning on and together we walk away without celebration. It'd only be months now until they arrive, if all goes well. But long months, they are.

* * *

JANUARY, 1919

WITH FATHER LARKIN'S VOICE BANKING OFF St. Ann's long ceilings so often, it seems as though the entire neighborhood is within reach of the ecclesiastical homily and the funeral rite. Again, we show up in force for what we all simply call "sayin' goodbye to people." The lot of us wearing our wake attire once more. With Sunday morning beer on our lips from the Dock Loaders' Club, we wash south up the Bridge Street hill again, little boys admiring us from windows upstairs, mothers shaming and appreciating us all at once, the Great Grippe taking another of the Lonergan brood, freezing and malnourished, just as it had taken Emma away from us, and many others too.

Again we are on the march through the neighborhoods, a Lonergan casket on a dray. Death everywhere, whether from grippe or war, death is the great constant. Fred Honeybeck last week. Gimpy Kafferty the week before that, died in France defending England, the both. And Quiet Higgins too. A pair of Simpson brothers to boot, Whitey and Baron, and many more. We just shaking our heads, for while we are funding a revolt with Germany in Ireland against England, they are fighting against Germany for England in France.

Today, the procession walks sullenly again in front of the open-shuttered refineries, half-opened stable doors, dusty stonecutter shops and wheelwrights and farriers and harness makers, the long and skinny smokestacks looking dolefully down on us all. Shuffling anew along the Navy Yard wall with the clopping feet of dour draught horses until we go west on Water Street. Beside the wood-fenced area in front of the giant Brooklyn Union Gas fuel tanks we continue, pulling the horses by the face and bits over the freight rails and rough cobbles. Looking over their shoulders, black-faced men inside foundries are lit only by the glowing orange of the smelting furnace and the casts pulled out by crucible tongs. The air smelling of ferric oxide and steam, we stop in front of St. Ann's Church again. Next door is Moore & Co. Paints that has for so long been there that its owners simply find it ineffective for its workers to honor each melancholic funeral cortege.

Especially during the war and the horrible sickness that falls drooling out of its gluttonous, toothy gob.

To her credit, Anna has not budged since May 1917 when she sent us from her home, and she stands here now arms crossed, sneering at our like. But we keep our heads low, cross ourselves respectfully, and fill the church with flowers, pay for the casket and the gravestone at Calvary Cemetery.

But here we part, half of us entering the house of God for the Requiem Mass, others remaining outside. Families separated too—Sadie and L'il Dinny heading in with the procession, the father breaking off.

Inside is silence but for the shuffling feet, the gentle dropping of kneelers from under pews, a distant cough, and the medieval ringing of the pipe organ extending notes long for to bless the bier that holds the child, feet facing the altar.

L'il Dinny is already squirming as he sits between myself and Sadie. Behind me is the Burke family, including the son who mouths wordless sounds every so often. Ahead I see Cinders Connolly with his pregnant wife and their four young ones. Philip Large among them. Detective Brosnan in civil clothes next to his daughter, and holding her hand is Patrolman Culkin. To our right is Mrs. McGowan and her remaining daughters—her son's widow still in her weeds four years on and her children next to her. The Lark and Big Dick Morissey as well as Red Donnelly, Henry Browne, Paddy Keenan, Beat McGarry, and many others sit amongst themselves and theirs. The Lonergan family in the front row, Mary surrounded by Anna on one side, the dead child's father at the other, arm wrapped over his wife's shoulder. The familiar scars of the mother ever-present. Burnt skin on one side of her face and scalded hair over one broken ear, tears and sobbing muffled. The eldest son Richie sitting with his fists in his lap, another new tie and coat over him for the occasion. Matty Martin and Timothy Quilty behind.

Then the voice of Father Larkin imitated by the reverberation.

> *Day of wrath and doom impending.*
> *David's word with Sibyl's blending,*
> *Heaven and Earth in ashes ending.*
>
> *Oh, what fear man's bosom rendeth,*
> *When from Heaven the judge descendeth,*
> *On whose sentence we all dependeth.*
>
> *Wondrous sound the trumpet flingeth,*
> *Through earth's sepulchres it ringeth,*
> *All before the throne it bringeth.*
>
> *Death is struck, and nature quaking,*
> *All creation is awaking,*
> *To its judge an answer making . . .*

We know these prayers in English and Latin. Some know them in Irish. And we know the incense and the holy water flung to the resting child. And we genuflect on call. And stand and sing and listen to Father Larkin in his black vestments, the prayer cycle of the Office of the Dead and his reading of the Liturgy of the Word. And over the child he stands on the altar, hands clasped, and into his homily he slowly gives for the young deceased.

"And as we know," he begins, voice sounding off the high ceiling and wood floors. With his palms open now, he is looking down to the child. "This earthly life fer which we are exiled is not permanent. Though t'is filled with pain and with sufferin'."

"I would like to spake today o' the one True God, and the Savior," Father Larkin's voice opens up. "Can we not all agree that there is only one God? Yes. We can. And in so bein', he has only one Messenger o' the Light. His son.

In our quest fer salvation, deliverance. And in places o' great darkness. In times o' great ruin and war. Poverty, hunger, disease, and death we sometimes believe in half-makers. For it is only in times of our greatest sufferin' that such a false deity may arise. T'is up to ye to listen to the Spirit o' God. To not be convinced by those that live only in the material world. Ye must remember that the Spirit o' God comes from the divine essence. The spark o' divinity. We are born ignorant o' this fact and must learn it. But this false deity is only concerned with the physical realities and at times such as these we are tested."

Ahead, Cinders Connolly turns his wide shoulders to me and stares. Stares without saying a thing, eventually turning back round slowly.

"This false messenger believes himself the one and the only. And although he is born o' wisdom, of a great mother, he does not even know her. Has never visited upon her and cannot prove even who she is. His own mother. . . . He is no more than an orphan with a divine sense o' himself. Exiled from the wisdom of his mother and from God. Arrogant, blinded by foolishness, he is a fashioner of ignorance. A creator, yes, but a creator only o' rules and morals and codes and schemes that cause us to remain attached to earthbound, material needs, enslaving us by his will. Enslaving us to our physical needs. Serving our people the lethal bev'rage that has for so long bound and imprisoned us—" A slight gasp comes across the flock. "And for which the state o' New Yark has just this very week endorsed a prohibition upon the production, transportation, and sale of. In one year from now, dens of alcohol will be drained and boarded up.

"And now I say, you have, all o' ye in the house o' God now, ye have the ability to ascend from this materialistic, sensate slavery. Ye may be liberated, if ye so choose. Spiritual freedom awaits ye for when ye pass, as this child has today, yer divine spark is sent up and if ye have not overcome the ignorance from which ye're born, and have not transcended from ignorance, which sin is the consequence, yer soul not accepted into the Kingdom of Heaven summoned by the last trumpet, it may be sent back to the pangs o' slavery in the physical world again, or worse."

Father Larkin above us on the altar walks in his black gown and headdress gently, intently.

"My children, the word o' God, it must be remembered, can only be taught by His apostles and t'rough the sacraments. I ask ye, all o' ye now, to look round. Shed light on he who seeks to hide in darkess and those archons that follow him, for they are not angels. Bring him to the open so that we may see him. See him for who he is and what he does. So that we know that he is a false creator, intent on enslavin' us in our born ignorance. Bring him to the fore so that we may use our common sense. With the faculty of our minds it is necessary to understand what is true and what is real. Expose him to the light, he who has no awareness o' the spirit o' God. No understandin' o' the world beyond matter and mind. It is he. He and his followers that seek to exile all of us in the pangs o' slavery, ad infinitum . . ."

After the ceremony Sadie is silent in thought, clutching her son's little hand and splashing kisses on his fleshy cheeks. The homily having swayed her, she crosses herself and ignores me entirely. Even refusing to allow me to let her and L'il Dinny walk ahead of me. When she finally does look up, she is gritting her teeth at me.

Dipping fingers in the font and crossing ourselves, she walks ahead of me in anger. As the double-doors open we are touched by the raw air and the slate grays and brickwork reds of late January in Brooklyn. And at the bottom of the steps of St. Ann's, The Swede, Vincent Maher, Mickey Kane, and others stand in a natural sodality behind Dinny as if they live for the weather, steely-eyed and happy. He looks up at Sadie and sees her face laundered with concern and doubt, then to the child. As mother and son descend,

Dinny reaches up for the hand of the boy but Sadie pushes it away furiously. "Don't touch 'em."

Watching her as she splits and parts the band of men, the child led by the hand toward the trolley stop a block away, Dinny sends two men to escort her home.

"Dada?" L'il Dinny calls out.

"What's the deal wit' her?" Mickey asks.

The Swede answers for Dinny, "Larkin."

From behind me, Brosnan, Culkin, and Ferris shoulder past and jostle quickly down the steps like muscular messengers prompted and aroused by some inner need to defend the sacrosanctity of their beliefs.

"Word with ye, son," Brosnan stands over Dinny.

"Son?" he answers.

Myself and the rest of us surround the tunics in their Sunday civvies to hear what is said.

"Silk truck went missin' last night, Dinny," Brosnan grits. "Ye band o' t'ieves know anyt'in' about it, do ye?"

"Who's Dinny?" a man yells behind me.

"Don' say that word again," Maher says to Brosnan.

Brosnan then grabs Dinny, throws him to the ground. Dinny does not try and defend himself. Does not even try to catch his balance and allows himself to fall, looks up to the middle-aged, red-faced man.

"Dinny Meehan!" Brosnan says with a screaming and a pointing. "The man right here, on the ground. Ain' no more'n a culchie an' a highwayman. A rogue of low degree by all accounts. Hillside men from a blighted breed o' diddicoys on top of it."

The Swede stands between Dinny and his aggressor, looks down to Brosnan. "We told ya, but ya looked away."

"We didn't know nothin'," Brosnan declares.

"Liar," The Swede mumbles.

"I'm off the wagon, Jimmy," Brosnan grumbles, his hair gray on the sides and jowls loosening in his age. "Ye've no hold on me'r us."

"Then we'll bring ye down," The Swede says as Dinny comes to his feet.

"G'on with it then. We'll have nothin' to do with yer likes no more. Go ahead and try and bring us down, ye feckin' bunch o' pikey shites. I got the right kinda men behind me now—yez all are the wrong kind," Brosnan says, wiping us away with the back of his hand. "I challenge ye, all o' ye."

Culkin suddenly pushes Mickey Kane by the face and neck, Ferris holds Vincent by the shoulder and a large crowd has gathered in a circle round the lot of us in front of St. Ann's.

"No, ye won't!" screeches Mrs. Lonergan pushing through the crowd. "Ye won't be settlin' a damned thing at me child's service, ye won't. Get on, then. Get on. Outta here. All o' ye."

"Get out!" Anna yells, again with her beautiful and angry face and her mother's child on her hip, screaming at the height of her lungs. "Damn you. Damn all o' you. I hate you, Dinny Meehan. I hate you. I hate you!"

As Richie limps through, a confused and emotionless look on his face and two of his followers behind him, a man yells out, "Shaddup, girl."

"You shaddup," Anna yelps and pushes through the crowd as her mother picks up a broken paver and heaves it toward the voice.

"Go 'way," Mrs. Lonergan continues. "Go 'way. Out. Out. Out!"

Heeding her, all the men turn slowly round, dour-faced and shamed and pulling their hats over their heads. Apologetic even, some are.

We meet back at 25 Bridge Street a few blocks away for a crisp, noontime drink and some talk. Eventually Richie Lonergan shows with all of his teenage devotees in tow. Sitting at a table along the wall they are glum and surly and I can see by the look on Petey's face when he looks at me that they are talking about us. Talking about how they hate us. Grumbling amongst themselves like ungrateful mucks. It angers me, watching them complain to each other about us, but I was looking for something to justify my anger. Something to justify my flying off the handle.

I look back at Petey with Tommy Tuohey on my thoughts. And I think of how much bigger I am than Petey now and all the time Tommy spent teaching me to fight. To fight Petey after I'd been beaten. To fight Petey, that's what Tommy taught me to do. And so I look at him again, little Petey Behan and his supposed tough self. Stare at him, do I. None too concerned this time about another challenge, me and him.

"Whatcha lookin' at?" he says.

"I'm lookin' at you and I don't like the look on yer face."

"So come take it off."

"Hey," Cinders yells toward me.

"I'll feckin' take ye down, I will," I say to him, throwing my drink to the ground and standing up.

"Today ain' the day for this," Beat scolds.

Red Donnelly picks me up over his head by my hips as everyone in the bar quickly stands, Cinders and Dance and Dago Tom and Philip Large and others between me and Petey, so quickly that neither of us have time to fight.

"Where ya goin', Poe?" Petey says, jumping up to everyone's shoulders so he can see me. "Poe. Nice fookin' name, Poe. Ya fookin' idiot."

"We're not done, ye'n I," I yell.

"Anytime."

In Donnelly's arms, he and Henry Browne walk me right out the front door, "Where the hell did that come from?"

"Came from Tommy," I say pacing.

"Tommy'n the drink too, eh?" Red says. "Go'n go for a walk, William. Walk it off."

"I'm not feckin' round with people no more," I yell.

"I know, I know," Red says.

"Feckin' tired o' this place. Fuck you," I yell up toward the Manhattan Bridge, which muffles my screaming with a passing train, *cha-chum, cha-chum, cha-chum*, rumbling and rumbling and shaking everything, then I whisper to myself, whimpering angrily. "Damnit. . . . Goddamnit."

"Walk it off, guy."

And so I do. I walk away. Walk and walk for hours at a time in the unsettled air, wind and bright breeze on my face. The cold. Always the cold and the wind. Always. I find my way to other drinking holes, and drink. And drink and sleep overnight on a bench in a saloon by Atlantic Avenue and Harry's place. Then wake up and do it again, hardly understanding what I am so angry about in the first place. Just angry. Deeply angry. And confused. For so long I'd worked to bring my mother and sisters here and now I feel I don't deserve them. That the things I've been a part of are horrible things. Shameful things and the dirt of death defiling and covering me. Hovering over me everywhere I go. That I grew up a good Roman Catholic and was taught what is right and what is wrong and still I was a part of murder, looked the other way in the deaths of others too.

I am ready to punish myself or anyone that crosses me. I spend all the cash I have on me and drink on credit, food foreign to me. I bite at the coarse liquid that chars my throat and fires my soul. Sitting still I am reeling and dizzy and stung with great barbs of rage, and I hope that any man round me has an ill word so to excuse my fraying with him. When uncle Joseph's face pulls up in my mind I close my eyes tight at the grisly and grim ways of the world. My own family, was he. The picture of his bony hips and bald spot haunting me. His bloodshot eyes and his drunken laugh. Mostly though, I remember the moment I looked back at him after I pushed a knife through the back of his neck, sticking him to the bar. Looking back to see him pull the chair quietly under him to wait out the last seconds of his life. How scared he must have been to die.

How horrified he must have been when we set the saloon alight with him still alive in it. God how he must have suffered. And all because of me. Me.

* * *

NIGHT AND FRIGID DARKNESS PIERCED BY the break of day and a floating afternoon all mix together and still I am run through with anger and madness and guilt and visions. I dream of holding Emma McGowan. Between death and living, sleep and wakefulness I can't tell. Can't see where I am. Drinks going down. Drinks coming up. A cement pillow, I dream. Of kissing her before she slips into unconsciousness. And I take her away for the gentle summer rain. The warmth of a humid rain on our northern bodies. And the flashing chance at the bliss of her trusting me, the kiss of her mouth. Trusting me so instinctively that she is ready to give herself entirely. I can see it in her and there is really nothing more beautiful in this life than what's in Emma's eyes. Her lips are round and they are soft on mine and she offers me her skin and there is no poetry better than this. Her love. Her body a treasure. Pressed against me, hip to hip. And as I make love to her I look and notice she is not there, and all that I hold in my hands, and that which had been close against my body was only the memory of her. My hands empty, filled only with imaginations.

"Wake up, asshole," a man says to me.

I smile, grab him by the throat and pull him to the ground by the coat. Punching and punching. Kneeing him in the face. Never letting go of him. Never letting go.

"Break his fingers, for fuck's sake," another man says. "Get him out."

And then I am again in the wind, stumbling. Onlookers staring at me. Gawking. Skirting out of my way.

"A drink," I tell another tender.

He sets me up and soon enough I am on the ground again. Death all round my mind. Faces and galleries and zoo bars in my memory and missing fathers and insane mothers and wayward children and Dinny Meehan haunting me and the butcher's apron flying above Ireland. My mother and sisters screaming as British soldiers kick in their door, licking their lips.

"William?" I hear Harry Reynolds's voice.

"Wha?" I say, sleeping on the ground of some saloon.

"C'mon, tomorrow's a big day."

"No."

"C'mon, tomorrow's Sunday."

"Today is Sunday."

"No it's not, tomorrow is."

"The Lonergan funeral."

"That was a week ago. The big day's tomorrow. Sunday. Tomorrow. Let's get ya ready."

I just cry. So angry, I cry. Confused. Undeserving as I am. Shaking my head and covering my face on the floor and bleating and blubbering and acting the fool. Harry yanks me up by the coat.

"Why did I survive and she didn't?" I ask.

"Ya didn' really know her all the way," Harry says coldly. "Think of it that way. Ya mother'n sisters, though—ya know them all the way. Drink this water and get some sleep."

"Does Dinny make people stay here? In Brooklyn?"

"Why do you say that?" Harry asks, quickly looking toward me.

"That's what Mrs. McGowan told me."

Harry turns his jaw, looks away.

I lie down, the engine in his room again put back together, the trunk of wood now in the perfect shape of a proper hobbyhorse for a young boy. With two wood-crafted curved runners for rocking back and forth, it looks as good a quality as any I'd ever seen. It's even been lacquered in different shades with little leather reins to hold onto and the face of the horse is in the shape of a smile.

I bathe in a wood-slat tub in the parlor. Sponge off.

Shave. Cut my hair. Drink more water. Coffee. Eat a meal.

"Ready?" Harry asks.

"I think so," sitting on my cot with a bowl and spoon in my hands.

* * *

SUNDAY AND WE ARE AT THE Atlantic Avenue Terminal, which is empty. I follow him through the maze of dock sheds, pier houses, the hodgepodge of odd storage units, worn wharf planks and wobbling empty steamers anchored by hawsers wrapped tight round cleats and all connected somehow, some way, and blocking out the general public from the jungle of the waterfront world where we reside.

Waiting for us is a tug and a paid driver for a taxi ride across the shipping lanes. The wind and mist in our faces and the skyline to our north, we lean forward, our elbows on knees as the vessel's stern is deep in the water churning below and behind us. Pegged, the mechanical engine struggles. Gargling with all its might, yet we move at the slowest pace.

"Why is Brosnan breaking ties?"

"Dunno," Harry answers quickly.

"That Waterfront Assembly meeting they had the other day? Remember?"

"Yeah."

"I bet it came out of that Waterfront Assembly meeting, like he was told to get in step or get out of the way. And all that in the papers too, about unsolved crime and . . . murders."

Harry doesn't answer, but he nods, which means that although he does not want it to be true, it is.

"And Father Larkin too. They reigned him in too, I'll bet."

No answer.

It's been more than three years since I've seen Lady Liberty this close. It's a different statue altogether now than when I was an unplanned immigrant coming from a feudal, agrarian past among the grassy hills of County Clare, Ireland, back in October 1915. She seems damaged now. Run-through herself, and hurt, and as we pass her I see she is pockmarked and wounded. Although I know it's from the explosion on Black Tom's Island and the weather always beating on her, I feel like she has changed. She still stands, yes, but more astute and with a heavier heart. Wary, yet wise. Angry and aching.

I think now, in my old age, of this exact day I tell you of now. Sitting upright, wiping away my old man's tears. The old memories that remain. Romanticized surely, but there they are. Seeing the statue on the island up close. Then Ellis Island again for the first time since 1915. Harry's profile and stern kindness. The mist in the air. All these memories. Always there.

The mother. Too many teenagers pull away from their mother, but I was the opposite. I missed her so much. Missed my family. And so a new family had adopted me in the interim. A family of men had brought me in and gave me a place in life. A wage to earn. A roof and food. But I think of my mother and her love for me. I think of her. And I think of how sad it made me to see my mother and sisters again after so long a wait. How different they were, also wary and wounded.

Their dresses are gray and long and handwashed too often and fraying. I am struck by how small the three seem. Ireland's diet during the war not much accommodating the physical growth in people, their clothes hang about them drably and they have that unplanned look about their eyes, staring at skyscrapers to the north and the sea air new to their noses—so many thousands of miles away from the only place they've ever known, and at the end of it, they are bitten by the ancient Atlantic crossing that our people have known so well. Tired and bedraggled, they look malnourished, pale and with windswept manes, but with flinty-faced pride holding high in them still.

My God how I remember how they looked when first I see them again after close on four years. I can't write at this moment and instead walk away for a tissue, my hands shaking like a helpless old fool. It took me this long to write this story, and now I know why. It's so close to the bone of me. These memories that I rush out here for you to breathe in. I sit back down and sigh deeply, try again to finish.

It isn't so much what my mother says, but rather her facial features and gestures and glances that catch me by surprise. Remind me for the first time in so long of my childhood growing up on the rainy farm out in the middle of the Irish countryside. And they have the smell of turf fires on them and soup and Ireland altogether. The smell of memory.

"Jesus, Mary and Joseph and Bernadette and John and . . ." my mother's voice summons every honored saint the church has, and there are a lot. "My bhoy. My bhoy, William James. We did it. We did it. We did."

"We did," I say, my face filled again with tears.

Abby and Brigid holding their hands over their mouths around us, hoping for some kind of welcome, but unsure if I am willing to touch them. Feeling as though the time is appropriate for such a thing, I open my arms to them and they jump into us. Harry leans against a wall watching us closely, tugging on his nose with a nervousness that I don't recognize from him. But he watches us and in trying to discourage any emotion, he crosses his legs and arms and looks down the long hall filled with others greeting their own people for the first time in many a year, employees walking by without notice, selfish in their New York City faces. I hold close to my family, mother on my chest, a sister on each arm until we begin coming into the recognition that we should get moving to the moment's concerns.

Gathering herself, my mother peers up at me, "Look at the size o' this one, won't ye? And with muscles abound, bhoy. Ye been werkin' hard, haven't ye?"

"This is Harry Reynolds, Mam," I say, waving him over. "I work with him a lot. He's a good man. Helped me out quite a bit."

Wiping tears from her eyes, she greets him and cordially he receives Abby and Brigid too as my mother offers an apology, "I'm so sorry for all o' this, Mr. Reynolds . . ."

"No worries," he smiles, which reminds of what my mother said to me before I left, so I repeat it now to her.

"Not to werry, Mam."

"Ya're in good hands wit' William," Harry assures.

"You're home now," I say as Harry and I pick up their tattered bags and rags. "Let's get moving—we still have to take a boat and a couple trolleys."

"Ye know, William, ye're bigger than ye're own big brother, ye know it? Ye are too," she says as we move toward the landings. "Ye were such a humble bhoy, ye were. So good, too. Sweet apple-cheeked little William followin' his da round the place, never once givin' me the lip. Ye should know, Mr. Reynolds, the bhoy was as gentle as the River Shannon is shy. I couldn't know how he's seen here in New Yark, but the bhoy was a pleasure round the home."

"We like'm here too," Harry smiles at my mother.

From the island, we get back on the tug and allow the women to ride inside the pilothouse with the driver while Harry and I ride in the back with the wind and the mist. I don't know why I think it remarkable, but Harry's facial features haven't changed at all. I suppose my surprise is only due to the big excitement I have with my mother and two sisters' arrival and everything else, but there is a safety I feel in Harry Reynolds's subdued strength. A safety that influences my behavior in front of my mother and sisters, even.

When we land back on Atlantic Avenue in Brooklyn, all three are helped off the tug onto the wharf. We walk back through the maze and while doing so, I think about how odd it is to escort my family through an area where I'd seen so many fist fights, men beaten, bludgeoned, and even killed. At the trolley station on the corner of Columbia Street and Atlantic Avenue, we wait with our bags on the ground in front of us. Reticently I look across the street at the saloon I spent a week inside, drinking my insides out.

The girls have never ridden a trolley before and are almost as enamored by the street train as they were the tugboat. Down the tracks, we change to the Flatbush trolley and afterward continue on down the Prospect Park West line and finally get off at Ninth Street. From there we walk the three blocks to 518 Eighth Avenue. Standing in front of the thin brownstone building built back in 1893, my mother looks up, then looks over at me.

"We're on the third floor," I say, knowing just how strange the stacked city tenement homes look to her.

We walk up the stairwell and eventually make it to the front door. I reach across everyone and unlock it, open it for my mother and sisters to enter.

"Oh my," my mother quickly says.

The new lace curtains are open for the natural light to come through the kitchen window, and a small folding table is flush against the wall with four chairs under it, a rocking chair to the side and a round rug in the center where the hole used to be. The floors are sanded and smell a bit of lacquer, the walls of fresh paint and new cabinets filled with glass dishes and one set of china, a new teapot on top of the Quincy oven. In the women's room there are three beds with metal headboards and footboards and bedskirts with new sheets and shams for the pillows and rugs under each one with small nightstands to the side. A closet we built with little running doors on them is opened, showing three Sunday dresses, and three hats, three pairs of new shoes, and two small dressers against opposing walls await their filling, a low window with lace curtains splayed open, showing the fire escape attached to the building and a view of Prospect Park a block away where the treetops can be seen swaying in the breeze over the building across the street.

"One day maybe we'll get something bigger, Ma," I say. "I know it's small, but . . ."

"No, no, no, no," she whispers, choking back her tears while sitting at the kitchen table alone, next to her rags and bags from Ireland.

"What's wrong, Mam?" Brigid asks, kneeling down.

My mother sits at the little table and buries her face in her hands as she weeps. She gasps and takes a deep breath as her face is swelling with redness and tears and exhaustion.

"Where will you sleep, William?"

"In there," I point to the door to the right where Harry and I built a room only big enough for a small bed and a small nightstand to its side.

Without even looking at it, she holds both hands over her face again, ashamed that she is crying.

"What ails ye, Mam?" Abby asks gently.

Catching herself finally, she manages, "I can tell ye two clean't the place spotless before we arrived here today."

"Yeah, we cleaned it up." I look at Harry with a smile.

"That means more than anyt'ing else in the werld to me, William. Anyt'ing."

We spend the late afternoon and dusk unpacking in the orange, swaying candlelight even as there are gaslights available.

"Would ye like me to wet ye a sup o' s'more tae, Harry?" my mother asks.

"Thank you."

We heat up some stew and open the table in the middle of the kitchen. Harry and I smile at each other as we are all sitting exactly over the hole that once reached down through the second floor. Without a fifth seat for Harry, he uses a nightstand to sit on. Abby smiles with Brigid while looking at him, and when my mother notices, she pokes the girls in the thighs. Sitting taller than the rest of us, Harry either does not notice them or ignores it all out of respect for their youthful age and his being a guest.

"Do you two work on the docks?" Mam asks.

"We do," I say.

"Must pay very well," she smiles. "This home is grand."
Harry and I look at each other again and with half-lies I
say, "In America, hard work pays."

Harry looks away, shame-faced.

A knock at the door echoes in the kitchen.

"Is someone here?" Mam asks quizzically.

Harry walks over to it, reaches across his waist for the
handle to his shiv as my sisters and mother watch him
closely. A second knock comes that scares them all.

"Who is it?" Harry asks.

"Burke. Is that you, Harry? Listen we have big . . ."

Harry opens the door quickly and lets himself out.

"What is all this about?" my mother asks.

"It's the man downstairs, he has a family. Very nice
people, I'll introduce you to them, but for now, I have to go
and see what is happening, all right?"

Instead of answering, she watches me closely as I
step outside.

Burke has the look of death on him while Harry has
already left. "Dinny and The Swede and Lumpy and
Vincent all have been arrested. They found a bunch of
shoes in the basement of Lumpy's brother's restaurant.
Hanan shoes, remember? Harry went to get Dead Reilly."

"Oh shit," I say, then look up. "Time for Mickey Kane to
step up. Us too."

CHAPTER 27

Everyone Knows

HARBOR TRAFFIC HAS DIED OFF A bit since the ending of the war. Contracts voided, bought out. No new ones needed. Still the wind rings up, yet there are not as many ships coming in. Not as many needed going out. The long-shoremen that load and unload goods are less in demand, but the jobs left are highly sought after. Money tightens up, for there is not as much in circulation. Still though, we own the rights to those jobs and the bites of money that come in, The White Hand.

Gathered outside the Dock Loaders' Club and at every terminal are angered labormen that are wanting for work, desperate for it. They line up and grumble when not picked. Cast slurs. Some pleading mothers come too, their hands holding the hands of children. Facing starvation and already malnourished, they brave the winter weather at the waterfront, keening for help to those that own sway. They don't give a care that our leaders are locked up. The Swede, Vincent Maher, and Lumpy Gilchrist. Least of their worries is that Dinny Meehan is not here. He who always knows what to do. The January cold is here, though. But the wind and the cold and the lack of work are no enemies to challenge, beat back.

The gusts are in my face. Make me blink. This is my day. My day on the docks. The day I become myself. Larger than myself. Bigger than how others have seen me. I stand up to the wind and the banshee screeching of the Manhattan Bridge above me.

I look across the icy East River toward Manhattan a block from the Dock Loaders' Club in front of the freight house of the marine-rail terminal at Jay Street. A float bridge is being pulled by a tug from the Lower East Side to us along the waterway. I can see it coming slowly. The first of six. We are to connect the train cars onto a locomotive that will take the thousands of bags of raw sugar to the Arbuckle Refinery at 10 Jay Street and unload them. This morning's work, though, Cinders Connolly is back at Bridge Street filling in for Dinny upstairs at his desk. I in Cinders's place here. Mickey Kane too, holding down the fort above the Dock Loaders' Club. Learning as they go, the two of them.

"You ready?" Burke says to me as a flag is shimmied up a dock shed by the super. A pier house whistle rips open the morning air and everything begins to stir. The metal stevedore's table is carried out and three men sit behind it, their backs to the water. A chain of train cars are slowly pulled from the walkway by a locomotive. Philip Large is licking his lips and holding a fist, and coming up from the Baltic Street Terminal I can see Big Dick Morissey here to help me like a good man. Many others begin strolling out of the Dock Loaders' Club down Bridge Street, and to the east, others saunter and amble half-asleep from row houses and framers in Irishtown.

"Liam," I hear, yet no one has called me by that name in well over a year. "Liam."

I see a man crutching down the ugly cobbles of Marshall Street from Hudson Avenue in the middle of the road. He has one leg, a shaved head, and is thin by all means of men.

"Liam, it's me. I heard ya takin' over the Jay Street Terminal 'til Dinny an' them get out," the man says, ably crutching at a quick speed and talking at the same time.

My first inclination is to ask who the man is. His shorn head has long, healed scars across it, and though he is younger than thirty, his jowl and throat are drooping with extra skin and his eyes are circled with a black that shows his lack of sleep or fair rest.

"Happy Maloney?" Big Dick says.

"Yeah, it's me. I'm back. Gee, ya sure are taller than I remember, Liam."

Big Dick and Philip and myself look down to his leg, though Burke has never met the man before.

"Got shot'n it infected so they cut it off. Listen, can I work wit' ya t'day? I ain't eaten since two days now and I knew ya guys'd help me so . . ."

"Ya heard about Johnny Mullen?" Big Dick asks.

"Eh, what about 'em?"

"Died."

"Oh, that's too bad. Him and I was good friends back when, but we got split up over there."

"Ya learn how to shoot a gun, did ya?" Big Dick says.

"Yeah, I did learn how to . . ."

"Take this then," Big Dick pulls out his revolver. "Sit right there on that cleat and hold that piece in ya hand. Look nasty too. If the tunics come, throw it in the river."

"Right," he says walking toward the water with the Manhattan Bridge above us.

"We'll get ya some breakfast here in a minute," Big Dick says, then turns to me as men are slowly gathering. "You're on, kid."

We shake hands. Behind us in a horseshoe shape are gathered more hungry men looking for work. Sixty, seventy day laborers, drunkards, and immigrants most of them.

I wipe a hand across my mouth and chin, gather my strength. Stomach turning. Burning. Nervous. Then turn round and yell from the belly, "We got six train cars t'unload s'marnin' and if there's a man among yez, I yet can't see'm. So in a circumstance such as this, we'll be happy to wait fer the man's willin' to werk like his name says he should, fer we don' need no feckin' navvies and we don' need no feckin' spalpeens loafin' their way t'rough the livelong day, so we'll wait then. And we will."

I cross my arms, Philip Large at my right, Big Dick Morissey to my left, and Thomas Burke supporting them with Happy Maloney scowling on the dock's cleat, pistol on his knee.

"I wanna work wit' ya, Mr. . . ."

"Kelly, as ye know me by," I say. "Patrick Kelly. Who else is interested in werkin' then?"

I see some hands spring up and move forward from the circle. I pick them and tell them to stand to the side and eventually all the men raise their hands and I now have their attention. But I hear a whisper. One head tilts toward the ear of another with arms crossed. And as we all know too well, there's more to hear in a whisper than a scream.

I tap on Big Dick and Philip's shoulders and as the whisperer passes in front of me, I grab ahold of the back of his coat and fling him to the ground. Burke grabs one of his feet, Happy stands up with the pistol, and Big Dick is smiling as he kicks at the back of the man's head.

"Ye got werds do ye?" I yell, as everyone turns round to see what is passing.

"Let the man go," one laborer yells out and before he can finish his sentence, Philip Large grabs him from behind. The man's hands are stuck at his side and there is nothing in the world that can loosen Philip's grip now that his hooks are sunk in.

"Hold him up," I say, as Burke and Big Dick and Happy and the stevedoring men and the gang of bedraggled laborers watch carefully.

"Don't, don't . . ." the man cries, his face uncovered and scared.

Barge horns bleating on the river, freight elevators chuffing, trains worming by in their maniacal metal

churning on the bridge above with the dank brine of waterfront in the mouth, the Manhattan skyline leaning over us
across. I wind my fist tight and strong, wrap it round my
head and grit my teeth as it thwaps on the man's face, then
with a left and then another right and an elbow to the brow
until Philip leaves the man for the cement to have, the stevedoring company men talking amongst themselves.

"Forty-five men we need. Which forty-five wanna werk?
Stand tall then. And at his attention along dis line where I
p'int here," I demand, Big Dick shoving men by their backs
and shoulders to it, Philip moaning and clapping his paws
together, and Happy is laughing and smiling as I point
toward the bridges. "West on John Street. Left on Adams.
Touch the Waring Envelope building and come back. First
ten's guaranteed a spot. Go."

"Don't trip on the tracks, fookin' fool," Big Dick yells at
a man who goes face down.

And the men run with all they have, pushing each other
out of the way in a dead sprint. All we can see is the backs
of their skinny hides chugging and competing against each
other for the right to work.

"Look at 'em go," Beat McGarry appears. "Just like the
good ol' days too."

I begin walking away toward the train car floats when
Beat hollers toward me, "Ol' Gas Drip Bard's talkin'
tomorrow night, Poe. Bring the fam'ly on over to the tavern
house on Hudson Avenue by the water and you'll get to
meet 'em."

"No time for that bunk," I yell back.

"Bunk he says."

With one foot on the dock and the other on a car float,
I help connect them to the Baldwin locomotive at the end
of the cement and wave toward the driver, who guides it off
the float bridge into the rail yard and then onto the cobbles and the neighborhood toward 10 Jay Street. Watching
them move from the float to land, I look across the East River

as the fog breaks. Look closer again, and I see a sign over a Lower East Side pier that says DAILY FERRY TO ALBANY: $2.

"Well anyhow," Beat continues. "The ol' man was lookin' forward to meetin' ya. Maybe another time."

* * *

WHEN THE JOB IS DONE, BIG Dick, Philip, Burke, Happy, and I report back to 25 Bridge Street where Mickey Kane is in charge, Cinders Connolly at his side divvying the day's small profits, Chisel MaGuire in Lumpy's seat.

"Problems?" Kane asks Philip and I from Dinny's desk.

Mickey is nervous. Before I can even answer, he is looking out the windows behind him at the men gathered in the alley. A toll is taken on him for not having slept for days since his cousin's arrest. Overseeing business at the Dock Loaders' Club day and night.

As Mickey's back is turned, I look up to Cinders. Downstairs there is a scuffle, loud voices, and before any of us can comment, Mickey gets up and leaves the room to check on it.

"Don' worry about him," Cinders says, walking past me to close the door Mickey left open. "He'll be all right. Tell me how things went today."

I shrug and look at Philip. "We can't do this forever. We're vulnerable here. Philip and Big Dick and the other guys that helped me were great, but they can't stick with me on the Jay Street Terminal forever. We need more men. Every day there's Polish, Russian, Germans, Finns looking for work and don't care who we are. They're ready to take us on. I have my family here now. They need me. I can't turn up dead or arrested, Cinders. When is Dinny getting out? And The Swede and Vincent and Lumpy?"

"Doesn't look good, but we been here before. Been t'rough this," Cinders says sitting on the desk in front of Philip and I. "Dead Reilly'll figure it out. The worst of it is, eh . . . the papers'r callin' him the leader now, Dinny. So now everyone knows. An' Brosnan's talkin'. Ya know ever since they did those stories on all the crime and murders in Brooklyn that go unpunished, that fookin' Brosnan's opened up. Talkin' an' gabbin' about how he arrested Dinny back in 1904 an' sent 'em to Elmira. Arrested 'em again in 1912 wit' Vincent'n McGowan'n Pickles. He's recitin' the Pledge of Allegiance to the Flag in the newspapers so everyone knows he's on the right side. Won' even talk to us anymore. He even told a reporter that Dinny's boastin' about how they'll never be able to send 'em up to the penitentiary."

"Dinny would never say anything like that."

"That's what I says. An' you know it too, right? But the readers? They don' know nothin' 'bout nothin'. At the trial for killin' Christie Maroney back then, they said he was unable to speak, ya know? Like he was deaf an' dumb like. Like he wasn't even there in the head. O' course, that was Dinny's plan, since he don' want nobody knowin' he's the leader, but now they know. Everyone knows. An' these yokes on the Waterfront Assembly'n Wolcott, Jesus. Fookin' Wolcott again. He's talkin' 'bout Dinny too, how he was the leader in 1916 when we hit Red Hook, remember? Burnt down McAlpine's Saloon wit' people in it, killt I-talians left an' right and that we're in like Flynn wit' the ILA. . . . That he ordered Silverman killt in 1917. That Dead Reilly represents us. The newspapers? They're even quotin' Father Larkin from St. Ann's about Dinny. It's Dinny Meehan this, Dinny Meehan that. . . . An' then there's them dried-ups say he's a saloon owner shillin' whiskey. Jesus, man. Goes on an' on. Everyone knows who he is now."

I look outside at the laborers in the alley below the window, "Should I be, uh . . . if I get arrested . . ."

"Chisel?" Cinders interrupts me.

"Yeah?"

"Give us a minute, yeah?"

Chisel stands from Lumpy's desk and walks out, but Cinders does not speak until he hears footsteps down the stairwell.

"Listen," Cinders says with Philip still behind me. "Here's what I do. I took a wad o' money I been savin' an' put it in a bank. Added my wife on the account so if anythin' happens to me . . . ya know?"

"I understand."

"You should do the same. Add ya mother's name to it and tell her where to go if anythin' happens."

"I don't really want to . . ."

"Gonna have to, William. Otherwise what?" He comes off the desk and goes back around to Dinny's seat. "An' keep a few bucks in ya pocket just in case ya gotta lam it. Things'll get better though, don' worry."

"Do you really think so?"

"Yeah, listen. I'm gonna see the ol' man on Hudson Ave tomorrow night at the tavern house. The Bard feller. A little time away from it all, ya know?"

"You are?"

"Yeah, sure, wit' the kids an' the wife too. Ya comin'?"

"Don't think so."

"It'll be good for ya. An' I was hopin' to meet ya fam'ly, right? Ya ma, sisters'n . . . any word on ya father?"

"Just missing."

"Yeah, just missin', hmm. Ah, sorry to hear that but uh . . . Philip's goin' tonight too, right, Philip?"

Philip moans in agreement as I look at him.

"Listen," Cinders says again. "Until ya talk wit' ya mother about a bank account, I'll make sure anythin' happens to ya, she's taken care of, uhright?"

I look up at him from the seat, "Thanks."

"Don' thank me, just return the favor."

"All right, I'll do the same, if somethin' happens to you I will—"

"Good, good. I don' wanna hear any details o' that. We're on then, you'n I, right?"

"Right."

By seven o'clock it's dark and Harry Reynolds, Burke, and I are struggling up flights of stairs at the Eighth Avenue building. Burke stops on the second floor and goes inside his home, and as Harry and I keep going up, all I am thinking about is my bed.

"There they are," my mother says welcoming me and Harry with a smile.

"Anybody knock on the door today?" I ask.

"Not a soul," says she. "Here's yer tae, William. And yers too, Harry."

"It smells so good in here," Harry says.

"Well that's because I found the grocer there round the block and I've put together a meat pie."

"Did you . . ."

"O' course, Liam. I told him to grind the meat right in front o' me or I wouldn't be buying it, I did too," she says, proud of herself.

"Well that's good, but I don't know if it's a good idea to go wandering around the neighborhood, Mam."

"Well then, ye'll have to find somethin' to keep us busy then. There's nothin' round here to cut the boredom, William. Hour after hour. . . . And we don't even know a single person. Haven't even met the people downstairs yet, what did ye call 'em?"

"The Burkes?"

"Well I wouldn't know what their names are, would I?"

Sitting at the table, Harry and I are given plates of food, but before we can take the first bite, I hear footsteps coming to the third floor. Harry looks at me. There are two other tenants on our floor, but they don't go out at night. Then a knock comes that scares my mother.

"Jaysus on the cross," Mam yelps.

"I'll get it," I say, already at the door while Harry stands from the table.

I hear a whisper from Thomas Burke on the other side.

"Who is it?" Mam asks.

"The Burke man from downstairs. We'll be right back," I say, knowing that it must be something important. Harry and I slip out the door before my mother can invite him in.

The three of us walk halfway down the stairwell when Burke says, "Sadie's downstairs."

Harry stops in the stairwell. "I can't see her."

"She's cryin'," Burke says. "Someone went to her home and she's askin' for help."

"William, you're gonna have to help her," Harry says. "I can't."

"What?"

"Dinny doesn't want me around her, especially when he ain't here."

"Why?"

"Get her outta here for a while. Outta Brooklyn," Harry says turning around and going back upstairs. "I'll keep ya ma'n sisters busy."

"Wait," I say, but the door closes.

Burke leads me downstairs where Sadie is in tears at the bottom of the stairwell with a bag of clothes in one hand, L'il Dinny pulling at the other in his short pants and boots.

"William, we can't go to our 'ome," she says desperately.

"Why?"

"It's terrible. They're everywhere and I'm alone, William."

"What happened?"

"Anna Lonergan, that l'il spiteful thing and one of 'er bruvas, I fink 'is name's Willie. Well, they stood outside on Warren Street for like two 'ours and next fing I know, a rock comes through the window, glass everywhere. I have a child in the home, William."

"I know, all right, all right . . ."

"And 'at's not the worst of it, William. I saw me cousin outside too."

"Which one?"

"Darby. And 'e was yellin' fings up into the broken window. . . ."

"Just calm down, he just wants to get into your head. Don't let him do it, all right?"

"All right but . . ."

"Just don't let him get to you. Don't let him scare you. Do you have money?"

"A little."

I turn to Burke, "Can you help us?"

"Sure."

"My mam and sisters have only been here a few days, and I really don't want them to think things are uneasy here. Can you take Sadie to the Long Island Railroad for a place called Rockville Centre. In a hotel. A nice one," I turn to Sadie. "It's a nice little town, I hear. Very quiet. Out in the country. You can take a taxi from there down to Long Beach, Sadie. It's really beautiful, and it has a board-walk and no one will know you're there. As soon as you get there, write me a letter to this address, all right?"

"All right, William."

"Take this." I hand her my day's earnings as a dockboss.

"I can't, William. I 'ave me own money."

"I would be very unhappy if you do not take this, Sadie. I'm going to send Happy Maloney down there to watch over you."

"He's back?"

"Minus a leg but yes. I want you to be comfortable and to have food brought to your room and I want you to go shopping too."

"Shopping for what?"

"Clothes or whatever you'd like. You're going on vacation, Sadie. . . . Until Dinny gets out."

Sadie looks up into my eyes and smiles. She wipes a tear away and hugs me. Holds me. And so does L'il Dinny, hugging me by the leg. But Sadie holds me close, pulls my ear down to her and whispers, "I always knew yu'd be good. Yu're good, William. Now yu need to start makin' a plan for yu'self an' yu family to escape 'ere."

"What do you mean?"

But she just smiles solemnly, leaves with Burke.

On the second floor I knock on the Burkes' room and gather them, including the eldest boy who can barely walk.

"I asked your husband for a favor, Mrs. Burke," I explain. "I'm very sorry for not asking you about it first, but it was a bit of an emergency."

"Oh . . ."

"Come with me though," I say, and help her son up the stairs to the third floor, step by step. His arm over my shoulder, scared out of his wits of falling down the stairwell.

"Don't worry," I tell him. "Not to worry, everything will be fine. I have you. What's your name, anyhow?"

"Joseph," he mumbles, petrified.

"Is that right? I used to know someone named Joseph," I smile. "I bet you're a lot nicer than he was though. Does your mam call you Joey or Joe?"

"Just Joseph."

"Joseph it is then. Do you like meat pie, Joseph?"

"Yes."

"Good, good. I bet you eat as much as a horse," I say.

"He does," his mother says.

And opening the door on the third floor I yell, "Mam, we have visitors."

"We do?" she says, her face lighting up. Harry sits at the table with cards, entertaining Abby and Brigid, who stand from the table with bright eyes to greet the visitors in the gentle and humble manner in which the Irish welcome people to their home.

"Yay!" two of Mrs. Burke's toddlers run in, a fat-cheeked baby on her hip, smiling, that is immediately taken from her and showered with adulation and blessings as our tiny home is filled to overflowing with family and friends. And tea. And I know that this is the life for me. And, if only for a moment, I let the peace we feel among ourselves take me over.

"And after church tomorrow, we'll go and see a sha-nachie," I say aloud.

"Here? In America?" Mam asks.

"Yay!"

"With Joseph?" Mrs. Burke asks desperately.

"We wouldn't go without him."

And Joseph, with his contorted features and glazed eyes smiles a distant smile, but a smile all the same.

CHAPTER 28

Deliberation

"ArEN'T wE A hANDSOME bUNCH ALL dressed up in the veins o' nicety. Now that Father Larkin? Is he from Dublin?" Mam asks outside after a late Mass at St. Ann's.

"I believe he is."

She harrumphs at the idea. "I knew it by his tongue. He's a bit of a swaddler, I'd say, goin' on and on about the baby Jaysus'n all. He is Catholic, is he not?"

"He appears to be," I say, lifting Joseph Burke into the horse-pulled taxi next to his mother and siblings.

It is only a few blocks to the tavern, but for Joseph it's quite a distance. The most of us walk alongside the taxi and though I know my mother has many questions, she resolves to keep them to herself. For the time being. The scar over my left eye only mentioned in passing and the other day when she found plumbing pipe fitted into my coat, she simply handed it to me and turned round.

"Oh, what it must've cost, all of this," she said one morning in our room. And knowing my mother as I do, I could see she was not only referring to money. "The price we'll have to pay, hmm."

And although we talk and talk as we meander through the old neighborhood, there is a great and still silence between us. The longer she is here, the more she finds out, the louder the silence.

"These'll break yer ankles, won't they?" she says, speaking of the rough cobbles of the old town.

"Take my arm."

We are greeted merrily in the tavern, women and children allowed in on storytelling nights. Hanging our coats by the door, we are met by soft-spoken old-timers along the stretch of the bar who hat-tip us and smile, grab our hands in salutation, and it seems once again we are back in the old country. The smell of pipe smoke, stale beer, turf, and whiskey. There are no windows and the darkness is only broken by amber light. In a back room there is a grand hearth-fire and candles on the floor and on the odd table. Mealymouthed children whisper to each other and know to tiptoe, as there are mothers and fathers here that waste no time in clouting them on the top of their heads for a lesson.

An old man sits by the fire smiling like a thin, close-shaven Santa rocking back and forth. He is the center of all attention here and all around him are chairs for people to sit and listen to him speak. His hair silver with experience, eyes drooping with knowledge. He seems well into his eighties but his mind is about him tightly, I can see. All call him The Bard, or The Gas Drip Bard, for he worked some fifty years or more as a gas works employee.

"Well," he begins, and quickly everyone becomes silent for to hear his words. "I see we've a good wheen o' childers here, but the child what can't sit still won't get a candy."

He starts off with two tales for the children, the first an old-country yarn from Killarney called "Peg the Damsel." Then he crosses the Atlantic with us to Irishtown in Brooklyn with the comical, pre-Civil War story, "Buxom Biddy Hoolihan and the Drunkard Goat of Shinbone Alley."

The room is quickly taken with his stories and not a child in the house is without full attention on him. His voice pitching high when he needs to make a point. Low with the slight sarcasm of the indigenous Irish. Some say his way of storytelling is like a magician's act. A true art form built through tradition predating Jesus Himself. Others describe it as catching words like birds in their flight from Irish to English. Yet the Irish ways still lived in the themes and plots that leave out the righteousness of the Anglo-Saxon's method. But in clear-spoken English, his stories are told.

Later I sit on an old chair by the fire with a Burke toddler asleep at my chest, cozy and warm. Mam and Abby and Brigid dozing. Only Beat McGarry, Thomas Burke, Cinders Connolly, and a few other men still awake, children sprawled across laps fast at their slumbering.

The Bard slowly sits back in his rocker. And so, a pillow behind him, warm tea, and his rubbing his workingman's hands together, pushes back his long white brows, tilts the candle to redden his cuddy and leans forward to a place where myths still carry.

"There was a murder in Brooklyn one time, where there often was before and I s'pose there will be again," he began to my surprise. "Dinny Meehan and t'ree others shot an' killed the tout Christie Maroney to bring the men o' the Irish waterfront together as one band, for there was a time in Brooklyn when street kings were so plentiful ye could hardly t'row a stone without raising a lump on one o' their heads."

I look over to Beat, who is smiling, which lets me know the old man is allowed to speak Dinny's name when so many others are not.

He nods toward myself. "I see the newcomer here has missed the last few stories leadin' up to where we are now, but we'll keep movin' forward. Son, ye can come back to me some day for the others, that all right?"

"That'll be fine," I say.

"Well then, t'was 1913 and Dinny along with his childhood friend McGowan and a young Vincent Maher and Pickles Leighton had been detained by Patrolman Brosnan o' the Poplar Street Police Station, as it were. And doesn't it sound familiar to ye? Doesn't it? Dinny and his men detained? Well the timing couldn't be better, so off we go. Just like today, t'was the papers that had a great time of it with the sensation of the trial and in great big bold letters they wrote:

"Jury Ready in Gang Killing: Great Gathering, Riot Expected after Deliberation of Sensational Trial

Not Since 1873 During the Great Whiskey Wars of Irishtown have the Marines Last Been Summoned from the Navy Yard to Keep the Peace'

"Could ye believe it? The Marines again. For what the police were callin' 'the most dangerous and eagerly awaited trial in Brooklyn since the turnin' o' the cent'ry.'

"'All rise,' the bailiff announces. 'For the Honorable Judge Francis Denzinger of the Kings County Court.'

A plume surrounds the Bard as he pulls the pipe from his face and continues, "Our men, youthful as they were in 1913, stand to pay the price for what is termed their 'dark roguery.' Can ye see them now? Can ye? Dinny, McGowan, Vincent, and Pickles. Four gorsoons bitten at the wrist by manacles and for what? Takin' down Maroney that paid the police to let him alone to his druggin' and enslavin' o' the women o' our neighborhoods? Oh no. And don't ye know if Maroney didn't personally hand out invitations to the I-talian to come to Irishtown? He did too. And is it any wonder he was shot in the women's entrance—to his dismay no doubt—of a saloon, fer givin' information to the tunics at his own betterment? Is it? No, it isn't.

"Well, back to the great trial of 1913 then. . . . In the gallery of the court's front row, Harry Reynolds stands next to Sadie Leighton and her mother Rose. And a cousin too, Darby, right behind 'em as Dinny Meehan himself looks over blank-faced and cuffed. And full o' nerves Sadie smiles for 'em, her hands shakin', for although she is with

Harry, it's Dinny Meehan that makes her feel the eternal tingles o' love and melancholy. Dinny then looks at Harry, who stares back, placin' his arm round the girl they both were courtin' after.

"'Dinny!' Sadie sings out.

"'Quiet,' the bailiff demands.

"And the courtroom is filled with gamely patrons. Disfigured rowdies from wild childhoods, young and old. Associates o' the murdered Maroney, oh yes, and o' course t'was them that'd like nothin' more than to give a high-hangin' to the four accused Whitehanders, and on a windy day too. But mostly the crowd was filled with devotees o' this band o' youngsters led by Dinny Meehan, that in the broth o' their generation long to take back the streets o' Brooklyn from the Maroney-led loogin pimps and gold-toothed larrikins that profit from the port city's great transience o' libidinous sailors and lascivious merchant marines and the deluge of bawdy immigrants. It was this new brood o' Irish American ruffian that sought to renounce the graft Maroney's ilk applied to the body o' our lasses. To clear the way o' touts and their tunic masters. And to wall off the world once again along the waterfront where strangers don't dare set foot beyond where the pier sheds and the docks begin. The White Boys, as their like was once called in the hills and stretches o' rock-strewn fences o' Ireland. Silence their biggest weapon. The silence. In their silence they are here to bring us together again. As we were when the casket schooners and the coffin ships fell into the port o' New Yark back famine-way when our like first came to New York. These young men of The White Hand sought to overthrow Maroney and bring us together again in our old customs kept dear and secure in auld Irishtown for so long. Against the inva-sion o' the I-talian Black Hand that Maroney courted into our neighborhoods, himself the most egregious breed o' stoolie and informant. In Brooklyn this new generation was created by one lad. Their leader a lone man, young as he was then. A chieftain among men. Aquirin' gangs like an entrepreneur does comp'nies. Piecin' 'em together like, from the smithy o' his soul. A creator o' pride and remembrance, yes. And a spirit, is he. More than anythin', he is a spirit. Who inherited a silent past. Whose history is obscured in lies by victors. And in the shame o' victims. Dinny Meehan was his name. The spirit of the auld ways, is he."

And listening to the old man, I know that I will tell this story too. That I will not allow it to be gone like so many other things in New York. In Brooklyn. Gone and forgotten. That I'd save the words that this man caught like birds. And store them away to be used afterward when it came my turn to tell stories. Beat McGarry sees it on my face too, and it all comes together. But I'll not tell it the same way as The Bard, because for him the rising of The White Hand in Brooklyn is an age-old lore. For me it is a scar, having lived through my springtime years during its heyday under Dinny Meehan's reign.

But before I can consider retelling the stories, I must seek this old man for the stories I've missed. That lead up to the arrest of Dinny, McGowan, Vincent, and Pickles. The stories that reveal the deepest motivation of our leader and the egg of our ways. But for those stories we'll have to circle back another time.

I look to my sleeping sisters, Abby and Brigid. And my mother dozing, her folded hands resting in her lap. And I am pulled away from The Bard for a moment. My mind taken from the gangs toward my family. And I know that all I've done is for them. We'd all do the same, of course. Any of us. Because we are human. Because we love people. Especially our family. That we will do anything we can to help them. Everything we can. For their survival. For their happiness, and when they are suffering and in need, we are there for them. And we give a piece of ourselves for them. Give everything we have to make up for their suffering. Throw ourselves into the suffering in order to relieve theirs. And I love my mother. And I want to tell her, but can't. I want to her to know it, but can't say it. Instead, I show her. And so I've shown her that I am willing to do terrible things to relieve her suffering. But now I see her contented. A home, she has. Food, she has. A church, she has. Safety from war too, she now has. And with these come a time for reflection on where we are to go next, our family. And I must make time for my own deliberation on who I consider family. I look back at my sisters, Mrs. Burke and Joseph and, finally, to my mother again . . . and the words come rushing to my mind: the gentlelife.

And I notice that my mother is not asleep at all, in fact. She is feigning sleep. Listening to the Bard's story all along, and knowing.

The Bard continues, "Guardin' the doors and standin' round the rim o' the courtroom are men dressed in military uniforms armed with bayonet rifles and pistols and black-jacks. And outside the Adams Street Courthouse there are seven hundred residents awaitin' decision. And round them too are a core o' two hundred riot-ready marines. The stand has been made. The line drawn.

"Nicely situated above all else, Judge Denzinger sits back onto his throne and speaks, 'Full house, we have. Let me remind all of you here today that regardless of the outcome, we are to remain respectful citizens to the flag of the Unites States of America and anyone seen to act in a less-than-dignified manner today will be hit with the full force of the law.'

"The crowd giggles among itself, grumbles too.

"'Quiet,' the bailiff demands.

"'Jury, are you ready?' Judge Denzinger requests.

"Timid nods respond from the jurybox.

"'Dennis L. "Dinny" Meehan,' Judge Denzinger announces, then asks the bailiff. 'Wait, which one is Meehan? He's the deaf and dumb one, right?'

"'The state of New York has determined he is an idiot, your Honor.'

"'Idiot. That's right," Judge Denzinger remembers.

"'He is unable to speak, is all,' Dead Reilly stands, insists.

More giggles from the court gallery.

"'Well, get him to rise when I say his name,' Judge Denzinger admonishes.

"Dinny is looking elsewhere, off in his own world as if he weren't there at all. Playing along, Dead Reilly touches him on the shoulder and points for him to stand.

"'Vincent J. Maher,' Judge Denzinger announces.

"'Charles M. McGowan.'

"'John F. "Pickles" Leighton,' Judge Denzinger finishes, then whispers to the bailiff, 'The loudmouth.'

"'The leader, your Honor,' the bailiff reminds.

More giggles are hushed by soldiers and patrolmen.

"The judge scans the rake o' mugs fillin' the courtroom wall to wall, raises his voice again, 'These four men are charged with the murder of one Christopher Lawrence Maroney one year ago on the morning of March 13, 1912. Jury?'

"The jurybox looks over.

"'Who will preside?'

"'I have been chosen to deliver the verdict, your Honor,' stands a small man, who is known as a business owner in the Jewish section of Williamsburg.

"'What is the determination in the charge of murder against Dennis L. Meehan?'

"Swallowin', the small man looks at the piece o' paper, though he already knows the answer. He then looks over and sees the lion-faced Dinny Meehan. The presiding juror then looks to Dead Reilly, who nods in his direction. The room is held in the small man's hesitation. . . .

"'Not guilty, your Honor.'

"The crowd erupts and stands and jumps and hugs and howls, and from deep inside the court's bowels is born an Irish hero. The spirit o' the people spoken for by the forsakin' o' the law. Thus is how an Irish hero is always born, is it not? And so the gavel comes smashin' down, and Sadie

Leighton holds Harry Reynolds close, who stoically looks on.

"'He's our man,' a woman screams out.

"'He'll buck your courts for all time,' another voice yells.

"And Judge Denzinger rings out, 'What is the verdict for Maher?'

"'Not guilty.'

"Again the crowd jumps against the slappin' and the whappin' o' the wooden gavel down.

"'McGowan?'

"'Not guilty.'

"'Leighton?'

"The crowd, quieter now but still congratulatin' itself, waits as the presiding juror again looks over to Dinny and Dead Reilly.

"'Guilty, your Honor.'

"'What?' Sadie yells.

"'Oh my,' Rose Leighton gasps. 'My nephew.'

"'Whad he say? Pickles's brother Darby demands.

"Chaos havin' taken the court, Judge Denzinger calls to attention, 'I will remind the crowd of its behavior. We'll meet again in two weeks for sentencing, good day,'

The Bard sits at the end of his rocking chair excitedly and continues, "And although Dinny is proclaimed not guilty, a riot ensues in the courthouse, spillin' into Adams Street and washes through the walled-off tenements toward the old town, horses let loose to their sprintin', bartenders put out of their saloons, taps opened, and the auld home brew brought out for to celebrate. But Jacobs' Saloon at 50 Sands Street, on the corner, below the Crown Hotel, 'tween the great bridges where Maroney held sway over the Brooklyn rackets is stoned. Its windows shattered and fiery bottles o' gasoline thrown within. Burned to the ground as everyone watches in awe. Even over the rails o' the high abutments of the Brooklyn Bridge to the west, the Manhattan Bridge to the east where the fraternal twin giants are only separated by a few blocks at Sands Street. In their hundreds, the parade o' waterfront residents hold Dinny, McGowan, and Vincent up as heroes, luminaries, guardians even. Exponents o' the auld Irishtown way. Paladins o' the poor. Champions o' change that over the next few weeks expelled the I-talians. Tamed the tunics and tossed the touts and pimps in their bawdyhouses out and once again implemented the auld code and its sanctionin' o' silence . . ."

Satisfied with his yarn, the Bard tamps his pipe and sits back. Slowly strikes a match so that we can see the wrinkles on his face and the command his eyes still own in the firelight.

He finishes, "And so t'was . . . just as it's always been with our like. . . . We celebrate against our enemy together—the vanquishin' o' the law that's held us back. For there is one thing we all know deep in us. And we know it from our history . . . the history that lives in us and speaks to us. That no Irish leader can be taken down by the moral indignations o' law, English or American. No reward nor penalty can stifle his silent beliefs. No, the only t'ing that can take down our leader is, of course, our own. From within. And oh how the begrudgers love their work too."

CHAPTER 29

Tunic and a Big Man

A SNOW HAS BEGUN TO CAKE Brooklyn as the crackling, icy air dips below ten degrees now. A sign, again. Children are covered by fearful mothers. The aged too, tucked into beds for protection. Old shirts jammed along breezy windowsills. Cold, empty fireplaces with broken flues are smothered with anything available. Potbellied stoves, too, sitting idly and without coal fires in rooms. The old working-class, treeless streets and sidewalks with red-bricked and clapboard tenement buildings facing each other are emptied out, whitened by a purity that removes the sick and the weak from this place. This blight of weather forcing the survivors to fight against each other for dominance over the available resources like caged prisoners.

But some see the catastrophic elements on the poor in New York and Brooklyn as a great opportunity. An unintended social benefit of the invisible hand. A divine judgment on the defective aspects of the national character, as they see it. An act of Providence from an all-merciful God against those that are selfish and turbulent in temperament. Their strict adherence to the utility of noninterference as it pertains to governmental economic relief of those suffering is a symbol of their disdain for weakness and dependency. To help is just too closely associated with socialism and Bolshevism. Yet this great indifference is slightly adjusted here and there. Sending agents below, secretly.

Inland, off the waterfront where Atlantic Avenue crosses Flatbush, the harbor winds are not as dialed. Snow has not been cleared of the streets or sidewalks and evenly settles—only footprints making human passageways through the whitening of the ground. In the polar air, Daniel Culkin is wrapped in his tunic and out of jurisdiction, Amadeusz Wisniewski dressed like a mammoth-sized businessman. They are walking together. When the big man Wisniewski speaks, it is so deep and low that it's barely recognizable to the ear. His face blanketed in thick wrinkles and lumbering with bulky strides above, Culkin looks up to watch his fleshy lips moving.

"We not killing 'em," Wisniewski says, noticing Culkin check his patrolman-issue revolver openly in his gloved hands.

"He already knows who I am," Culkin says, his neck bent up as they cross Flatbush. "He's a mental case. Got no idear how he'll react to this."

"He don' know me, dough," Wisniewski growls. "Wolcott says . . ."

"I know what he says, I was there," Culkin cuts him short. "I been lookin' for this guy for mont's. It can't go wrong, but if it does, I'll kill 'em. Ya can't trust 'em. Fookin' certifiable, this guy."

"Ya can't trust 'em, then why we—"

"Just doin' a job's all," Culkin says. "Someone thinks it's right, I dunno."

They knock on the second-floor door and a small, handsome female in her early twenties opens it as far as the rusty chain allows. Her eyes are drunk-blazed and her ratty hair matted on one side, she huddles cold in the crack of the door. The chain partially obscuring her view, she looks up to the giant bending down to her.

"Maureen Egan," Wisniewski grumbles in his chest.

"How do you—"

Wisniewski palms the door and pushes it open, ripping the chain from the wall as she falls backward. Culkin walks through, revolver pointing toward her on the ground, then points it toward the dark hallway inside the room.

"Where's Garry fookin' Barry?" he demands.

"He's dead," she yelps.

"No he ain'," Culkin says. "Ya lyin', where is he? I know he's alive."

"Fookin' asshole," she screams, kicking up at him as he walks by.

"Jesus, man," Culkin says as Garry Barry appears with James Cleary behind, holding their arms high and stepping out of a doorless closet. "Ya face is fuckt, Barry."

Maureen Egan comes from behind Culkin with a knife and just as she is about to swing it, Wisniewski grabs her by the back of her red curly hair, yanks her backward and lifts her over his head with one arm, pushing her face into the ceiling. She swings the knife behind her rabidly, but Wisniewski uses his other hand to grab her by the wrist, snapping both the radius and ulna. The kitchen knife dropping helplessly to his feet. Then she is dropped to the floor too as Wisniewski steps on the knife.

Garry Barry's eyes are blank and shameless, murderous. Mouth slightly open, he holds his hands slack over his head, less than fearful of a gun pointed at his face. Unconcerned of pain, it is seen in his eyes that pain has been a bedfellow since childhood and with death all round, always there, it too is no source of concern or urgency. But now, his face has long surgical scars through the eyebrows where his sinuses were reconstructed. His nose having been opened up, then sewn back together crudely, leaving obvious stitch-scars from tear duct to upper lip.

Culkin speaks, "The man that ordered this done to you . . ."

"Is in jail," Barry nasally finishes the sentence.

"You ands me," the oddity of Wisniewski's barely intelligible Polish accent and baritone voice fills the room. "We go burn Meehan brownstone on Warren Street, you ands me do now."

"I ain' goin' nowheres," Barry mumbles.

Groaning, Wisniewski hands Barry a pregnant envelope, "Ya da new leada o' da Whitehant."

Barry looks up to the giant. The only thing he ever wanted—to be leader of the gang—and it's handed to him along with an envelope full of cash by a tunic and a big man.

"We go now," Wisniewski says.

CHAPTER 30

Vin

"VISITOR," THE SCREW CALLS OUT AS Vincent Maher stands from the cell bench.

"Sixto? Jack?" he says.

Then a third man walks behind Jack and Sixto Stabile.

"Don' say his name, please," Sixto asks kindly and with the accent of Anglo-American gentry. "It wouldn't be the smartest thing you've ever done. We like you, Vincent. Let's keep it a like-like relationship."

"Uhright."

Frankie Yale, the shortest of the three visitors, is wearing a large overcoat and many rings and shakes a pointer finger calmly at Vincent, "You . . . you part Italiano, are ya?"

Vincent comes closer to the bars to see the man he's only heard stories of. "I don' think so."

"Wid a name like Vincent?"

"No."

"So, Vin, ya eva been to Chicago?"

"No."

"Maybe ya should go sometime. I got friends there. In high places. They got lots o' bawdyhouses out there, ya know. Bawdyhouses need guys like ya. Right?"

"I was offered that job once already."

"Lemme ask ya a question, Vin," Yale says. "Ya know dey call me the Prince o' Pals, right?"

"I've heard it."

"I give you a pal's advice, yeah? All right. Here it is. Do ya rememba guy named Pickles Leighton?"

"I know 'bout him, yeah."

"Still up in the stir to dis very day. . . . How 'bouta guy named uh . . . Non Connors?"

"Yeah."

"Bill Lovett?"

"I know 'em."

Yale nods his head in agreement, "What dey all got in common? Dem?"

"You tell me."

"Not to be rude, he's your friend, Vincent," Sixto says with a polite smile.

"All t'ree got set up by Dinny Meehan, ain' dat right?" Yale says while looking down at his manicured fingers.

"I don' know no one by that name," Vincent says bowing his head.

Frankie Yale smiles and points his finger at Vincent again, then gently touches his forehead with it, "He ain' no secret no more. Ya know, someone's gonna have to fall fa dis here Hanan Shoes debacle. Ya know dat right? Well, word is it's you, Vin."

Vincent does not answer.

"One more name," Yale says, changing his stance and opening his long coat. "McGowan."

"What about 'em?"

Yale looks over his shoulder at the screw down the hall behind him, "Ya rememba how McGowan got killt? Eh? Back in 1915? Couple guards I heard, right?"

Vincent looks over at the screw, who can't hear them.

"I dunno," Yale says. "Bein' on the inside o' da ILA, ya know, maybe gives us opportunity. Ya rememba Paul Vaccarelli, right? He's a VP wit' the ILA."

"I know about 'em."

"He knows 'bout you too, Vin," Yale says folding his

ringed hands. "And he likes ya. Just like I do. And uh . . . gonna be a big strike comin' up. The longshoremen wanna raise. Can ya blame 'em? A lotta dime to be made in strike-breakin'. We're gonna need men. Lots o' men."

Vincent looks at him confusedly, "Ya gonna call a strike and break it too?"

Yale nods at Vincent's openly stating the obvious, makes a smirk on his mouth and lifts his eyebrows. "The dime, Vin. In America, it's all about the dime. Not blood no more. The dime's all. Don' matta how ya get it. Ya wanna future?"

CHAPTER 31

Treasurer, New York

SLICK BLACK HAIR, BIG LOOSE SUIT, the drooping and aggressive face of a Rottweiler, King Joe leans back in his rogue throne in the Chelsea Clubhouse on West Fourteenth Street in Manhattan, head of the ILA in the New York Harbor. A man brazenly walks into his office unannounced.

"Thos Carmody?" King Joe says startled, noticing the shrapnel wounds on the side of Carmody's face. "Ya made it back alive."

"That ain' my title," Carmody says coldly.

Puzzled, King Joe asks, "What ain' ya title?"

"Ya made it back alive."

"What?"

"My title's Treasurer, New York. Remember? Before the war?"

King Joe laughs, stands at his desk, and extends an arm for shaking. "I kinda like that. I'll getcha a nameplate says THOS CARMODY, YA MADE IT BACK ALIVE."

"Again."

"Yeah, THOS CARMODY, YA MADE IT BACK ALIVE, AGAIN."

"Nah," Thos says. "Just get me the one that says TREASURER."

King Joe nods. "We might do that. We'll have to look over ya resume."

"I got credentials, and a foothold on the Brooklyn docks ya gonna need before the ILA puts a stop to any loadin' or unloadin' o' ships in New York Harbor," Carmody says, his lip forever torn along the right side of his pockmarked face. There are tiny bald spots over his ears too where the cricket-ball grenade that exploded near him had sent small pieces of hot metal into his right arm, shoulder, face, and head, splicing open his lip.

"Is that right?"

"Guess who I saw'r in France?" Thos asks.

"Who?"

"Bill Lovett and his buddy, Non Connors."

"Yeah?"

"Yeah. We made pals, him an' I. He's got the right idears about a general strike. He'll be on our side. Not on the side o' wops like Vaccarelli and Yale down in Brooklyn—ya know what I mean?"

"The I-talian element in the ILA? I think maybe I do."

"T. V. O'Connor appointin' that Vaccarelli guy VP o' the ILA?"

"Dumb," King Joe agrees.

"Necessary at the time, maybe," Carmody says. "But when the day comes that Vaccarelli works wit' the shippin' companies and the Waterfront Assembly to provide strike-breakers, maybe that'll be the nail in O'Connor's coffin. Then the ILA'll need a new president."

"An' I t'ought ya was a T. V. O'Connor guy," King Joe says slyly.

"I was, 'til I wasn't."

"Never really understood why ya made a deal wit' Meehan when he was the one put a hit on ya."

"Times change an' so do the angles. Some people look to the past to see ahead. Never was a lackey for that way o' thinkin'. I look to the now," Thos says, staring forward at King Joe. "So does Bill Lovett."

Standing again from his desk with a big hollow grin, King Joe reaches forward for a handshake, "Treasurer? Welcome back, Thos."

"Thanks," Carmody says pulling out the bullet Tanner Smith gave to him back in April of 1916, then looks at King Joe before leaving. "Tanner Smith still around?"

"Yeah," King Joe says. "He came lookin' for ya once, 'bout a year ago."

"I'll be payin' him a visit, otherwise he'll be payin' me one."

CHAPTER 32

Cinched by Blood

THE REVERE SUGAR REFINERY LOOKS LIKE some metallurgic rendition of a Roman oculus dome but for the great mechanical arm protruding from the top, elbowing down toward the seawall and jetty below. On the dock jutting out even further into the Erie Basin is tied an empty ship ready to be loaded by some one hundred Italian longshoremen in the blustery, slanting snowfall. Been almost two years since they were invited by Dinny Meehan to cross the Gowanus Canal and have since taken over the south terminal of Red Hook.

With the Italian language muttering and laughing in the distance, Darby Leighton stands against a brick wall and watches them, snow gathering on his shoulders. A wandering introvert compelled to make his own way in a communal world, he stands out on the periphery, always. Looks out at them gathered along as if amassed for war on the Red Hook bulkhead, open-stance and proud. Short men and flabby-muscled, unlike the tall and wiry Irish that long ruled here, the Italian cannot work long hours in the elements. The snow here coming down too heavy and the angular wind biting bitter and stinging their southern ears. But they are willing to work for less. The stevedoring company and the ship's captain not complaining there. Italians roosting in the old territory of the incumbent Irish. And holding the same union card as any man in The White Hand.

"Dinny Meehan," Darby says, shaking his head, then leans and spits and turns round, goes back north. "Sold us outta south Red Hook."

* * *

"Richie?" Matty Martin whispers, with the cold Atlantic Basin and whitened Governor's Island behind. "Richie, Darby's out there wantin' to talk wit' ya."

From Commercial Wharf, Richie looks beyond Truck Row lined with tire tracks through a dirty snow, past the twin New York Dock Company buildings where a man is smoking a cigarette against a warehouse wall, hat over his eyes.

"I vill distlact Kane," Abe Harms says and walks toward the pier house.

With the waterfront wind at his back, Richie limps across a slushy Imlay Street east toward Van Brunt, and when he reaches Darby Leighton, they wordlessly walk around a corner, wide-legged due to the icy pavement.

"Bill's back," Darby says, a bilious and steamy smoke running quickly over his shoulder. "Connors too."

Richie does not answer.

Darby Leighton's face is weatherworn and his lips chapped and white. His eyes are black and sunken and has aged much more than the six years it's been since the trial of 1913, when his brother Pickles took the fall in the killing of Christie Maroney, and when Dinny took his cousin Sadie as bride, and finally when he, Darby Leighton, was banished from The White Hand forever.

"Ya heard anythin' about Dinny'n them gettin' released yet?" Darby asks.

"Nah."

"Come close to me," Darby says, opening his coat to a .45 tucked in his belt.

Richie comes closer, takes the gun as he looks over his shoulder and Darby's too.

"Gillen'n' Kane," Darby whispers.

"Ain't seen Gillen t'day. Prolly up wit'. . ."

"Then Kane."

The bright wind washes across Richie's face, illuminating his gray-blue eyes where under the left one is an open scar, blood dried from the arid air. The left of his sullied white collar is stained a browned red too from some unspoken affray of late. He sucks in his stomach to nudge the gun into his own belt and closes his coat.

"Bill wants to know who ya really are," Darby says, then walks toward the sound of ringing pulley chains from the grain elevators north of the basin, vaporous steam running again over his shoulder.

Richie ambles back through the slush to the piers. As he enters the dark pier house, he sees straight through the arched pier door across the water toward Manhattan. Abe Harms and Mickey Kane are talking with their backs to Richie in front of the doorway. The Statue of Liberty reaching over Governor's Island ahead. Richie's wooden leg pegs the pier floor at every other step as he approaches the door and the light. Harms and Kane look back, hands in pockets. Kane looks again out onto the water, his broad upper body and the clothes that cover his athletic frame ripple in the gusting flood of glacial air whipping toward him. Whips too into Richie's face as he looks to Harms, who nods in agreement at his approach. Richie slants the .45 up under the back of Kane's neck toward his skull.

"The fuck?" Kane says.

Bursting out of an open fissure in Mickey Kane's forehead and right eye are three spouts of blood, a large dollop of twirling brain and shattered bone matter, all lobbed and issuing into the churning Buttermilk Channel as

Kane's faceless body crumples to the flooring, flops out the pier house door. And with a flaccid plopping into the icy water, he is dead and gone to time and memory, never to be found.

Hearing the hammer blast of a .45, the other teenagers, Martin, Petey Behan, and Tim Quilty, enter the pier house as Richie turns round without comment, gunsmoke at the end of his arm, Harms at his side.

Bleating and maaing like sheep and oxen in the countryside, the moiling current of barges, transport steamers, tugs, and converted warships that feed the city here traverse the sea lanes coming to, leaving New York Harbor. Great buildings on the islands and adjoining lands watch over their circulating like the blood of life *pa-pum, pa-pum, pa-pum*. The heart of it all the men and women who want for better lives—if not in their generation, or the next, no matter. Still wanting, regardless, for the summer of life, and cinched in their day by both the pure blood of the old world, and the hope for a new and better world only imagined yet.

* * *

THE GREAT SILENCE OF OUR STRUGGLE coursing through the memory in your blood, only. For the stories of the things we'd done were not told by our children, or their children. Like the shame of victimization, starvation, and loss being none too inspirational for the present, we perhaps do not exist to you. The past being so easy to forget in America, for it is known. The future a treasure of unknown hope. Our fathers and grandfathers, like their fathers and grandfathers, speaking to us in our blood the horrific acts committed upon them and the horrific acts committed in return.

And me now with my mother here. My sisters too. Thankful to have them away from the bloody war of independence and the following civil war coming to Ireland.

Thankful to have them in my reach. But yet still now coming to New York are great disturbances, too. And it's a war is what I'd brought them away from, but what is coming can't be called anything less than a war. Mickey Kane's death will cause a stirring among many other things stirring in the city. The murder of a blood heir. The last heir. Dinny Meehan is now alone. He knows it. Sadie knows it. Harry Reynolds knows it too, yet no one else does at the time. Not I. Not Beat McGarry nor The Gas Drip Bard. No one but those three: Dinny, Sadie, Harry. That he is the last of the Meehans now and forever, because the boy is not his. The boy cannot be his, for Dinny Meehan does not exist to anyone at all, at all.

"I don' know no one by that name," Vincent Maher had said, bowing his head.

"Never heard o' the man. He live around here?"

"Ya don' know no one named Dinny Meehan," Cinders Connolly told me when I was jailed. "Just don' say nothin'. . . . We're all Patrick Kelly."

"There are ghosts of our past, ye know," Mr. Lynch from the old County Clare protective declared. "They live among us too. Ye t'ink they don't? Even if they are mostly just remembrances. They live on. Within us all."

Once seen as a force of benevolence where the needs of many weren't being met, he hid in the silence of things to help our people here. To free them. To quell the rattles of hunger. And to be ourselves, alone, by creating and fashioning an existence and a territory within the boundaries of the enemy's deeded properties like fighting, wandering gypsies. Within the dominant culture like animals in a trance of instinct brawling each other in a human's world. Dinny Meehan now known for who he is, or who he is perceived, the nous, or the faculty of our old-world ways exposed. He will be perceived again this time as a force of malevolence. The trinity only completed with a horrific cleansing. A blood cleansing. A division assembled by the

old Anglo-Saxon ascendency in New York that conquers.
Always has conquered. And he will remind us, Dinny will.
Speak to us in our blood of the clashing of the early morning's night and the bright of day, in that constant position
of change, the inequitable polemic where we live, hovering
between the darkness of the past and the unknown future.

And I owe him. I owe Dinny Meehan, the man what
raised me in my father's absence. Brought my family across
the great flood of the Atlantic Ocean. We all owe him, and
he will summon me, as he will summon us all for a rising
against an enemy we cannot defeat. Summon our honor.
To break our strength. He will always summon us, against
time and change. He will make us remember that outsiders
and foreigners are no more than invading gangs too.
Police gangs. Union gangs. Corporate gangs. Italian gangs,
and the gangs of traitors among us. He will not let us forget
the egg of our discontent, forever being a great hunger
thriving. That we were starved from our real mother's
tearful reach, her scent still in our noses, her milk forever
on our lips. When he finds his last blood heir has been
killed, he will summon us. He will assume our promise to
him, and he will make us kill again, and we will die too.
The blood sacrifice, a martyr's wish. Dinny Meehan and
his green-stone eyes, gentle and knowing and wet with the
aura of timelessness, will throw his great weight against it
all. For him, the poetry of the past is endlessly repeating
itself in the now. The poetic, oceanic unsettled air in his
hair always.

"They can never kill me off," he told me.

They can never kill him.

ACKNOWLEDGMENTS

Special thanks to: Katherine Cesario, Mandy Keifitz, John Smart & family, the Moody family, Dennis Sullivan, Dennis Lynch, Dan Lynch, Jill & James McNamee, Jenna McNamee, Todd McNamee, Jessica Lynch-Goldstein & family, Kit & Tom Leppert and family, Marilyn Rogoff-Lynch, Judy Steele, Jeannine Edwards, Peg & Bob Edwards and their eight boys, Patricia Meehan, Julie Meehan, Patrick Lanigan, Peter Quinn, Terry Golway, Malachy McCourt, T. J. English, Colin Broderick, John Duddy, Larry Kirwin, James Terrence Fisher, Richard Vetere, Tyler Anbinder, Maura Mulligan, Kevin Baker, Terence Donnellan, Tom Deignan, Terrence McCauley, John Lee, Jennifer Richards, Kevin Davitt, Maura Lynch, everyone at Irish American Writers & Artists Inc., Fultonhistory.com, Charles Hale and everyone at Artists Without Walls, Sheila Langan, John McDonough and WBAI Radio-NYC, Conor McNamara & Meredith Meagher, Ireland's Great Hunger Museum, Theresa Nig Loingsigh, Levi Asher at litkicks.com, John Malar, Owen Rodgers, Michael James Moore, Nick Mamatas, Stacey McCuin, Alex Resto, Rocky Sullivan's of Red Hook, Marie Flaherty, Laura Motta, Andrew Cotto, Declan Burke, Fiona Walsh, Steve Mona, Tara O'Grady, Sean Carlson, Jim McGlynn, Jimmie Buchanan, and Patricia Carragon.

ABOUT THE AUTHOR

EAMON LOINGSIGH'S FAMILY EMIGRATED FROM COUNTY Clare, Ireland in the late nineteenth century. His great-grandfather was a sandhog, digging for the New York City subways and opened a longshoremen's saloon in Greenwich Village in 1906 at 463 Hudson Street, which stayed in the Brooklyn-based family until the late 1970s. Loingsigh is a trained journalist that has written extensively on Irish American history. His work includes the novels *Light of the Diddicoy* and *Exile on Bridge Street* (both Three Rooms Press)—which comprise Volumes One and Two of the Auld Irishtown Trilogy. He is also the author of the novella *An Affair of Concoctions* and the poetry collection, *Love and Maladies*. He lives in Brooklyn.

Recent and Forthcoming Books from Three Rooms Press

FICTION

Meagan Brothers
Weird Girl and What's His Name

Ron Dakron
Hello Devilfish!

Michael T. Fournier
Hidden Wheel
Swing State

Janet Hamill
Tales from the Eternal Café
(Introduction by Patti Smith)

Eamon Loingsigh
Light of the Diddicoy
Exile on Bridge Street

John Marshall
The Greenfather

Aram Saroyan
Still Night in L.A.

Richard Vetere
The Writers Afterlife
Champagne and Cocaine

MEMOIR & BIOGRAPHY

Nassrine Azimi and
Michel Wasserman
Last Boat to Yokohama:
The Life and Legacy of
Beate Sirota Gordon

James Carr
BAD: The Autobiography of
James Carr

Richard Katrovas
Raising Girls in Bohemia:
Meditations of an American Father;
A Memoir in Essays

Judith Malina
Full Moon Stages:
Personal Notes from
50 Years of The Living Theatre

Phil Marcade
Punk Avenue:
Inside the New York City
Underground, 1972-1982

Stephen Spotte
My Watery Self:
Memoirs of a Marine Scientist

PHOTOGRAPHY-MEMOIR

Mike Watt
On & Off Bass

SHORT STORY ANTHOLOGIES

Dark City Lights: New York Stories
edited by Lawrence Block

Have a NYC I, II & III:
New York Short Stories;
edited by Peter Carlaftes
& Kat Georges

Crime + Music: The Sounds of Noir
edited by Jim Fusilli

Songs of My Selfie:
An Anthology of Millennial Stories
edited by Constance Renfrow

This Way to the End Times:
Classic and New Stories of
the Apocalypse
edited by Robert Silverberg

MIXED MEDIA

John S. Paul
Sign Language: A Painter's
Notebook (photography, poetry
and prose)

TRANSLATIONS

Thomas Bernhard
On Earth and in Hell
(poems of Thomas Bernhard
with English translations by
Peter Waugh)

Patrizia Gattaceca
Isula d'Anima / Soul Island
(poems by the author
in Corsican with English
translations)

César Vallejo | Gerard Malanga
Malanga Chasing Vallejo
(selected poems of César Vallejo
with English translations
and additional notes by
Gerard Malanga)

George Wallace
EOS: Abductor of Men
(selected poems of George
Wallace with Greek translations)

HUMOR

Peter Carlaftes
A Year on Facebook

DADA

Maintenant: A Journal of
Contemporary Dada Writing & Art
(Annual, since 2008)

FILM & PLAYS

Israel Horovitz
My Old Lady: Complete Stage Play
and Screenplay with an Essay on
Adaptation

Peter Carlaftes
Triumph For Rent (3 Plays)
Teatrophy (3 More Plays)

Kat Georges
Three Somebodies: Plays about
Notorious Dissidents

POETRY COLLECTIONS

Hala Alyan
Atrium

Peter Carlaftes
DrunkYard Dog
I Fold with the Hand I Was Dealt

Thomas Fucaloro
It Starts from the Belly and Blooms

Inheriting Craziness is Like
a Soft Halo of Light

Kat Georges
Our Lady of the Hunger

Robert Gibbons
Close to the Tree

Israel Horovitz
Heaven and Other Poems

David Lawton
Sharp Blue Stream

Jane LeCroy
Signature Play

Philip Meersman
This is Belgian Chocolate

Jane Ormerod
Recreational Vehicles on Fire
Welcome to the Museum of Cattle

Lisa Panepinto
On This Borrowed Bike

George Wallace
Poppin' Johnny

Three Rooms Press | New York, NY | Current Catalog: www.threeroomspress.com
Three Rooms Press books are distributed by PGW/Ingram: www.pgw.com